Love Walked In

Love Walked In

a novel

Marisa de los Santos

DUTTON

DUTTON
Published by Penguin Group (USA) Inc.
375 Hudson Street, New York, New York 10014, U.S.A.
Penguin Group (Canada), 90 Eglinton Avenue East, Suite 700, Toronto, Ontario, Canada M4P 2Y3 (a division
of Pearson Penguin Canada Inc.); Penguin Books Ltd, 80 Strand, London WC2R 0RL, England; Penguin Ireland,
25 St Stephen's Green, Dublin 2, Ireland (a division of Penguin Books Ltd); Penguin Group (Australia), 250
Camberwell Road, Camberwell, Victoria 3124, Australia (a division of Pearson Australia Group Pty Ltd); Penguin
Books India Pvt Ltd, 11 Community Centre, Panchsheel Park, New Delhi - 110 017, India; Penguin Group (NZ),
cnr Airborne and Rosedale Roads, Albany, Auckland 1310, New Zealand (a division of Pearson New Zealand
Ltd); Penguin Books (South Africa) (Pty) Ltd, 24 Sturdee Avenue, Rosebank, Johannesburg 2196, South Africa

Penguin Books Ltd, Registered Offices: 80 Strand, London WC2R 0RL, England

Published by Dutton, a member of Penguin Group (USA) Inc.

First printing, January 2006
10   9   8   7   6   5   4   3   2   1

Copyright © 2005 by Marisa de los Santos
All rights reserved

Grateful acknowledgment is made to reprint the following song lyrics:

BUT NOT FOR ME, By: George Gershwin and Ira Gershwin © 1930 (Renewed) WB Music Corp. (ASCAP).
All Rights Reserved. Used by Permission. Warner Bros. Publications Inc., Miami FL 33014

EMBRACEABLE YOU, By: George Gershwin and Ira Gershwin © 1930 (Renewed) WB Music Corp. (ASCAP).
All Rights Reserved. Used by Permission. Warner Bros. Publications Inc., Miami FL 33014

HOW LONG HAS THIS BEEN GOING ON?, By: George Gershwin and Ira Gershwin © 1927 (Renewed) WB
Music Corp. (ASCAP). All Rights Reserved. Used by Permission. Warner Bros. Publications Inc., Miami FL 33014

LET'S DO IT (LET'S FALL IN LOVE), By: Cole Porter © 1928 (Renewed WB Music Corp. (ASCAP). All Rights
Reserved. Used by Permission. Warner Bros. Publications Inc., Miami FL 33014

YOU'RE THE TOP, By: Cole Porter © 1934 (Renewed WB Music Corp. (ASCAP). All Rights Reserved. Used
by Permission. Warner Bros. Publications Inc., Miami FL 33014

THREE IS A MAGIC NUMBER, by Robert Dorough. Used by permission of ABC Music Publishing.

LIBRARY OF CONGRESS CATALOGING-IN-PUBLICATION DATA
De los Santos, Marisa, 1966–
    Love walked in : a novel / by Marisa de los Santos.
      p. cm.
    ISBN 0-525-94917-8 (acid-free paper)
    1. Motion pictures—Appreciation—Fiction. 2. Fathers and daughters—Fiction. 3. Custody of children—
Fiction. 4. Philadelphia (Pa.)—Fiction. 5. Restaurants—Fiction. I. Title.
    PS3604.E1228L68 2006
    813'.54—dc22   2005003281

Printed in the United States of America
Set in Fairfield LH Light

For David Teague

You're the Nile
You're the Tower of Pisa

Love Walked In

1

Cornelia

My life—my real life—started when a man walked into it, a handsome stranger in a perfectly cut suit, and, yes, I know how that sounds. My friend Linny would snort and convey the kind of multipronged disgust I rely on her to convey. One prong of feminist disgust at the whole idea of a man changing a woman's life, even though, as things turned out, the man himself was more the harbinger of change than the change itself. Another prong of disgust for the inaccuracy of saying my life began after thirty-one years of living it. And the final prong being a kind of general disgust for the way people turn moments in their lives into movie moments.

I do this more than I should, I'll give her that, but there *was* something backlit and sudden about his walking through the door of the café I managed. If the floor had been bare and not covered with tables, chairs, people, and dogs, the autumnal late-morning sun would have slung his narrow shadow dramatically across the floor in a real Orson Welles shot. But Linny can jab me with her three-pronged disgust fork all she wants, and I'd still say that my life started on that October morning when a man walked through the door.

It was an ordinary day—palpably ordinary, if that makes any sense, like it was asserting its smooth usualness. A Saturday, loud, smoke already piling up and hovering like weather over me and the customers in Café Dora. I sat where I always sat when I wasn't waiting on someone—on a high stool behind the counter—and I watched Hayes and Jose play chess. Everyone said they were good players. They themselves said they were. "Not prodigy good," said Hayes. "Not Russian, Deep-freakin'-Blue-playing good. But hell." Hayes was from Texas and wrote the wine column for the *Philadelphia Inquirer*. He liked to swear in offbeat ways, liked to walk in, turn a chair around backward with a bang, and straddle it.

As I watched, Jose lifted his shaggy head, gave Hayes a liquid-eyed, sorrowful look, and moved a chess piece from one square to another. I don't know the game well, but whatever Jose had done, it must have been something, because Hayes tossed back his head and hooted, "Hot damn, boy! You pulled that one *right* out of your ass!" Hayes looked at me with a wry smile and a genial cowboy twinkle in his eye, and I lifted one corner of my mouth in a kind of rueful facial shrug. "What can you do?" my face said.

But don't get attached to Hayes. As he was already in the room, he's obviously not the man who walked into it bearing the new life on his shoulders, and he doesn't finally figure into this story much. Not sure why I started with Hayes, except that in lots of ways he's a neat little embodiment of the old life: a self-invented, smartish, semialluring wine snob disguised as a cowboy, not un-nice, with fairly amusing comments tripping off his tongue and probably a real person under there somewhere, but possibly not. In college, I read *Piers Plowman* in which this man Will goes on a journey and runs into characters like Holy Church and Gluttony. Think of Hayes as a character like that: Typical-Denizen-of-Cornelia's-Old-Life. I've always found allegories kind of comforting. When you encounter people named Liar and Abstinence, you might not be crazy about them, but you know exactly what you're getting into.

Another regular, Phaedra, made her entrance, all blowsy auburn curls, leather pants, and nursing-mother breasts, and tugging a giant black pram behind her—one of those English nanny prams with high, white rubber tires. Five people jumped up and nearly cracked one another's skulls trying to hold the door open for her. Phaedra directed a beseeching look at the couple sitting at the table nearest the door, a look that turned out to be unnecessary. The man and woman were already hustling up their cappuccinos, jackets, camera bags, and backpacks on metal frames, not minding a bit.

"Cornelia!" Phaedra sang at me across the room in just the sort of musical voice you'd expect to come out of her mouth. "Could you? Café au lait? Loads of sugar? And something sinful!" We don't have table service. Phaedra made a helpless, sighing gesture with her shoulders and her long hands, indicating her child, her exhaustion, the whole ancient weight of motherhood. Phaedra was a pain. But Allegra was a different story. Bearing the coffee and a croissant, I came out from behind my counter and made my zigzag way around tables and dogs for the sake of Phaedra's baby, Allegra.

And there she was, wrapped in a leopard-print blanket, just waking up. A blue-eyed, translucent, bewitching witch of a baby, fresh as new bread in that smoky room. Allegra resembled Phaedra, same white skin, same glorious Carole Lombard forehead, but with carrot-orange hair that flew out in all directions. I waited for the pang; the pang came. I never saw Allegra without wanting to touch her, specifically to sleep with her in the crook of my right arm. I put the croissant and the coffee in front of Phaedra, then cradled my elbows with my hands. Allegra was asleep and making nursing motions with her mouth because what else would babies dream about?

"Face it. You want one," said Phaedra. With effort, I shifted my gaze from gorgeous child to gorgeous pain-in-the-ass mother. "See that?" said Phaedra. "You had to literally drag your eyes away from her." Ouch, I thought, and then sat down to talk for a minute, Phaedra's misuse of the word "literally" having created a warm spot in my heart, tiny but large enough to prompt a five-minute conversation.

"How's business?" I asked. Phaedra was a jewelry designer.

"Not good. I'm starting to think people just don't *get* it," said Phaedra. Her signature pieces, or what would be her signature pieces if anyone bought and wore them, were made out of sea glass and platinum, a juxtaposition of the ordinary and extraordinary, Phaedra claimed, that forced one to rethink one's perceptions of "value" and "preciousness." Maybe people didn't get it. Or maybe they got it but didn't feel sufficiently moved to shell out eight hundred dollars for a bracelet made of old Heineken bottles.

Phaedra lifted her coffee to her lips, eyeing me brightly through the steam. "Cornelia, what if you wore some of the pieces in the café, just to generate in-ter-est?" Her tone suggested the idea had just popped into her head. In fact, this was the third time she'd asked.

"I can't wear jewelry at work," I said, not elaborating but rolling my eyes in a way I hoped suggested some unseen powers-that-be who hovered over me, forbidding jewelry. The truth was that I never wore jewelry anywhere, ever. I'm five feet tall and built like a preteen, eighty-five pounds soaking wet, as my father says, and my fear is that, given my smallness, jewelry will make me look like a geegaw or doodad, a spangly ornament to hang on a tree. It's a shame, too, because I adore it. Not so much Phaedra's kind—cool, angular objects—but serious jewels: diamonds, cuffs and chokers, brooches like shooting stars, tiaras. Jean Harlow jewels, Irene Dunne on the ship in *Love Affair*.

Allegra stirred in her leopard-print nest, yawned, and shot out a fist. Phaedra lifted her onto her lap, instantly dipping her swan neck, dropping her face into the orange hair, breathing in her child's scent. An authentic gesture, automatic, unstudied. I felt prickles shoot down my arms. I touched a finger to Allegra's hand, and she gripped it hard and hung on.

"You *should* have one, you know," said Phaedra, harping, and this instantly got my hackles up, until I saw her face, which was something like kind. Phaedra was always a better person with Allegra in her arms. So I just trilled a little laugh and said, breezily, "Me with a baby. Can you imagine?"

"Of course, I can. Perfectly," said Phaedra. "And so can you."

While I resented her smug smile, and while I'd have died before admitting it to her, I had to admit to myself that she was at least partly right: I couldn't imagine it *perfectly*, but I could imagine it. Had imagined it, in fact, more than once. But, every time, what brought me to my senses was my conviction that before a person dropped a new life into this world, she should probably get a real one herself.

The truth was, I was treading water and had been for some time. If you're wondering why a thirty-something woman who had gone to all the trouble of attending a university and slogging through medieval allegorical texts had risen no higher on the career food chain than café manager, I don't blame you. I wondered myself. And the best answer I'd come up with was that I hadn't figured out anything better—not yet. If I were to ever have a full-fledged vocation, as opposed to a half-assed avocation, I needed to love it and, in my experience, it isn't always easy to figure out what you love. You'd think it would be, but it isn't. Also, if you stay in it for any length of time, like anyplace else, a café becomes a world.

I felt suddenly weary, looking at Phaedra and Allegra and the shining black pram. And if a woman weighing less than ninety pounds can be said to heave herself, I heaved myself out of my seat and lugged myself back to my spot behind the bar.

All of which is meant to demonstrate the ordinariness of the day and how the ordinariness was even taking on shades of dreariness and futility. Because you have to understand what my life was like in the "before" in order to see just how much it changed in the "after." Ordinary, ordinary. Except that—and I honestly believe this, Linny's pooh-poohing of movie moments notwithstanding—just before, a minute before the café door opened one more time, the ordinary day turned itself up a notch, in preparation.

The light falling through the high, arched windows went from mellow to brilliant, turning the old copper of the espresso machine to pure gold. And the music—Sarah Vaughan, whom I worship, singing

George and Ira, whom I worship—was suddenly floating and dipping like some kind of bird in the clear space above the cigarette smoke and chitchat. The coffee smelled sublime, the flowers I'd bought that morning pierced the air with their blueness, the coffee cups lost their chips and glowed eggshell-thin, and standing in my red sweater and vintage suede skirt, my boots solidly on the floor, I felt almost tall.

The door of Café Dora opened, and Cary Grant walked in.

If you haven't seen *The Philadelphia Story,* stop what you are doing, rent it, and watch it. It's probably overstating the point to say that until you watch it, you will have been living a partial and colorless life. However, it is definitely on the list of perfect things. You know what I mean, the list that includes the starry sky over the desert, grilled cheese sandwiches, *The Great Gatsby,* the Chrysler building, Ella Fitzgerald singing "It Don't Mean a Thing (If You Ain't Got That Swing)," white peonies, and those little sketches of hands by Leonardo da Vinci.

If you have seen it, then you know there's a moment when Katharine Hepburn as Tracy Lord steps from a poolside cabana. She's got a straight white dream of a dress hanging from her tiny collar-bones, a dress fluted and precise as a Greek column but light and full of the motion of smoke. A paradox of a dress, a marriage of opposites that just makes your teeth hurt it's so exactly right.

I was fourteen when I first saw it. It was three days before Christmas, which in my family's house meant, means, and will always mean, Yuletide sensory overload: every room stuffed to the gills with garland and holly, the whole place booming with Johnny Mathis, and a monstrosity of a tree towering in the living room, weighed down with ornaments of every description, including dozens defying description that my brothers, sister, and I had made in school over the years.

Fourteen was not a good year for me. I was the latest of late bloomers, of course, about two feet high and scrawny as a cat, still shopping in the children's department, profoundly allergic to every member of my family, and convinced that nothing could make me happy.

But then my grouchy channel-surfing landed me in the middle of a black-and-white heaven: Tracy, the dress.

I was so struck, I forgot how to swallow and began to truly asphyxiate on a sip of 7-Up. And when, a little later, Tracy unfastened the belt from her willow waist and slipped her faultlessly formed self out of that faultlessly formed garment, I stood up and yelled, "Holy shit, that's her *bathing suit cover-up!*" which my father, who was sitting on the floor fastening—no joke—jingle bells to the collars of our cats, did not appreciate.

I turned every atom of myself over to the rest of the movie. People must've gone tearing through the room, because people always did go tearing through rooms, especially my brothers Cam and Toby, who were eight and nine at the time. But a volcano could have begun spewing molten rock inches away from me, and I would not have noticed. I sat. I watched. If a girl could sling a poem over her swimwear as though it were an old T-shirt, what else might be possible?

I slid my fingers over my face, feeling for Tracy's winged cheekbones. And when Dexter (Cary Grant) took Tracy to task, saying, "You'll never be a first-rate woman or a first-rate human being until you have some regard for human frailty," I recognized it as wisdom and wondered whether I had it, that kind of regard, and just how to get it if I didn't.

In college, I took a film studies class subtitled something like "Turning the Formula on Its Head" in which the professor talked about the trick *The Philadelphia Story* pulls off. It should never have worked: creating a fantastic love scene between two characters whom you know are not in love with each other, getting you somehow to root for them wholeheartedly during the scene, but then to feel completely satisfied when they end up with other people.

Before you get the wrong impression, you should know that I'm not and never was one of those film people, the kind who argue into the wee hours about the auteur theory and whether Spielberg is the new Capra, or whether John Huston impacts, in unseen ways, every second of American life. I don't know from camera angles, and I don't have an encyclopedic knowledge of pre–World War II German cinema, but I fell a little in love with the film professor when he looked upon us with shining eyes and proclaimed, "No, it should not work. But work it does!" because he was so passionate and right.

When I heard Mike (Jimmy Stewart) say to Tracy in that tender, marveling voice, "No, you're made out of flesh and blood. That's the blank, unholy surprise of it. You're the golden girl, Tracy," I clasped my hands under my pointy chin, prayed that she would run away with him, and swore to God that someday a man would say those words in that voice to me or else I would die. But then, at the movie's end, my father heard cheering and left water running in the sink to watch his lately distant, disaffected teenage daughter bang her fists on the arms of her chair and turn to him crying, "with a face as open as a flower" (my dad's own improbable words), saying breathlessly, "She's marrying Dexter, Daddy."

I'll admit it. I've always been more than a little proud of myself for having been fourteen and deeply benighted about almost everything, but having had the sense to recognize what is surely a universal truth: Jimmy Stewart is always and indisputably the best man in the world, unless Cary Grant should happen to show up.

His name was Martin Grace. An excellent name, which, you may have noticed, shares all but three letters with "Cary Grant." Of course, if you're not a freak of nature, you probably didn't notice, and you'll be relieved to know that it didn't even spring to my mind right away. It was later, as I lay in bed that night, that I figured it out, mentally crossing out letters with an imaginary pencil, concentrating pretty hard, but sort of affecting an offhand, semi-interested attitude about it, cocking my head casually on the pillow, even though there was no one in the room to see me.

Truth be told, I'm a little superstitious about names. Back in college, I dated an enormous, blond, dumb fraternity boy from Baton Rouge with a voice like a foghorn purely on the strength of his being named William Powell, whom everyone knows from the *Thin Man* movies, but who is even better in *Libeled Lady* and is one of those men whose handsomeness you believe in completely even though you know it doesn't exist.

My mother met the boy and knew instantly what I was up to. "Your nose looks like Myrna Loy's," she'd said. "Be satisfied with that." Even so, I didn't ditch Bill until a few nights later when I stood in his Georgian-mansion-turned-dank-cave of a frat house and watched Bill dancing shirtless on a tabletop, his bare, unfortunate belly pulsating like an anguished jellyfish. The bellyfish pulsated, and William Powell, with a delicate shrug, chose that moment to detach himself from Bill forever and slip out into the honeysuckle-scented night.

Slippery things, names. Still: Martin Grace. Good. Very good.

He'd stood dark-eyed and half-smiling in the doorway. Tall. Suit, hair, jawline all flawlessly cut. "Imperially slim," is the phrase that jumped out of my fourth-grade reading book into my head. But the man in that poem ended up shooting himself, I remembered later, while this man, *my* man, clearly had only a seamless, sophisticated, well-shod life ahead of him. I'm exaggerating, but not much, when I say that as he walked to the counter—walked to me—the dogs, chess players, prams, etcetera parted before him like the Red Sea.

"Hello," he said, and his voice wasn't mellifluous or stentorian or melting or sonorous but was nonetheless unmistakably leading-man. As you knew he would, he had a dimple in his chin, and for a wild second or two I considered touching it and asking him how he shaved in there, because if you're going to rip someone off it might as well be Audrey Hepburn. I didn't, but I distinctly felt the dimple impress itself upon my unconscious, if such a thing is possible.

"Hi" is what I said.

"A coffee, please. Black." And you could just tell that's really what he liked and didn't sense a self-conscious backstory involving a Marlboro Man masculinity obsession trailing like a long, stupid tail behind the request.

When I handed him his coffee, I let my hand linger on it an extra beat, so that it was still there when he reached for it. I like to pretend to myself that the cup became a little conduit and that our electricity shook it. Anyway, coffee spilled on my hand and I yelped and pressed it to my mouth like a two-year-old.

He looked at me with real concern and said, "I should be kept in a cage."

"Occupational hazard." I shrugged. "It's fine."

"It's fine? Really? Because if it's not, you have to tell me so I can go drown myself in the Delaware."

"Don't be silly," I said. "The Schuykill's closer."

"The Delaware's deeper. I don't have the guts to drown myself in shallow water, even for you."

Even for you, even for you! my heart sang.

"Except," he said.

"Except what?" I snapped, snappily.

"Except it'll have to be the Thames. I leave for London in two hours."

This might not sound so earth-shattering to you, so fabulously clever or romantic, but trust me when I tell you that it was. Right from the start, we just had a cadence, an intuitive rhythm that I might possibly compare to the sixth sense that jazz musicians sometimes have when they're playing together if I knew the first thing about jazz. You've seen Tracy–Hepburn movies, yes? It was the conversation I'd been waiting for all my life.

And it kept up, that back-and-forth. He talked about his business trip—four days in London, finance something or other—and about fog, how the thing of it was it really was foggy in London.

I felt taut and tingly and flushed, as though I were wearing a new skin, but I wasn't exactly nervous. Miraculously, I was up to the challenge of meeting this man, perfect as he was. I was "on." I even had the presence of mind, in the presence of Martin Grace, to continue doing my job, which was fortunate because that's the way life is, isn't it? Even as you and the Embodiment-of-All-Your-Hopes stand percolating your own little weather system, two teenaged boys with skateboards under their arms are bound to walk up, splash a pile of dimes onto the counter, and order triple mocha lattes. And usually, it's not when your eyes are locked with the black-lashed, chocolate-colored stunners the dream man apparently carries around on his face all day as though they were ordinary eyes, but when you're busy jittering the dimes into the cash register that you'll hear him say, "Why don't you come with me?"

Because he said that, Martin Grace did. To me.

I heard it again, an eerily precise aural memory, as I lay in bed that night, turning over the all-but-three-letters/Cary Grant idea for the first of you don't even want to know how many times. At the sound of Martin's voice in my head, I sat up, got up, walked over to the window, my white nightgown floating like a ghost around me, and sat in the chair I'd covered last spring with figured, lead-heavy green silk that had once been a monster of a fifties ball gown hanging in a resale shop in Buena (pronounced Byoona) Vista, Virginia. I cranked open my third-floor casement window, looked at Philadelphia—my piece of it—and let my affection for it lift lightly off of me like scent from a flower and drift out into the cool air. Spruce Street: cars and lights; the synagogue on the corner; the hustlers in front of it, male and heart-breakingly young. I felt the two tugs I always felt when I looked at those boys: the tug toward wanting the cars to stop, the tug toward wanting them not to stop.

I could be in London right now, I thought. Right now, lying back on unfamiliarly English pillows with Martin Grace beside me.

Why I wasn't is a long story—so long that it probably isn't a story at all. It's probably just the way I am. But the next thing I said, a major-league clunker, the conversational equivalent of falling on my face, pretty much sums it up.

I stood there in tumult, weighing common sense against desire, trepidation against adventure, caution against impulse, while inwardly banging my head against the wall because, tumult or no tumult, my answer was a foregone conclusion:

"I want to, but I can't. My mother wouldn't like it."

"So we'll leave her home this time. She can come on the Paris trip."

As I sat at my window replaying this conversation, lonely, night-gowned, face burning, but still somehow happy, I watched a helicopter in the distance drop its beam of searchlight and swing it slowly back and forth. I imagined a couple in evening dress doing a song-and-dance number in the street below, the woman's skirt blooming like a white carnation as she spun.

Then I tried to imagine a world in which my mother would accompany me and my older (by maybe fifteen years?) lover to Paris, and blew out a single, sarcastic, "Ha!"

My mother alphabetizes her spice rack, wears Tretorn sneakers, and never puts eleven items on the ten-item express grocery counter, ever. She is a garden club president, and I mean that both literally and figuratively. On the outside, my life doesn't look much like hers; I've made sure of that. But the truth is that I am my mother's daughter, literally, figuratively, forever.

Still, I made sure Martin Grace did not walk out the door without my number. I leaned over, folded back his lapel, and placed it in his inside breast pocket myself. Then, I gave him a look so worthy of Veronica Lake, I could almost feel my nonexistent blond tresses falling over one eye.

2

Clare

It started with towels. Ten full sets, thick Egyptian cotton-dyed dark plum, pale yellow, flamingo pink. Her mother dropped the huge white shopping bags heavy with towels on the floor of Clare's room, then ran back to the car for more, until there were ten bags lined up like teeth on Clare's rug. "Wait until you see them all, sweetheart. So beautiful. The best. The very best."

Clare leaned against the doorjamb, let the wood press into her shoulder, half inside, half outside the room. She listened to her mother chatter and watched her toss the towels onto the bed, really pitching them so that the bath sheets unfolded like banners in the air and the washcloths fluttered open like little birds. Apple green, crimson, hydrangea blue. The bed was heaped with them. Clare put her thumbnail between her teeth, didn't chew it, but held it there.

"Have you ever seen such beautiful towels? I feel the colors in my bones. Right inside my bones. Don't you, Clarey?" Clare's mother was breathing hard, almost panting, as though looking at the towels were like running or dancing.

Clare said, "We have towels already."

Her mother walked over to her and swaddled her in a towel the soft brown of a brown egg. The towel was huge. Clare was going on eleven and was tall for her age, but the towel wrapped around her twice and puddled at her feet. Inside it, she felt skinny and hunched. Clare's mother took Clare's face in her hands, gently. Under her makeup, her cheeks were flushed. "It's important to wash them before you use them the first time. And to wash each set separately so you don't spoil the colors. Do you understand that?" Her voice was hushed and serious, so Clare nodded. Her mother took her hands away and looked over her shoulder at the bed covered with towels.

"We'd better go down and have lunch now, Mom," Clare said.

"Oh, they just make me want to weep," said Clare's mother, and she lay down on the towels and wept.

The next morning, Clare sat in her fifth-grade classroom making lists.

Orphans. All of Clare's favorite characters were orphans, and she wrote their names in the back of her notebook while her teacher went over the reading-comprehension questions for the Helen Keller autobiography the class had read. The questions were on a sheet of paper on Clare's desk, with Clare's answers penciled in underneath each question.

Clare's mother called her worksheets "soulless," not because the questions were stupid and reduced the readings to a bunch of lumpish facts; not because for what her mother was paying for the fancy Main Line school, they should have been coming up with something a lot fancier than worksheets; but because the sheets were copied on a Xerox machine. She recalled for Clare the mimeographs of her youth—the curling, slick paper, orchid purple smudgy ink, and the odor, a fragrance like none other. "I'd pick up the worksheet first thing and just *breathe* it, Clarey! That smell was the smell of *school*."

Clare had wanted to say something good in response to this, something original and declamatory about her own school, how it smelled or didn't, something to let her mother know that they were a team, two interesting people who noticed smells and soullessness. Clare tried hard to toss off sharp, quirky comments in front of her mother, to quip, is how she thought of it, the way girls in books were always quipping.

Anne of Green Gables was a big quipper, for example. Once in a while, at school or with their cleaning lady, Max, who wasn't a lady really but a nineteen-year-old with a tattoo of a phoenix rising from smoldering ashes across her bony shoulder blades, Clare was capable of quipping. But often, with her mother, conversation was tricky. Clare found herself trailing after, while her mother's mind and voice dashed ahead, doubled back, ping-ponged in amazing ways.

Anne Shirley, Sara Crewe, Mary Lennox. These were the top-three orphans, with Anne miles ahead of the other two, so Clare wrote their names in inch-high lettering that came as close to calligraphy as she could manage given her number two pencil and limited artistic talent. When she was younger, she would sometimes draw pictures of each next to their names: three pale, big-eyed faces, each almost perfectly triangular, and topped, consecutively, with red hair, black hair, blondish hair. After the Big Three, there were others. Heidi. The Roald Dahl orphans: James and Sophie. Wild, vaguely creepy Pippi Longstocking, if you believed, as Clare did, that Pippi's father was drowned and not a cannibal king. Tom and Huck. David, Pip, Estella, Oliver and the rest, struggling through fog, grim streets, and their twisting, thickly populated stories. The Boxcar Children. Unforgiveable Heathcliff; Hareton, who hanged the puppies from the back of the chair; Jane Eyre. Recent, bestselling orphans: Harry Potter, the sad-faced Baudelaires. There was also a subcategory of half-orphans, usually motherless, and a subsubcategory of half-orphans with kindly housekeepers: Scout and Jem; all four Melendy kids (five after they adopted Mark, a full-fledged orphan); even Nancy Drew, who was almost an adult and barely counted.

Clare grouped and regrouped the orphans, categorizing them by age, sex, hair color, country of origin, economic status. Clare was starting a list of the poor ones who ended up rich when she heard her teacher stop talking. Worksheets notwithstanding, Ms. Packer was nice and was maybe even a good teacher, Clare thought, although she was no Anne Shirley, who—once she'd grown up and become a teacher—loved every student as her own child, who won over the wicked Jen Pringle, and who inspired handsome Paul Irving to become a famous poet. Ms. Packer had a loud voice, was thick-waisted, thin-haired, and her fashion sense ran to Birkenstock sandals with socks, thumb rings, and what was whispered to be bralessness. But she seemed to care about books, and she sometimes talked about the characters as though they were real people, with tears in her eyes and a choke in her throat. She wasn't married, and Clare understood that it was because she was madly in love with Charles Darnay and no other man measured up.

The night before, upon Ms. Packer's suggestion, Clare had stuffed cotton in her ears and worn a blindfold for two straight hours. After she caught her finger in a drawer, busted her shin against the Biedermeir table, and spilled an entire glass of iced tea, she'd sat in a chair for a long time and afterward understood that being blind and deaf meant being alone with your thoughts and feeling a tide of worry rise around you.

Ms. Packer stood, arrested midsentence, pencil in the air, looking at the back of the room, and when Clare twisted around with the rest of the class to look, she saw her mother standing in the doorway. She wore a wrap dress, heels, sunglasses, lipstick. She was lithe and elegant, and her hair fell like a sheet of silk to her shoulders. When she looked at Clare and smiled, Clare felt a knot she hadn't realized was under her ribcage loosen. My mother, she thought. Look at her. Who would worry about a woman like that?

But then she saw Mrs. Jordan, the assistant to the Head of the Lower School, hovering behind her mother, looking put out, and Clare remembered that parents never came to the classrooms. They waited in the reception area, and Mrs. Jordan sent a helper down to retrieve their children. Clare imagined her mother striding like a runway model down the school hallways while Mrs. Jordan pattered after her, apprising her of the rules in a tense but polite voice. The knot tightened.

"Sorry to interrupt, Ms. Packer, but I need Clare," said Clare's mother, turning her smile on Ms. Packer.

Then, Clare's mother dropped like a dancer or a panther into a crouch and shook back her hair. She held her arms out to Clare, as though Clare were a toddler. "I need you, Clare," she said.

As Ms. Packer and Mrs. Jordan exchanged bemused, disapproving looks over her mother's shining head, Clare chose the side she was on. She looked from teacher to administrator, then grinned at her mother, a grin she made sure wasn't just the fashioning of her mouth into a shape but that went all the way to her eyes. Then, she shoved books and notebooks into her backpack and stood up.

"You'll e-mail me with the homework, please, Ms. Packer?" she said briskly, just tipping her voice up ever so slightly at the end of the sentence to turn it from statement to request.

She glanced at her friend Josie, whose desk was next to hers, and noticed that Josie's expression was familiar, the combination of admiration and friendly envy with which Josie always regarded her when they spent time with Clare's mother. Josie had once told Clare that she thought of her mother as a cross between a fairytale princess and an exotic animal like a peacock. Josie was a bright girl, but not especially creative, and this was definitely one of the most interesting things she'd ever said to Clare, which showed just how much Clare's mother fascinated Josie. Even when Clare's mother did some ordinary mother thing, like give them a plate of cookies, Josie gazed at her in amazement as though she'd just performed magic. Even though Clare's mother showing up in their classroom was peculiar, it probably didn't seem particularly so to Josie, who saw everything Clare's mother did as special and unexpected. Rules that applied to other mothers didn't apply to her.

Ms. Packer nodded at Clare, her brows still knit. Then, Clare turned on her heel, as pertly as any storybook heroine ever did, walked to the classroom door and, as she hadn't done for years and not caring what the kids in her class would think, took her mother's hand.

Clare stayed stride for stride with her mother, head high, ponytail swinging, down the hallways of the school, through the oak-paneled entryway, and out the door. They were coconspirators stepping out together into the sunny afternoon. But, in the parking lot, her mother looked down at Clare's face and said, with a hint of irritation in her voice, "Nothing to worry about, Clarey. I'm your mother. I'm allowed to take you out of school without jumping through hoops."

"No, Mom. I'm not worried. I'm really not worried," said Clare, inserting what was almost a skip into her step. "Ms. Packer and Mrs. Jordan, they'd be okay, if they weren't so—conventional." Clare's mother squeezed Clare's hand.

"Sometimes, darling, a mother just has to let everything go, and take her daughter to lunch."

"I agree," Claire almost sang, and she felt everything was fine—better than fine. She'd used a good word, "conventional" and, in a breezy, laughing voice, her mother had called her "darling," a luxurious, old-fashioned endearment that Clare had read a thousand times but had never been called.

Inside the rose-colored walls of the restaurant, before her mother said unthinkable things, Clare was happy. At first she was happy because she had decided to be, and then she relaxed into her happiness and just felt it.

The restaurant was cool and high-ceilinged, with waiters in creaseless white shirts, and with tight bunches of purple flowers in tiny vases on the tables. It was the sort of place that is sure enough of itself to be noisy and bustling rather than hushed, and Clare thought it was wonderful. The way the water sat in the glasses; the menus that didn't open but were a single pale yellow card; the small, brightly colored, evenly spaced paintings that hung across one wall—all of it dazzled Clare.

"If you can tell us which of these two wines you'd recommend and why, you're our man," said Clare's mother to the handsome, black-haired waiter. She handed the wine list to him and pointed to the two selections, her hand lightly touching his, her fingers looking tapered and delicate. She spoke in a low voice, and the waiter smiled. His front tooth was chipped, causing Clare to notice how young he was. This is the way men smile at beautiful women, she thought, and she felt proud that even this guy who was almost a kid, almost a boy, could fall under her mother's spell.

When he brought the wine, he filled her mother's glass, and then held the bottle over Clare's glass. Clare started to tell him no, but he was looking at her mother, not at her and, astonishingly, her mother nodded. Clare watched the dark wine rise in the glass, watched the waiter's hand give a slight twist at the end, then sat staring at the wine, unsure of what to do next. Should she remind her mother about her own mother's sister, Aunt Patsy, who at age nine, after a dinner party, had sneaked downstairs and drunk the dregs of every guest's drink? "They found her in the front yard, laughing at the moon. From that moment on, she was a hopeless drunk. Hopeless." Her mother's words, her mother's cautionary tale; it seemed impossible that she'd forgotten it.

But her mother was raising her own glass and looking at Clare, eyebrows arched. It was a large glass, long-stemmed, like nothing Clare had ever held or drunk from, and she wrapped her fingers gingerly around the stem, then—glancing at her mother—cupped her hand under the globe and lifted. Her mother nodded approvingly. Maybe it was all right, then; it must be.

"It's as important to know when to break the rules as it is to know when to obey them. Here's to playing hooky!" Her mother touched her glass to Clare's, and Clare drank, tasting the odd, rich harshness, but swallowing anyway. Tears started in her eyes, and she blinked hard. Please don't let me be a hopeless drunk, she prayed, then snatched the prayer back. It must be that some people can become hopeless drunks and others can't, Clare thought, and her mother must know this and know Clare to be the kind who can't. If her mother didn't know that, she would never allow Clare to drink, not in a million years. She imagined her mother knocking a glass from her hand, just as Clare was raising it to her lips, the glass shattering, the wine purple on the wall.

The food was interesting, little complicated creations resting in the centers of large plates, sauce drizzled in gleaming patterns, meat placed on top of vegetables instead of next to them. Clare would just begin to dismantle or eat around the edges of one creation, when another plate would come. It was too much food—much too much—but that was OK because her mother was eating with gusto, really digging in, and it hit Clare that her mother hadn't been eating much lately. She would flit around the kitchen at dinnertime, perch—legs crossed, one swinging—on a countertop, but would rarely sit for long. Clare tried to remember seeing her mother actually chew and swallow food. Her mother had always been slim, but recently Clare had noticed how thin she was: hands grown translucent, almost clawlike, skin pulled tight over her cheekbones, hipbones jutting alarmingly under her dresses. She looks like a model, Clare had reassured herself, but it was still a relief to see her mother eat, and Clare was happy.

"Listen, Clarey," her mother said suddenly, "this Christmas, we leave all the god-awful American yuletide tedium behind and go to Spain. Madrid"—her mother took a deep sip of wine, then shook her head—"no, no, no. Barcelona! Gaudi! You won't believe your eyes. It's like fairyland! What do you think?"

And Clare felt so honored, being asked what she thought, so she said, "I think definitely yes!" even though she loved their Christmases in Philadelphia. It was always just the two of them. Clare's parents were both only children and both orphans, even though they didn't acquire full-fledged orphanhood until they were already grown up, and Clare never saw her father at Christmas. They had a tradition of eating dinner together on New Year's Day, but it hardly counted as a tradition because it usually didn't happen. Clare's father was away or busy most years, which was all right with Clare.

So every year, Clare and her mother would take the train in and watch every tree lighting in town, then sit on the floor together at Lord & Taylor to watch the light show over and over, shop, and hear as much carol singing as they could. They both loved carols, and Clare's mother had taught her verses to "Silent Night" and "Hark, the Herald Angels Sing" that almost no one else knew. On Christmas Eve, they would eat dinner at a country inn, where a married couple named Juno and Lars would serve a Christmas-carol dinner that included goose, pears, chestnuts, and real figgy pudding. Clare would feel safe and peaceful, at a table with her mother in a room filled with noisy, laughing, dressed-up strangers, the country sky arching over the roof, and Christmas arriving around them little by little like snow.

But her mother was so uplifted, describing candy-colored spires decorated with knobs and swirls, shaping them in the air with her hands, and planning lessons in Catalan for them to take together, that Clare didn't mind giving up one holiday season to Spain. If her mother's voice sounded higher than usual, contained a hectic note, Clare thought, it was just excitement and probably a burst of energy from all the food.

Then, Clare's mother suddenly stopped this vivid, bubbling chatter, looked around at the pink walls, and said, "My husband used to bring me to this place," in a new, hard voice that stopped Clare cold. Clare's parents had divorced when she was two years old. While Clare saw her father occasionally, Clare's mother never talked about his leaving, never talked about him much at all, and had certainly never called him "my husband." What shook Clare more than this, though, was the way her mother's voice and face changed so fast, as though she were a different person interrupting herself.

When the waiter walked up a second later, Clare's mother's eyes softened as she turned her attention to him and the corners of her mouth curled. To Clare's amazement, her mother took the man's hand between the two of hers, turned it over, examined his palm, turned it back, then lifted his cuff with her fingers to look at his watch.

"I see you have the time," she said in the same low voice she'd used before. The waiter glanced at Clare, then smiled at her mother.

"Would you like your check?" he said. His hand still rested lightly in hers, and as she nodded, she opened her fingers, releasing it like a bird.

Just after he walked away, Clare's mother stood, folding her napkin carefully and placing it on the table. Her expression was full of affection for Clare, "Ladies' room. Wait here, darling," she said, and now the "darling" sounded all wrong, like she wasn't talking to Clare at all. Abruptly, she sat back down in her chair and leaned toward Clare. In a loud whisper, almost a hiss, she said, "Never let anyone tell you men want sex more than women. Your father was nothing in bed, but with the right man, sex is exquisite. Exquisite! Listen to your body, Clare." Then she stood up and walked away.

Clare felt punched, gasping and sick. She crossed her arms in front of her chest, holding on to her own shoulders to stop herself from shaking. What could be happening? She wanted her mother to be drunk, but she knew she wasn't; her glass of wine was almost full. The mother she knew would never have spoken those words, would never have taken her out of school to go to lunch, wouldn't have given her wine, wouldn't have touched a waiter. Should she tell someone? Who? Would her mother get in trouble if she did?

Clare knew what you did when someone you loved died. You pulled yourself tall and straight like a princess, received condolences graciously, dry-eyed, and then later sobbed stormily and cleansingly into your pillow. But all the books she'd read had taught her nothing about what you do when your mother doesn't die but turns into someone you don't know, someone who doesn't take care of you anymore.

3

Cornelia

If you're not a big believer in signs, then, trust me, we have that in common. If your impatience with people who are forever telling stories containing a fairly ordinary coincidence that they interpret (after a pregnant pause) as *a sign* borders on nausea, I'm right there with you. And if you've noticed that such people almost invariably opt to take as signs only those things that point them in precisely the direction they wanted to go anyway, while ignoring plenty of other seemingly valid sign options, well, my friend, we're three for three.

For example, this arrogant, slick-haired guy Luka from the café showed up one day fairly gyrating with excitement about a woman he'd just met in New York, whom he called his "soul mate," letting the phrase hang in the air for a moment as though it were freshly minted rather than so shopworn as to be entirely without meaning to any thinking person. Then he recounted their meeting, unsubtle-innuendo-laden interaction, and subsequent minimal-but-promising sexual contact. And the big finish, the shiny tack that was meant to pin his little story to our brains forever, was the fact that they were both wearing entirely brown ensembles. Brown shirts, brown pants, brown socks, brown shoes. Brown *belts*! Brown *watch bands*! (It was the small leather goods that really seemed to get him.) After a pause, Luka breathed reverently. "It was a sign we belong together."

The sad part is that at least five people heard this story, and not one called him an idiot, but instead sat wordlessly smiling and slow-nodding at him. No one liked Luka because he was wholly unlikable, but people were a bit in awe of him, as he was the richest person any of us knew personally. Though Luka was a dog-walker by trade, his grandfather set up the entire family for countless generations by inventing a grommet or wing nut or gasket or some other of those tiny Dr. Seuss–sounding gizmos. Because it had to be done, I fought through the money fog that surrounded Luka and said, "What about the fact that she's married with two small children? What was that a sign of?"

So, you can imagine my embarrassment in telling you how the day after meeting Martin, I set about compiling my own collection of signs. It wasn't a large collection, I'm happy to report. It contained three items; I'd say three *measly* items, but while the first two were definitely measly, the third was really quite spectacular—downright cinematic.

The first sign didn't even strike me as a sign until I was stepping through the door of Fringer's Antiques on the heels of my friend Linny at about ten the next morning, which was roughly twenty-four hours after the sign dropped into my life. Actually, it didn't drop into my life as much as fall out of my mouth. I'm talking about the reference to my mother, the one I made when Martin asked me to go to London with him.

I almost never talk about my parents to anyone. They're fine people. I love them. Don't sit there waiting for me to disclose some dark childhood secrets—and I hope and pray I'm not one of those tiresome underachieving, unabused offspring who blames her parents for her limping career, designer-knockoff shoes, and broken toaster oven (my shoes are generally quite good, just so you know). Let's just say that, from a fairly early age, my home life felt like a movie set I'd stumbled onto by accident. If you've seen Katharine Hepburn as a Chinese revolutionary in *Dragon Seed*, you know what I'm talking about. Good intentions, talented players, everyone trying hard. Just bad casting.

In any case, my bringing up a topic to Martin that I only ever broach with my most intimate of intimates was remarkable. I took it as a sign.

"I take it as a sign," I said to Linny.

"A sign that you're deranged," belted Linny into the cool silence of the shop. She tapped her finger on the side of her head, a head that was wrapped in a scarf. It was an awful scarf, a horror of polyester silk printed with Monet's waterlillies.

"Shhh!" I hissed as Mr. Fringer inclined his head to shoot a look over the tops of his glasses at us. His shop was not one of the truly elegant ones on Pine Street, no mint-condition eighteenth-century writing table posing tiptoe like a ballerina in his window. No mint-condition anything. But a good shop—my favorite. The garbage, the not-bad, the godforsaken, sat cheek-by-jowl with the stunning-but-for-a-ripped hem, -missing knob, -water stain, -torn cover—the only unifying principle being that at one time or another, old Mr. Fringer had taken a shine to each and all.

Mr. Fringer was severe, but I liked him for two reasons. First, he was unabashedly gaga over his wife, had photos of her in gilt frames hanging behind his desk, and would work the fact of her beauty into almost any conversation. She *was* beautiful, too, in a broad-shouldered, duchessy, Ingrid Bergman–type way. What was so great about Mr. Fringer's love for his wife was that she wasn't dead, as one might have expected. I'd even met her a couple of times. I found it quite moving that a man could be so awe-filled and celebratory about the woman he came home to every night.

The second reason I liked Mr. Fringer was that he was a reasonable man, a man who could be bargained with. I'd once talked him down from five hundred dollars to two hundred for a great big, Depression-era chandelier—a wreck, but a salvageable wreck, or so I'd thought upon seeing it, even though I know squat about antiques. And I was right. Not to boast, but it's the kind of thing I have a knack for being right about. I polished up the brass, hunted down crystals that matched it, and talked my landlord into hanging it from my apartment's high ceiling. Every day, I could look up and watch it sparkle like my own personal galaxy. So if Mr. Fringer wanted his store, his precious merchandise, swaddled in reverential hush, I was happy to oblige.

"But you were right to turn him down. He could be a homicidal maniac," stage-whispered Linny.

I picked up a black, asymmetrical, upside-down tornado made of felt.

"Could be. But wasn't. You don't know; you didn't see his eyes. They were brown," I whispered.

"Well, why didn't you say so before?" snorted Linny. "Did you give him your number? And what the hell is that?"

"A hat. I did. I wrote it in my very best penmanship." I set the hat down. Very Ninotchka, but like every other human being besides one who's ever lived, I'm no Garbo. Besides, some things just can't make the leap from past to present, and that hat was not a leaper.

A young man in what can only be called a blouse—paisley gauze and piratelike with poufed sleeves cinching at the wrists—entered the shop with what can only be called a saunter. He carried an overloaded backpack over one shoulder that he probably called a rucksack because he was just the type. I saw Mr. Fringer sharpen his gaze and aim it toward the backpack, watching its proximity to breakables; he leaned his head and shoulders back, a cobra ready to strike.

The young man's glance settled on Linny. His face darkened with recognition, and he approached, sleeves gently burgeoning.

"Your poetry selection is for the birds," he declared, his eyebrows arched. Linny had deferred her acceptance to law school a few years back and worked in a bookstore.

"Tweet," tweeted Linny loudly, after a pause of just the right length. Linny is a master of the pause. The man stared, blinked twice, then wafted out of the store. Mr. Fringer gave Linny an approving smile. She smiled back, with a modest, one-shouldered shrug, before turning to me, wide-eyed.

"His shirt," said Linny.

I shut my eyes to block out the memory.

"I loved it," said Linny. I opened my eyes and looked at Linny in her scarf, striped engineer's overalls, and embroidered Chinese slippers. A wave of love splashed over me. Linny is truly the only person I know who wears whatever the hell she likes. If ever she hauled off and went to law school, they'd probably send her home to change clothes. Maybe not, though. She'd apparently rolled out of bed one morning, stretched, taken the LSAT practically on a whim, and gotten a score that had the whole Ivy League drooling like a basset hound.

"I love *this*," I said. Divine, perfect, made for me. Made maybe seventy-five years ago, but definitely for me. Black, sleeveless, narrow, dropped waist, a touch of black beading, possibly real jet. Light as a feather and no bleaching under the arms, thank you, God. A first-date dress to die for; a first-date dress Louise Brooks would die for. I knew it would fit.

"That wouldn't fit a Chihuahua," said Linny.

Like a glove. Sign number two.

What surprisingly few people know is that before Joan Crawford was terrifying with eyebrows like two shrieking crows, she was adorable and sylphlike and funny. At the end of *Forsaking All Others,* a film that will charm you but will not alter the warp and woof of your life's fabric, Joan finds out it was old pal Clark Gable not, as she had supposed, lifelong love Robert Montgomery who, on what was supposed to be her wedding day, filled her room with cornflowers, her favorite of all flowers. When a friend informs her of this, her pretty face fills with light, the scales fall from her eyes. The flowers are a sign! She is transfigured! Clark is her man! Put aside the fact that, despite Robert Montgomery's goofy cuddliness and nice posture, a choice between him and Clark Gable is no choice at all; put aside the fact that RM got drunk and married a floozy with an appallingly artificial speaking voice the night before he was supposed to marry Joan. It's the flowers that send Joan out the door, stranding RM on their would-be second wedding day, and onto the ship that's about to carry Clark away forever.

It was my day off, but after Linny reminded me one more time that Martin Grace did not step off some movie screen into my life and after I'd rolled my eyes at her and shoved her through the doorway of her bookstore, I popped my head into Café Dora.

And there they were: two dozen, in full bloom. Sent by a man to whom, in our whole half-hour conversation, I had never breathed a word about flowers. A cloud, a flock, an aria, a *glory* of peonies, as lush as hope, as white as a promise. I nodded at them, and twenty-four snowy heads nodded back.

Sign number three.

4

Clare

Clare sat on her bed with her notebook, sorting examples. The examples seemed to fall into two categories: girls who used sweetness and girls who used pluck. *Little Women* contained both kinds of girls. Beth March was gentle and shy, so scary Mr. Laurence next door gave her a piano. When Jo March looked him right in the eye and told him he wasn't as handsome as her grandfather, he laughed and said she had spirit.

It was important that Clare figure out how to get a man to like her, because she had decided to call her father. Clare's father wasn't frightening in any ordinary kind of way. He wasn't ugly with wild hair, he didn't shout, and she couldn't remember him ever getting angry at her. Clare wasn't even sure that she was scared of him, but the thought of calling him made her heart pound. She had never called him before. When she told Max the cleaning lady this, Max started puffing and sputtering and cleaning the kitchen table with swipes that were more like slaps.

"Jesus Christ, almost eleven years old, and you've never called your own father! The bastard must go out of his way to make you feel pretty goddamn comfortable with him." Clare smiled at Max's back, jolted out of her fog of worry for a few seconds by Max's rapid-fire tirade. Clare thought Max had the most unexpected voice to ever come out of a person. While Max was all cool, art-girl edges to look at—skinny, pierced, inky black bangs in a mid-forehead, straight-across chop above cat's-eye glasses—her voice was a cartoon airhead chirp. Instead of sounding harsh, her expletives streamed like little silver bubbles in a fish tank.

"Guess he thinks he can just write a check, and his fatherly duties are done. Forget connection. Forget sharing your child's life. *So* wholly fucked-up, as I'm sure you'll agree." She paused and looked at Clare.

"Pretty fucked-up, I guess," said Clare with a shrug, enjoying the tang of the forbidden words in her mouth, but not really sure they were accurate. Clare hadn't called her father before not because he'd told her not to but because it hadn't occurred to her before. She wondered whether she was supposed to want to call him up to tell him about a new friend or a good book or her role in the school play. Maybe she was the one who was fucked-up. Clare considered asking Max about this, but decided against it.

As Clare watched Max, she thought about how Max dusted in the same way she did everything, with square-shouldered authority, but also with care. She imagined the little muscles of Max's arms rippling under their tattoos. What if Clare scrapped the whole idea of calling her father? What if she just told her problem to Max instead? Maybe Max could help.

But Clare decided not to tell Max, after all. Although she considered Max an adult, Clare knew that not everyone would; some people would think of her as a kid, and kids had trouble getting listened to, especially if they had tattoos and funny glasses. Besides, even if someone would listen to Max, in order for Max to get someone to help Clare's mother, she'd have to tell them how wrong things had gotten, how Clare's mother wasn't being a very good mother anymore, and the thought of this scared Clare.

Clare tried to imagine living with her father instead of her mother, and she just couldn't; she was sure her father couldn't imagine it either. If Clare knew anything about her father, it was that he would never let anyone take Clare's mother away from her. If he decided to help, he'd figure out a solution that would keep them together.

"I'd truly love to get my hands on that asshole," tinkle-belled Max, and Clare thought maybe Max would be just what her father needed. That she'd be like Maria bursting into the Von Trapp household with her satchel and funny haircut, waking everyone up, making clothes out of curtains, and making Captain Von Trapp fall in love with music, his children, and her. Clare doubted it, though. She remembered how the captain's lips twitched when his little daughter Gretel forgot to say her name during roll call. You got the feeling right from the beginning that Captain Von Trapp had a soft heart under his cold, unsmiling exterior, and Clare had never gotten this feeling from her father, even though he smiled all the time and called her "Clare-o the Sparrow." Besides, Captain Von Trapp had the excuse of being grief-stricken and a widower, and Clare's father wasn't either of those things.

"He's not mean to me or anything," said Clare. "He just has this . . ."

"This what?" said Max, stopping her cleaning and turning to look at Clare. She pulled off her fisherman's sweater and sat down on the floor next to Clare, sticking her blue-jeaned, pipe-stem legs out in front of her. Max was usually bundled in layers of clothes: hoodies, long underwear, flannel shirts, child-size tank tops, and sometimes an oversized funny purple-and-green poncho on top of it all. Once Max had left the poncho at Clare's house and Clare had walked around her backyard in it, loving the way it made her feel cuddled and safe and, at the same time, like a butterfly. Now Max wore a tiny black T-shirt that said HAUSFRAU in pink gothic print.

"This way of looking at me. The way my mom looks when we go over to the Shrewsburys' for dinner; she smiles and talks and laughs, but you can tell she's really bored. That's how my dad looks at me, like he can't wait for me to be over," said Clare. She was glad she'd told Max this, and glad she'd thought of the right way to say it. She hadn't actually put it into words before, even inside her own head.

Max put her arm around Clare and said, "His loss, honey-pie."

When she was nine, Clare's best friend Molly had moved to Taos, New Mexico. Among all the losses this meant for Clare—and it ranked, until recently, as the heartbreak of her life—the most painful loss was Molly's family and her great, ramshackle Tudor house.

Clare's mother had owned a party-planning business—still did own most of it, in fact, though she'd gradually turned the day-to-day work over to her partner Sissy Sheehan and had become a kind of figurehead. Back when she was running it, though, Clare's mother did most of the planning, ordering, arranging—the daylight work, she called it—but sent Sissy to the actual event. Clare wondered how her mother could stand it: choosing the candles, food, plates, flowers, music, sometimes even creating a theme like Ali Baba or the Roaring Twenties, paying attention to details like the color of the lighting or whether to hang tapestries on the green walls to keep everyone from looking jaundiced, but then never getting to see how it all turned out. When Clare asked her about it, her mother had said, "I do see it, Clare. In here." She'd tapped her head, then smiled and tilted up Clare's chin with her finger. "Anyway, I'd rather see *you,*" she concluded, so that Clare understood why her mother did the daylight work.

Sometimes, though, especially during the holiday season, an event was so important that Clare's mother had to be there herself. Then she would put on a long crepe or jersey dress, usually black, nothing bright or sparkly, except maybe her chandelier earrings if the event was very special. The point was to be invisible, Clare's mother told Clare, even though Clare knew her mother would shine like a star no matter what. And she would drop Clare off at Molly's house, sometimes coming out to talk to Molly's mother, Liv, or her father, Jim, maybe doing a funny, self-mocking spin or curtsey in her dress, and then would pick Clare up the next morning. Her mother usually arrived when they were still at the breakfast table, and she would sit for a minute and have coffee with Liv and tell vivid little stories about the party: a minor avalanche of profiteroles, a drunk guest's profanity-studded toast, a hostess swooning in her tight-cinched corset-bodice dress. Clare treasured these moments: the taste of cinnamon toast, flowers on the table, her mother's dancing laugh, the two girls, the two women, happy and friends.

When Molly's family moved, Clare had no place to stay, so her mother hired an assistant named Seth for Sissy and they began doing all the night work. First, though, Clare's mother had to attend one more function—a big getaway weekend at a mountain resort to celebrate the marriage of the children of two feuding society families.

"I have to be there to make sure they're not slipping poison into each other's martinis. When the guests leave the party on a stretcher, it's bad for business." Her mother's voice softened. "It'll just be this one time, Clarey."

So, after six years of short day visits, Clare had ended up at her father's apartment in the city for an entire weekend. It hadn't been so bad, at first. Clare's father had filled every second with activity: the Natural Science Museum, the art museum, a picnic in the park with restaurant food in fancy little boxes instead of sandwiches, a shopping trip during which her father bought her a pair of high-heeled leather boots that her mother thought were unsuitable for an eight-year-old and never let her wear and a red double-faced wool coat embroidered with flowers around the cuffs and a matching hat that might have come right out of Sara Crewe's closet. The first night, they had gone to dinner at the Four Seasons and afterward Clare had fallen asleep with a new white teddy bear the size of a three-year-old child.

But the second night, she'd awakened around midnight and felt suddenly scared of the unfamiliar room with too much light coming in through the tall windows. She stepped over to one of the windows and looked down at the moving cars and the people on the sidewalks. It felt lonely to be in the room, with all the lit-up busyness down there, all its noises she couldn't hear. She thought about why she wanted to go home, even though her father was nice to her. Maybe it was because he forgot the names of people she'd just finished telling him about and because he sometimes asked the same questions twice. But the thing that made her feel dull and almost invisible was the way his gaze would drift sideways or over her shoulder as she spoke. His attention was like a child's when there's a television on in a room, and Clare could sense his eyes scanning as though another, better daughter might skip into view at any moment.

After a while, Clare had decided to get a drink of water and glided carefully past her father's bedroom door to the kitchen. It had taken her a while to find a glass and just as she finished filling it, she heard a low, animal-like sound coming from the living room. She almost made a run for it, back to the guest room, but thought of Mary Lenox from *The Secret Garden*, how she'd heard crying somewhere in the English manor house she'd been sent to after her parents died of cholera and had marched boldly down spooky hallways looking for the source of the sound.

Clare had held her breath and inched into the living room, holding the glass of water in front of her as though it were a candle lighting her way. She'd almost dropped it when she saw the woman, a stranger, half-lying on the loveseat, hair tumbled to one side, a hand dangling, face slack, mouth wide open as she snored. A sharp noise jumped from Clare's throat, and she ran to her father's bedroom, water splashing over her hand onto the floor. The room was empty. Crying, she called her mother's cell phone, and her mother left the mountain retreat that minute. Clare packed her bag, heart banging, and took the elevator to the lobby where she waited for her mother. In the two hours it took for her to get there, for Clare's hot face to be pressed against the soft wool of her mother's coat, her father never came back, and the woman he'd left to watch her never noticed she was gone.

After that, Clare felt something new for her father, something that might have been anger but that came out as unease and watchfulness and didn't leave much room for sweetness.

So it would have to be pluck, Clare decided. She sat looking at the phone. The vacuum cleaner was a distant, reassuring whine and tangled up with the sound was Max's sprightly, off-key soprano: "You are lost and gone forever! Dreadful sorry, Clementine!" Max's voice made the words sound jolly.

Clare listened to Max sing a second longer, then shoved the books off her bed with a decided bang; plucky or not, she'd rather call with Max in the house.

Besides, her mother might be home soon, with bags full of quirky, expensive food she'd culled from various groceries and specialty stores. The past week or so, Clare's mother had been on a cooking tear, had taken to buying armloads of cookbooks, issues of *Food & Wine* and *Gourmet*, as well as cooking tools that were expensive and exquisitely specific in nature, like a huge paella pan with its own circular propane burner.

Clare would watch her mother unpack grocery bags, cradling the food in her thin hands as though each item were a fragile precious gift, an offering: morels; saffron; white truffle oil; Dover sole; a bag of small, purple potatoes; a long, thick stalk with Brussels sprouts growing around it like a spiral staircase. Then, she'd cook in a fevered, chattering way, sometimes tumbling half-finished dishes into the sink and beginning over, sometimes pulling golden, fragrant soufflés or loaves out of the oven and arranging them before Clare in a gesture that seemed oddly far removed from feeding someone. Sometimes, Clare would wake up in the middle of the night and hear her mother chopping. On these occasions, Clare would wait until her mother went to bed, then would tiptoe downstairs to turn off the lights and, once, two of the burners on the stove.

Clare dialed her father's office, and when his secretary answered, Clare said firmly, "This is Clare. Please put my father on. It's imperative that I speak with him right away."

There was a pause, and then the secretary said, "Oh. Well, how are you, Clara?" She sounded young, not intimidated by what Clare hoped was her own forcefulness, and also . . . what? Sympathetic, maybe. Despite getting Clare's name wrong, the secretary sounded nice. Clare felt a little thrown off. It was easier to be plucky in the face of opposition.

"Fine," said Clare, the edge in her voice smoothing in spite of herself.

"Your father's not in the office, but I can have him call you back. OK?"

Clare felt deflated. No. She didn't trust him to call back, but even if he did, it might be too late. Her mother might be home. Her mother might even answer the phone.

"No," said Clare, her voice rising, "I need to talk to him now. Please."

After another pause, the woman said, "Well, look, sweetie, I just got off the phone with him, so I bet I can catch him. He'll call back in a few minutes. How does that sound?"

"It sounds good," said Clare, softly. "Thank you."

She hung up and waited for what felt like a long time, with one hand on the phone. When it rang, she jumped and pulled her hand back as though the phone had suddenly caught fire. Then, she answered.

"Hello."

"Sparrow!" said her father's voice, "Good to hear from you! How's your afternoon?" Just like that—"how's your afternoon"—as though he talked to her every day instead of almost never. Clare wondered if there were someone else in the room with him, listening.

"I need to talk to you," said Clare.

"I've only got about five minutes, sadly enough, but for five minutes, I'm all yours."

Clare gathered herself. "This is important. It might take longer than five minutes. It's about Mom."

Clare expected him to say something, ask something, but he didn't.

"She's sick, I think. Or maybe she's"—Clare faltered—"she's changing; she's not acting like herself. And this has been going on for a pretty long time."

"I'm sure it's nothing to worry about, Clare," he said. "People change. You're different every time I see you. You took maybe two tiny sips of your egg cream last time you were here, and you remember, don't you, how you used to love them?"

Clare felt a flash of hatred for the playfulness in his voice. "No. No. It's not like that. It's not any kind of regular change. Listen to me!"

"I'm listening." Her father sounded tired.

"She cooks all the time, all night sometimes."

"Well, that doesn't sound so bad. Go on," said her father.

"And she buys things, weird things. Big pans and cookbooks."

"Well, she never did seem to have any trouble spending money," he said dryly.

"No, you don't understand. Like—towels. She bought all these towels, in every color." This sounded ridiculous, even to Clare. She heard her father cover the mouthpiece and speak to someone. She began to fill with panic; she was losing him.

"And she took me out of school for lunch. She gave me wine!" She didn't want her voice to sound the way it did, desperate. But she was desperate.

"Well, I think that's wise. French children younger than you drink wine, Clare. What did you think of it?"

"What did I *think* of it? I hated it! And she flirted with this really young waiter; she held his hand. And she said things to me that she wasn't supposed to say. That she wouldn't say. Things about, about . . ." Clare was crying now.

"Calm down, Sparrow. About what?"

Clare shut her eyes. "Sex." Now I've done it, thought Clare. Now I'm a traitor. Unbelievably, her father laughed.

"Look, Clare, your mother is a grown woman, a single woman and, if memory serves, a beautiful one. If she wants to flirt with a waiter or anyone else, that's her business. It might make you uncomfortable, but it's perfectly natural. And you're nearly eleven years old. I only wonder why she hasn't already had a conversation with you about the facts of life."

Clare ignored this. "All I can think is that it was the bat."

"Bat?"

"We woke up one day last summer, and there was a bat in the house. Mom told Dr. Aduba about it, and he said, just to be safe, we should both get a round of rabies shots. Not the stomach kind. Mom didn't think you could get bitten by a bat and not know it, but she made me get the shots anyway. But she didn't get them. And now she's sick."

"Your mother doesn't have rabies, Clare." His voice now was the voice of a person who is making a show of being patient. For a moment, despite Clare's efforts, desperation won out over pride. When she spoke, her voice was smaller than she wanted it to be.

"Dad? What's happening, it's scaring me. I can't sleep."

"There is nothing to be afraid of. I promise you that. And now I have to go. I'm sorry." He was about to hang up. Pluck, Clare thought, pluck, pluck.

"You're not sorry. But you're my father. You have to help." There was a pause.

"I'm telling you, as your father, that everything's fine, Clare. I'll talk to you soon." He hung up.

Clare looked at the phone in her hand, then stuck it under her pillow, so she didn't have to look at it. She slid onto the floor, tucking her knees up under her shirt, holding them hard.

It didn't make sense to feel more alone after this conversation, she thought. It wasn't like she'd lost something, because there was never anything there to lose. But she felt more alone anyway.

5

Cornelia

Less than twenty-four hours after I got the flowers, he called. Didn't just call, but called from London, thank you very much. When I heard his voice, I could just *feel* the presence of scones and lemon curd on a tray next to him and the red double-decker buses lumbering by outside.

"Hello," I said.

"Do you eat?" he asked.

"Sometimes," I said.

"Did I just say, 'Do you eat'? I meant, 'What do you eat?'"

"Oh, things," I said. I pressed two fingers to my wrist. Pulse leaping. Voice cool.

"Vegetarian?"

"Omnivore."

"Omni means all. Do you eat all things?"

"No tongues of any kind. And no licorice."

He laughed a pure, warm, amber-colored laugh that made me feel pure, warm, and amber-colored.

I wore the dress, with a short, lightweight, cranberry wool coat with bracelet sleeves (but no bracelets) over top, and my favorite knee-high black boots. The sole advantage to freakish smallness is that the feet that accompany it are also freakishly small, enabling one to make out like a bandit at shoe sales. (Don't be alarmed, I don't plan to regale you with descriptions of every outfit I wear, although I remember, as a kid, loving that about Nancy Drew books: "Wearing a dainty, ice-blue blouse, Nancy opened the door"; "Nancy tossed a soft yellow cardigan over her slender shoulders and slipped into her convertible"; "Nancy removed her blouse, skirt, and shoes, and put on a pale green shift dress and a pearl necklace." But the fact is, sometimes clothes are *significant*.)

Being my mother's daughter, I turned a deaf ear to the inner voice screaming at the top of its lungs, "Trust this man completely!" so that when Martin asked where he should swing by and collect me, I told him I'd meet him at the restaurant. Five days later I walked up, and there he was, waiting. I won't gush about his appearance, except to say that he was beautiful in the way certain handcrafted wooden objects are beautiful—so seamless, smooth, curved, lustrous, so fully realized and self-contained that it only strikes you seconds later and with the force of a lightning bolt: "Oh my God, that's a chair!" At which point, you sit down and want to stay forever.

The restaurant was of the jewel-box variety: tiny, booths and chairs covered in silver-gray velvet, a fireplace hanging on the wall like a picture in a frame. The food was superlative, I'm sure it was, no doubt made with fresh, seasonal ingredients, no doubt appropriately crusty on the outside and melting on the inside, inspired but unpretentious, simple but original. I vaguely remember being surprised by the taste of figs, and I'm pretty sure I lifted a spoonful of something creamy and the color of a sunset to my lips. But my senses, hijacked by Martin, barely registered what was maybe the best meal of my life.

We talked and talked and talked. Maybe love comes in at the eyes, but not nearly as much as it comes in at the ears, at least in my experience. As we talked, lights flicked on inside my head; by the end of the night, I was a planetarium.

He told me he loved my name, how there were a handful of women's names that turned all other women's names into cotton candy, and my name was in the handful.

"Along with what?" I asked him.

"Eleanor, Mercedes, Augusta," and he reeled off four or five more like a man reciting a poem, so I told him about my first college roommate, a purebred palomino of a girl from Savannah with unimpeachable calves and an antique amethyst the size of a walnut on a chain around her neck. She could fling a Frisbee like a pro, speak flawless French, and had a sweet, long-and-pointy-canine-toothed smile that threatened to collapse half of fraternity row like a house of cards. If she'd been slightly less pretty or if her family's money had been slightly less ancient, I'm sure she would've turned up her turned-up nose at me every chance she got. But because her own social position was unassailable, she could like whomever she chose. She liked me; I knew because she told people in the lilting, slightly hoarse (due to years of yelling across lacrosse fields or from horseback to others on horseback, I'm guessing) voice all future Tri-Delt presidents have, "Cornelia's a great girl!" I liked her, too, because she was nice and also because she cast a golden glow that fell on everything around her, including her ant-sized roommate.

But she decided within a couple of weeks that my name was just too "out there" and set about pulling a nickname out of "Cornelia."

"Well, the obvious choice would be . . ." said Martin, wincing.

"Don't say it. Don't even think it," I told him. "Are you thinking it?"

Martin shook his head and crossed his heart. I told him that she'd settled on C. C., even though my middle name, being Rose, did not begin with a C, and my last name, being Brown, did not begin with a C. For two semesters, I was C. C. Brown.

"Throw in a 'Little' or a 'Blind' and you've got yourself a bluesman," said Martin, helpfully. "This roommate of yours, what was her name?"

"Selkirk Dalrymple," I told him.

He laughed his molten laugh, and I felt like the kid at the party who whacks open the piñata. Victorious and with treasures raining down on me.

He told me about his own first college roommate, a guy who had a thing for the "beret set" girls and whose pièce de résistance seduction technique was to casually mention having read Proust's *Remembrance of Things Past*, all seven volumes (and, yes, Martin did use the French title at one point, pronouncing it accurately but not in an Alex Trebek kind of way, so stop worrying), which worked like a charm. When I asked Martin if the roommate had really read it, Martin said that was the beauty of it: The kind of people who were most jealous of him and who would have been, consequently, those most scathingly skeptical of him, were also the kind of people who would've preferred death over anyone's discovering that they had not themselves read it or at least not gotten any further than *Swann's Way* and so had no idea of what questions to ask to test him.

This is the kind of conversation it was: convivial, both of us making gifts to each other of little funny stories, sort of shining them up and handing them over and being nice to each other about them. We didn't drag out our secret souls and let them dance naked around the restaurant, but our little stories were glimpses into the interior, colorful postcards from the lands of Martin and Cornelia. A good way to begin.

Afterward, Martin walked me to the door of my apartment building. Under a streetlamp, he looked at me and ran one hand over my head, cupping the place above my neck for a second or two.

"It suits you, this cap of hair," he said.

"And look at you," I said. "Your eyelashes. They're like miniature whisk brooms." Then he laughed, reached for my hand, and placed a kiss in the center of my palm.

The next morning:

Linny: Let me guess, you watched him walk away, then took the stairs two at a time, singing "I Get a Kick Out of You."

Cornelia: Wrong. Wrong, wrong, wrong.

Linny: "Embraceable You."

Cornelia: Fiend. Hell-fiend friend from hell.

Linny [warbling smugly]: *"Don't be a naughty baby. Come to mama, come to mama dooooooo."*

On our second date, we ate with our fingers at a gold-and-red-draped Ethiopian restaurant; gaped at the otherworldly, ultrarefined, long-necked, sloe-eyed beauty of the entire restaurant staff from hostess to busboy; walked for an hour, my hand tucked into the crook of his arm in a way that cried out for me to be in pearl-buttoned, wrist-length gloves; and then, in the foyer of my apartment building, we filled five minutes with kisses so delicate, so intimate and gentle that, afterward, I walked up the stairs to my apartment, carrying the moment carefully as though it were a glass globe full of butterflies.

The next morning:
Linny: I know. Ethiopians are amazing. Can you believe that Peter Beard photographer guy gets so much credit for discovering Iman? Boy, finding a beauty in *that* country was tough! *That* took a real discerning eye!
Cornelia: I believe Iman is actually from Somalia.
Linny: Tomato, tomahto.
Cornelia: Nice. Very nice. Very culturally sensitive.

Sure, I could've told Linny about the wrist-length gloves and the butterfly globe, or else I could've just gone ahead and plunged an hors-d'oeuvre fork into my ear.

On our third date, we went to a Tom Stoppard play about A. E. Housman that left me awed and exhilarated. On the way out of the theater and for blocks and blocks, I gushed about the braininess and wordplay and passion and compassion and ruthlessness and how I'd sat in the theater and trembled with the sense that what was happening onstage was turning me into a better person. Martin said he felt the same way, "Except that you were watching the play, and I was watching you."

Amazing, right? How could there be more, right? There's more.

"I love movies, but usually plays make me restive," I told Martin, after a pause both elated and shy.

"Oh, restive. One of *those* words," said Martin, nodding.

"I know," I said, almost certain that I did.

"One of those words that mean the opposite of how they sound," said Martin.

"I know," I said again, because I did know, exactly. "Like enervated."

"Spendthrift," said Martin.

"Attrition."

"Obviate."

"Cleave."

"Cleave," said Martin, who didn't miss a trick.

On my doorstep we kissed, urgently, for somewhere in the neighborhood of twenty minutes.

The next afternoon:

Linny: So you and your new boyfriend are unregenerate dweebs in exactly the same way. De-lovely.

Cornelia: De-fuck off.

But I took that word *boyfriend,* folded it right up, and tucked it into my back pocket to think about later.

Over Vietnamese food on our sixth date, I somehow hopscotched from describing the best Halloween costume I'd ever worn (Charlie Chaplin; I was the spitting image, same too-small jacket—not easy to find for a too-small someone like me—big shoes, big eyes, cane . . . all but maybe three people thought I was Hitler, but *I* knew, which is what truly matters, right?) to confessing what I suspect is my worst personality trait.

"Fearfulness," I said. "I'm fearful. Fundamentally fearful, overly cautious, lacking an adventurous spirit. A fraidy-cat."

"You're not fearful, Cornelia," said Martin.

"I bailed out of my junior year abroad three days before I was supposed to leave for Spain, even though I was dying to go. I don't go in the ocean because I might get attacked by a great white shark. I've never owned a dog because those suckers can turn on you in the blink of an eye. I went to college in the town I grew up in. The same college in whose medical school my father teaches. I'm the only person I know who has never lived in New York City. And I turned down your offer to go to London."

"Fearful's not so bad. Fearful's good, actually, in some ways," said Martin, dunking a summer roll into the summer-roll sauce. I reached across the table and touched his cheek with my hand, ostensibly to thank him for the attempt at consolation, but really, secretly because I could and was relishing that fact. His skin was taut and warm under my fingers.

"My ex-wife used to tell me I was fearful," he said, "but I had a pug named Puggy as a kid, so she must've been wrong." I kept my hand on his cheek for another beat to demonstrate my coolness upon hearing the ex-wife news, then lifted it away with mothlike lightness. He bit into the summer roll. Not even the tiniest bit of vermicelli, not even the smallest drop of sauce fell; Martin was the tidiest eater I'd ever seen. I thanked my stars I'd neglected to include the fear of men with ex-wives on my fears list.

"So how long were you together?" I asked, examining a fragment of peanut on the tablecloth with my finger, casually, I hoped. Although, when I thought about it later, devoting any attention at all to a fragment of peanut is probably a dead giveaway that one is not feeling casual.

"Just over a year. She had that respiratory thing and breath like rotten cauliflower. I went camping for a week, came back, and she'd been disappeared."

I looked up at him, finger on the peanut.

"She was also hopelessly incontinent."

I kept looking.

"Four years," he said.

"What happened?" I asked.

"Nothing very interesting. We had a good run. Just weren't meant for the long haul." So gallant and good-natured, so feather-light and civilized, so Cary Grant. It was an answer I should have savored; instead, it gave rise to that moment. You know what I mean. The moment in a relationship in which at the same time you discover you've been floating in air for five and a half weeks, you also discover that your feet have dropped a little closer to the earth.

"You make her sound like a racehorse. Or like a play," I said. Teasingly, I hoped.

"Now that you mention it, Viviana was a little of both. Leggy, overbred, no shortage of drama, some of it melo-."

I am leggy insofar as I have legs.

"Viviana. She's Latin, then?" Jennifer Lopez, Salma Hayek, Penelope Cruz. They began slinking around my head on endless legs. Cameron Diaz, too, although it's unclear to me that she's actually Latin, and if Natalie Wood in *West Side Story* made an appearance, well, all I can say is I was a little agitated.

"Viviana Hobbes. Her first name being one of those things Anglo-Saxon aristocrat families do to exoticize themselves." And, instantly, there was Grace Kelly, shooing the Latin and pseudo-Latin lovelies away with one swipe of her Kelly bag.

That night, when I kissed Martin good-bye, over his shoulder (I was standing a few steps above him), I imagined I caught a glimpse of Grace Kelly as Viviana Hobbes looking at us. But her gaze, when it met mine, wasn't the cool blue regard we all associate with Grace, not the gaze of *To Catch a Thief* or *High Society*. Instead those eyes were Georgie Eligin's from *The Country Girl*, all rue, patience, and loneliness.

Over poached eggs on toast at Linny's:
Linny: Can I ask just two questions?
Cornelia: No.

Linny: First, you hear "Anglo-Saxon aristocrat" and torture yourself with Grace Kelly. Why do you *do* that? Is Grace Kelly the only Anglo-Saxon aristocrat in the world? Did you ever consider Jackie Frigging Bouvier Kennedy? Did you ever consider that Viviana Hobbes just might have eyes on the sides of her head like an otter?

Cornelia: I'd have to say, no.

Linny: I didn't think so.

Cornelia: Anyway, that wasn't it, the Grace Kelly thing, that wasn't what bothered me. It was the breeziness.

Linny: Breeziness?

Cornelia: His tone. Like marriage was a restaurant.

Linny: I need a little more.

Cornelia: Or tennis. Or two-button suits. Something he tried or used to do and just doesn't do anymore.

Linny: Like, "I was married, but it was nothing personal."

Cornelia: Like four years of marriage weighed nothing at all.

Linny: OK, but at least he wasn't like that one guy in that one movie, the one you made me watch.

Cornelia: . . .

Linny: The guy obsessed with his dead wife.

Cornelia: True. Especially since he was obsessed with her because he'd drilled holes in her sailboat and sent her dead body to the bottom of the sea.

Linny: Question number two: Did someone pass a law against sex?

Six dates. I had to admit she had a point.

And then came date seven. A little date I like to call *Date Seven* or *It Happened One Night.*

6

Clare

For three days following her conversation with her father, Clare lived inside the storm—the black, spinning hurricane of her fear. At night, she lay down with its roaring in her ears, and if she slept, she heard it again before her eyes were even open. She didn't read. She didn't go to school. When the school secretary called, Clare heard her mother say into the phone that she, Clare, was sick, and the clarity and sureness of her mother's voice made the storm around Clare grow blacker. That her mother could sound all right and be all, all *wrong* was as terrifying as the fact that her mother had never even taken Clare's temperature, never brought her a blanket or a cup of tea, seemed almost not to notice she was there.

Clare's skin felt wind-burned and prickly; her eyes and cheeks were hot all the time, but there were moments—especially moments when Clare imagined too far into the future—when her body was seized by a hard shivering. "I am sick with dread," Clare told herself. "I am heartsick." But while giving names to things that frightened and confused her had helped Clare in her old life, it didn't help her now. She rubbed her hands up and down her arms to warm herself, feeling the bones underneath, then rolled her fingers over the knobby places on the sides of her elbows, pressing down until it hurt. "Underneath, I'm a skeleton," she whispered to the daffodil-yellow walls of her room.

On the afternoon of the third day, Clare heard her mother step quickly and lightly up the stairs and go into her bedroom, heard the sound of drawers sliding open and shut. Her mother was half-singing half-murmuring a song, and Clare kept still, listening with her whole body. As she listened, almost shaking with effort, Clare felt something stirring in her chest, the tiny beginnings of anger. She slid off the bed, and her bare feet on the floor were surprising—faraway and strange, just shapes, yellow rug showing in the little space between her first two toes.

Clare walked shakily down the hall to her mother's room. The door was standing open, and Clare stopped just outside it, not looking in yet, holding her breath and listening to her mother sing. "Wild Is the Wind," a song from the Nina Simone CD Clare and her mother used to love listening to in the car. "Wild Is the Wind" was song number ten. Number two was "Mississippi Goddamn," and she and her mother adored that one, turned it up loud, and sang it, both of them, at the tops of their lungs, rolling the "god" around in their mouths, slinging the "damn" out with gusto. They could have been on the highway, cars zooming all around them, but they were in their own world, too, at those moments, it seemed to Clare, the interior of the car, that shared space of air, charged with their two voices, almost shimmering. Now, she listened to her mother sing one of their songs—hers and Clare's—in a stranger's voice, a voice that slid disturbingly back and forth between raspy and velvety and seemed so much to be sung *to* someone that Clare found herself stepping into the room to see who it was.

The room was empty, of course, except for her mother, who had just slipped a narrow summer dress over her head and was shimmying it into place, her hands running over her hips and down the sides of her legs. She didn't look up as Clare entered.

"It's December," said Clare. Her voice was creaky and hoarse, an old woman's voice.

Her mother seemed not to hear, but just kept singing in that new voice, as she sat down in her burgundy leather reading chair, "claret" is what she used to call the color, to put on a pair of high-heeled, strappy sandals. Clare saw that the shoes were precisely the same creamy color as her mother's feet. A shopping bag and a shoebox lay on the floor, and Clare saw them with the same kind of distance with which she'd seen her own feet moments before. Uncomprehendingly, she stared at the two shapes, the crumpled shape of the bag, its heavy, matte, sage green plastic with darker green lettering on the side and the clean lines of the black rectangular shoe box. Clare stared, concentrating, needing to understand what the two shapes were. Months later, Clare would read the William Carlos Williams poem about the red wheelbarrow and the chickens and would remember those two shapes. So much depends on—what? Two ordinary objects. A shopping bag, a shoe box.

When Clare realized what they were, they stopped being what they were and simply became two things too many. Something inside Clare gave way. The anger that had uncurled like a tendril at the sound of her mother's singing surged, filling her lungs, all the cells of her body, like smoke. Clare started screaming choked, clotted screams, a terrible sound in her own ears. She pitched herself—her thin, skin-covered bones, her wild hair and shaking head—into the room, kicking the shoe box, stomping on it, twisting the bag and trying to rip it to shreds. The plastic bit into her palms. "I hate you!" she screamed again and again. Then, "You're killing me!" And finally, dismally, and without inflection, "You don't even care, you don't even care, you don't even care."

After a long time, Clare dropped onto the floor at the foot of her mother's bed and pulled—clawed—at the edge of the duvet, yanking it off. It was weighty and full of feathers and covered with beautiful fabric—a Florentine pattern in dark corals and pinks and light greens. Clare wrapped it around herself, then sat inside it and looked at her mother, feeling almost shy.

Her mother had stopped singing and was looking back. Clare realized how long it had been since her mother had looked at her, right at her face. Her mother's eyes weren't shocked or afraid, and they did not seem to be the eyes of a woman who could go shoe shopping while her daughter lay in her room almost delirious with loss and fear. Her mother looked at her with a gaze full of kindness.

"Mommy," said Clare, quietly. "Mommy. You can't go outside in that. It's winter. It's cold."

Clare's mother smiled at her, a mother's smile.

"Your new shoes," whispered Clare, wonderingly, "they shouldn't sell summer shoes in winter."

Still surrounded by the duvet, Clare walked on her knees over to the claret-colored chair, paused for a second or two, then put her head in her mother's lap. "Please stay here, please stay, please stay. Don't leave. I miss you all the time," pleaded Clare.

Her mother lifted Clare's head from her lap gently, using both hands, as though Clare's head were made of glass, and stood up, stepping around Clare, around the tumbled fabric that formed a kind of landscape on the floor. Clare looked up at her mother, waiting.

"Oh, Clarey," said her mother, tenderly, patiently. "Resort. You remember."

Clare shook her head.

"Resort wear. In stores. That's how you can buy summer clothes in winter."

Clare's mother walked out, her heels loud on the oak plank floor of the hallway, then loud again on the stairs.

Clare sat on the floor, dazed. Her mind stayed empty for a while, and then she began remembering a slumber party she'd been to the previous spring, just before the end of school. Two popular girls had been there, twelve-year-olds with plucked eyebrows and long, swinging hair. They'd decided to play "makeover" on the plainest girl at the party, a girl with whom Clare had gone to school since she was four and whose dreadful shyness had, by first grade, stopped even the sternest teachers from calling on her. Her name was Candy, a name so wholly wrong for her it seemed cruel to say it, and hardly anyone did. The older girls covered Candy's face with awful, garish makeup—an orange, pink, and blue mask—and curled and teased her thin blond hair into a knotty mane. "You look gorgeous, Candy! Just like a movie star, I swear to God," the girls told Candy lovingly, looking around and nodding at the other girls at the party, prompting them to join in. Some of them did, crowding around Candy in a cooing, patting cluster as Candy, flushed and speechless, blinked her gummy eyelashes in happiness.

Exhausted on the floor of her mother's room, Clare recalled her own shame at having watched Candy's transformation without saying a word. When she finally spoke up, it was the disaster she'd known it would be. "Shut up, you guys. You know she looks terrible. Why don't you leave her alone?"

All the girls glared at her, then one of the twelve-year-olds said, "Bitch! You must think you're really hot. Look, you made her cry." And that was the worst of it, the way Candy looked, desolation creeping over her face as she realized they'd been making fun of her all along. As Clare left the room to call her mother to pick her up, she saw one of the twelve-year-olds putting her arms around Candy to comfort her and Candy letting her do it.

Clare should have known better—*had* known better—but it was the way the girls had spoken to Candy, the texture of their voices. Such meanness served up in the sweetest tones, and to someone whose need for love was terrible in its completeness.

The worst thing, Clare thought now. Worse than hitting. The worst thing anyone can do. And then her body jumped, jerked like a person's body who wakes up from a dream of falling. Again, her mother's voice was saying, "Oh, Clarey," tricking Clare into trust and hope, mocking her. There may have been a tiny piece of Clare that knew it wasn't true, but the rest of her ached, pulsed with the idea of her mother as a bully, of her mother hating her.

Back in her room, lying on her bed, Clare heard the front door open and shut, and she looked out the window to see her mother setting off across the lawn, her step jaunty, almost dancing. Coatless, her mother swung her long, bare arms as though it were summer, a picnic basket in one hand, a thermos in the other, and entered the woods that separated their house from the house next door.

By the time she came back, it was late at night; Clare was in a thick, dull sleep, so the huge front door's slamming was just a thud in her head, muffled—almost no sound at all.

And because Clare was eleven years old, alone, and in trouble she could not see her way out of, on the fourth day—a Sunday—Clare woke, breathed for a minute or two, got out of bed, and reentered her daily life.

"First a shower, then breakfast," she instructed herself firmly, as though she might refuse. As soon as she stepped into the shower, she realized she'd gotten it backward. Her head had been hurting for days, but under the falling water, the headache opened like a rose— bright red, layered, and complicated. The pain beat inside her face, her ears, down the back of her neck. Clare turned off the water and sat down on the edge of the tub, gasping, her ears ringing. Food. She needed food.

Downstairs in the kitchen, wrapped in her bathrobe, she grabbed the first thing she saw—a banana—wolfed it down, then threw up in the sink. Chocolate milk, next. Better. While she sipped it, she made herself two pieces of toast, buttered all the way to the edges and cut diagonally the way she liked, then sat down and ate with her eyes closed. It was one of those moments when eating is like prayer. Clare gathered her strength. She put her faith in the crunch of bread, in the saltiness of butter on her tongue; she took their goldenness into her body and, afterward, felt that her soul had been restored—at least enough so that she could mount the stairs, take a real shower, and put on her clothes. As she brushed her teeth, she examined her reflection in the mirror.

"Same old Clare. Same old face," she told her face, reassuringly, and it was almost true. Skin pulled a little tightly across her cheek-bones, faint purplish smudges under her eyes, but basically the same as ever.

"Same old Clare," she said again and almost laughed with relief.

Clare put a notebook, two pencils, and, for company, a copy of *Anne of Avonlea* (the Anne book with the fewest sad events in it, apart from *Anne of Ingleside*, which Clare despised for its silliness and over-use of points of ellipsis and which she believed in her heart had not been written by L. M. Montgomery at all) into her backpack. Then she went downstairs to the library, where, for reasons unknown to Clare, her mother had started sleeping at night.

She was there now, on the sofa, covered with the brown, fringed cashmere blanket they'd had forever, and curled in toward the sofa's high back. Clare was glad she couldn't see her face, but she stood looking at her mother's hair falling over the edge of the sofa, honey-colored and gleaming like a waterfall even in the semidarkness. That was how her mother was, catching all the available light in any room and making it part of her. Grief was there suddenly, all around Clare; the room was filling up with it, so she held her breath like a person un-derwater and turned her attention to what she'd come for: her mother's purse. It sat neatly on a bookshelf. Clare removed the wallet and took out her mother's ATM card and then, without even a glance at the sleeping woman, she ran out of the room. When she had gulped in enough air to speak, Clare called herself a cab.

She had the driver pick her up in her next-door neighbors' driveway. The Cohens were a couple in their late sixties, who spent their win-ters on a Caribbean island the name of which they made a big deal about keeping secret, but which Mr. Cohen had once told Clare be-cause he liked her so much. "Keep it under your hat, sis," he'd said, winking. "If the whole town starts showing up, we'll have to find a new place." This made Clare wonder what the Cohens did down there that they didn't want their neighbors to find out about. But, except for writ-ing the name down in her notebook, Clare did keep it under her hat.

The Cohens were away now, but there were some men replacing slate shingles on their roof. One of the men waved at Clare. He was young, with a tan face and yellow hair like a surfer, and Clare thought someone so summery looking must be especially cold up there on the roof. She waved back.

The cab driver was a tiny person sitting in the center of an enormous puffed-up parka. He looked too young to be driving, but Clare saw his cabbie license posted on the little window that separated the back and front seats, so she asked him to take her to the bank downtown. During the drive they didn't speak, but sat listening to a woman sing opera; Clare could tell by the way the woman's voice soared and then dropped quite suddenly that, whatever had happened to the woman, she had started out angry and ended up sad.

Clare's mother usually bought things with credit cards, but when she and Clare were going someplace together, Clare's mother would let Clare get cash with her ATM card because Clare was still young enough to find the process magical. The password was Clare's own birthday. Clare entered the numbers and stopped cold, staring at the four Xs on the screen: 1202. December second; today was the third.

Clare felt a pang of self-pity, then made herself shrug. "Whatever," she told the four Xs—a word most kids said all the time and one that, for this reason, Clare chose never to use, but she felt the power of it now. Refusal, short, sharp, and hard, like a silver pin that could take the air out of anything; something to add to her arsenal. She pushed another button, and the four Xs disappeared. For most of her life, Clare hadn't had much occasion to feel sorry for herself but, standing at the ATM, she realized that this feeling loomed huge and possible, like a forest she stood on the edge of. If she entered it, she might never be able to leave.

When her mother's name appeared on the little screen, Clare felt like a thief and an imposter, but she got the money out anyway, because she had to. Clare didn't know much about being alone in the world, but she knew that people alone needed money. A hundred dollars. A lot of money—more than Clare had ever held in her hand before. Quickly she folded it into her change purse, dropped it deep inside her backpack, and started off down the street away from the bank.

Clare's downtown was really just one long street lined with pretty shops and restaurants. Even the hardware store was pretty, with its wooden sign shaped like a saw and gold lettering on the window. Clare hadn't been to that many places, but she knew enough about downtowns to understand that this one wasn't typical. The sidewalks were brick, for one thing, and there were giant stone planters here and there with plants that changed with the seasons. Today, they were full of greenery and tiny Christmas trees strung with lights.

There was a toy store full of handmade wooden toys, astonishing old-fashioned Lionel trains, and dolls with smocked dresses and the faces of real children. There was a clothing boutique her mother called "Instant WASP" that sold crisp, expensive clothes in candy pink, daisy-eye yellow, tree-frog green, and also sold matching mother-daughter Lilly Pulitzer dresses that made Clare and her mother roll their eyes at each other and say, "I wouldn't be caught dead!" There was a bakery with fragrant breads and the world's best birthday cakes (Clare's mother had once gotten her one shaped like a castle), and a real Italian gelateria featuring flavors like persimmon, cinnamon, espresso, and rose. You could get pepperoni at the pizza place, Pizza by Edie, but you could also get toppings like caramelized onions, prosciutto, shaved manchego, and a sauce made of yellow heirloom tomatoes.

Clare knew that even ordinary downtowns almost didn't exist anymore, that they stood around like abandoned movie sets, falling apart, and here it was as though someone had taken an ordinary downtown, waved a magic wand, and made everything a little bit or several times better-made, fresher, lovelier, costlier than ordinary. If Clare had been a few years older, she might have felt guilty about this. At newly eleven, she just felt lucky to live in such a nice place.

Naturally the diner Clare went into, called Lorelei's Down Home, served diner food made beautiful and interesting. Clare had been there many times with her mother for dinner. Her favorite was turkey meatloaf stuffed with sharp provolone and fresh basil served alongside potatoes smashed with garlic and cream. Today, it was Sunday— brunch served all day. Clare recognized one of the waitresses, who nodded at her and pointed toward a window table set for two. On the table was a cream pitcher, a sugar bowl full of pale brown chunks of raw sugar, and a vase of gerbera daisies.

When the waitress came with two menus, Clare said in a clear voice, "It's just me." The waitress paused for a moment, a puzzled line between her eyes, and Clare started to make up an excuse in her head. "My mother's shopping, and I got hungry" is what she was about to say, but the waitress smiled and said, "Good enough, love. Coffee? Hot chocolate?"

Clare smiled, "Hot chocolate, please."

After the hot chocolate arrived and Clare had given her order, a "Farmer's Frittata" with smoked ham and buffalo mozzarella, and after Clare had asked the waitress if buffalo really lived on farms and the waitress had laughed, Clare got out her notebook and began to make a list. CLARE'S TO-DO LIST she wrote in bold letters at the top of the page. Under it, she wrote:

1. Call Josie's mother. Ask for ride to and from school. Tell her M starting to work mornings. Tell her M not calling herself because she's in the middle of cooking dinner. Be sure to call around dinnertime.

2. Bring note to school giving permission for me to go home with Josie's mother. Type note on computer so only have to forge signature.

3. Call Jordan's Grocery for delivery. Get pasta, sauce, canned vegetables, peanut butter, jam, butter, Quaker oats, things that won't go bad. Get Parmalat milk in boxes. Can get bread and put in freezer. Maybe get cookies, too. Multivitamins to stay

healthy. Ask them to deliver early in morning before I go to
school. And before M wakes up.

4. Call Max. Cancel again, so she won't see M sleeping on sofa.
   Say going out of town. If she asks where, say New York City.
   Don't say seeing show because Max might ask about it.

Between bites of frittata and sips of hot chocolate, Clare broke her
life into twenty-four hour pieces and drew up a plan that she hoped
would get her from one day to the next.

And it worked. It worked more or less. There were a few glitches.
Once, Sissy Sheehan, who ran her mother's business, worried that her
mother had been out of touch and had failed to return the phone call
of a client they'd worked with for years.

"It's so not like her, Clare, you know? Is there something going on
with her I should know about? I mean, you'd tell me if she were sick,
right?"

Yes, I know it's not like the her that you know, but it's exactly like
the her she is now; yes, there's something going on; no, you shouldn't
know about it; or, yes, maybe you should; yes, I'd tell you if she were
some kinds of sick; no, I wouldn't tell you if she were other kinds of
sick; yes, yes, yes, she's sick in a way you can't even imagine. Clare
stacked up these true answers and put them aside. There was no reason to be angry at Sissy, but Clare was angry. I'm eleven, she wanted to
scream, I'm a kid. This is not my job. Look for answers someplace else.

"Sissy," Clare began carefully, "my mom's fine, but I think she's—
she's in transition."

"Transition? You mean, she's thinking of selling the business?" Sissy
sounded excited. Clare knew Sissy had wanted to buy her mother's
portion of the business for some time.

"Maybe. I'm not sure. She's doing some—introspection."

"Oh, God, aren't we all. Or shouldn't we all, rather. Seth and I were
just discussing that the other day. You just go on day after day, per-
forming the—what?—the *acts* of your life, and you get caught up, and

you lose track, don't you? You lose track of your self, your needs, your—what's the word . . ."

"Priorities?"

"Exactly! Jesus, Clare, sometimes you are truly not a child. You're that prescient! You just *know*, you know?"

"I know," said Clare. So this is how you talk to adults, she thought, Just throw out a few vocabulary words, and let them do the rest.

"So, OK then, tell her to take her time. Seth and I are holding down the fort, no problem. Give her my best. Godspeed and all that, OK?"

"OK. She'll be in touch, I'm sure," said Clare, although that was the very last thing she was sure of.

Clare's own friends were not quite so easily satisfied. One afternoon, Josie and Marie, another girl from their class at school, showed up at Clare's door unexpectedly. They'd ridden their bikes from Marie's house, which was just down the road, but it was a curvy road and was still quite a long way for two eleven-year-olds to ride their bikes. As they stood there, red-faced and panting, Clare understood that they'd come for a specific reason, and she stepped outside, shutting the door behind her, and waited. She didn't ask them to come in because, although her mother wasn't home and hadn't been home since early that morning, she might drive up at any moment. Josie and Marie couldn't be there when she did.

"Do you, like, not want to be friends with us anymore or what?" Marie was the one who asked, because that's the kind of thing Marie did, even though she wasn't especially good friends with either Clare or Josie. Clare thought of Marie as a girl who took up a lot of space, and she had a loud, throaty voice and T-shirts that already pulled tightly across her chest. She also phrased questions in such a way that no one was ever quite sure how to answer.

"No." Clare decided on "no," but threw in, "I do still want to."

"Because you never invite Josie over to your house anymore," said Marie. "And you're at hers all the time? You, like, live there?"

There was truth in this. Besides riding to and from school with Josie, Clare had begun doing her homework at Josie's house after school sometimes. No one seemed to mind. In fact, Josie's mother, Mrs. Arthur, was nicer to her than usual, bestowing upon her the kind of pitying looks and low, solicitous tones Clare imagined adults usually reserved for orphans and kids with cancer. Clare knew Mrs. Arthur didn't suspect that Clare's mother was going crazy or whatever she was doing; Mrs. Arthur just regarded Clare as the neglected child of a single mother.

Once, as Clare sat at their kitchen table helping Josie with a worksheet, Mrs. Castleberry, who had older children at Clare's and Josie's school, stopped by and, because they were the kind of adults who know much less about children than they think they do, Clare was able to overhear much of their conversation about her.

"Almost every day," said Mrs. Arthur.

"Her mother's otherwise occupied?" asked Mrs. Castleberry, but as though she already knew what the answer was. Even though they were in the next room, Clare could just feel Mrs. Castleberry's too-thin eyebrows going up as she said it.

"Working," sighed Mrs. Arthur. Like most of Clare's friends' mothers, Mrs. Arthur didn't have a job.

"She doesn't have to, you know. She's got more money than God. The only child of rich only children. Talk about silver spoons," said Mrs. Castleberry. Jealous, thought Clare.

"I just don't know why she doesn't get married. Lots of men would want her," said Mrs. Arthur. Clare looked at Josie, who rolled her eyes and mouthed the word "bitch."

"Oh, there are men all right," and then they dropped their voices. Clare's face burned. She wanted to rush in, tell those women precisely what she thought of them in her coldest voice, and then slam the door on her way out, rattling the stupid framed family photos taken at some stupid photo studio that Mrs. Arthur had hung on every wall. But if she couldn't be at Josie's house, she'd have to be at her own instead, and she couldn't face that, not every day. Besides, Josie's mother was her only way home.

"Sorry," Josie leaned over and whispered, and because Clare knew Josie was a nice girl, and also knew better than most kids that daughters aren't responsible for their mothers' behavior, she shrugged and smiled and said, "That's OK."

And as Josie stood next to Marie in Clare's front yard, Clare could tell that Josie felt helpless and wished none of it were happening, that she'd said a few words to Marie and then had gotten swept up in indignation and a plan that didn't really belong to her. Clare decided to forgive Josie, both because she knew Josie was weak, not bad, and because Clare needed her.

"My mom's just been really busy lately," Clare said, looking Marie right in the eye.

"Doing what?" asked Marie, for whom the concept "none of my business," was nonexistent.

"Working."

"Nobody has to work that much," said Marie. "I bet she's dating some guy she doesn't want you to know about."

Clare thought how strange it was that everyone seemed to think the same thing about her mother. Maybe it was because her mother was beautiful in a way most mothers aren't. Maybe being beautiful like that made people feel as though they knew all about your life. You don't know anything, thought Clare, and she wanted to laugh a bitter laugh. What people assumed was nothing compared to what was actually happening.

"Whenever she dates anyone, she tells me. I get to meet him, if I want," and this was true, although Clare's mother didn't have boyfriends very often or for very long. What her mother had said in the restaurant about sex popped into Clare's head, but she shook it away.

"Whatever," said Marie, which didn't surprise Clare. This was the word all conversations with Marie came to sooner or later. Clare turned to Josie.

"Are you mad at me?" she asked, and Josie darted a glance at Marie, took a breath, and shook her head.

"No, I'm not mad," said Josie. Clare felt proud of her.

"I have to go in, now," said Clare.

"Whatever," Marie said again and, as they started to get on their bikes, Clare went back into her house. The visit had worked out in her favor, she decided, as she knew about Marie's "whatevers." Like a stone dropped into a pool, her "whatever" on the subject of Clare and her mother would ripple outward, until the worst any of her classmates would think is that Clare's mother had a boyfriend—a mystery man. Clare didn't love the idea of everyone believing this, but it would be convenient, an umbrella explanation for her mother's absences or odd behavior. Besides, she knew Marie's imagination to be narrow and sluggish, incapable of any kind of leaping. No one would end up thinking her mother was dating a serial killer or the president or an international spy. Clare found this thought both comforting and mildly disappointing.

The final glitch in Clare's plan was simply that Clare had neglected the nuts and bolts of how she would go about being with her mother in the same house, as the mother she had always known slipped away more every day. She should have made lists of tones of voice, conversation topics, aspects of her mother's behavior to ignore, places for Clare to rest her hands or eyes while she was busily ignoring these aspects, and lengths of time she could allow herself to look into her mother's face to see what was or wasn't there.

For the first twenty-four hours or so, it didn't matter. Their house had always been ridiculously large for just two people, full of rooms no one went into much except Max, who went into them to dust untouched furniture and vacuum un-stepped-upon rugs and to "chase out the ghosts." Max played jokes on them sometimes, like hanging a painting upside down to see if anyone would notice. Now, with one occupant trying to be alone, and the other occupant spinning through days and rooms like a planet encircled by the atmosphere of her own distraction, the house was perfect. It colluded with Clare, who needed all the allies she could get, to keep them apart.

But on Wednesday morning, as Clare was finishing her toast, her mother walked into the breakfast room with the newspaper and sat down across from Clare.

"Morning, Clarey," she said.

Clare put her toast down and thought how everything had become a decision. The decision to put down her toast. The decision to look at her own mother. She looked. In her soft, fawn-colored sweater, no makeup, her hair in a ballerina knot at the nape of her neck, her mother looked totally normal. That is to say, she looked extraordinarily beautiful. But Clare wasn't fooled. Prettiness could be a lie, like anything else, and hope was not a game Clare played anymore.

She was right not to play it. Her mother began reading her bits of news from the paper, which seemed normal enough at first, and Clare responded with "ohs" and "reallys," but, eventually, all the stories were sad or violent. Boy-soldiers in Africa. Suicide bombers. Snipers shooting people as they put gas in their cars or took their children to school. Clare's mother would begin one story, break off mid-sentence, start another, her voice full of urgency, like a person crossing rushing water by jumping from stone to stone.

"So much heartbreak and disorder. How can the world hold all of it?" her mother said mournfully. Clare brushed the crumbs from the table onto her plate and stood up. Look around, Mom, she wanted to say, heartbreak and disorder are right here. Instead, she walked to the sink with her plate.

Then, her mother began to talk about the president, to rail against him, which wasn't actually so strange, since she had always regarded him as both stupid and dangerous, but this time, the words had an odd rhythm, as though her mother were so angry, she could rant instead of breathe.

"Give me one day in the White House, just one day," her mother said. Clare blew out a harsh laugh. "Oh, yeah, Mom. You'd make a terrific world leader. We sure would be in capable hands if you were in charge!"

Clare had never spoken to her mother like this, and almost immediately, she wished she could take the words back; they were so biting and vicious. One glance at her mother told her that she hadn't even heard but, just because someone can't notice that you're being mean, doesn't mean you're not; in fact, Clare decided, their not understanding makes it worse, like you're hurting a child. I have to be careful, Clare thought, not to become a very bad person.

As she sat at her desk at school that morning, Clare opened her notebook and wrote: W. H. A. T. E. V. E. R. If nothing mattered to you, nothing could change you into someone terrible and cruel. Then, Clare turned to a clean sheet and began a list: Miss Havisham, Aunt Sponge and Aunt Spiker, Miss Minchin, Uriah Heep, Voldemort, Snape. People who had let life make them hateful. The characters no one wanted to be.

Clare did not make a list of the things she had lost. If she had been able to face making such a list, she would have left off it the most obvious, the most searing losses. Mother, for example, would have been excluded because that word at the top of that list would have been a black hole, sucking everything into it and leaving no light to see by. She would have focused on daily, livable losses, would maybe have narrowed the list itself to something like "Lost Things I Hadn't Even Realized I Had." Near the top of this list would have been silence. Or maybe not silence, but that reliable quiet in which she, her mother, her house and everything in it had hung suspended every night of her life. After she'd gotten too old for lullabies, this quiet itself was her lullaby.

In her new life, night became a time for listening, for lying awake or half-awake, awaiting the bang of pans, the opening and shutting of doors, music playing, the creaking of floorboards as someone walked through a part of the house where she should not have been walking doing something she should not have been doing. "Whatever" didn't work at night. At night, for Clare, bereft of quiet, everything mattered.

One night, a little over a week after Clare had sat in Lorelei's Down Home planning out her days, she woke up not knowing what she'd heard or that she'd heard anything at all but knowing with certainty that there was a stranger in her house. Bleakly, without considering her options, Clare got out of bed, walked into the hallway, and then turned back to get her telephone. If the person were dangerous, she could call the police; quite apart from this was her need to hold a familiar object in her hands so that she wouldn't be alone.

As she walked slowly down the stairs, avoiding almost automatically the creakiest spots, the faint scraps of sound began stitching themselves into a fabric. Nothing in Clare's experience had taught her to recognize what she was hearing, but she believed she knew exactly what the sounds meant. She could have turned around then, gone back to her room, but she wanted to be brave. It's better to know, she thought, to know and then, knowing, decide what to do next. "How bad is it?" sick people asked. "How long do I have?"

Even though Clare expected to see what she saw, it took a few seconds for her to understand. The letter L, her first thought, an L made of people's bodies. Or a T, upside down. Her mother's long hair dark against her white back, swaying as she rocked. A sound that wasn't laughing and wasn't weeping. The man lying under her, stretched out. Moonlight coming in through the windows, drawing a long shadow down the side of the man's muscular thigh, shining on the man's face. It was his face that struck Clare, struck her so that she vibrated like a struck bell and felt sick. The surfer from the Cohens' rooftop, the one who had waved to her. Somehow, her recognizing him made what she saw worse and more real. Until then, she'd been OK; recognizing him made her unable to stand it.

They didn't see her. She reeled away, heading straight for the back door. Her mother's fur coat, a coat that had once belonged to her grandmother, hung on the coat stand next to the door and she grabbed it on her way out. Outside, the air was cold and smelled like snow, but the sky was clear. Clare dropped the telephone, put the coat on, and stared at her yard—at the box hedge, at the swing hanging from the oak tree, and finally, blankly, at the high, burning white moon. She didn't cry, just sat on the ground like a squirrel or a raccoon in her fur coat. With her eyes open and her back against a tree, Clare waited for morning.

7

Cornelia

If you've ever considered having a conversation about your sex life in a South Philadelphia cheese shop, stop that thought in its tracks right now and wring its scrawny, little neck.

Why?

I'll tell you why, you know I will. But first I should say that I have nothing against such cheese shops, in general. In fact, I love one particular South Philadelphia cheese shop—the very one that figures into this story—with a love so exalted and sweet that the place has shown up more than once in my dreams. A couple of years ago, when I succumbed to overwhelming peer and societal pressure and took a yoga class, the instructor asked us to begin by imagining ourselves in a beloved, familiar place. While others were probably mentally transported to the seashore or their grandparents' farm or their childhood tree house, I settled in among the wheels of Parmigiano Reggiano, the semisoft wedges of Bel Paese, the gorgeous white fists of Mozzarella di Bufala, and the giant provolones dangling from the ceiling like punching bags.

It's not that I am on familial terms with the people who work there. I can't keep them all straight, to tell you the truth, as there seem to be a great many of them in rotation, all loosely or closely related to one another, all equally nice. They talk about cheese—and not just cheese, but olives, charcuterie, pâté and so forth, with that combination of

Marisa de los Santos

offhandedness and passion more commonly associated with reference librarians. ("We all know *The American Heritage Dictionary of Idioms,* but have you tried *Brewer's Phrase and Fable, Millennium Edition?* Well, hold on to your hat; you're in for the ride of your life!"). It's the plenty of the place that speaks to me, and the language—*artisan, ash-coated, washed rind,*—and the unlikeliness of it all. From someone's hands in France, Wisconsin, Italy, Argentina, Ireland, Greece, to this single, singular, well-lit store on South 9th and to me, if I can afford it. My head knows this to be true of many stores, that it's the result of making phone calls, placing orders, but in this particular store, my heart sees only serendipity. In this store, I believe in luck.

Except, this time, the day after *Date Seven,* I'm unlucky enough to enter the store with Linny, who decides in her maddening Linny way to pick up the thread of a conversation we'd started two streets back, the thread she'd dropped in order to rush into a shop and buy a neon green watch cap right off a window mannequin's head. The mannequin looked glad to be rid of it.

Anyway. For reasons that will soon become clear to you, I prefer to tell this story in the third person, thus keeping as much distance as possible between it and me. Here we go. The cheese store on a quiet afternoon. Two middle-aged men behind the counter. Linny and Cornelia enter. And boom:

"So, I'm sorry sex with Martin was no good," chirrups Linny.

The middle-aged men smile sympathetically at Cornelia.

Cornelia hisses, "The sex wasn't 'no good.'"

Middle-Aged Man Number One says, "Any good. The sex wasn't *any* good."

Cornelia protests, not shrilly (not yet), "The sex was fine!"

An ample elderly woman, possibly the mother of the aforementioned men, drifts in from the back of the store to smile sympathetically at Cornelia.

"'Fine?' Around here, we call that damning with faint praise," says Middle-Aged Man Number Two.

68

"You do?" says Linny, impressed.

"Fine's not exactly what I meant," Cornelia tries to insert. No one notices.

"He didn't make that up!" the ample woman roars, poking Middle-Aged Man Number Two in the chest with her finger, as though he'd been an incorrigible plagiarist for years and she couldn't stand by and watch it a second longer.

Shrewdly seizing the opportunity to turn the conversation away from her sex life and her grammar usage, Cornelia jumps in. "Shakespeare?"

"Pope," Middle-aged Man Number One corrects, gently, his voice heavy with sympathy, almost sorrowful. She can't read, she can't speak, and she can't have sex, is what he's thinking.

The ample woman flaps two circular slices of *sopressaeta* at Linny and Cornelia. Linny takes hers, breathes its aroma for a second, and then pops it into her mouth. Suck-up, Cornelia thinks, and she starts to shake her head, but the ample woman's eyebrows shoot up and Cornelia doesn't wait for the emotion—anger or pain, she can't tell which—to travel down the woman's face. She takes; she eats.

"Feel better?" the ample woman asks her.

"Yes. No. I mean, I couldn't feel better. I really mean, why would I feel 'better'? Wait, what I'm saying is, I'm perfect. I feel perfect!" and now Cornelia is shrill, as you knew she would be, given time. Not shrill by nature; she's been driven to it, you have to admit, by a relentless onslaught of pity and understanding.

"That's it, then, for Martin, I guess," says Linny with a sigh.

Apart from Cornelia, everyone in the store, perhaps everyone on the sidewalk outside the store, perhaps everyone in the entire city nods, knowingly.

"No, that's not it. Of course that's not it!" How did this happen to me? Cornelia thinks. She feels like the subject of her sex life is a puppy or a ferret, something she'd never in her right mind let off its leash, but which is now somehow running amok among total strangers. Pushed to the edge, she throws decorum to the four winds.

Her voice blasts through the shop like a foghorn, only higher. "It was the first time! Just because there weren't fireworks the first time doesn't mean there will never be fireworks. We're human; we're adults; we teach each other; we communicate; fireworks don't just go off, wham-bang; fireworks *evolve!*"

Awestruck by the utter, asinine nonsense of this metaphor, everyone is still. Into the stillness, the ample woman drops the word "Wrong." Then she says it again. "Wrong."

"Oh, jeez, now she'll start in about her sexual history," moans Middle-Aged Man Number One.

"I'm not talking about my sexual history, although I could. Fireworks! I've known fireworks. I'm talking about science."

"Science?" says Linny.

"Pheromones." The woman turns to Cornelia. "The chemicals in his body call out. The chemicals in your body answer. It either happens or it doesn't."

On top of being dumb, Cornelia is dumbfounded. The woman turns to Linny.

"She's never heard of pheromones?"

"I've heard of pheromones," whines Cornelia. She is pathetic beyond all imagining.

"Cornelia's not a science person," explains Linny to the ample woman. "Her sister Ollie, she's the scientist in the family. Some kind of star geneticist. Beautiful, too. Tall. And you should see her husband."

The ample woman clasps her hands together and nods, as though this explains a lot, which it probably does, but that's another story and none of her business, goddammit. And, not to put too fine a point on it, but Cornelia would not call five foot six "tall."

"For your information, I got excellent grades in science! All through high school, excellent grades!" the hapless Cornelia bleats.

This is why you don't discuss your sex life in a cheese store in South Philadelphia. Because it can only end one way: with you standing in the middle of the shop, thirty-one years old, head thrown back, screeching about your report card at the top of your lungs.

On the way back to my apartment, Linny and I stopped, as we always did, outside the playground at 11th and Lombard to watch the children through the fence. It was December and heading toward evening, but the kids who were there didn't seem to notice the cold. They ran around with open coats and climbed all over the jungle gym, mittenless. I was wearing leather gloves and holding a paper cup of hot coffee but, all on their own, my palms remembered the feeling, the burn of the metal monkey bars under them, the numbness moving outward to my fingertips. I watched one kid cry as his mother peeled him off the pole he clung to. He wanted to keep playing; he didn't want to go home, and I remembered that, too.

"Remember that?" said Linny, "That feeling of never wanting to stop even when you were freezing cold? Where do you think that feeling goes?"

She always does that, says the thing I'm thinking. I wanted to tell her about after sledding, how Cam, Toby, Ollie, and I, and sometimes our friends Star and Teo, too, would sit on the mudroom floor soaking wet, taking off our boots, and how it wasn't until our feet and hands started to hurt with that bad, coming-back-to-life hurt that we'd realize we'd been cold at all. But I was punishing Linny for the cheese shop, so I just shrugged.

"You can't stay mad at me, Cornelia. You know you never can, so why bother trying?"

I didn't say anything. We kept watching the kids. One boy, three years old or so, in a lime green parka and a ridiculous, multicolored fleece jester's hat was still swinging. His mother was pushing him, and he was singing, unaccountably but with great brio, "Gonna lay down my sword and shield, down by the riverside, down by the riverside, down by the riverside." I'll take him, I thought.

"I'll take that one," said Linny, pointing to the boy, "But only if the hat comes with him." I looked at her.

"It's not that I can't stay mad at you," I told her, "it's that I can't *get* mad at you. If I could ever get mad at you, I'd definitely be able to stay that way. Just so you know."

We kept walking, "I ain't gonna study war no moooore!" sailing over our heads like a streamer.

It wasn't that the sex was bad. It really wasn't. It's that the evening was so exquisite, so without flaw in every other regard that the sex should have been a revelation; it should have thrown us over the moon. And it didn't—not quite.

When I told Linny this, back in my apartment, she'd said, "So you're saying that the only thing missing from a night of otherwise perfect, unbelievable sex was perfect, unbelievable sex."

In the allegory of my life, I can never decide if Linny is Snark or Truth.

"That's not what I'm saying at all. You should have seen the dinner he made. The flowers on the table. The way the lights came in through the window. If you could have seen his face when he looked at me. And heard the things he said, not just before, but after. As a matter of fact, after was great. I loved after, and you know how awkward after can be." I talked; then I stopped talking.

In the allegory of my life, if Snark and Truth turned out to be the same character, well, it would not surprise me a bit.

I'm a fan of suggestion, obliquity, discretion, the cut to the morning after, the camera's eye turning upward, outward—to the sky, to the cuckoo clock over the bed, to the rushing river, away. Forget those slick bodies tangled on the floor or grappling on kitchen tables. Sexy is Jimmy Stewart and Donna Reed talking into the same telephone receiver, their anger tipping reluctantly over into desire, the desire as much in the distance separating their two mouths as in their proximity to each other. What I'm saying is, you're not getting details—not detailed details anyway. If you're anything like I am and, like most people, I assume most people are like I am, this is just fine with you.

That being said and at the risk of your believing me insane or at least supremely weird, I'll tell you how I think of *Date Seven,* how it's parsed out and catalogued in my memory. Bullets, they call them, right? Here are the bullets:

- Compliment One
- Almost *Rear Window*
- *Notorious*
- Not *Casablanca*
- Compliment Two
- Food
- Sleep/No Sleep

Compliment One: It didn't get me into bed, if that's what you're thinking. Not because I'm not susceptible to flattery; I am, at least to the right sort of flattery, and this was very much the right sort. But because, precompliment—very precompliment, in fact—as soon as Martin had asked me to dinner at his apartment three days prior to the night in question, the going-to-bed part felt inevitable. We both knew it would happen, and we both knew that we both knew it would happen, but we didn't mention or even hint at the possibility of its happening, which we both appreciated.

His apartment was perfection—no surprise there. "A bachelor pad," he'd warned me, but its only bachelor-pad quality was its complete consistency. Every piece of furniture from the chaise to the sofa to the dining room chairs, and every other item in it—lamps, plates, martini shaker, pepper grinder—was clean, curvaceous, ingeniously put-together. My own apartment was uneven, overfull, raggedy in patches, but it grew around me organically, by accretion, like the shell of a chambered nautilus. I loved it and everything in it—loved every specific item with a specific love. But nine-and-a-half people out of ten would certainly prefer Martin's ripped-from-a-magazine décor, its having so obviously lived as a vision in some visionary designer's head before it became an actual living environ. And even I, tiny half-person clinging stubbornly to my funny, messy, personal idea of home, enjoyed the sensation of being a tiny, half movie-star on Martin's elegant set.

Martin made drinks while I stood by a long window overlooking Rittenhouse Square, now aglimmer with Christmas lights, distance turning it into an underwater city. On a table next to the window, an orchid plant with a single white flower glowed.

"I bought the view, really," said Martin. He handed me a cold shimmering martini in a cool shimmering glass. I looked at him as he looked out the window.

"The agent was waxing poetic about moldings and noiseless dishwashers in one of the most amazing displays of eloquence I'd ever heard. Scripted, probably, but it seemed completely extemporaneous. There was a whole stanza, I think, on the parquet floor, beautifully delivered. Hand gestures and everything. But all I did was go from window to window, looking out." His voice was like music, low and warm. An oboe, maybe, or a French horn.

He turned to me. "She hates me, that agent. I've seen her around town a few times over the years, and she snubs me cruelly. You know what I love best about you?" Just like that.

It took a minute for me to say "What?" because that word *love* was flying around the room like a bird, flashing its wings. I looked at the small luminous face of the orchid for help but, like all orchids, she was entirely self-involved, enwrapped in her own beauty.

"Your stillnesses. Those listening stillnesses. I don't know anyone who keeps herself so still while other people are talking."

The compliment, the view, the lights, the orchid, the drinks in our hands, Chet Baker quietly singing "Time After Time." It was one of those dropped-from-the-sky silvery moments when you stand there believing that every last thing in the world is delicate, lovely, and precise, including and especially you. I set down my drink and gave the mouth that had just bestowed such fine words upon me a truly sterling kiss.

*   *   *

Almost Rear Window: Grace Kelly can be a lot like an orchid herself, gazing at the world from several gold-and-white removes away. But she can smolder, too; she can flirt like nobody's business. That's what I like best about *Rear Window*, how flesh-and-blood she gets when she comes on to Jimmy Stewart, the gleam in her eyes when she opens the secret compartment of her Mark Cross bag to reveal the peignoir set and slippers she's brought with her. *Does she ever have plans for you, mister,* say the peignoir set and slippers, with delicious frankness.

As I leaned into Martin with my sterling kiss, we bumped into the orchid's table. The orchid didn't budge, of course, didn't blink an eye, but, at the other end of the table, my handbag went flying onto the floor, spilling out—not its entire contents, but just two items. Martin and I swooped down to retrieve them, almost bumping heads. I got the toothbrush; he got the fresh pair of underwear. I considered going the embarrassed excuses route. Instead, I chose the knowing, can-you-handle-this smolder. I smoldered, and Martin—God bless him—smoldered back.

Notorious: The smoldering was interrupted by the chime of the kitchen timer, and my first thought was, Please, please, please don't let him say "Saved by the bell!" because it would have been too obvious, amateurish, but he didn't of course, and I could tell it didn't even occur to him, which evidently is more than one could say for me. He walked away, turning once to toss me my underwear and flash me a grin, and I returned my workaday version of slippers and peignoir to my handbag, then followed him into the kitchen.

It was duck, glistening darkly and smelling like heaven. Martin stood poking it with the kind of authority I rarely feel while cooking, even though I'm quite a decent cook, which made me want to stand behind him and put my arms around him. So I did. Thanks to my ridiculously high heels and a lifetime of practice standing on tiptoe, I was able to rest my cheek against his shoulder. His sweater was sage green and the softest sweater I'd ever felt.

"I love men in sweaters," I said.

"I'm a man in a sweater," he said.

"Tell me about the duck," I said, and he turned around in my arms and began to do just that, beginning with the market where he bought the duck and the alleged purity of the duck's diet, thus sparking the *Notorious* segment of the evening. Hitchcock again, I know, but the man knew his way around a love scene. Ingrid and Cary kissing and laughing their way from the balcony to the living room, straight through a telephone call, and all the while talking about dinner—that they would stay in; she would cook a chicken; they'd eat it with their fingers. Kissing him, laughing, she accuses him of not loving her. "When I don't love you, I'll let you know," he says, kissing her. We didn't say anything like this to each other—I threw it in because the line is just so great—and we talked about duck instead of chicken, but the moving from one room to the next, the smiling into each other's mouths, the shadows sliding into all the right places, under cheekbones, along jawlines, and just the pleasure of it all, happiness suffusing every glance and touch, we got that spot-on, exactly right.

Not *Casablanca*: "The chief beauty of the duck is that it can wait," Martin told me, mid-kiss, and this is the point at which the camera turns away, maybe running over the sensual lines of the Art Deco and Modernist furniture, taking a peek at the street beneath the window, resting on the duck cooling in its pan, before switching off altogether.

If you've been wondering whether Martin was one of those men who looks so divine in clothes that he is diminished and somehow nakeder than naked without them, he was not.

He had delectable sheets.

We hit that hard-to-hit balance between intensity and kindness, demand and generosity. We really did.

There was not one awkward second, not a single readjustment, no

"Ow, my arm's sort of twisted under . . . that's better" business. Our rhythm was as effortless as the ocean's; we waltzed; we tangoed.

And the earth did not shift on its axis. It should have. Clearly, it should have. The stars could not have been more aligned. But it did not.

I'm not sure why. But just afterward, before either of us had even caught our breaths, I looked at his faultless profile, at his lashes resting on his cheeks, and at the hollow at the base of his throat that is one of my favorite parts of the human anatomy as it is one of everyone's favorite parts of the human anatomy, and in the presence of all this loveliness, the words that came into my head were these: "Who are you really? And what were you before? And what did you do and what did you think?" Except that when Rick says this to Ilsa in the Paris flashback, you know that they already know everything that matters about each other. You know because you've seen them together in Casablanca, seen Rick's eyes when she walks into the room in her white dress, his dark, broken, longing gaze, and you've seen her tilt her face up to see him, her eyes lit with tears, and you understand that, in spite of Nazis and husbands and distance and leave-takings and history, they are connected to each other in the deepest way and for all eternity.

I wasn't disappointed, exactly. But I lay on Martin's bed and knew in my bones that this night was not ever going to give rise to a moment in the future when Martin and I would stand together, alone and outside of time, with the world going mad around us, and say to each other, "We'll always have Philadelphia." It wasn't that kind of night.

Compliment Two: Martin said my face was pretty.

Something you should know about me: I have a pretty face. I do. I'd be lying if I said I didn't.

Although I'm not remotely blond, I get a lot of Mia Farrow circa *Rosemary's Baby*. And Jean Seberg. Jean Seberg was a name thrown around a good deal at the café—you probably guessed that—mainly because the desire to discuss Jean-Luc Godard was simmering just under the surface of everyone's interactions and they'd give themselves any excuse to let that desire boil over.

That's what people do; they compare people they see every day to famous people. The guy who delivers pastries has Humphrey Bogart's hairline and slightly buck teeth; the girl roller-skating outside the museum is the spitting image of June Allyson in the 1949 version of *Little Women;* your parents' accountant, from a distance, looks so much like Sidney Poitier in *The Lilies of the Field,* it takes your breath away. That sort of thing. So any famous woman with a little triangular face and big eyes who, being a famous woman, is way more beautiful than I am, that's what I hear.

Oh, and I've gotten Audrey Hepburn from exactly two men. While there's not a drop of truth in the comparison, I gave them credit for at least knowing on which side their bread was buttered.

So, I'm pretty—pretty enough. The trouble is that my kind of pretty is not the kind I'd have chosen. I've heard all those words: gamine, piquant, waifish, what have you. I've heard elfin; elfin stings. And pixie . . . *pixie?* A word to the wise: The grown women who want to evoke pointy-eared beings scaling mushrooms and wearing acorn caps for hats are few and far between. We all know what those words truly mean; they mean I'm teetering on the edge of cute. And cute is death. Denigration, death, and decay.

Still, every boyfriend I've ever had has told me I have a nice face. (I dated one misbegotten guy who said, "You're definitely a face girl, Cornelia." Translation [as if you or anybody else would need one]: "You've got no body to speak of. Your face was a bone thrown to you at conception, and not every man would appreciate it, but I do.")

But Martin, Martin, Martin. As I lay there thinking the "Not *Casablanca*" thoughts, Martin did something that pushed all of those thoughts not out of, but certainly to the back of, my mind, to a shadowed little corner where their own mothers wouldn't recognize them. Martin propped himself up on one elbow and, seriously and with great care, began to run his finger lightly over my face. He did this for a long time, and in his eyes and in his fingertip was reverence, just the sweetest kind of awe. My bones and skin turned golden under his touch.

Finally, he said, "The trouble with your face is that it's ruining me for other faces. It's making me rethink every face I've ever liked."

Then he smiled, and his eyes didn't say "What a cunning little chin!" His eyes murmured, "Garbo, Gardner, Bacall, they've got nothing on you, Cornelia."

Food: We talked; we laughed; we ate the duck. It was the last word in ducks. That duck was a marvel.

Sleep/No Sleep: We went back to bed. Martin held me. He slept. He was the kind of sleeper you knew he would be: serene, dignified, no snoring, no talking, his profile casting its elegant shadow on the wall, the bed, the woman in his arms. I was the woman in his arms, and all night long I didn't sleep a wink.

8

Clare

The story was called "Annika and the Bears."

The beginning of the story is really the end, and Annika is staring wide-eyed into new velvet-black darkness. The eyes she stares with were brown once, sparkling and the exact color of root beer, but are now an empty ice-blue, almost white. Annika is waiting for her body to grow warm so that she can fall asleep and, as she waits, she remembers life outside this darkness, remembers the world she loved and how it changed. Once, her home was called the Land of Spring and Fall because that's what it was, a place in which the seasons didn't turn in a circle, but moved like a seesaw, Fall becoming Spring becoming Fall becoming Spring. And there had been a moment every year when the seesaw hit a perfect balance. This was Annika's favorite time because blossoms burst from branches alongside red and gold leaves, crocuses opened between rows of corn, and baby animals were born under autumn skies. In the Land of Spring and Fall, it was never too cold or too hot to play outside; brooks never froze or dried up; leaves never fell from the trees; and people and animals never grew old or died.

But then a witch appeared in the land, a witch who was furiously angry, but for no reason anyone could understand, and the witch cast a spell that plunged the land into a never-ending winter. In Winterland, terrible things began to happen. People and animals got sick, with wrenching coughs and burning fevers. Desperate for warmth, the people began to kill their friends the animals in order to wrap themselves in fur coats. Food became scarce, and everyone began to fight over what little there was. And strangest of all, one by one, every living, breathing creature in the land began to turn white as chalk, as colorless as snow with no sun shining on it.

One day, Annika sat at her window, looking sadly at the blank world, when she saw, trudging across the snow, her beloved friend John the bear and his family of bears. Some of the bears were white, some were a dull gray, but only John was still a rich chestnut brown. The bears walked with their immense heads hanging down and some of them cried, dropping tears onto the snow. Before they hit the ground, the tears turned to ice. Annika ran outside, calling John's name. He stopped and looked at her with his kind eyes and told her that they were going away, to a cave deep inside one of the high hills that surrounded Winterland. "To sleep," he said. "To wait." Annika threw her arms around John, buried her face in his beautiful fur, and then stood and watched as the procession of bears patiently resumed their long journey.

That night, Annika woke up with a start. She sat up in bed and saw that the hair falling over her shoulders was as white as milk, and she ran to the mirror. As she stared at her reflection, the pink began draining from her cheeks. "Oh, no," she whispered. "It's happening. I'm turning into someone else. A winter girl." In a flash, she had on her shoes and her thickest wool cloak and was out the door. The trail of crystal tears the bears had left gleamed in what little moonlight could force its way through the clouds and, slogging through snow, cold eating into her bones, Annika followed the trail.

When she got to the cave and moved away the rock that blocked the entrance, all the bears were asleep, except John. He rested his paw on the patch of soft dirt next to him. "For you, dear heart," he said sleepily. Then he moved the rock into place and lay back down. Annika curled up between John and another bear, listening to their slow breathing, readying herself for sleep. The bears' bodies warmed her own from the outside in. The last thing to get warm was her heart, and then Annika fell asleep.

The story ends this way: "Imagine the deepest sleep you've ever slept. Multiply its deepness by the number of stars in the sky and the number of fish in the sea. Then you will know the sleep of Annika and the bears."

It was the best and longest story Clare had ever written. She had worked on it all term, filling pages of a notebook during every free period at school. Ms. Packer followed the story's progress, sometimes asking Clare to read pieces of the story aloud to the class. Ms. Packer was crazy about the descriptions of the Land of Spring and Fall and wrote "Wonderful simile!" next to the seesaw section. In December, when the story was nearly finished, Ms. Packer suggested Clare make it a Christmas present for her mother.

"What's the matter, Clare?" she said. "It's an amazing story. I just know she'll love it, don't you think?"

Clare smiled then, and nodded, and that day she began to copy the story over onto creamy, unlined paper. In art class, she worked hard on a cover for it, first drawing the face of a brown bear on light blue card stock and then cutting out tissue-paper snowflakes and gluing them all over the cover, over the bear's face. She paintbrushed the whole thing with watered-down glue to create a kind of glaze, and when she was finished, the bear looked out from the cover—blurred and difficult to see through the snowflakes, but there.

Ms. Packer read the end of the story while the rest of the class was at lunch. Not hungry and eager to hear what she was sure would be praise, Clare asked permission to stay in the classroom. She sat at her desk, pretending to write in her notebook. After Ms. Packer finished, she sat down next to Clare and, with alarm, Clare saw that her teacher's eyes were filling with tears. Ms. Packer took both of Clare's hands in hers.

"Oh, sweetheart," she said in a choked-up voice.

Clare turned her face away. Her hands felt like two cold stones inside Ms. Packer's thick, warm, square ones. Clare wanted Ms. Packer to let go, but she didn't.

"What happens when Annika wakes up?" Ms. Packer asked.

"What do you mean?" said Clare, startled by the question.

"I thought Annika would figure out how to break the spell, but she doesn't." Clare shook her head and looked at Ms. Packer's shoes. They were red canvas sneakers with white rubber across the toes. Dumb little-boy sneakers, thought Clare fiercely.

"She just goes to sleep," continued Ms. Packer, and Clare felt Ms. Packer's eyes on her face, felt how hard Ms. Packer was waiting for something from her. Clare tried to imagine what Ms. Packer wanted her to say.

"Right. She goes to sleep and waits for the winter to be over," explained Clare. "I think it's a good ending." Clare pulled her hands away. "I thought you liked the story," she said. Don't cry, don't cry, don't cry, she told herself.

"It's not that I don't like the story. It's a brilliant story. Really great. I just want to know, what happens when Annika wakes up? Is the spell broken? Is it spring again?"

Clare shrugged. "Maybe. I don't know. It's just a story."

Ms. Packer hesitated, then touched Clare's chin with her fingers to turn her face toward her own. Without meaning to, Clare flinched away from the touch.

"I want to go to lunch now," Clare said, starting to stand. Ms. Packer stopped her with a hand on her shoulder. Her hand was firm, not rough, but Clare shrank under the light grip and sat down. Stop touching me every two seconds, she wanted to yell, but she kept quiet.

"Everything's not all right at home." Ms. Packer stated it like a fact.

"Yes, it is," said Clare automatically. She could feel her heart beating in her neck and the sides of her head, and she concentrated on keeping her breathing normal, pulling the air all the way down into her chest. Clare had seen Ms. Packer staring at her in the past few weeks. *The same way she stares at the crossword puzzle during free time,* Clare had written in her notebook, *like I'm some problem she's trying to figure out.* But even as she wrote the words, she felt their injustice. Ms. Packer cared about her; she knew that. Ms. Packer believed there was something wrong in Clare's home, and she was right.

But, although Clare would not have been able to say exactly why, the something wrong had become a secret, and keeping the secret had become the one clear goal of Clare's life, the point of every single day. And the secret was not the small hard kind you could hide at the bottom of a pocket or in a closed fist. The secret was a living creature. It followed her everywhere, fluttering in the curtains, squatting in the corner of the room, or darting across the floor, and Clare's hours were spent distracting people from the secret's presence. It took all of her energy, but she was succeeding. She believed that.

She smiled a lot, laughed and gabbed with the girls in her class during lunch and in the courtyard before school started. She packed herself large, healthy lunches, completed every bit of her homework, and paid meticulous attention to her grooming, scrutinizing her full-length reflection every day before leaving the house. Clean, ironed clothes, neat ponytail, scarves, hats, and gloves in cold weather. She bathed and brushed her teeth more often and more thoroughly than she ever had before. In short, Clare became the picture-perfect child, obviously well-cared-for, obviously loved.

So when Ms. Packer started in with her questions, Clare was able to say with confidence, "Why would you think there's anything wrong? I feel fine. I look fine. Don't I?"

Ms. Packer puffed out a small sigh. "You look . . ." Then, she seemed to change her mind about something. "Yes, you look fine." She smiled. "I didn't mean to worry you, Clare. Go eat your lunch."

Clare had this conversation with Ms. Packer three days before the start of winter break, and although she'd hated every second of it, the experience turned out to be good, in a way. In a way, helpful. Because Clare had been dreading the end of school with a terrible dread. Like a person dangling from an edge, Clare had held on to school's familiar shape. School meant a pattern, an arranged life, a predictable amount of boredom. Winter break lurked like an enemy: almost a month at home, the loose hours, her mother—every day, her mother—the feeling that anything could happen, nothing was too bad to happen, and on top of it all, a Christmas that would not be a Christmas—a mean joke of a Christmas. Clare did her best to keep these thoughts away, but they could crowd around her in an instant, at any moment, a buzzing swarm from which she was never safe.

Then Ms. Packer said the words "Everything's not all right at home" and turned school into the enemy. Suddenly, weeks at home meant relief; home gave Clare a fighting chance to keep the secret. She only had to make it through three more days.

On the third day, just before they went home, the kids in Clare's class took the holiday gifts they'd made for their parents off the walls and out of the cases in which they'd been displayed. Clare took down "Annika and the Bears" and slid her palm lightly across the cover. A story is only words living inside a person's head, she thought, floating and invisible. But she'd written the words down and made a book, an object that took its place in the world of objects. She was proud of the book's weight. Never had a project turned out so precisely as she had envisioned it. She slung her backpack over her shoulder and started down the hallway, keeping the story in her two careful hands. Kids flowed by her, rushing and buoyant. Someone shouted, "Merry Christmas!" and then everyone was shouting, their voices wide-open and joyful. Clare listened.

Clare stopped walking and stepped to the side, out of the stream of children. She leaned back against the wall, bent one knee, and rested her backpack on her leg, yanking the zipper open. In one fast, angry motion, she folded the story over like it was nothing—a magazine you'd smack a fly with—and shoved it into her backpack, ruining the cover. "Good," she said out loud. When Clare looked up, she saw Ms. Packer staring at her, and Clare took off down the hall, running.

Out in the air at last, breathing hard, Clare looked around for her friend Josie; she whisked her head from side to side, scanning the crowd like a frantic person in a movie. She was a frantic person. Clare forgot to care how she looked to other people; all she cared about was leaving. Then she saw the dark blue Volvo at the front of the pick-up line—Josie's mother's car, Clare's ride home. She started running toward it, but before she even got close, the car started pulling away. Horrified, Clare waved her arms, and yelled, "Stop! You forgot me! You forgot me!" But the car was gone. Clare let her arms fall to her sides. She stood there. The crowd thinned as all the children got into cars and headed for home.

A horn started beeping. Beeping was not allowed during pick-up, but someone was beeping over and over again. The noise came from the teachers' parking lot close to the school's entrance. "Ms. Packer," Clare whispered, and because she was sure the beeping would go on until she did it, she turned slowly around and looked.

Not Ms. Packer. Her mother. Not in their white Land Rover, but standing next to it. Her mother standing there, upright as a queen, with one hand through the open driver's side window beeping and the other hand high in the air, waving at Clare. "Oh, no," said Clare. "Oh, please, please, please, please."

Clare ran toward the parking lot. "Oh, please, please, please, please."

When her mother saw Clare coming, she stopped beeping, got in the Land Rover, and started the engine. "Please, please, please, please." Clare was still saying it as she got in the car and slammed the door. She bent her head down and put both hands on her forehead, rocking a little.

"Please, what, Clare?" asked her mother in a normal voice, but Clare didn't know. The word was connected to nothing specific or nameable, because that would make what was going on in Clare's head hoping. Clare didn't hope. In Clare's mouth, "please" was pure wish.

Clare sat like that for a few minutes, holding her forehead, her knees pulled up, her elbows pressed tightly against her body, as though she were literally keeping herself together. When finally she unfolded and looked up, she didn't recognize the road they were traveling, traveling fast—a narrow road with curves and dips and great brown blurs of trees on either side. Clare heard heavy *thunks* as objects in the back of the vehicle bounced and slid. Instinctively, Clare reached for her seat belt.

"Slow down," she said, also instinctively, knowing her mother wouldn't listen.

Her mother said something Clare didn't understand, a string of meaningless sounds. Clare kept her eyes on the road. Clare's mother said the sounds again, more loudly, and she seemed to be laughing. Out of the corner of her eye, Clare saw something blue waving back and forth.

"What are you saying?" she asked. "You're not saying anything." Clare took a breath and turned to look at her mother. Her mother was wearing a soft, thick, white turtleneck sweater, dark blue jeans, and diamond stud earrings. Her hair was tucked smoothly behind her ear. Clare hated her for looking like that, like a model or an actress on vacation. In her hand, her mother held two blue envelopes.

"Bon Nadal i un Bon Any Nou!" her mother sang out again, "Merry Christmas, in Catalan, darling. You didn't forget?"

Plane tickets—two plane tickets in blue envelopes. Luggage thumping in the back. Barcelona. Clare's throat released a high-pitched moan, and her mother turned to look at her.

"No, no, no, we can't go to Barcelona, Mom. You're sick. We can't be on an airplane or in Spain or anyplace when you're sick. Don't you understand that there's something wrong with you? Stop the car, Mom. Please." Clare spoke as though her mother were a child. She knew she couldn't give in to panic. If she gave in, they would be lost. But as Clare spoke, it came to her that something was strange about her mother's face: Her right eye was wide, black-lashed, her left eye was different, smaller, incomplete, almost erased-looking. The two sides didn't match, and this imbalance broke Clare. The bottom dropped out of the moment and she fell. For the second time in her life, she was overtaken—possessed—by screaming, by rage she didn't own. In the grip of this rage, she screamed the word "Stop!" and she kicked and she slammed her fists against the dashboard with all her strength.

Miraculously, her mother did stop, pulling to the side of the road and putting the car in park. It took some time for Clare's anger to subside and for her to come back to herself. Even after her breathing slowed, her head and body shook with intermittent sobs, something Clare had only ever seen happen to babies. She felt like throwing up. She wrapped her arms around her stomach and looked at her mother.

To her amazement, her mother was weeping. Tears poured down her face, wetting her sweater. Her cheeks and the corners of her mouth trembled, and the trembling went on for a long time, and then her mother opened her mouth and cried long sounds, "Ahh, ahh, ahh," over and over, like a machine.

"You're right, Clarey, it has to stop. It has to stop. All of it. All of it. You're right." Her mother's voice was the saddest voice Clare had ever heard.

Clare's mother reached across and opened Clare's door.

"I'm so sorry. How did everything go to hell? I don't know. I didn't mean to do it. I'm so sorry, Clare." And she was, Clare could tell; her mother was sorry for everything in the world.

There was nothing else to do. Clare unbuckled her seat belt, pushed the car door wide open, and stepped down into the weeds and gravel. Clare's mother was still crying, her head tilted back against the headrest, her eyes closed. "Mommy," said Clare flatly, leaning forward in order to leave the word inside the car. Then she stepped back and pushed the door shut. It's click was the most final sound Clare had ever heard.

The Land Rover pulled away. Clare watched it until the road curved and it was gone. The sky overhead and behind the treetops was an uninflected pale gray. "It's over," she told the trees and the sky. There was no relief in her voice. Clare slid her backpack over both shoulders and started to walk.

9

Cornelia

"*What* breaks your heart? Has your heart been broken? Tell me. When has your heart been broken?" I asked Martin. Because if you're going to ask a stupid, graceless question, you may as well ask it three times in succession with very little variation. A rotten question. I knew that before I asked it, before it reverberated in the air around me like a wrong, wrong note, before I saw the "Oh, no; here we go" look flicker over his face then disappear. No way to make such a question sound nonchalant, particularly as I'd asked it in triplicate, more particularly as I'd asked it in bed—mine, not his, thus taking advantage of home court advantage—and most particularly as it came on the heels of yet another story of my own heartbreak. Another unsolicited story, if you insist upon accuracy, and I know that you do. I depend upon it.

Before I asked Martin that question—days before, as I contemplated asking it—I was already bored with myself, with how deeply unoriginal the question made me. Like a wicked fairy—*poof*—the question turned me into a first-name-only, hypothetical character in the pages of a self-help book. Exactly the kind of book we all disdain because it reduces to formulae our irreducible human selves, but which we at least think about buying (thus abetting the book's piranhalike devouring of the *New York Times* bestseller list). That time we had a terrible cold and were listlessly switching channels on the *tiny* television we hardly ever watch and even forget we have, we happened upon Oprah discussing such a book and found that, as much as we hated to admit it, the book rang true—at least, some of it rang somewhat true, truer than we'd ever expected. "He doesn't talk to me," Cornelia whines and, looky there, she is not Cornelia but the universal, allegorical Whining Woman. Suddenly, Martin is from Mars, and Cornelia, God help her, is from Venus.

The only comfort I can take is in the fact that I put my own little spin on the whining, tinted the whining a vaguely Cornelia-like color. It's not that Martin didn't talk to me. He talked, he shared, he was forthcoming, regularly coming forth with loads of information about himself.

Apart from the facts about him you already know, I knew that he was born and raised in Rye, New York. I knew he'd been blond as a child. I knew that he'd gone to the University of Chicago and had gotten an MBA at Harvard. I knew the things he felt he should like but secretly did not: horses, Russian novels, recycled paper products, Langston Hughes poems, French cinema, the city of New Orleans, cheese for dessert. And the things he felt he shouldn't like but secretly did: sports cars, those chalky orange circus peanuts, seersucker (never wore it, but wanted to), Olympic figure-skating, and the Jerry Lewis film *Cinderfella*. (I know, pretty tame as far as guilty pleasures go. You were expecting monster trucks and Japanimation?). I knew *The Exorcist* still gave him nightmares and that the only time he felt truly patriotic was when he heard instrumental versions of "America the Beautiful." I knew that at age thirteen, he'd been airlifted out of the Maine wilderness after stumbling upon a bees' nest on a summer camp nature hike. I knew he spent astronomical sums on custommade shirts and felt guilty about it. I knew he found me funny and beautiful and smart.

He talked to me. I talked to him. Rarely, in fact, did we stop talking. Conversationally, we were Fred and Ginger—spin, slide, shuffle, bend. Giddy. Effortless. *Tappity tappity tappity tappity boom boom slap*, went I. *Tappity tappity tappity tappity boom boom slap*, returned Martin, and then he'd set me spinning like I'd never spun before, my dress flaring, my hair platinum blond and shining like the moon.

But I thought I'd figured it out, why our sex life wasn't more spectacular; or to be specific, was several worlds away from spectacular. For all our talk, all our exchanges, we never handed over anything of real importance. We were all laughter and lightness and glow. We liked each other till the cows came home, but I never saw his broken places, nothing soft or stinging or half healed-over. He'd never seen mine, either. And I decided that truly stellar sex wasn't possible without that kind of knowledge. Love either, although, at that point, I wasn't ready to do more than give the subject of love a passing glance, a nod of acknowledgment. "Be patient," I told love under my breath. "I'll tackle you eventually."

I didn't take the clunky direct-question approach to begin with. He'll reveal himself if I reveal myself, is what I thought. So, I waited for an opening, the slightest invitation. But the invitation didn't come, which is when I started the aforementioned unsolicited storytelling. One afternoon, I told him about my best friend Andie who died of leukemia at the start of fifth grade. After the funeral, her mother gave me the new winter coat Andie never got a chance to wear—a purple parka with fur around the hood that I hung, tags and all, in the coat closet of every place I'd ever lived, including my current apartment.

I told him about having dropped out of graduate school after half a semester, which wasn't in itself so hard because I hated all my classes and believed if I stayed another minute, I'd never love another book. Afterward, though, I lived inside the four grim walls of my failure, my first huge failure, for weeks, unable to tell anyone.

I told him about my sister Ollie, two years older than I am, and how passionately we'd loved each other as kids, but that somehow we didn't seem to anymore. It wasn't even a story, really, because there was no drama, no plot, no climactic falling-out I could put my finger on, which was maybe the worst part about it. We just stopped being sisters. I was making a salad while I told him this, and when I started to cry, I blamed it on the onions and dumped the salad in the trash.

It wasn't easy, since I don't like being vulnerable any more than the next guy, possibly less than the next guy, and also since all the above events and conditions are among the few topics the importance of which I am unable to undermine with jokes and a mocking tone. Which shows you how much I wanted Martin. I just wanted him.

Not that he made any of it any easier. Each time I began to give him one of my heartbreaks—and I was straightforward, not dramatic, used as few words as possible, only cried the one time—I could almost see him deliberately settle the parts of his body, one by one, into an attitude of what was meant to be interest but ended up as something more like patience, forbearance. He forbore, I think, and looked tender and handsome enough while doing it. And afterward, each time, he'd give a rueful little smile that crinkled the corners of his eyes, and he'd touch my cheek or run a hand along my forearm. Nothing wrong with that—entirely appropriate and above reproach, except that the touches ended up feeling to me like pats on the head.

Just before I came out with "What breaks your heart?" et al., I was telling Martin about Mrs. Goldberg—Suzette Goldberg. I'd arrived at Suzette's story more or less naturally, although, once I got started, I had no qualms about incorporating it into Project Drawing-Martin-Out. Which would have been just fine with Mrs. Goldberg, of that I was sure.

As I told you, Martin and I were in bed, propped up on pillows, my head leaning against his shoulder; we were being quiet, for once, and I broke the silence by saying, "*Mousquetaire.*"

"Musketeer or Mouseketeer?" asked Martin.

"*Mousquetaire.*" I pointed to the far wall of my bedroom. "Opera glove," I said. "They used to call them that."

They were framed, the opera gloves. Late nineteenth-century, white kid with pearl buttons. I'd lined the back of the frame with lavender velvet. If my apartment ever caught fire, the gloves in their frame would be the first thing I grabbed.

"Mrs. Goldberg gave me those gloves," I began. She was our neighbor, and although she was much too old to be my mother—I can't remember a time when she didn't seem old—she felt like my mother in ways my real one never did. There's too much to tell about her and not enough. As I described her to Martin, my descriptions struck me as ordinary and flat, even clichéd, and Mrs. Goldberg and the feelings I had for her were none of these things. She fed me madeleines and fresh figs. She told me stories about her life in New York City and her husband, Gordon, with whom she'd fallen in love when she was eleven and he was seventeen.

We'd sit for hours in her bright attic looking at her carefully stored belongings, everything nestled in boxes or swathed in pieces of soft cloth. A painted fan, Venetian lace, four strings of luminous pearls, each with a clasp shaped like a different insect: a ladybeetle (her word), a dragonfly, a butterfly, and a bumblebee. She and her three sisters had each received one upon turning sixteen. There were albums of photographs and countless family portraits, some postage-stamp size, others larger than life. Mrs. Goldberg had magic in her hands, so that every object she touched was instantly rare and profound, an artifact from Atlantis or Troy.

And each object had a story attached—or not attached, but glowing delicately around it like a halo. Mrs. Goldberg's stories were dense and rich with details, bristling with New York lights, wars, music and dance, travel, and even sex, although Mrs. Goldberg was not one of those adults who makes a big show of talking to children as though they were adults. When we talked, I felt singled-out and specific. "You see how this heel curves, Cornelia?" she'd say, placing a shoe in my hand. "Not made for hiking, certainly, but I walked for miles in these shoes, at Gordon's sister Lizzie's country house, the summer I turned nineteen."

I'd never not known her, but my true friendship with Mrs. Goldberg began when I was eight, and even after I started college, I'd visit her once a month, at least. I loved her more than I needed her, but I did need her. Her life had been so splendid, so intensely and atten-tively lived, that connecting with it made me feel rich, excited, hope-ful, even when I was at my most muddled and drifting.

The fog began to float in when I was in my last year of college—a barely perceptible haze, but it thickened over the years. Alzheimer's, I guess, although no one, not my parents or either of her children ever said that word in my presence, and while I know how both futile and presumptuous it is to assign intent to nature, I envi-sioned the bad genes sitting on some remote arm of whatever tan-gled chromosome they called home and cursed them with all my strength. Impossible not to see malice in that particular disease at-tacking that particular woman, a person who was a receptacle, a liv-ing jewel box—if you'll forgive the disconcerting metaphor—of so many memories, exquisite and surprising, regular Fabergé eggs of memory. Her children chose a perfectly nice assisted-living facility, tucked into a little bowl of a valley in the Blue Ridge Mountains not far away, and because she couldn't stand to sell her house, they didn't. Her daughter Ruth called me in Philadelphia. "She wants you to help her choose some things to take with her. It can't be much, though," said Ruth. So I went.

It was a good day. Actually, it was a terrible day, but good insofar as Mrs. Goldberg's illness seemed to recede a bit, enough so that we could glean from her Ali Baba's cave, one terribly small box of treasure. She gave me the opera gloves just before I left. "They were my mother's and then they were mine, and now they are yours, child of my heart," she told me. A good day—a gift of a day—but brutal, brutal.

Martin patted my head. OK, he didn't pat my head. A stroke is not a pat, and it was a stroke—two strokes actually, as though two were better than one, as though it were a two-stroke story. The truth is that, Project Drawing-Martin-Out notwithstanding, I'd almost forgotten he was there. So when I pulled away from him, really I jumped away from him, and stared at him. I was stung. Stung and desperate, even angry, and the three-headed, hangdog dog of a question just fell out.

"What breaks your heart? Has your heart been broken? Tell me. When has your heart been broken?"

I hope my tone wasn't challenging, but I can't promise it wasn't. Or petulant or demanding, although, a demand is a demand no matter how you slice it. I hope it didn't have overtones of "tit for tat," which would've been awful. Plaintive, I'm quite sure it was plaintive. There's an old Sheila E. song—stay with me, here—in which a woman is shopping for if-you-have-to-ask-you-can't-afford-it lingerie, and I'm not entirely sure why I bring that up and very obviously shouldn't have, but it has something to do with my question(s) to Martin. Do you see what I mean at all? Questions the asking of which erases the reason for asking, yes? Something like, "If you have to ask, no way are you ever getting the answer you're looking for." Or maybe more like, "If you have to ask that question in order to keep him, girl, he's already gone."

After the barely-there exasperation left his face, Martin recovered. He smiled, cupped my face in his hands. Tenderly, all charm, laughter gilding the edges of his voice, he said to me, "I guess I've been keeping it in cold storage. Saving it for you, C. C. Brown."

He was as sweet and as giving as he could be. I still believe that.

What followed Martin's leaving the next morning—a blithe leaving on his part, as he never suspected a thing—was a miserable forty-eight hours. I wore my bathrobe and shuffled around my house crying and consuming tea and hot soup and other types of invalid food. I opened books and shut them. I lifted the phone receiver and put it down. I remembered his voice and all the extraordinary things it had said to me. I listed on the couch, blown sideways by my own unhappiness, and tried to watch *Meet John Doe* because, despite what anyone thinks, no one does dark the way Capra does dark, and tried to remind myself that compared to everyone's disappointment and isolation, my disappointment and isolation were puny, not even garden variety. The movie backfired on me, though, because, as in all Capra films, love saves the day, and what I was pretty sure of was that it was not going to save mine, not this time.

On Saturday morning, very early almost-morning, I woke up to an unearthly glow coming from the window next to my bed. Snow. Snow under streetlamps and a lightening sky. Bluish and clean and muting every edge. A day had never looked so new. "Silly girl," I whispered to myself. "What is the matter with you?" How had I convinced myself that everything hinged on a single question? I'd blindsided him, caught him off guard. Shame on me. All wasn't lost. All? Had I really thought that? Nothing was lost, not one thing.

I stood at the window, letting the relief wash over me. Then I took a shower, devoured an enormous breakfast, and walked to work in the snow.

It was going to be busy at the café, busy with holiday shoppers and out-of-town guests, but it wasn't busy yet. Jacques, the not-discernibly-French college kid I'd hired recently, was late, but I didn't mind. I couldn't have minded anything. Bathed in radiance, walking in beauty like the night, I did all the setup, breathing in the fragrance of cinnamon and chocolate, pouring the thick white cream into pitchers. I greeted Bob the pastry guy like a long-lost brother, sang an aria over the croissants and fruit tarts, and when Hayes and Jose showed up, I gave them both beatific smiles.

Ten minutes later I was slicing lemons, and I glanced up. In front of me stood Martin Grace, looking exactly like himself. And standing next to him was a tiny, chestnut-haired apparition in an antique floor-length mink coat.

I blinked and shook my head to clear it—I really did—and then I looked at the tiny woman again. A child, a pretty little girl. She had the most remarkable expression in her eyes: fierce and furious and terrified and bottomlessly sad. No one would need to ask this girl if her heart had been broken.

I noticed the expression in her eyes before I noticed the eyes themselves. When I noticed the eyes themselves, I knew them in an instant. An unmistakable resemblance.

"Cornelia, this is Clare," said Martin, smiling a little. The girl began to tremble, and she lifted her chin.

"Clare Hobbes," she said in a clear, proud voice, and then she burst into tears—exploded into tears. Long wails and deep, tearing sobs. Martin took the smallest step away. Hayes got up, signaled to Jose, and they walked out, their coffees still steaming on the table. The three of us were alone, two adults and one child. And because somebody had to, I ran over to Clare Hobbes and took her in my arms—we were exactly the same height—and I held on as hard and as well as I knew how.

10

Clare

Clare lay on her side on the guestroom bed in her father's apartment, not sleeping, trying to imagine herself as a piece of driftwood. She tucked in her knees and circled them with her arms, pulling in tight, making herself small. She wanted every part of her body to be touching another part of her body so that she was aware of all her edges, all the places Clare ended and the rest of the world began. Float, she thought, drift, although she wanted not to think at all. She looked at the lamp on the bedside table, an object that never had to think a thought, that only was. Thinking, imagining, deciding, worrying—Clare was through with all of that. Drift. She even rocked a little on the bed, letting waves and swells undulate beneath her, carrying her wherever they would.

But even as she lay there becoming an object, letting go of everything, she knew it wasn't working. At that moment, true letting go would mean falling asleep, which her body wanted desperately to do. But as she began to blur and grow heavy, to sink away into sleep, the old human girl Clare was suddenly right there, saying, no—saying, last time, I said I would never sleep in this place again and I won't. Never.

Who cares about that? She tried to tell herself. Who cares anymore? Drift. Float. Let what would happen, happen. It did anyway, didn't it?

But there were those words in her head, insisting on themselves. "No. Never. No. No. No." Reluctantly, Clare sat up, and as she did, what had been a kind of undefined rustling and hum in another room became voices. Her father and his friend, that very small woman with the boy's haircut who had hugged Clare as Clare cried.

Clare hated having done that, having bawled out loud like a baby in front of her father, but she couldn't help it. The crying had happened the way everything happened now, like weather—a thunderstorm that hit, then rushed away. The small woman had kept her skinny arms wrapped tightly around Clare, even as Clare sank to the floor. When the crying ended, the woman helped Clare into a chair and, never taking her hands from Clare's shoulders, gave some calm instructions to a tall, astonished-looking, shaggy-haired boy who must have entered without Clare's noticing. Then the woman had crouched in front of Clare, looking Clare in the eye. "Are you ready?" she'd asked. After a moment, Clare nodded, and without another word, not even to Clare's father, the little woman led Clare out the door, down the street, through the square, to Clare's father's building, and finally into his apartment.

They're talking about me, Clare thought. And even though she wanted so much not to do it or anything else, silently Clare slid off the bed and walked down the hallway to hear what they were saying. She sat on the floor and rested her chin on a chaise made of leather and metal, a piece of furniture that Clare remembered from last time she was there. Then, back when she was a child, she'd thought it resembled a caterpillar. Clare sat like that, not hiding really. Her father and the woman were at the dining room table, facing each other. Clare could see the woman's face, but not her father's. If the woman had glanced in the right direction, she'd have seen Clare.

"These past few months, I've been learning how to read your face, Cornelia. It speaks a subtle language, that face."

Cornelia. The name took Clare by surprise. She hadn't realized she'd been thinking about the small woman's name at all, but as soon as her father said "Cornelia," Clare knew she had been expecting something else: Meg. Kate. Jill. Something short, like the woman and her hair were short, something snappy and take-charge. *Cornelia.* Long—three syllables or even three and a half—and old-fashioned. There was a character in *Anne's House of Dreams* named Cornelia. She was Anne's friend. This Cornelia was her father's friend, and Clare wasn't sure she wanted to know her at all. But if Clare ever decided to call her anything, Cornelia was a name Clare could use.

"Martin," the woman—Cornelia—tried to begin. Clare decided it was all right to use the woman's name inside her own head, where no one would know she was doing it.

"I was getting it, though, I think I was getting it. But I must be reading it wrongly now because I can't find any anger in it. You have to be angry at me. Anyone would be." His voice was low and serious. Clare thought he was right: Cornelia's face was something, but not angry.

"Angry." Cornelia said the word neutrally, as though considering it. She sat very still.

"For showing up like that, with her. This situation, I don't understand what it is yet, but I know it's a mess. And I know it's not your mess, and now you're in it." Clare's father reached across the table and slid his palm under Cornelia's hand. He examined the hand for a few seconds and then said, "You were good with her, you know. Thank you for that."

"Don't thank me." Cornelia's voice seemed strained and her face tightened. "Do you think I mind that? Helping a little girl? Your daughter." Cornelia spoke the word "daughter" as though she had just learned it, as though it were a foreign word she was working to get right. Clare saw Cornelia look down at their hands on the table. Then Cornelia took her hand back and sat up a little straighter in her chair.

"We're talking about the wrong things, Martin. We'll have to talk about me and us and whether I'm angry and all of it, but not now. What happened? What happened to Clare?"

"I don't know very much. A girl called me early this morning—a spitfire of a girl, mad as hell. At me, I think. About what, I'm not sure. She'd come to clean and found Clare alone. All Clare would say is that her mother left."

"What do you mean, 'left'?" asked Cornelia.

"That's it. Left. Clare wouldn't say anything more than that. When I got to the house, this girl—Max was her name—she was waiting with Clare. Clare was sitting next to her on the sofa in that coat with her backpack on her lap, just sort of staring into space. Max walked out to the car with us, and for a minute there, I didn't think Clare would let go of her hand."

Clare noticed that Cornelia's eyes were full of tears. "Poor Clare. Poor little scared girl," but in a way that didn't make Clare feel mad at her, even though she didn't want pity.

"Max whispered to Clare and put something in Clare's coat pocket. After that, Clare let go. She got in the car."

"And did she say anything more about her mother? About what happened?

"She didn't speak at all, and I thought it best not to push her. When I asked her if she'd had breakfast, she shook her head."

"So you brought her to the café. To eat breakfast," For the first time, Cornelia's voice sounded angry or accusing, maybe, just a tiny bit, but when Clare's father spoke again, his voice was regular, as though he hadn't noticed the change.

"Yes. I thought maybe she'd like a croissant, some hot chocolate."

Cornelia stared up at the ceiling and let out a breath. "Never mind," she said. "Can you think of why her mother would have done this? Has she ever done anything like this before?"

"I really can't say for sure. I don't think so, but Viviana's always been—"

Clare hated hearing him say her name. She stood up, then, and shouted, "No! She wouldn't leave me. She didn't mean to. Something happened to her."

Cornelia pushed away from the table and stood up, knocking over her chair. 'We should call the police, Martin!" She turned to Clare, "Did someone come and take her? She'll be OK, I know she will, but you have to tell us. Did she just go out and not come home? Was she in the car?"

Clare froze, trying to figure out how much to tell. She'd been keeping the secret for so long, and she didn't even know these people—not even her father. She couldn't trust them. But she couldn't let them call the police.

"Don't call the police. You can't do that. No one took her. She was sick. She wasn't herself. And she left. And I don't know if she'll ever come back. But you can't call the police because she didn't mean to do anything she did." The words came out in a rush, and Clare saw Cornelia begin to walk toward her. Clare held up her hand to stop her.

Clare looked right at her father, who was still sitting at the table. "She was sick," Clare said in an icy, deliberate voice. Cornelia looked at Martin, waiting.

"I didn't know," he said to Cornelia, lifting his hands in the air, as if to demonstrate their emptiness. Clare listened to him say it. He didn't matter. He had never mattered, and he didn't now.

"I want to go home now," said Clare to Cornelia. "She might come back."

Cornelia said, gently, "Do you think she will?"

Clare remembered her mother in the Land Rover, saying she was sorry in that sad, sad, final voice. Clare shook her head. She felt tears sliding down her cheeks, so she covered her face with her hands.

"Your father will go back to the house, and he'll leave your mom a note," said Cornelia. She was standing close to Clare now, but not touching her. Clare didn't want to be touched. "That way, she'll know you're here and she can find you. But even if she doesn't come back, we'll find her. We'll find her and help her get well."

For weeks, Clare had worked hard to let go of hope, had been very stern with herself about giving it up, so, although she was tempted, she didn't allow Cornelia's words to make her hopeful. Still, Clare was glad Cornelia was there, saying those words to her. If Cornelia weren't there, Clare would be alone, so when Cornelia said, "OK?" Clare nodded.

She sat down on the caterpillar lounge and Cornelia sat next to her. "But I won't stay here. I hate it here. I'll stay at a hotel or something. Maybe I can stay with Max. She gave me her cell phone number." Clare took the card from her pocket. "Any time" was written next to the number. The "any" was underlined three times. "But I won't stay here."

Cornelia looked at Clare's father. He shook his head as though he were confused by it all and then clasped his hands and put them on top of his head. He made his face look unhappy and helpless. Then, he got up and went into the kitchen.

"Why don't we go someplace else right now and talk about that?" Cornelia said to Clare.

"OK," said Clare, dully, even though she was finished talking. She felt tired. Her eyelids felt heavy. The fur coat felt terribly heavy.

"Wait here just a minute, then. I want to talk to your father." Cornelia got up and went into the kitchen. Clare could hear them. They might have been arguing, but she couldn't tell for sure. When Cornelia came back, her eyes looked tired too, but she smiled.

"Your father is going to leave the note for your mom at your house. And we'll go to my apartment, if that's all right with you. It's not far. He'll come later, won't you, Martin?"

"Of course, I will," said Clare's father. He was talking to Cornelia.

Cornelia and Clare walked across the apartment, and Clare's father walked with them. As they all three stood at the front door, he started to say something, stopped, and then reached out a hand to touch a lock of Clare's hair, one that hung next to her face. He didn't give it a playful tug or tuck it behind her ear as her mother might have done, but held the ribbon of hair between his thumb and forefinger, one second, two seconds. She waited for him to take his hand away, and then she and Cornelia walked out the door. Outside, Cornelia started down the snowy sidewalks, turning now and then to be sure Clare was still there. Clare, in her fur coat, her breath hanging in the air in front of her, walked a few steps behind, weary like the bears in her story.

When they got to Cornelia's apartment, Clare stood just inside, swaying slightly. A chandelier sparkled overhead, but everything else in the room felt smudged, fuzzy, half-real. Cornelia took one look at Clare, then caught hold of her elbow and guided her into the bedroom. Clare fell onto the bed, kept falling and falling and falling. When she woke up, it was dark and, into the dark, Clare was calling for her mother.

11

Cornelia

"*Be* not afraid of parenthood; some are born parents, some achieve parenthood, and others have parenthood thrust upon 'em."

And yes, cheese-shop snafu notwithstanding, I know enough about William Shakespeare to know that this is not how the quotation actually goes. I matriculated two months in a Ph.D. program in English Literature, did I not? I did. And *Twelfth Night,* if not my favorite play by W.S., is in a dead heat for first place: *Twelfth Night* for wit and charm; *King Lear* for heartbreak. A balanced diet, the major mental and emotional food groups brilliantly represented. I have been to dinner parties at which saying this would be like dropping a bucket of bleeding fish into a shark tank: a lot of vicious snapping, grim hangings-on, and no one getting away unscathed. The sort of argument I both appreciate and avoid because, on the one hand, art does matter and is something to get riled up about; on the other hand, I could batter someone over the head repeatedly with the Lear/Cordelia reunited in prison scene or the line "And my poor fool is hanged," and someone could batter me back with "To be or not to be" and where would that get us? In my experience, people love what they love. They just do.

Or fail to love what they fail to love. Which naturally brings me back from what you've no doubt noticed was a pathetic attempt at digression and diversion, which are generally two of my specialties, as you also may have noticed. But even I can't escape the fact that there is only one possible topic here, a topic that is not a topic at all but a child, Clare Hobbes—once Clare Hobbes Grace, daughter of Martin as Cordelia was daughter of Lear.

I brought up the previous tweaked quotation mainly to discuss how it's only partly accurate because, as far as I can tell, no matter what the circumstances, parenthood is thrust upon a parent. No one is ever quite ready; everyone is always caught off guard. Parenthood chooses you. And you open your eyes, look at what you've got, say "Oh, my gosh," and recognize that of all the balls there ever were, this is the one you should not drop. It's not a question of choice.

Before you get your political hackles up—and I like those hackles; they're fine hackles, I have a set myself—I should clarify that I'm not talking about choice as we ordinarily use the word. Not Choice as in Pro-. I'm talking about post-choice, the embodied baby, the done deal, the child trailing clouds of glory, etcetera. And, of course, because I see said hackles rising again, I know there are plenty of people with done deals who are smart and brave enough to recognize that they need to thrust parenthood upon someone else, someone with more resources. I'm not talking about those people or taking them to task. If I'm taking anyone to task, and apparently I am, it's those people who have the material resources (and then some; if you can afford a penthouse, more than one signed and numbered Edward Weston photo, and a Mies Van der Rohe chaise, you can afford a child, yes?); who are grown-up; who are in splendid, chiseled, glowing, shockingly handsome health; and who are in all ways suited not to be let off the hook.

I'm talking about Martin. Obviously, Martin. Because as his eleven-year-old daughter slept the sleep of the spent and brokenhearted in the next room, in a strange bed, Martin sat next to me on the couch and said, "I'm just not cut out to be someone's parent. I never was," neatly lifting himself off the hook, without so much as a wrinkle in his English custom-tailored shirt.

Except that I couldn't let it go. I could have admired his candor. I could have eaten up this long-awaited snip of self-revelation, savored its sweetness on my tongue, and moved on. It would have been so easy to let it go, but I couldn't do it.

"Father," I said.

"What?"

"Someone's father. You said parent, not father," I said.

"Does that matter? Is there a difference?" he asked, not completely rhetorically, thank goodness. Still, the Sheila E. song was back in my head; *"If you have to ask, you can't afford it . . ."* I forwent singing it aloud, for which I drearily awarded myself a couple of dreary points.

"Maybe being a father isn't something you do because you're cut out for it. Maybe it's something you do because your child needs you to do it." I said that. Afterward, there was a long silence.

"We haven't known each other very long, Cornelia. But we have something. I think we have something. Enough so that you are a person on whom I wouldn't rush to judgment. I'd give you the benefit of the doubt. Can you do that for me?" His voice was so quiet, and there were so many other things he could have said to me. Things like, "You're the thirty-one-year-old, single, childless manager of a coffee bar, Cornelia. What the hell do you know about being a parent?" Or "Let's think. Have you managed every last thing in your life in the best possible manner?" Or "Must be nice up there on your moral high ground, Cornelia. Nice clear air up there lets you see other people's faults in crystalline detail."

But he was tender and sad and far more fair than I deserved and, disenfranchised child in the next room or no, I wanted to be in love with Martin, still. I hadn't given up on that. I wanted our being in love to remain in the realm of the possible. Apart from that, I knew that all the things he didn't say but could have were true responses, entirely just, and I felt bad about that. I don't mind being wrong, but I can't bear to be *in* the wrong, or on the side of wrong.

"I'm sorry, Martin," I said. "I'm sorry, and yes, I can do that." There were tears in my eyes, and I took his hand and kissed it. "But, because we're talking about us, I want to ask"—shut up, shut up, shut up, Cornelia—"why didn't you tell me about Clare?" Good God, can I ever just keep my mouth shut? Is that ever possible?

And that's when I saw it, the befuddled, unguarded look on his face. The look that said "I didn't tell you about Clare because it didn't occur to me to tell you," with the follow-up, "Because it didn't seem important enough to tell you." With this look still on his face, Martin began, "I don't know. I didn't think it . . ." and the word hanging in the air was "mattered." I could see it hanging there, black and jagged, but Martin recovered.

"I wanted to tell you. I meant to. All I had to do was put one word in front of the other, but I couldn't seem to do it. As you can tell, it's not a happy or a simple relationship, mine and Clare's. Maybe I was afraid you'd run away from me."

Obviously, this was a good answer. A grade-A, magnificent answer. He was expressing vulnerability; that's what I wanted, right? Also, expressing the desire to keep me—wanted that, too, right? But it came too late. I'd caught a glimpse behind the curtain, at the little lever-pulling man behind the Great and Powerful Martin.

I would have to think about this—definitely would have to, no doubt about that. But, though it doesn't come easily to me, I can avoid hard truths, at least for a while, and Martin's being a man capable of misplacing the idea of his child like an old set of keys was the kind of hard truth for which the word "later" was created. Besides, I had more pressing issues before me. The facts were these: There had never been a little girl asleep in my bed before. Yesterday, no little girl. This morning, no little girl. Now, there was a little girl; now, there was Clare.

"What are we going to do now, Martin? For Clare," I asked.

"Right. Well"—Martin was brisk, all-business—"we need to find Viviana, of course. I should file a missing-persons report, I know I should. If Clare's right and Viviana's ill or having some kind of break-down, she could be a danger to herself. I almost called the police this

afternoon, but I didn't do it. I don't know the law, but it's possible Viviana could be in serious trouble for abandoning Clare. Legal trouble.
There could be far-reaching consequences. Also, Viviana is a fairly
prominent figure in social circles around here; it would be difficult for
her and for Clare if these problems became public knowledge. Clare
needs her mother. She needs her life to return to normalcy as soon as
possible, with the least amount of messiness."

As do you, I thought uncharitably.

"So I took a rather bold step today and engaged a private investiga-
tor," said Martin.

"You did?" I asked, and Sam Spade, Philip Marlowe, and every film
noir detective to whom the word "hard-boiled" was regularly attached
began gumshoeing his way around my mind. As I looked at him, the
usual refined, sparkling, spotless Martin became a little grainier, his
immaculate edges the tiniest bit roughened up. I was intrigued.

"A good detective firm, I think, very reputable. I got the name from
a guy at work who'd used them a few times with good results. I guess
the job itself involves an inevitable amount of sleaziness, but this place
seems as discreet and above reproach as most businesses ever are. Do
you think it was the right thing to do?" I caught myself loving, as I'd
loved before, the way Martin asked my opinion, as though my input
were of immense value.

"I suppose so," I said. "If the agency is really trustworthy." I wasn't
sure, though, not at all sure. As I've mentioned before, I'm my mother's
daughter, and my mother is as merrily careful and law-abiding a soul
as ever lived. No way she'd call a private dick, a shamus, a hard-boiled
anything. She would contact the proper authorities and let the cards
fall where they may. That's what I was brought up to do. But when
you're mired in confusion as I was, it's wisest to hold close those things
you do know. The one crystal-clear fact here was that Clare needed
her mother, and because it was the one crystal-clear fact, the proper
action to take was whatever action would bring them back together.

"But, meanwhile . . ." I said, because until Martin had started in with his private detective solution, I had hardly even been thinking about finding Viviana. I'd been thinking about the child in the fur coat on the bed who wouldn't sleep forever or even just until her mother returned home, although I bet she wanted to do just that. Clare would wake up. She would wake up needing what children needed. "What about Clare?"

Martin was thrown off, even stricken. "I don't—I don't know. I don't know what to do. She needs . . . well . . ." Martin floundered. Then his brow cleared for a moment. He picked a backpack up off the floor and handed it to me. It was L.L. Bean, colored two shades of pink, and had CLARE stitched on the front pocket. "She left this in the car. Maybe there's something in it she needs."

I opened it and found a spiral notebook full of writing and some sort of book, crumpled, an art project maybe. I didn't read either. Martin looked at me, hopeful.

"She'll probably want these, Martin," I said gently. "But I was thinking more along the lines of toothbrushes and sweaters. Pajamas. Food. A bed. You'll need to take time off work to be with her, I guess."

Never underestimate the power of physical beauty. Physical beauty is sly. It works on you in ways of which you are not even aware and over which you have little control. There's probably a genetic or evolutionary reason for beauty and our response to it, about which I could ask my geneticist sister who explores precisely that sort of question as a fellow at some fancy lab on Long Island and who explores it in her own life, too, probably, as she's no slouch in the pretty department. But, as I've mentioned, Ollie and I aren't exactly close.

In any case, there's just something about a terribly beautiful man in distress that is irresistible, and when I asked Martin what we should do about Clare, Martin became a terribly beautiful man in distress. I was moved.

"Oh," said Martin in the smallest voice I'd ever heard him use. He opened his mouth to speak, shut it without speaking. He looked around himself, casting about for answers to the question of Clare, but found only couch cushions. He rapped the knuckles of one hand lightly, repeatedly, against the dimple in his chin. *Think, think, think,* I could almost hear him thinking.

Then from under his classical forehead, from under his black, thick-but-not-too-thick, shapely-but-not-in-a-manicured-feminine-way eyebrows, he lifted his dark eyes in their remarkable frame of lashes to meet mine, and what I saw in their wondrous depths was simple, naked panic. I'm not made of stone. I said, "She can stay here. With me. If she wants to."

"I'll come over a lot, of course, as much as I can. I'll do whatever you tell me to. Thank you, Cornelia. Thank you for helping." Martin was just this side of jumping for joy. His gratitude was tremendous, oceanic. "I can't thank you enough."

"You have. You've thanked me enough." Martin was never one of those people who are oblivious to the ways others might perceive him, and, right now, the magnitude of his relief was unseemly, clearly unseemly. That it wasn't clear to him is an indication of just how carried away he was, of how much he dreaded spending time with his daughter. It made me angry.

Focus on Clare, I reminded myself, on what Clare needs. And the irony of that struck me with no small amount of force. In my entire adult life, I'd never even owned a pet. How could a woman who'd never trusted herself to meet the needs of a hamster have any idea what to do for a child? I pushed the thought aside. Focus.

"Clothes. Did you get some for her when you went to the house to leave the note?" I asked him.

He looked sheepish.

"I told her you would go. You didn't go," I said.

"I'll go tomorrow. All I could think about was finding Viviana. I spent the day hunting down the detective agency and hiring the detective. Anyway, the detective—his name is Lloyd—he needs to go to the house, find out what he can. I'm taking him there tomorrow. We want to give him all the help we can."

"And you'll bring back clothes for Clare," I said, reminding him.

"And I'll bring back clothes for Clare. And whatever else she wants. Ask her. I'll get whatever she wants," he said.

Just then, there came from the bedroom the most lost, the most forlorn sound I'd ever heard. Clare. Telling us what she wanted.

"Mommy, Mommy, Mommy."

I jumped up. And then stopped. I looked at Martin, who slowly stood and walked to the bedroom. He was in there less than a minute.

"She doesn't want me," he said. "She's asking for you. She wants you."

I don't think she did, not particularly, but she didn't want him, I knew that much.

"Go. Go on. Go home. It's OK. Call me in the morning," I told him. He took my face between his hands, kissed me, and left.

So for the second time in one day, I put my arms around a child while she cried her heart out. I stroked her hair and said "Shh, shh," and what was amazing is that this seemed to help. Holding Clare, whispering soothing words, this seemed to make her feel better. Maybe that's just how children are. But, what was more amazing is that it felt pretty good to me, too. Twelve hours ago, I'd never seen this girl. I could count the number of words we had said to each other. She did not belong to me. But she fit inside my arms; she fit. I didn't love her. But, I suddenly understood, to my bewilderment, it wouldn't take much.

There's a kind of ease in darkness, a soft, blurring quiet that smudges the lines between one person and another. The broad light of a kitchen is quite a different matter. When Clare stopped crying and we walked out and stood among shiny surfaces and sharp edges, I suddenly felt charged with prickly nervousness, like static electricity; if I touched Clare, I believed we'd both get a shock. So I stood, looking at her, waiting to know what to do. Her face had that clean, almost incandescent look children get after they cry, and this glow seemed to place her fur-

ther out of my reach, as though she were half-angel, hallowed by sadness. Tell me what to do, I thought, and in a few seconds, and in a reassuringly human voice, Clare did.

"My stomach's growling," she said. "I think I'm hungry. Are you
hungry?"

"Famished," I said.

I had made some chicken soup the day before, and I heated up two
bowls full of it. While we ate, I told Clare that her father had not
called the police but had hired someone very smart to help find her
mother. I asked her if she wanted to stay with me, and she nodded. I
didn't tell her that her father had not left the note as I'd promised he
would, but I did say he was going to her house tomorrow to pick up
some things, whatever she wanted. I had a thought.

"Clare," I said, "when I was a kid, I loved to make lists. Do you ever
make lists?"

And I'm almost positive that when I asked her this, Clare smiled.

12

Clare

Clare sat at a table in Café Dora watching two men play chess. One of the men was tall with a crooked nose and blue eyes, and he wore a red shirt with white piping and pearly snaps all down the front and on the pocket flaps. A boy in Clare's class a couple of years ago had dressed as a cowboy for Halloween and worn a similar shirt to the class party, and Clare found it interesting that they made such shirts for adult men. The other man had a head of thick, black, springy curls, sad eyes like a basset hound, and a smile that surprised you— a big girly movie-star smile with corners that turned up and dimples on either side. Once, the cowboy startled Clare by clapping his hands and shouting, "Yee-haw, Josie, you caught me nappin'!" to which the other man, whose name was evidently Josie, responded by shaking his head, the curls bouncing much more wildly than you would expect, as though they were alive, and letting the smile spread slowly across his face.

When this happened, Clare glanced over the counter to meet Cornelia's eyes. Cornelia's eyes were wide and turned up a little at the corners like cats' eyes, but they weren't gold or green or blue, as cats' eyes tended to be; they were medium-brown, with maybe a smidge of hazel, but mostly just brown. Cornelia's nose was nice, slightly tip-tilted; her smile was rectangular so that you saw her bottom teeth as well as her top, and her chin was pointed. In fact, her face was shaped very much like the pictures of Anne and Sara and Mary that Clare used to draw in her notebook. An orphan face, although Clare didn't know if Cornelia was an orphan. When Clare looked at Cornelia over the coffee bar, Cornelia rolled her tilted brown eyes at the cowboy's loudness and, though she didn't quite smile, Clare rolled her eyes in return.

More than ever, more than when she was living in her house with her erratic and unrecognizable mother, Clare's fears were a roaring, blinding storm that could lift her up and suck her in before she knew it was happening. "My mother might be dead," shrieked the storm, and in that second Clare would be overtaken, lost, whisked out of the sunlit world in which other people lived.

The night before, as she'd sat eating chicken soup—rich and delicious soup with little fat dumplings—and buttered toast in Cornelia's apartment, Clare had discovered a way to keep this from happening. She found that if she paid extremely careful attention to what was around her, really concentrating, and noticing every detail, the terror would fall back.

Clare had observed the gold-flecked sheen of the soup's surface, the rippled edge of the glass plate on which her toast sat, the peacock-blue-and-gold embroidered shawl draped over the back of Cornelia's velvet couch and, on one wall, a grouping of small antique paintings, all portraits of women. Looking closely, Clare noticed that there was something quirky in each painting: an ugly lap dog with an almost-human face, a cracked brown egg in an eggcup, a flock of pecking chickens and a pig outside a window. One woman had tight bunches of curls on either side of her face that dangled like clusters of grapes and around her was an arbor with twisting grapevines hung with clusters of grapes. Clare had thought at first that these women might be Cornelia's ancestors, but after noticing these funny details, she imagined Cornelia's happening upon them over the years and just liking them.

After dinner, Cornelia had asked Clare if she might like to take a bath. Clare almost never took baths anymore, just showers, but she was still tired and didn't want the commotion of a shower, so she'd agreed. For a few seconds, she'd gripped the lapels of the mink coat, reluctant to take it off, until Cornelia said, "Let me show you something," and Clare had followed her into the bedroom. Next to the bed was a coatrack hung with hats, scarves, shawls, a little fur stole, and a couple of jackets; Cornelia showed Clare a bare place on the rack.

"We'll hang it here and, that way, if you want it during the night, you'll just grab. You won't even have to get out of bed."

Clare had taken the coat off, then, and immediately wished she hadn't. She liked the way it made her feel part-bear, on the verge of being something other than herself, and she liked that it made her feel large, as though she took up a great deal of space and, especially, she liked that it made her feel held. Also, of course, it belonged to her mother, but that was not something Clare wanted to think about just then. Clare had looked at Cornelia, who nodded encouragingly, and Clare had hung the coat up.

After the bath, Clare put on the pajamas Cornelia had left for her—pajamas so pretty they seemed to be something else. Everything in Clare's apartment is like this, Clare had thought as she looked in the mirror at herself. Peculiar and pretty and so obviously *chosen.* Cornelia had stood in a store, letting the white, gliding fabric cool her hands. "I won't take those, but I'll take these," she'd said. "Elegant," Clare said to her reflection. "I am elegant." She noticed the mirror's carved edges, the flower-shaped buttons on the pajamas, the way the pajamas themselves caught the light.

In this way, Clare anchored herself in the moment, the here-and-now, and kept the future, the unknown, the worst-case scenarios at bay. So, the next morning, when Cornelia told Clare she would take the day off, Clare had thought about it, and then asked, "Do you think you could take me to work with you? I'll stay out of everybody's way. I promise. You won't even know I'm there." Because being out in the ordinary, busy world, in a place with new things and people to look at sounded good to Clare. When Clare asked this, Cornelia wanted to hug her; Clare wasn't sure why, but she could tell this by the look Cornelia gave her. Cornelia didn't hug her, but she did say, "You know what? We'll go to the café, but only if you promise to get in the way as much as you want to."

Clare's father had stopped by after that to pick up the list Clare had made—a detailed list. With some adults, Clare could just write "clothes" and rely on them to find what she needed, but not with her father. Her father had kissed Cornelia, called Clare "Sparrow," and asked her if she'd eaten dinner, if she'd slept more, and if there was anything special he could get Clare from the house, even though he held her list in his hand as he'd asked the question.

After he left, neither she nor Cornelia talked about him at all. Instead, Cornelia had turned to Clare, smiled, and said, "How about I lend you some clothes?"

Cornelia had let Clare choose, and Clare ended up in a thick, soft, powder-blue sweater, chocolate brown corduroy pants, and brown boots, all of which fit to a T, and all of which made Clare feel sophisticated and adult. She'd even let Cornelia talk her into leaving the mink hanging on its wooden hook and into wearing an amazingly lightweight brown shearling jacket instead.

"You look wonderful," said Cornelia.

"I feel like I'm wearing a costume," said Clare, adding quickly, "but I like it."

As Clare looked around the café, it seemed to her that *everyone* was wearing a costume or part of a costume. There was the cowboy. There was a man with an Amish beard in a gas-station-attendant shirt with "Bub" stitched on it. There was a man with a goatee and a black beret; a fragile blond girl in immense black, square glasses; and a beautiful auburn-haired woman in a blue silk cheongsam (Clare knew what a cheongsam was from multicultural week at her school) with jeans underneath. The cheongsam woman kept popping pieces of pastry into the mouth of her tiny, red-haired daughter who sat on her lap in a wool sailor dress and cap and red shoes, waving imperiously at people and blowing the occasional kiss.

Cornelia sat down at the table with Clare. As the black-beret man at the next table took out a cigarette and prepared to light it, Cornelia tapped him lightly on the shoulder.

"No, Egon," said Cornelia, shaking a finger at him. "Children on board. You know the rules."

Egon growled like a vicious dog, then turned to Clare. "Watch out for this one. She's a dictator. She rules with an iron fist."

Clare gave him a very serious look and said in a very serious voice, "I will. I'll watch out for her. Thank you very much." Egon threw back his head and laughed uproariously, then shrugged on his coat and went outside to smoke.

"Was I that funny?" whispered Clare to Cornelia.

"No offense, but no. You were funny, but not that funny. It's unclear that anything in the history of the world has ever been that funny. However, if Egon just laughed like a normal human being, would the whole roomful of people turn to stare at him and wonder what joke they were missing?"

"No?" said Clare.

"No," affirmed Cornelia. "Are you dying of boredom?"

"I like it here," said Clare, "But does everyone always look like this?"

"Like they're on break from twenty different movie sets? Pretty much. That's why my friend Linny never comes here. Also, she says she'd have to lose ten pounds, get cheekbone implants, and change her name to Luna before we'd let her in. But guess what?"

"She's coming," guessed Clare.

"She is, indeed," said Cornelia. "And here's my prediction. She'll fall head over heels in love with . . ." Cornelia pointed to the cowboy.

"She'll fall in love with the cowboy?" asked Clare.

"No, not with Hayes. His name's Hayes, and he's not a bad guy, all things considered, but no, the shirt. That god-awful, dingbat, nightmare of a shirt he's got on. Linny will love it. She'll covet it."

"Thou shalt not covet," recited Clare.

"You tell that to Linny," said Cornelia.

"Can I ask you a personal question?" Clare asked.

Cornelia gave her a rueful little smile. "That only seems fair," she said. Clare didn't quite understand what this meant, but she decided to go ahead and ask.

"You don't have to answer, but I was wondering, did you go to college?"

"Yep," said Cornelia. "College and two months of graduate school."

"Because you seem really smart," said Clare.

"I'm pretty smart. Not blisteringly, blindingly smart," said Cornelia.

"That's good. Who wants to be blistered and blinded? I wouldn't," said Clare. Talking this way with Cornelia felt easy and good. Maybe it was the grown-up clothes. Or maybe it was because she was keeping herself inside the moment and inside the conversation with all her might; she was saying things that she sometimes thought but didn't say, or only thought of later when it was too late.

Cornelia laughed a real laugh.

"There's another part of the question, but you really, really don't have to answer this part," said Clare.

"If I'm so smart, why do I work here, serving coffee to a bunch of pretentious, self-involved, Europhile maniacs?"

"I wasn't going to say Europhile," said Clare.

"Because you're too polite," said Cornelia.

"I don't know what it means," said Clare, and Cornelia laughed again, then got serious.

"When I was a few years older than you are, I fell in love with a movie. *The Philadelphia Story*?" Clare shook her head.

"Well, I guess we know what goes at the top of Clare's must-see list. Anyway, that's why I came to Philadelphia. Isn't that silly?" asked Cornelia. Her tone was light, but Clare could tell that it was a real question.

"No. Probably you didn't have reasons to go other places and since you had a reason to come here, you did," said Clare.

"That's exactly right. The movie's not set in Philadelphia, really, more like out on the Main Line, but still. I thought I'd try it. After I left grad school, I didn't know what to do. I wanted to be around interesting people who said interesting things in interesting ways about interesting subjects, but I was too chicken to go to New York or Paris, so I got a job in a place where everyone came from or appeared to come from or appeared to be on their way to someplace fascinating," explained Cornelia.

"That makes sense," said Clare.

"You are a very nice girl, Clare. I came here and eventually became a manager and eventually couldn't think of anyplace else to go," said Cornelia.

"Do you think you'll stay?" asked Clare.

"No, I don't. I'm not sure what I'll do next, though. The problem with me is that I like to work; I like to do what I do well and completely; I just don't have a calling. Not yet, anyway," Cornelia puffed up her cheeks with air, then let the air out. "If you think of anything, though, let me know."

"I will," said Clare solemnly. Cornelia smiled, then jumped to her feet to wave at a woman who had just entered the café.

Clare turned and saw a woman in a long burgundy cocoon of a coat, a Sherlock Holmes hat, a rainbow striped wool scarf and the kind of high rubber boots men wear to go trout-fishing. The boots were neon yellow. She looked like she was on break from four different movie sets, not just one.

"Linny," said Cornelia, "Speaking of blinding and blistering."

From the doorway Linny looked around the room, then at Cornelia. "You've got to be kidding me!" she shouted across the room. Cornelia gestured for her to come in, come in. Linny came in and stamped across the floor, pausing once to give Hayes's red-and-white shirt the once-over. Cornelia raised her eyebrows at Clare.

When Linny plopped down in the chair next to her, Cornelia said, "Don't start. About the shirt."

"*Magnifique!*" said Linny. "Happy Trails to Me. You're Clare." Clare nodded.

"Nice Wellies. I have to get back," said Cornelia. "But don't you tell stories about me when I'm gone, Linny. And Clare, take everything she says with a grain of salt." Linny pushed a big shaker of white stuff across the table to Clare.

"How's that?" asked Linny, smiling sweetly at Cornelia.

"That would be sugar," said Cornelia and started to turn away. Clare put a hand on Cornelia's arm, and Cornelia looked down at her, then immediately crouched low so they were face-to-face.

"Barcelona," said Clare, softly. "We were in the car, and she was crying, and she stopped to let me out. I walked for a long time, until it was dark. And some teenagers picked me up and drove me home. But she had two tickets. For Barcelona. She wanted to spend Christmas there. So maybe that's where she went." Cornelia was perfectly still, listening to Clare. Then she put her hands on the sides of Clare's face and nodded.

"Good. Thank you. That will definitely help. Brave girl," She kissed Clare on the forehead, which surprised Clare and seemed to surprise Cornelia, as well. But it was OK, Clare decided, and she smiled—not a carefree, dazzling smile, but the best one she'd smiled in what seemed like a long time. At any rate, it felt real.

Left with Linny, faced with the hat and the boots and what turned out to be a fairly ordinary Fair Isle sweater and jeans underneath the monstrously huge coat, Clare felt shy.

"Now that she's gone, the pest, what do *you* think of the red cowboy shirt? Honestly. Brilliant, right?" Linny leaned in conspiratorially.

Clare looked at the shirt again and said, "Well, if *you* like it, you should ask him where he got it."

Linny said, "Very diplomatic, missy. I just might do that."

"His name is Hayes," Clare told her.

"Of course his name is Hayes," groaned Linny. "No normal names in this joint."

A cream horn, a fruit tart with impossibly perfect berries on top, and a fat chocolate croissant materialized on the table in front of Clare and Linny. Then another hot chocolate for Clare and a foamy-topped coffee for Linny appeared. Clare turned to see the fast, little bustling form of Cornelia slip back behind the counter.

"She's a feeder," said Linny. "Gets it from her mother. Both of them devotees of the philosophy that all the world's ills can be cured if you throw enough food at them, although Cornelia would probably not admit that."

"So she does have a mother," said Clare, thoughtfully, almost to herself.

"Have you heard of Plato?" asked Linny after a pause, during which she'd broken off a hunk of cream horn and bit it.

"Sort of," said Clare. "We mostly did myths this year, but next year, I think we do philosophy."

"Myths are better. All those people turning into other things—trees, cows, swans. I'd be a peacock, I think. Nice to be gorgeous and dumb for a while. Anyhoo, Cornelia's mother, Ellie, she's the Platonic form of the mother. And not appreciated enough for it, if you ask me. Her father's a peach too."

"Is Cornelia my father's girlfriend?" asked Clare.

"Hmmm. Yes, I'd say that's a fair description of who she is. For now, anyway," mused Linny, her mouth full.

"Do you think they'll get married?" As she said this, Clare realized that it was incredibly important for her to know this. Later, she'd sort out why.

Linny appeared to be trying to decide between two answers, or maybe appeared to be trying to decide what answer Clare wanted to hear. Finally, she sighed. "We haven't talked about that specifically. But if you want my honest opinion, I'd say no, I don't think Cornelia will marry your dad. I'm not always right, though. I'm right a lot, but not always. She's starry-eyed about him, that's for sure."

Clare didn't know what to say next, but it turned out not to matter because at that moment, she happened to glance over toward the café entrance and standing there, tall and lean, in a plain dark blue peacoat and duck boots—not a costume at all—was the handsomest man Clare had ever seen. He had a light brown face, he needed a haircut, and even from all the way across the room, Clare could see that his eyes were bottle green.

"Oh!" Clare gasped. Linny turned to look.

"Well, look who's here," she said. "Suddenly, I'm feeling starry-eyed myself."

The man looked in the direction of the coffee bar. He smiled.

And then, above the noise of the café, a voice rang out, joyfully singing a tune Clare recognized right away. It was Cornelia's voice: *"Taaayyyyo! Tay-ay-ay-yo-oh!"*

A number of people, Linny and Clare included, joined in. *"Daylight come and me wanna go home."*

The man standing in the door ducked his head a little, shyly, smiling again. Again, Clare gasped. Then, as the other people in the café went back to their conversations, the man walked across the room to the coffee bar, and Cornelia stepped out from behind it, and the two of them hugged so hard, Cornelia was lifted right off the ground.

13

Cornelia

I'd never been so happy to see anyone in my life. I know that sounds dramatic, but it's a fact.

The shock of the new. I like it; you like it. There's no jolt like a new jolt. But, I'm an even bigger fan of the shock of recognition, and when Teo walked through the door of the café, I'd had my fill of newness; newness was old-hat. I wanted my pleasures as familiar as they come, and, for me, they don't come much more familiar than Teo. Even though I hadn't thought about him in quite some time, as soon as I saw him, in that coat he's had for eons and with his hair falling in his eyes, I realized that no one else would do. No one but Mateo Sandoval. Teo. Taaayyyyo. My brother-in-law. A little piece of home.

And, when I think about it, I don't mean actually that I hadn't thought about him in quite some time. Instead, I mean that I hadn't thought about him *directly* in quite some time. Because he is not one of the myriad people I've known in my life or continue to know who enter my mind, stay awhile, and leave. He's just in there, like Linny or my mother or father or siblings. So long ago I don't know how long ago, Teo took up permanent residence.

Even "brother-in-law" sounded wrong to me, and not just because his and Ollie's elopement two years earlier had come utterly out of the clear blue sky and thrown us all into confusion, but also because I'd known him for so many years before he became my brother-in-law. His family moved down the road from mine when I was four and Teo was seven. Like my father, his father was a doctor. They still played golf together. And our mothers were best friends, fellow garden-clubbers, tennis partners, and co-pillars of the community—despite the fact that, unlike my mother, who is definitely a pretty woman, Teo's mother, Ingrid, was and remains a Swedish blond bombshell whom you'd think would fit in better at the Cannes film festival on the arm of a star director twenty years her junior than at a Junior League meeting in a twinset from Talbots.

Teo and Estrella (his younger sister, whom we all call Star—a name that suits her to a T) and Ollie, Cam, Toby, and I lived our childhoods in and out of each other's houses, yards, and even beds, in a purely nonsexual way. (Although Teo did give me my first kiss for the simple reason that I was fourteen years old and desperately in need of being kissed, after which I thanked him and we went back to pounding each other and the rest of the neighborhood kids with snowballs.) "Brother-in-law" didn't scratch the surface. More like brother-in-arms. Or just brother. Whatever the title, I loved the guy.

Loved not, apparently, in the same way my sister, Ollie, loved him, although not one person in their mutual acquaintance could have guessed this fact. When they showed up together at our house in Virginia one Christmas morning, married, my dad demanded to see the marriage license before he'd believe them. "Since when are you even in love?" blurted Cam, who is a dear boy, though distinctly lacking in subtlety—a question that made Ollie laugh and Teo look sheepish, but one that neither of them answered, although we all were dying to know.

But once the two families got over the shock, some of us rejoiced mightily at the union of the two nice, bright, successful young people and of the two nice, bright, successful families, and others of us all but forgot about it, since the man in question had seemed like a member of our family forever and since the two lovebirds were not particularly lovey-dovey around us and seemed to relate to each other in pretty much the same way they always had.

As far as I could tell, the only two differences were that they slept in the same room at my family's house and, a couple days after Christmas, left together, returning to Teo's Park Slope apartment which was now Teo's and Ollie's Park Slope apartment, even though she stayed out at her place near the lab when she was working.

But when I saw Teo standing in the café, I didn't think about Ollie or our families or any of that. In fact, I didn't think much at all; I just felt, and what I felt was glad.

I pulled Teo across the room, dragged another chair up to our table, and made some fluttery motions with my fingers in the air to Jacques to indicate that he should carry on without me, as I've found that people respond better to being bossed around when their boss appears vaguely idiotic while bossing them.

"You're looking wonderful, Teo," Linny said, a bit breathlessly. "I mean, hi, Teo. You're looking—wonderful."

Teo is the only man in the universe who can render semi-incoherent my otherwise inexorably coherent friend Linny. She claims that Teo is the most beautiful human alive, that there should be a law against being so beautiful, that Teo glows with an unearthly, possibly radioactive light, that beauty alone will win Teo a place at the right hand of God. I am not making these statements up. Linny uttered them and other similarly hyperbolic utterances after seeing Teo on various occasions and, as she spoke each time, her face shone with the kind of divine ecstasy that had surely transfigured Sir Galahad's features when he'd achieved the Holy Grail.

"Outbreeding" is how my sister, Ollie, sentimental fool, explained his appearance, referring to Teo's being the product of a Swedish mother and a Filipino father—a genetic combination that in all likelihood also makes him less vulnerable to diseases like Alzheimer's and malaria. (OK, so maybe I'm not remembering what she said exactly right, but it was something like that.)

While I knew that Linny's response to Teo verged on the insane, I also knew that he was handsome. But I knew it the same way I know George Washington was the first president of the United States. I did not doubt it, but beauty is something you know objectively and also something you experience, and I just didn't experience Teo as beautiful. Linny maintained that I saw Teo the way certain autistic people see everyone, as a collection of separate features. She claimed I saw the sum of his parts and not his whole, a whole that turns intelligent women—not all intelligent women, but it isn't just Linny—into howling lunatics. Maybe she was right. When I saw him, I saw a quiet, green-eyed man with messy hair whose personal style had not evolved much since his prep-school days, if it had evolved at all. But mostly, what I saw was Teo—just the regular, standard-issue Teo. Instead of a being drenched in celestial light, I still saw the kid who spent an entire sweltering summer in a Spider-Man costume, pretending to stick to walls.

"It's good to see you, too, Linny," said Teo, apparently oblivious to the fact that he was flapping the unflappable Linny. Even if he'd noticed, it wouldn't have made much difference. The only effect Teo's effect on women like Linny seemed to have on him was embarrassment, which no doubt only served to make him more adorable to them. A cycle too silly to even call vicious.

"Well, thanks, Teo," Linny bubbled, giving her hair a small, unconscious fluff.

"And I don't think I've had the pleasure of meeting you before," said Teo to Clare. He said it in a natural way, not in a manner designed to charm and flatter, but when I saw Clare blush, I saw that charmed and flattered she certainly was. In fact, it was glaringly obvious that Clare had been bitten by Linny's bug, and how.

"Clare, this is my brother-in-law, Teo. Teo, this is Clare," I said. Clare couldn't speak, but nodded with great and tremendous vigor, as if to verify that—yes, I was right! She was Clare!

"Let's give these two a minute to get their bearings, Teo. It'll help if you refrain from smiling at them," I said. "So tell me what brings you to my fair city."

"A medical conference. An amazingly boring medical conference. I was sitting there listening to some amazingly boring lecture, and I felt my bones starting to petrify. So, I ducked out to visit my friend Cornelia," said Teo.

"Good decision. And where's the DNA goddess? Out ruthlessly hunting down the Nobel Prize like a dog?" I asked, and I may have been mistaken, but I thought I saw Teo flinch, ever so slightly. It occurred to me that maybe my flippant attitude toward his wife might pain him, which was the last thing I wanted. He's in love with her, I reminded myself. I should be able to understand that, as I'd spent much of my life being in love with her too.

"Sort of. I guess," he said, with a wry smile. "She's away right now, doing some research. Won't be back for a while."

"What about Christmas?" asked Clare, having rejoined us on planet Earth and sounding worried.

"Overachieving types like Teo, Ollie, and myself exist on a plane above what you people call the 'holiday season,' " said Linny, having also rejoined us on planet Earth and sounding snarky.

"Yeah, well, Ollie does work pretty hard," said Teo. Then he perked up. "Hey, Cornelia, remember that holiday season you made the whole neighborhood watch It's a Wonderful Life every day for—wait—was it a month?"

"Don't be silly," I said.

"At least a month," said Teo. He turned to Clare. "You're lucky you weren't born yet, Clare. She would drag children still in diapers out of their warm homes by force and plunk them in front of the television. It was brutal."

Clare laughed—a gorgeous sound.

"I've only known her a day, and she's already making a list of movies for me to watch," said Clare, laughing again.

"Great, now you've got her in cahoots against me." I reached over and gave Teo a pinch.

"It's good for her, don't you think?" Teo asked Clare. "Being cahooted against?"

"I think so," said Clare, nodding sagely.

"So what *are* your Christmas plans?" I asked Teo, and right away, I knew I'd made a mistake.

"Don't have any. My parents are spending Christmas with Star in London. Ollie and I had talked about going to your parents' house, but once this research thing came up, I decided not to make the trip without her. I might go down for a few days in January. What about you? Who are you spending Christmas with?" We'd all been intent on keeping things light, on keeping Clare smiling her sweet smile, but it was bound to come along sooner or later, a question bearing a freightload of other questions, all requiring heavy, difficult answers.

"Well, Teo," I could have said. "I didn't plan a trip home because I had an inkling my emotionally distant boyfriend had a romantic getaway up his sleeve, during which I hoped to bridge said emotional distance, but then his daughter whom I didn't know existed and whom had just been abandoned by her mother showed up at the café yesterday and is sitting right here, in all her misery and loveliness, so what we're doing for Christmas now is anybody's guess." But I didn't say this, of course. I didn't say anything. No one said anything. Clare dropped her gaze to the center of the table, then to her lap.

Linny looked around the table. She stood up. "Excuse me," she said. "I need to see a man about a shirt." Before walking away, she rested her hand on the top of Clare's head. Linny wasn't bailing out on us, I knew that. I'd filled her in on enough of Clare's story for her to know that the story, what little I knew of it, was full of sorrow, and, if it—or parts of it—were going to get told here in a crowded café, the smaller the audience, the better. Linny walked in the direction of Hayes, calling, "Halliburton!"

Clare lifted her eyes, and they met mine. "His name is Hayes," Clare said in a flat voice.

Without meaning to, I sighed. "I know," I said to Clare. It's a cliché to say that the air was thick with all our unsaid words, but sometimes, clichés speak truth. I was finding it difficult to breathe.

"Clare," said Teo softly, "watch." And he began to send a quarter rolling and flashing over and between the fingers of one hand, then the fingers of the other, back and forth. It was a trick I'd seen him do before, seen other people do too, although usually just with one hand, and I knew it wasn't the hardest trick in the world. But Teo did it exceptionally well, so that the quarter rippled like water over his long fingers. If you were a worn-out, hurting child, the trick might look like a miracle.

Clare's eyes widened. "Can you teach me?" she almost whispered and, even though nothing had been explained, the air in the room suddenly felt like ordinary air.

They worked at it for ten minutes, and Clare wasn't really getting it, but that didn't matter, because with each minute she was looking more like an eleven-year-old child. I left to check on Jacques, and when I got back, Teo was saying, "There are two stages. First, you have to learn how to do it. And second, you have to forget how to do it and just do it. Turn off your brain and trust your hands." Clare nodded, and I could tell she was writing this down in her head, word for word.

Then Clare did an amazing thing: She put the quarter between her two palms, clasped her hands together tightly with the quarter inside, and said, "Teo, have you ever known anyone who went crazy?"

It was a surprising question, but Teo didn't look especially surprised, just thoughtful. "Yes, I guess I have."

"Did they ever get better?" asked Clare.

"They did. The ones I knew did. The ones I knew were themselves for a long time, and then they started to change. They got confused or started to forget things, and they would behave in ways you'd never expect. Sometimes, they were even scary."

"They stopped being themselves," said Clare. She never took her eyes from Teo's face. He never looked away either.

"Well, no, not really, although it seemed that way. They still carried inside all of what made them themselves and nobody else. They had lived lives and loved people, and all that was in there somewhere."

"Do you really think they still loved the people they'd loved when they were well?" asked Clare.

"I really do. They may not have been able to get to the love very easily, and they may not have acted all the ways the love would usually make them act, but the love didn't disappear. No way. What happened to the people I knew was that the delicate chemicals in their brains got thrown off balance, so that there was too much of one thing and not enough of another."

"Like being sick?"

"Exactly like being sick. And medicine and good, listening doctors helped them get well."

"Does everyone get well?"

Teo hesitated.

"Not everyone. But a lot of people do. And scientists are learning more all the time about how to make even the sickest people better." In Teo's calm, even voice, the answer wasn't a howling wilderness. I watched Clare pass through it and emerge on the other end, whole. Then she set the quarter down and took hold of the table's edge with both hands.

"My mother is sick like that. She started changing in the beginning of October. It was just the two of us in our house, and I watched her get worse and worse. She would buy all kinds of strange things, and she took me out of school for a day for no reason and, one time, she gave me wine to drink." I listened to Clare, astonished. She had the most expressive face I'd ever seen, and what was in those dark eyes, in the set of her jaw, and across her smooth forehead was unmistakable: trust. I'd seen a flicker of it earlier, when Clare told me about Barcelona. This was no flicker, but a steadfast, shining lantern of trust, shining right at Teo. Under other circumstances, I might have felt slighted—why Teo, why not me?—but this was far too important. Good choice, Clare, I thought, good girl.

"That must have been hard," said Teo, and Clare nodded, her eyes glazing with tears. No storm came, though, no breakdown. The tears didn't even fall.

"She stopped taking care of me. She'd always taken great, great care of me, and she stopped. But she didn't mean to. That's why I had to keep everyone from finding out she was sick."

"Because you were afraid people wouldn't understand? That she might get in trouble?"

Clare nodded.

"She picked me up at school on the last day before vacation, and she was different again. Different from the way she'd been different before. She cried so much, and told me she was sorry. And then she dropped me off by the side of the road. That's why I'm here."

"Is Cornelia your mother's friend?" Teo asked.

"No, her father is my . . . ," I began. I paused, rifling through the standard labels, rifling through and discarding. Suddenly, all those words felt broad and clumsy, seemed to either carry too much weight or too little. I thought, briefly, of my personal favorite of the *Piers Plowman* allegorical character names: Tom-True-Tongue-Tell-Me-No-Tales-Nor-Lies-For-To-Laugh-At-For-I-Loved-Them-Never. Exactly the kind of precise nomenclature I needed, but before I came close to piecing anything together, Clare jumped in.

"Boyfriend. Cornelia's my father's girlfriend," said Clare.

"I see," said Teo but, of course, he didn't see, not the whole complicated picture, and I fought the urge to explain. Why did I want to explain to Teo what didn't even make sense to me, yet? I'm not sure, but I'd sat at this table and witnessed two people being as brave and honest as people ever are. Maybe I wanted to be brave and honest too. For now, though, I kept my unpeaceable peace.

"You know what I think?" said Clare, her face brightening. "I think you should spend Christmas with us, Teo. Cornelia and I can sleep in her bed, and you can sleep on the couch." She remembered something, and turned to me. "If it's OK with you, Cornelia."

I laughed. "It's OK with me." Clare turned back to Teo.

"It's a really big couch," she said.

Then the smile she gave Teo turned Clare into a girl only the hardest-hearted among us could refuse, so my old friend Teo, good man, didn't stand a chance.

$$\frac{14}{}$$

Clare

In Cornelia's kitchen, Teo was teaching Clare how to chop.

While Cornelia was still working, they had walked around China-town together, buying a big bag of fragrant rice, small yellow mangoes, and the ingredients for a Filipino noodle dish called *pancit*. They'd also had fun choosing desserts Clare had never seen before, made with unexpected ingredients such as rice, coconut milk, and, most un-expectedly of all, root vegetables like cassava, sweet potato, and a pur-ple yam called *ube*.

The gruff, elderly woman at the bakery had allowed Clare to sam-ple some of the desserts before choosing, even though she said she didn't usually do that and made a big show of being reluctant. Clare knew the woman wanted to do it because Teo had asked her. He'd told her his father was from Manila, and he let her shake her finger at him and tease him about his green eyes and his inability to speak Tagalog. Teo taught Clare how to say one of the few phrases he knew, *"Mali-gayang Pasko"*—Merry Christmas—and just before they left, he had taken the elderly woman's hand and pressed it lightly to his forehead. *"Salamat,"* he said. Thank you. The gesture was called blessing, he told Clare later, and was something children did to adults to show respect. Clare loved it. When no one was looking, she tried it out by lifting one of her own gloved hands in the other.

After shopping, Clare had pushed Cornelia's little cart back toward the apartment, and Teo had carried the bag of rice over his shoulder like Santa, except that he looked nothing like Santa, of course. He didn't look like anyone else in the world, as far as Clare could tell, but she didn't find herself marveling every single second at how handsome he was as she'd thought she would after first spotting him in the café.

As they walked through the city's Christmastime streets, what Clare did marvel at was how easy it was. The muscles in her body, especially in her neck and between her shoulder blades, relaxed for the first time in a long time. Her body felt like something she was, not something heavy she had to carry around from place to place. The big tree at the courthouse; all the red, green, and gold; the garland and lights wound around everything on Broad Street and down Walnut didn't hurt her as she'd feared they would. The sky stretched above it all, a single clean blue like a laundered sheet. Out in the snow-scented air, under the sky, she could even think about her mother and of all the Christmases they'd spent walking around those streets together, without slipping into panic.

Clare was not such a little girl that she could spend one morning in a café talking with adults and feel that everything was going to be fine. But after her conversations with Cornelia and Teo, Clare stepped out into a world in which fine was a possibility, in which fine didn't feel like a distant, dimly shimmering universe she would never enter again. Watching Teo ahead of her carrying the bag and turning around to smile, she understood suddenly what the difference was, such a simple change: She'd been alone for a long time; she wasn't alone anymore.

She caught up with Teo. She didn't want to talk—not really. She liked the bubble of easy quiet they walked in, but she wanted to ask one question.

"It's OK to feel happy, right?" She hoped he'd know what she meant.

"Right. Very OK," he answered, not looking at her and not slowing down or stopping but smiling into the distance a private smile—more eyes than mouth—more to himself than to her. Then he said, "How are you at chopping?"

Not bad, as it turned out. After Teo showed her how, she rocked the big knife like a seesaw over the scallions, staying at a slight angle, and left a trail of small, fairly precise pieces.

"It's kind of like the quarter trick, right? You turn off your mind and trust your hands?" asked Clare.

"Kind of. But don't trust your hands too much. Not yet." Teo grinned.

Teo was wonderful at it, amazing to behold, so fast and controlled at the same time. *Zip, zip, zip,* and the carrot became a line of discs, overlapping one another like fallen dominoes, and all just the same width.

"Showoff!" called Cornelia from the couch.

"Are you a surgeon?" asked Clare, a little out of breath from just watching him.

Teo laughed. "If surgeons cut like this, they wouldn't stay surgeons for long. No, I specialize in therapeutic radiology."

"What does that mean? X-rays?"

"He's an oncologist," said Cornelia, walking up and popping a carrot piece in her mouth. "He treats cancer patients. He just doesn't like to say it."

"But treating cancer patients is good," said Clare.

"Sure it's good, but saying the word 'cancer' can put quite a damper on a dinner party. I've seen it happen. 'Pull up another chair, dear, death just showed up!'" said Cornelia.

"It's like a magic spell. You say it, and instantly everyone around you gets depressed," said Teo, chopping up a Chinese sausage effortlessly, like someone signing his name or shuffling a deck of cards.

"You should become a coffee-bar manager. When I say I'm a coffee-bar manager, instantly everyone around me just thinks I'm an underachiever," said Cornelia.

Just as Clare was worrying that Cornelia might be talking about what she'd asked that morning, Cornelia put an arm around her shoulders and squeezed. "And don't you think I'm talking about you, honey. Besides, there are worse things someone could think about me. At least the term 'underachiever' hints that I'm capable of ever so much more. Ever, ever, ever so."

"On the other hand, maybe you're flattering yourself. Maybe they're just thinking you're a loser," said Teo innocently, and Clare was rather shocked at this, but Cornelia laughed and threw a piece of sausage. It hit Teo right between the eyes.

"Remember a few hours ago, when I said you were a nice guy? Backspace. Delete."

"Here's Cornelia's story," began Teo to Clare.

"Oh, a lovely way to begin what I'm sure will be a lovely character assassination," said Cornelia. Clare wasn't worried anymore about their being mean to each other. She imagined that someday she'd be part of a friendship in which she and the friend thought so highly of each other and were so sure of this that they could say anything.

"Cornelia's story is that she's unquestionably smart," said Teo.

"Unquestionably. Without question," agreed Cornelia.

"Growing up, every kid in our neighborhood heard, 'Why can't you get grades like that little Cornelia Brown?'"

" 'Little' being the operative word," said Cornelia. "When you're thirteen and look like you're nine, you develop that which is developable."

"And she's talented, too. But her personal favorites among her talents, the ones she's decided to make the most of, are not necessarily the kinds of talents that lend themselves to a career," said Teo.

"Readily," corrected Cornelia. "That lend themselves *readily* to a career."

Teo lifted just his eyes from the cutting board and flashed Cornelia an evil grin. Clare almost gasped, but stopped the sound in the back of her throat and held it there, like a kid caught with a cigarette and a mouthful of smoke. She'd been telling herself she'd gotten used to Teo's face, but she'd been wrong. By the time she realized she was holding her breath, she had no choice but to pant a little to get enough air. When she noticed Cornelia noticing this, Clare turned the panting into a cough.

"While the rest of us were in med school and law school and grad school and business school or whatever," Teo continued, "Cornelia was studying hard too, but subjects like funny conversation. Sarcasm. Cleverness. What am I leaving out?"

"Wit. At least, give me wit. And making light of serious matters. And flattery—backhanded, of course," Cornelia said, pretending to count on her fingers.

"And personal style. According to my sources, Cornelia doesn't have a ton of money to throw around, but she's always had great personal style," said Teo, gesturing around at the apartment.

"You do." Clare nodded enthusiastically. "You have great personal style. Great plates and pajamas."

Cornelia laughed. "I was born in the wrong century. I could have been an ace courtesan." Then she looked at Teo with a serious, wondering face. "But here's the thing, Teo. You're right. You're exactly right. What you just said, that *is* my story."

"Of course it is," said Teo.

"I just never thought anyone else knew that. If I can apologize in advance for sounding like some idiot high school girl, I'd just like to say that I feel so—*gotten*." Cornelia pressed her hands to her heart and made her voice high and gushy when she said this last part, but she wasn't really joking.

Teo shrugged, said, "Apology accepted," and looked down at the chopped meat and vegetables, his face pleased but shy, as it had been that morning when he'd stood in the doorway of the café. Teo, Cornelia, and Clare stood there in the kitchen for a moment, hushed— Teo looking at the vegetables, Cornelia looking at Teo, and Clare looking at them both. For a few seconds Clare felt so warm and peaceful and normal, like she was suddenly standing in a pool of sunlight in a familiar place. Home. For a few seconds, this spot felt like home.

Then there was knock at the door, and Cornelia answered it, and it was Clare's father. Before he noticed anyone else was there, he hugged Cornelia and leaned down to rest his forehead on her shoulder briefly, then he kissed the top of her head. When he pulled away, his arms fell to his sides, and Clare saw that his face had a somber expression on it, maybe even a sad expression. He looked worried, too—his eyes looked worried. Clare thought about how her father had said he'd been learning how to read Cornelia's face. Clare didn't think she knew much about her father's face, but whatever the expression was, it was real, she could tell.

Then Clare's father noticed her standing there, and then noticed Teo. "Hello, everyone," he said, and all the sadness was gone. His smile was assured, expectant, and perfectly symmetrical.

"Hi," said Clare. And then, because she had seen him standing there, unhappy, in his coat with his arms hanging inside its sleeves, and had felt sorry for him, and because feeling sorry for her father was a new feeling, she added, "Dad."

"Martin, this is Teo Sandoval, my sister Ollie's husband. He appeared at the café this morning hungry and with petrified bones, so we took him in," said Cornelia, brightly. "Teo, this is Martin Grace."

"Nice to meet you, Teo, petrified bones and all." Clare's father put out his hand. "Or are they better?"

Teo rubbed his hands together, then shook Clare's father's hand. "The bones are better, but the hands are pretty garlicky. Sorry about that."

"What's cooking, Sparrow?" Clare's father unbuttoned his coat, and Cornelia slid it from his shoulders. She tossed it over the back of the couch first, but then picked it up.

"You'll stay for dinner, Martin?" she said, "I mean, naturally, you'll stay for dinner." She ran her hand over her hair, then took Clare's father's coat and hung it in the coat closet.

Clare found herself talking to her father about the shopping trip with Teo and about how they'd brought the groceries back in the cart, with the sack of rice over Teo's shoulder, and about the dish she and Teo were making. It was easy to talk to her father now, and she remembered that much of the time, in the past, talking to him had been pretty easy. For most of Clare's life, there'd been so much distance between her father and herself, an empty space across which she could send stories or information because telling him mattered so little. She only ran into difficulties when she wanted him to like her, which she'd fallen into now and then over the years, or when she'd needed something from him, which she'd never done until recently, or when she was furious at him, as she'd been just yesterday. At least for now, that fury had fallen away. He was just the near-stranger he'd always been.

She told him about Teo blessing the woman in the bakery.

"Why don't you show him?" suggested Teo. So Clare did what she'd wanted to do since they'd left the bakery: She walked over to Teo, carefully put her palm under his, lifted his hand, and touched it to her forehead. Teo smiled at her, but then looked quickly over at Clare's father. Clare saw concern in Teo's face. Puzzled, Clare looked at her father too. He was leaning casually against the wall, one leg crossed over the other, and had started in about some other country he'd been to in which the children performed some similarly charming gesture. Her father was fine.

Even so, she was glad her cooking project kept her too busy to talk to him much. Teo showed her how to peel and de-vein the shrimp and then cut them lengthwise. As she worked on this, he chopped cooked pork and chicken and cabbage. The sharp blade through the cabbage made a lovely sound. Then he cut the ends off each crisp snow pea.

While they were cooking, Cornelia made two small platters of snacks: wedges of cheese, pieces of French loaf, clementines, and grapes so purple they were nearly black. She put one platter in the kitchen for Teo and Clare and set the other on the coffee table; then she joined Clare's father on the sofa.

Cornelia had left a couple of feet between them, and Clare's father reached across and rested his hand on the back of Cornelia's neck, as though to draw her to him. Cornelia didn't move closer, but she reached up and pressed his hand with hers, briefly. Then she reached for a clementine and began to peel it with her swift, delicate hands. Clare thought how disappointed her father must be. If none of this had happened, if Clare weren't here, he would have had Cornelia to himself. He'd probably made all kinds of fancy Christmas plans for the two of them—romantic plans. Clare imagined air travel and boxes within boxes. Even though she didn't want to be with him, either, and of course didn't want her mother to have gotten sick and left her, Clare felt a short, mean rush of satisfaction. Even her father couldn't have everything the way he wanted it all the time.

Cornelia gave half the peeled clementine to Clare's father. He didn't eat it, but rocked it distractedly back and forth in his cupped hand.

"I spoke to Lloyd. The good news is that the Barcelona tickets were never used. In fact, there's no indication that Viviana got on a plane going anywhere," said Clare's father. "The bad news is that before she picked Clare up at school that day, she withdrew a large sum of money from the bank. If she's using cash, we won't be able to track her credit-card charges."

"I can hear you," Clare wanted to call across the room. "I'm not deaf. You know that, right?"

Immediately, Cornelia turned her attention from Clare's father to Clare. Their eyes met.

"Clare," said Cornelia, waving her over, "your father was just filling me in on the search for your mom. Come sit with us?"

Clare's father looked startled, which disgusted Clare. He never realized how old she was. She remembered being in the car with him the morning before, after they'd driven away from her empty house, how he'd said, "I bet some really good hot chocolate would fix you right up." Now she imagined him thinking, *The baby's over there, busy with her noodles and shrimp; she won't notice we're discussing her life right in front of her.*

"No, thanks," Clare said nonchalantly. "Maybe you can just tell me about it later, Cornelia." She popped a grape into her mouth, turned her back on them, and stood there wishing she had something to do with her hands when Teo handed her a big pan and said, "Ready?"

As Clare sautéed garlic and onions, she focused on distilling her feelings down to simple gladness that her mother had not left the country. Everything they didn't know about where her mother was or what she was doing tried to crowd in with its darkness and clamor, but she willed herself to ignore it, to push it out and slam the door. It was only when Teo put his hand over hers, the one that held the funny metal spatula that resembled a child's sandbox shovel, that she realized how hard she was gripping it.

"There you go," he said, shifting the garlic and onion around in the pan. "Perfect."

The pancit was delicious; everyone said so, even Teo and Clare—especially Teo and Clare. Clare said it was better than spaghetti, lo mein, pad thai, and spaetzle put together, and Cornelia congratulated her on her sophisticated palate.

"When I was eleven, I didn't know spaetzle from pretzels," Cornelia said.

"Or pad thai from bad pie," said Clare's father.

"Or lo mein from Rogaine," said Clare, who had thought of this in the nick of time, and everyone laughed.

"When you were little, did your mother make this?" Clare asked Teo.

"My dad makes it. My mother tells this story about how, before they got married, a whole troop of my dad's aunts came to meet her. They brought her a big pearl ring and some other stuff to wear at the wedding, but she figured out pretty fast that this was just an excuse. Their true mission was to teach her how to cook."

"Did she learn?" asked Clare.

"Sure. She learned. And then, after the wedding, the aunts boarded the plane to go home, and she promptly forgot everything. Turned the kitchen over to my dad, for which we are all eternally grateful," said Teo.

Cornelia shook her fork at Teo and began chewing furiously so that she could say what she wanted to say.

Teo groaned and set his forkful of *pancit* back on his plate with a clink, waiting.

Cornelia swallowed, then cried, "Teo!" reproachfully.

Teo rolled his eyes, then held up his index finger. "One dish," said Teo. "One."

"I will not sit idly by. I can't. Ingrid Sandoval is a tremendous cook! Huge!" said Cornelia, indignantly, but her face glowed, vivid and lit up with unlaughed laughter.

Teo laughed and shook his head. "One dish. Not even a dish really," he said to Clare and her father.

"Swedish pancakes. Teo's mother's pancakes are to die for," said Cornelia, glaring at Teo. "Whenever I'd spend the night at Teo's house, his mom would make them for me. Pancakes for *dinner*, which at my house would've been a departure on par with pruning bushes in the nude. Pancakes for dinner was *heaven*."

Clare noticed her father watching Cornelia and Teo talk, his eyes going from one of them to the other, as though he were watching a tennis match. There was an amused smile on his face, but Clare thought he looked uncertain, thrown off—only by inches, maybe, but until today, she couldn't remember having seen him be anything but confident and at the center of things.

"With powdered sugar and lingonberries?" he asked, which surprised Clare and then annoyed her. The pancakes belonged to Cornelia and Teo, not to him.

"Lingonberries when she could get them, but usually strawberries," said Teo.

"Or sometimes strawberry syrup. Remember that strawberry syrup?

And they were thin—whisper, whisper, whisper thin . . ." Cornelia's voice trailed off, and she fell back in her chair, limp, her eyes shut.

"A shame about Cornelia," said Teo. "Death by pancake."

"Death by memory of pancake, by virtual pancake. Poor girl," said Clare's father, correcting Teo, or so it seemed to Clare, and she burned with resentment. She turned to Teo, but he didn't seem to be burning with anything. He smiled at her, and she noticed that his eyebrows were darker than his hair, that they were very straight like dashes, but slanted slightly upward. *Accent grave, accent aigue,* she thought. But even as she thought about Teo's eyebrows, she felt anger at her father simmering inside her.

Cornelia sat up, blinked, and smiled at them all with the look of someone awakened from pleasant dreams.

"She lives!" said Clare's father. "And a good thing, too, because we need to discuss important issues."

Abruptly, without a glance at her father, Clare got up to get the desserts she and Teo had bought. She'd spent time arranging the desserts on a large plate in what she believed and hoped was an artistic way. They were so pretty.

"Such as?" asked Cornelia.

"Such as tomorrow is Christmas Eve," said Clare's father. He reached for one of the desserts, without asking what it was or saying anything about the platter. The dessert had rested on a bit of banana leaf, and Clare wondered, angrily, what kind of person would take a dessert off a banana leaf and not ask what it was.

"Teo, I expect you have plans for the holidays, unlike the three of us who are flying by the seat of our pants this go-round." Clare's father turned to Clare and smiled. "Which, as everyone knows, often turns out to be the best way to fly."

"That's a piece of *bibingka*," said Clare, coolly. "The dessert you're eating. It's cooked on a banana leaf. And Teo's staying here with me and Cornelia. He's spending Christmas with us."

Clare's father looked thrown off again, to Clare's satisfaction, although it only lasted a moment. He glanced at Cornelia, then returned his attention to Clare.

"Excellent," said Clare's father, graciously. "The *bibingka and* Teo's plans."

"They weren't his plans, actually," explained Cornelia. "He was railroaded. Ollie's away working, and we couldn't have Teo spending Christmas alone, watching football and eating tuna salad out of the bowl, could we?"

"We definitely could not," said Clare's father. Not *you,* Clare thought hard in her father's direction. Cornelia's "we" hadn't included him; "Clare and I," that's what Cornelia meant by "we."

Her father went on. "Since it's Christmas Eve, Clare, and you may not have had time to do much shopping before you got here"—Clare saw Cornelia glance at her with concerned eyes—"I thought maybe you and I would go, make a day of it. Maybe take in the light show at Wanamakers?"

"It's called Lord & Taylor now," Clare corrected. "And I don't think I should go without . . ." No way was Clare going to cry in front of him again, no way. "I don't think I want to go this year."

"I understand," said her father. Inside, Clare felt herself grow cold and taut.

"You don't understand anything," she said in a hard voice. Saying this didn't give her any relief or satisfaction. Still, although later she might wish she hadn't said it, she didn't wish it now. She lifted her chin.

"And I already have shopping plans. Teo's taking me," she said. And as she said it, she remembered that it was only what she'd been hoping, not what she and Teo had been planning. They hadn't discussed Christmas shopping at all. Oh, no, she thought. But Teo didn't look mad or even taken off guard. He didn't say anything. For what seemed like a long time, no one said anything.

"Clare." Cornelia almost whispered it, and Clare saw that her face was troubled and was asking Clare for something. Clare thawed, just a little. Clare knew she hadn't hurt her father, because nothing she said to him could ever hurt him. He'd been embarrassed probably, to have Teo hear how she'd spoken to him, but his feelings hadn't been hurt. Clare knew that, but Cornelia didn't, and Clare didn't want Cornelia to be upset.

"Teo's taking me because I have to get a present for you, Dad." Clare spoke to her father, but looked at Cornelia. Cornelia nodded almost imperceptibly at Clare, and the two lines between her eyes grew less pronounced.

"Oh, I see," said her father. "OK, then, Clare." His expression and tone were carefully kind, carefully patient, as if to say, "I am an adult talking to a poor damaged child."

"And that works out nicely because . . . Martin, do I have to remind you about the butternut squash incident?" Cornelia took Clare's father's hand as she spoke. The lines between her eyes had smoothed out completely, but Clare saw how Cornelia's words drew her father gently into a circle of two. Whatever the butternut squash incident had been, it had belonged to the two of them. The words and the way she held his hand were meant to comfort. Maybe that was Cornelia being in love, Clare thought.

Clare's father laughed. "If you have to you have to, but I wish you wouldn't."

"So you know that if I'm left alone to buy groceries for Christmas dinner, I'll get enough to feed twenty-five adults. We'd have to rent a truck, and how easy would that be on Christmas Eve? I need you with me."

"Twenty-five ravenous linebacker adults, you mean," Clare's father said with a laugh. "You're right. You do need me." He lifted Cornelia's hand to his mouth and kissed it, seeming happier than he had all evening. Cornelia looked relieved.

The thought just appeared in Clare's mind: If Cornelia married Clare's father, then Clare would have her. They would belong to each other in official ways. Visits to her father would mean visits to Cornelia. She remembered how, in the later books, Anne Shirley would play matchmaker and everyone would end up happy. Maybe Linny was wrong about her father and Cornelia. Maybe with some help from Clare, they would end up married to each other. Why not try? She pictured a scene in which she and Cornelia ate breakfast at her father's dining room table in gleaming pajamas, laughing and drinking hot chocolate out of identical white mugs while her father sat behind his *Wall Street Journal* a small distance away, on the very edge of the scene.

As Clare held this thought in her mind, Clare's father took another dessert from the platter, cut it in half, placed one half on Cornelia's plate and popped the other into his mouth. Cornelia lifted the dessert, a tiny, precious cake filled with *ube* paste, and asked, "Now, Clare, Teo, what makes this one purple?"

The scene of the three of them together lost its bright colors and blurred. Cornelia was so nice. She deserved better than Clare's father. Clare sighed and allowed the scene to vanish altogether.

15

Cornelia

They went to the light show after all, Teo and Clare did. They'd shopped for a while and talked for a while—Clare especially had talked—and over slices of pizza, Clare had suddenly said, "Do you know about the brass eagle? The big brass eagle between the shoe department and the jewelry department?" And Teo thought about this and then, in his uncanny Teo way, asked, "At Lord & Taylor?" Even though I'm pretty sure he'd never been there, since Teo doesn't live in Philadelphia; is a less-than-exuberant shopper; and claims to be allergic to large department stores—literally, not metaphorically, allergic. I've heard him say this more than once or, rather, mumble it apologetically, usually while declining an invitation to enter just such a department store. The standard mumble includes incoherent references to ventilation and cleaning fluid, which oddly enough people seem willing to accept, possibly on the grounds that he is a physician or maybe just because they are disarmed by his general disarmingness. Although, I have to say that Teo doesn't exploit his ability to disarm nearly as often as most people would.

Anyway, despite his well-guarded ignorance regarding department stores, Teo asked, "At Lord & Taylor?" And Clare said, "Yes. Just to the side of the eagle, that's the best place to sit. If you're closer, it hurts your neck, and if you're farther back, you get stepped on by people shopping for hats and scarves." So they went. They sat on the marble floor, just to the right of the brass eagle to watch a light show that's been going on, in some form or another, since something like 1955. You'd think kids these days, with their easy access to Pixar animation, Imax, and video games that break clean through their computer screens and scramble around their rooms, would fail to be transfixed by organ music and nutcrackers and sugarplum fairies in lights raising one leg, then the other in their stiff little dance. You'd think so, but you'd be wrong. They're transfixed.

"Was she transfixed?" I asked Teo.

We were sitting on what would be Teo's bed for the second night in a row but what was at that moment still my couch. Clare was asleep in my room.

And he said, "Yeah, that's the perfect word for what she was."

That struck me as such unequivocally good news, and hearing it caused me to feel relief and hope, which in turn caused me to ramble excitedly and at some length about the wonderful resilience of children, until I noticed that Teo's expression bespoke not relief and hope, but worry and puzzlement.

"What?" I said.

"I hadn't thought about it that way," he said.

"What way did you think about it?" I asked, nervously.

"Do you know that Clare's been to that light show every year since she was born? When she asked to go today, I just thought, she's eleven, it's Christmas Eve, her mother is God knows where, and she wants to go to the show they've seen together every year since she was born. I almost said no," Teo said, with the air of someone who wishes he'd said no.

"You couldn't say no," I told him consolingly.

"I couldn't. That's the only reason I didn't. But when we were sitting there, with about a million happy families, waiting for the thing to start, all I could think was, 'Where did you get the idea that you had to be so brave? And what is it going to cost you?' "

"Oh," I said, and for a while this was all I could think of to say. Then I added, "I bet you're right. I bet it was too much." And as it turned out, he was right. Of course, he was. But before I get to how it turned out, and what happened as a result of how it turned out, I want to stop and fill you in on what was happening to me about the same time Clare was cross-legged on a marble floor awaiting a light show that might further break her heart.

And it's funny because I feel guilty about stopping and filling you in on what, not so long before, would have been a shining moment in my life, possibly *the* shining moment, possibly the diamond-bright point around which everything else would turn. There was a time when I would have sung full-throated from the rooftops what Martin said to me in the park on Christmas Eve.

But it seems somehow wrong that while the story of Clare's heart-break was unfolding itself in my presence, the story of my romance with Martin didn't come to a respectful halt. It didn't wait discreetly in a corner until a more appropriate time. Instead, in its uncertain, un-settling way, it continued to unfold as well.

Do you know that Auden poem about suffering? The one where he talks about how at the precise moment Icarus was splashing into his ocean death, the ploughman went on ploughing his field, undis-turbed? Well, about suffering, and most other things as well, Auden was never wrong. I think you see where I'm going with this. While Clare suffered, Martin and I continued ploughing, although in a rather subdued manner and certainly not in the metaphorical sense à la Shakespeare, Sophocles, etcetera, which would have been abominable of us.

Here's what happened. We were walking through the square on our way to buy, among other items, a turkey of reasonable size when, quite suddenly, Martin pulled me down next to him on a park bench and let his gaze travel searchingly over my face. I may have men-tioned that his eyes were astoundingly beautiful, a fact of which, at that moment on that bench, I was not unaware. In fact, I was acutely, achingly aware of it. And Martin had a certain way of looking at me that made me feel exactly as though he were touching me, even when he wasn't.

He looked. Then he said, "It's the wrong time to tell you this," and I knew what he was going to say, and I felt pulled in so many different directions that I couldn't go in any of them and was frozen. I should say I knew the general gist of what he was going to say because, as usual, Martin's language was pure Martin.

"Every day, I live with wonder. I walk around with it and lie down with it and wake up with it every morning, no matter where I am. I've never known anyone like you because there isn't anyone like you. And because there isn't anyone like you, I've never wanted anyone the way I want you."

The words weren't silky; they cost him effort and had weight. They didn't sound rehearsed, if that's what you're thinking.

"Cornelia, I love you. It's the wrong time to tell you, but I'm telling you. I love you. And all of what's going on with Clare, as hard as it is and will be, I think it could turn out to be a good thing for us because if we're going to share our lives, you need to understand what my life is—all of it. And I want us to share our lives, Cornelia."

Alarm. At this, I felt alarm. "Martin," I began.

But he stopped me by giving me a wry smile and saying, "No, I'm not proposing. Even *my* timing isn't as bad as that. And I don't want you to say anything right now. In fact, I strictly forbid it. I wanted to tell you that I love you, that's all."

He kissed me, then, and I said, "Am I at least allowed to say thank you?"

"No," he said, smiling.

"Thank you," I said, smiling back.

You might think you know what I should have felt and wanted, where Martin was concerned. No doubt it is crystal clear to you. But what you have to understand is that all of those clichés and dead metaphors people use to describe confusion were suddenly alive and kicking: My life was a roller coaster; everything was happening too fast; I didn't have time to catch my breath; my head was spinning; information overload; cannot compute cannot compute cannot compute.

No, Martin was not exactly the man I'd hoped he would be. Yes, he was chilly to his daughter, even in her time of great need. Yes, this chilliness disturbed me. And yes—I hadn't forgotten this—my doubts regarding his rightness for me had begun rearing their unfortunate heads before Clare ever appeared in our lives. In my life, I mean, as she had been in his since her birth—although obviously not in the way one would expect and wish.

But while that sounds simple enough, when you think about it, it wasn't simple at all. For one thing, all of the above reasons for at the very least keeping Martin at a distance and at the very most breaking it off with him on the spot did not erase everything else that was true about Martin and about me and Martin together. If they should have erased all that, they did not. When it was just the two of us, in so many ways, Martin lifted and lit me up; he made me quicker, smarter, funnier; he was gentle when I needed gentleness; we loved the same things in the same ways, at least mostly, and that is nothing to sneeze at.

For another thing, he wasn't a list of attributes, but a flesh-and-blood man, as physically present a presence as anyone I'd met in my life. When he told me he loved me, he said it in his particular voice with catches in his particular throat, and the bones and muscles of his face moved in familiar ways and also in ways I'd never seen. Can you understand what I'm saying? I'm not just talking again about the power of physical beauty. Less-than-fantastic sex notwithstanding, we were intimates; I'd breathed his breath; my skin knew his skin; my nerve endings had sparked under his touch. That kind of knowledge was deep and had never been something I could walk away from with ease. And he had taste and humor and effortless elegance. He was downright debonair, and how many men could you say that about? And, OK, he was. He was so beautiful.

A reminder: Strangers stopped him on the street to tell him he looked like Cary Grant.

And he was in love with me. Come on.

I was in turmoil. I didn't know what to do, so what I did as soon as I got the chance was behave like a horse's ass to the person who least deserved it.

After he'd told me about the light show, after a long silence during which Teo and I sat together, sharing mute, mutual distress at Clare's distress, Teo turned to me and asked, "Cornelia, are you sure about Martin?" It wasn't a question I was ready to answer or even to hear with the smallest amount of grace. I was overwhelmed and over-wrought, dry brush ready for a spark. I knew the question was real, but I pretended to think it was rhetorical, and doing that is mean—mean and unfair, not to mention cowardly. "Chickenshit" is what Linny would say. When faced with direct questions about Martin, I was plain chickenshit.

I'm not proud of my behavior. The spark caught. I blazed.

I blazed, but my voice was pure ice: "So you're here two days and you're an expert on Martin?"

What would most people have done in response to this response? Gotten mad, probably, which would have been entirely called-for, or backpedaled, tap danced, apologized, made a self-effacing joke, but Teo knows his way around a silence. He can keep quiet in an eloquent, watching, unfidgety way, and he knows an unanswerable question when he hears one. I've always admired these traits in Teo, but I wasn't in an admiring mood. I set about filling up his steady, green-eyed quiet with my venom.

"You've decided he's a bad father and a bad man. You've decided he's emotionally stingy and detached and God knows what else."

Silence.

"But what exactly do you know about having a kid, Teo? It's pretty easy to arrive in a child's life at a vulnerable moment and be a hero. But thinking you're now an expert on Clare and Martin, thinking it's your place to pass judgment, well that's going a bit far, don't you think?" When I finished, I was winded.

"I don't know Martin," said Teo. "I was wondering how well you knew him." Teo was angry; I recognized the tightness around his eyes and the red stain spreading down the centers of his cheeks. But angry or not, when discussing important matters, Teo tends not to stoop to sarcasm, and he wasn't being sarcastic now. It didn't matter. I was wildfire, out of control and, apparently, there was nothing to which I would not stoop.

"Ah, so you're not judging Martin's relationship with Clare, but with me. Is that right? Do I have that straight now?" It gets worse. "That's great. That's just fine. And what about you? You're so happily married that your wife leaves you alone during the holidays. Just how well do you know Ollie, Teo?"

This would have been unkind under any circumstances, but it wouldn't have been so wretchedly awful, so lowdown, had I not harbored serious doubts about Teo's marriage. In my defense, as little as I deserved defending, my suspicions regarding this were only suspicions. It's possible that Teo and Ollie had been spending the last two years in the most blissful marital bliss imaginable, in which case my poisoned arrow of a question would have bounced off the armor of his happiness without leaving a dent. My mother certainly thought they were happy. But I had my doubts.

And, unlike most of my doubts, these didn't arise out of my own natural and well-developed cynicism, because while I can be a cynic about some things, you may also have noticed that I can be a bit of a romantic about others. I believe in true love. On the list of things I believe in, true love is tops.

And as far as I can tell, Ollie believes in true love too, because not two months prior to her marriage to Teo, she introduced me to her "soul mate" (her phrase, not, God forbid, mine). He was her fellow fellow and fellow fast-rising star at the laboratory and was gloriously good-looking, which is probably why Ollie wanted me to meet him. Six and a half feet tall, Jamaican-born, Oxford-educated, a serious cyclist who probably did not win the Tour de France only because his broad shoulders, otherworldly cheekbones, and massive IQ weighed him down.

Even more breathtaking than his physical and mental attributes was the way my cool-as-a-cucumber sister became a lovesick, spellbound, eyelash-batting girl in his presence. When he entered a room, Ollie was just a hairsbreadth away from turning into one of those Beatles-Come-to-America girls, the ones who weep openly, clutch their cheeks with both hands, and scream. In the hour and a half I spent with them, she even deferred to his intellect on matters of science, twice.

Anyway, at some point, they'd applied jointly for a hefty grant to go work on some project in the Galapagos Islands, and what killed their relationship is that the grant was given to Edmund (that was his name, Edmund Battle) only, and he accepted it sanguinely without insisting that Ollie come too, her not inconsiderable charms losing out to the siren calls of turtles and finches and career opportunity. Edmund up and left, and next thing I knew: Ollie and Teo, till death do them part. Draw your own conclusions.

Zap. The poisoned arrow struck. And even though my behavior was indefensible, I want to jump to my own defense once again by saying that even before it struck, before I saw Teo's slight but undeniable recoil and grimace of pain, I wished I could have taken the words back. Teo got up, went into the kitchen, and just kind of stood there, leaning on the countertop with one hand and looking at the floor. I watched him stand like that, the man who had walked through the door of Café Dora into a tangled, tangled mess, and who hadn't walked right out again, as anyone else would have, but had set about untangling what he could as though it were the most natural thing in the world to do. The man who'd just devoted Christmas Eve and all his energies to making his sister-in-law's boyfriend's lonely, heartsick daughter less lonely and less heartsick. My oldest friend, a man of uncommon kindness.

I made my way over to him, wading through the swamp of shame I'd created and into the murky depths of which I deserved to be sucked down and forever lost, and I took his hand and begged for forgiveness as I'd never begged before.

And Teo forgave me.

He smiled at me, even though his eyes still had the bruised look, the look I'd put there, and he said, "This is a hard time for you. I wish it didn't have to be so hard. I like it when you're happy." Then his smile got bigger. "You're nicer."

"You're right," I said, and we ended the night laughing.

Teo was right about Clare, too. Her bravery wasn't without its price. At four a.m., I awoke to the sound of sobbing.

I sat up and rubbed her back with the circular motion I've always found soothing. After a while, she put her head in my lap and said, "I want my mommy."

I thought about those words, how they contained so much more than they seemed to contain, more than any four words could hold. They meant what they meant and were also a universal cry, maybe *the* universal, plaintive, openhearted cry for comfort. Soldiers in the heat of battle; death-row prisoners; explorers stranded in deserts, jungles, on mountaintops; anyone sick or lost or just tired and bewildered: we all wanted our mothers. I thought about my own mother—straight-backed, eternally smiling, never without tissues, Band-Aids, lipstick, aspirin, optimism, and reassurance. Mothers—why didn't they all collapse under such weight? I shivered.

Clare wanted her mother to be here and, also, she wanted her mother to comfort her for the loss of her mother. Temporary. Temporary loss. Please, God.

"I know you do," I told her.

"She might come home for Christmas," Clare said. "She wouldn't want to be away from me on Christmas."

No, she wouldn't want to be. I felt sure of that. I looked down at Clare's profile in my lap; in the dark, I could just make out the curve of her jaw and the sweep of her eyebrow over her wide eye. Viviana's child, I thought. Viviana must love this face so much.

"Do you want to go home?" I asked.

Clare nodded. Under the quilt, her whole body was shaking.

"Then, we'll go," I said.

Which is how I ended up in the Twilight Zone—i.e., cooking Christmas dinner in my possibly-soon-to-be-ex-possibly-not-boyfriend's missing ex-wife's Main Line restaurant-caliber kitchen with my brother-in-law—God bless him—while my boyfriend (my would-be fiancé, actually, although I was quite sure he would not be) and his all-but-estranged and until recently, to my knowledge, nonexistent daughter redecorated my Christmas tree in the right-out-of-*The Philadelphia Story* missing ex-wife's Main Line living room. And if you had trouble following what I just told you, imagine what it was like to live it.

Not that morning, exactly, but as soon as the sky outside my bedroom window showed hints of becoming at some point in the not-so-distant future something other than pitch black, I woke up Teo, who pushed his overgrown hair out of his eyes, blinked maybe twice, and then started taking ornaments off my Christmas tree. "She'll want it, don't you think?" he asked.

Clare was already dressed and packing her things in the bedroom. She had blossomed into the very incarnation of Christmas spirit— bright eyes and flushed cheeks and humming "Joy to the World"—at the prospect of our going, a transformation that would have both moved and worried me more had I had time to process it. But I was loading—feverishly—turkey and pies (it had seemed like a good year to cheat and buy them) and a pan of cornbread (for stuffing) and fresh herbs and potatoes and wine and whipping cream and butter and so forth and, in my haste, plenty of unnecessary items as well, like two jars of Nutella and a box of Cheerios, into shopping bags and cardboard boxes I'd pilfered from the basement of my building.

About halfway through, I remembered to call Martin, who, after a long pause, responded to my somewhat deliriously cheerful announcement "There's been a change of plans!" and consequent description of the changed plans with a brittle "I have to say, Cornelia, that that is a ridiculous idea." Upon hearing this, I stopped in midpack, put down the bag of green beans I was holding, and took the phone out in the hallway so that Martin's daughter wouldn't have to overhear me remind her father of the universal rule regarding heartbroken children: If it is within the realm of human possibility to honor their requests, you do it.

I knew Clare might end up getting hurt—more hurt. I knew her mother was almost definitely not going to arrive at the moment when the carving knife was poised in the air, candlelight glinting off it, "We Wish You a Merry Christmas" tinkling on the stereo, as Clare may have been picturing; but I also knew that Clare wanted to be home. I knew it felt wrong to her not to be at home for Christmas. And I also knew that even Clare, child though she was, really didn't believe her mother would come. She only hoped, and her hope was slender—a wisp of hope, a ghost. I knew this because I'm wise, but also because, just before I went in to wake up Teo, Clare had put her hand in mine and said, "Don't worry. I know she probably won't come."

I was all set to tell Martin this, to allay his fears regarding Clare, when Martin said, "When I went to pick up Clare the other day, it was the first time I'd stepped foot in that house in seven years. Spending Christmas there would just be too awkward," and then he softened. "You understand, don't you, Cornelia?" And I did, I understood all too well. I understood that Martin's fears regarding Clare didn't need allaying by me or anyone else because he wasn't thinking of Clare at all.

I took this grim fact and filed it grimly away under "Reasons Not to Be with Martin," a file that was growing fatter by the day and that I vowed to peruse from start to finish later, in a future when I had time for hard truths and contemplation, sometime after I'd stuffed Teo's car full of Christmas dinner and strapped a Christmas tree to its roof.

"Martin, we're going. You can go with us," I said, keeping my voice steady, "or not."

"I see," said Martin, and he didn't sound angry, as I'd expected. That was the thing about Martin, he was gracious and civilized when most people would fail to be. Whenever you were tempted to believe him a bad man, he would remind you that he wasn't one. "I'm sorry. I didn't know it was so important. Give me fifteen minutes."

Despite all the strikes against it, that Christmas Day went better than you'd imagine for longer than you'd imagine.

The house was immaculate, thanks to Max, and showed remarkably few signs of having been inhabited, for several months, by a woman whirling downward into her own strange world and a desperate child doing everything she could to hold on to the ordinary one. There were a few giveaways—painful ones. At one point, Teo led me wordlessly to the pantry to show me the carefully arranged rows of canned peas and carrots and chicken soup and the three shelves loaded with boxes of Parmalat milk. I found the receipt later pinned to the bulletin board in the kitchen; Clare had had the groceries delivered and charged them by credit card. The pantry hurt. Worse than the bomb-shelter resemblance was the sheer quantity. I covered my mouth with my hand and my eyes filled with tears as I imagined my sweet girl (I thought of her that way already; I couldn't help it) anticipating months, maybe endless months, of isolation and secrets.

And when I helped Clare carry her suitcases to her room, I didn't mean to snoop, but after she left, I lingered and saw another bulletin board and, pinned to it, another artifact of a lonely and frightened life.

A list. It was called "CLARE'S DON'T-FORGET LIST" (with "don't" underlined three times) and said:

1. Eat a big breakfast; can't seem hungry; can't lose weight.
2. Take shower every morning; hair washed, brushed, neat.
3. Clothes: Shirts tucked in, sweaters on cold days. Check for holes in clothes, even socks. Raincoat and umbrella for rain. Snow boots for snow. Always hat and gloves when cold. Scarf when temperature is in thirties.
4. Watch weather report every evening; check again in morning if time.
5. Forge: permission slip for Nutcracker trip, note for M missing parent-teacher conference.
6. M missing Christmas pageant because???

The list went on and included trash pick-up days, bill-paying information, reminders to call and cancel with Max who apparently cleaned the house every other week, a list of foods (chicken soup was one) and vitamins to prevent colds and thus prevent a trip to the doctor, which I imagine would've been nearly impossible to pull off without a parent. In the margin, Clare had written in block letters: FORGOT TO SEND CHRISTMAS CARDS! NEW YEAR'S INSTEAD? LIST ON COMPUTER?

Clare was a marvel, resourceful and imaginative and brave, the kind of girl you usually only found in books organizing orphan uprisings or saving the world from the forces of evil. Thinking this made me feel hopeful; girls like that always won in the end, always. But I ached for her aloneness and wondered at her deep, deep need to keep her secret. It struck me that perhaps keeping the secret was vital not only because she was afraid of what the world might do to a mother like hers, but also because it was a project, a big detailed, consuming project. A way to be in control of something.

But even Clare couldn't have kept it up for long; the list told me that, too. Even right that minute, there might have been someone out there saying, "You know, dear, Viviana didn't send a card this year and, come to think of it, we haven't heard from her in a couple of months, and remember how she was acting a bit odd last time we saw her . . ." Even if Viviana hadn't disappeared, someone would have come to Clare's rescue, as unwilling as she was to be rescued. Those rows of Parmalat and canned food—the thought that most of that would've ended up untouched on the shelves no matter what was a comfort.

As I stood looking at the list, Martin came into the room. That is, he didn't exactly come into it, but stood in the doorway and studiously avoided resting his gaze on everything in the room except for me. That was how he would seem the entire time he'd spend in the house, balanced on the threshold, tentative, never wholly arrived. When I pointed to the list, he read it quickly, then said, "I wish I'd known what was happening. I wish she'd told me," so ruefully that I wanted to touch him and did. I ran a finger from his ear to his chin. I'd always found that jawline remarkable and precise; now, I noticed how remarkably and precisely it resembled Clare's. He took my finger and pressed it to his lips.

As I said, the day went surprisingly well. We were all trying hard, Teo and I—and Martin, too, I suppose—were trying hard for Clare's sake, and she was trying hard because she saw how much we wanted her to be happy; she was that kind of child. Also, maybe the day went well because Christmas is Christmas. I'm not a sentimentalist—OK, I am a sentimentalist about some things, but not about Christmas—but when a holiday has been sold as merry year after year after year, it gains a kind of momentum. The idea of merry carries you along for a good distance. It carried the four of us nearly all the way through dinner—a dinner that turned out to be, if not the most exquisite Christmas dinner ever cooked, not at all bad. At any rate, the turkey was not dry, not even the breast meat, which is not so easy to achieve under any circumstances, and is further testament to how hard we were all trying.

But it couldn't last. Clare had been thinking of her mother all day—of course she had—and she'd pulled me aside at one point to show me a picture of the two of them together. In nearly every room of the house, there were framed photographs of Clare, who had been a lovely baby and who, apart from a brief snaggle-toothed, messy-haired interlude, had lived eleven years of continuous prettiness. There were no photographs of Martin and, until Clare showed me the one in the library, I'd seen none of Viviana, which, after seeing the photo of her, I took as a sign of enormous modesty and restraint on Viviana's part because, if I looked like that, it would take *Herculean* modesty and restraint not to plaster every wall with my own image. I'd pictured Grace Kelly, and I was off, but not by that much. In fact, Viviana bore a striking resemblance to a not-so-well-known film-noir actress named Lizabeth Scott, who is sometimes referred to as a poor man's Lauren Bacall, but who was a beauty in her own right and who steals scenes from the likes of Barbara Stanwyck in *The Strange Love of Martha Ivers*. Besides, how poor is such a poor man, anyway? After all, it's Lauren Bacall we're talking about. At the worst, he's a guy with just one vacation home and a smallish yacht. Save your sympathy.

In the picture, Clare is about eight years old, her hands are lifted to chin-level and open in a way that meant they'd just been cupped, and she's staring upward as though amazed, and her mother is next to her, looking not upward, but at Clare's face and, as striking as Viviana is, her expression is the really beautiful thing in the picture. It's that loving. I wanted to cry, thinking how that woman would never have meant to become someone who would frighten her child and abandon her.

"It was a butterfly. But it flew away at the last minute," explained Clare, and as she stared at the photograph, smiling a little secret smile at the memory, she didn't look like a conquering heroine in a novel, but like a very, very little girl—much younger than eleven. I wanted to hug her, but I held back. I know when a moment doesn't belong to me.

So, even though Clare spent the day being as solid and cheerful as I'd ever seen her, I knew being back in her house meant her mother felt to her both more present and more absent. Even I half expected Viviana to walk through the door, so what must Clare have been feeling?

It didn't happen just as the carving knife was poised to cut. Our bird was already sliced, distributed, and being tucked away by all four of us. And the music on the stereo wasn't "We Wish You a Merry Christmas" but the Vienna Boys' Choir sending "Silent Night" in German lofting into the air on their luminous voices. But the moment felt absolutely like a moment, and not just in retrospect, I don't think. Clare had just discovered that I'd adored L. M. Montgomery's *Anne* series as a child, and she may as well have discovered a diamond mine, her face was so radiant. I felt like I'd accomplished something pretty fabulous, even though all I did was read some books twenty years ago. Clare actually clapped her hands and was staring at me raptly when into this lull in conversation came a knock at the door.

Everyone froze, turned to look at the door, then turned back to look at one another, electrified. If we were animals, our fur would've been standing on end. It occurred to no one that Viviana would've been unlikely to knock at her own front door, least of all to Clare, who was sitting bolt upright with her arms crossed—clutching each other—across her chest and was breathing so hard I could hear it over the music.

Then, she flew to the door, threw it open, and took several steps back. A man in his late twenties or so, with longish hair, Ben Franklin glasses, and a ski jacket, stood there, looking very surprised. At the same time Martin stood and said, "Lloyd!" Clare made a terrible choking sound, and both Teo and I were up and out of our seats. He got to her first and put an arm around her hunched shoulders, but she wrenched free and tore out of the room. We heard her run up the stairs and looked at each other.

"Let her be alone?" asked Teo, and I nodded. For a little while, we'd let her be alone. It was hard to know what to do because, here in this house, we were interlopers, the wrong people, no matter how much she liked us.

Martin said, "Come in, Lloyd," in a tired voice, and Lloyd stepped inside and shut the door, but made no move to take off his coat, and no one asked him to, not even Martin, for whom impeccable manners are a kind of reflex.

"Sorry to show up like this, folks. Christmas and all. Drive by the house now and then, just to check. Saw the lights on." Lloyd didn't look like any hard-boiled detective I'd ever seen, but he talked like one, sort of. Choppy phrasing. Absence of the personal pronoun.

"Of course," said Martin. "Lloyd, this is Cornelia Brown and Teo Sandoval. My daughter, Clare, opened the door for you. She's been bearing up remarkably well, but it's a difficult time."

"Nothing new to report. No mail delivery. She must've had it stopped. Saw a couple of people come to the door here." Lloyd took a spiral notebook from somewhere and flipped it open. "Lady with a kid about Clare's age. Drove a Ford Expedition. Black. Pennsylvania plates. Tall lady in a white Mercedes. Left a plate of cookies and a card. 'Merry Christmas. I'm spending New Year's in Barbados with Zach. Remember him? Cable guy? Tom Cruise look-alike? Seth's minding the store. I'll call when I get back. Love, Sissy.' " Most people could not maintain an utterly expressionless monotone while speaking the phrase "Tom Cruise look-alike," but Lloyd was not most people.

"Sugar or chocolate chip?" I asked, because I'd been standing there mutely and feeling a bit idiotic about it. Unsurprisingly, the question left me feeling as idiotic as ever, but it did jolt Lloyd into using a fully formed sentence.

"They were sugar cookies shaped like Christmas trees and stars. Decorated with icing," he said and blushed. "I . . . well, I thought . . .

if they sat here, they might attract, you know, bugs and animals and such."

While I nodded, inwardly speculating as to what "and such" might refer (street urchins, carnivorous plants?), Martin patted Lloyd on the shoulder with a reassuring chuckle. "Absolutely right, Lloyd, I appreciate that. Well, you'll keep me posted, I expect."

Lloyd flipped his notebook shut and nodded, tucking in his lips and jutting out his lower jaw slightly in that, you-bet, TV-sheriff kind of way. Then he left, and Martin, Teo, and I just stood there, uncertain of what to do next.

"Is everyone finished eating?" Teo finally said and, because it would have been ridiculous to go back to the table and start eating as though nothing had happened, and also because we'd probably all lost our appetites, we said yes.

Teo went into the kitchen, and I began to pick up plates from the table when Martin said, "Can we talk a minute?"

"Sure," I said, feeling unaccountably nervous, and then called out, "Teo, I'll help in a sec, OK?"

Martin led me by the hand into the library—a warm, oak-paneled room—and we sat down on the leather sofa. Then he took two plane tickets out of the breast pocket of his jacket and handed them to me. They were to London.

"These were meant to be my Christmas gift to you, Cornelia, the trip you turned down the day I met you." He smiled at me. "I have some business there and in Paris, but I'll finish every day by late afternoon. I thought we'd take a couple of days in each city."

I sat looking at the tickets, letting myself imagine, for a few seconds, what the trip would've been like. Glorious, I allowed myself to think. I would've brought along my doubts about Martin's ability to connect (and please take that word "connect" as it was intended— strictly in the spirit of E. M. Forster, whom I revere, rather than as a reflection of our self-help, men-are-from-Mars, etcetera, culture), but surely he'd have put them to rest in Paris, the city where lovers are practically required by law to bare their souls, right? But even as I thought it, the thought turned wan and listless and drifted away like smoke. It seemed forever ago, the ante-Clare era and, as romantic as that era was, I couldn't wish it back without wishing Clare away, which just wasn't possible. I sighed and looked up at Martin.

"You could still go with me. A colleague of mine has a college-aged daughter who would stay with Clare; she's very reliable"—he must have seen the expression on my face—"but I'm sure it's a bad time to leave Clare with someone she doesn't know."

"It's impossible," I said simply, and then I had a thought. "Did you say I could still go *with* you?"

Martin nodded, staring right into my eyes instead of dropping his gaze with shame, which he surely should've done.

"You're not still going?" I asked, and even then he just held steady.

"I tried to get out of it, but there's just no one else they can send. I leave the day after tomorrow," he said. Then he began, "I hate it that I have to ask this," and he left it there, not asking.

There was nothing else to do. I said, "I can take a few days off. I'll stay with Clare. Here or at my apartment, whichever she wants. Although if we stay here, we'll have to come up with an excuse as to why I'm with her instead of Viviana. But, Martin . . ."

His composure broke then, didn't break dramatically, but cracked perceptibly, "Cornelia, she doesn't want me. Anyone could tell that." He rubbed his forehead with his hand.

"Don't you think I know that the time for me to be there for Clare passed by long ago? I missed it. I had a hundred chances, and I missed them all. Now, I'm is no help to her. If anything, I make things worse." I'd never seen Martin so unhappy. There was nothing I could say to make him feel better. Every last thing he'd just said was true.

"I'll stay with her. You know I'll stay," I put my arms around him, tightly, and we sat like that for a long time. I wasn't in love with him, and I believed it was good for him to be feeling this particular hurt.

But to understand that you've blown it, that you can never fix it is one of the worst feelings ever. I wouldn't leave him alone with that.

When we went into the kitchen, Teo had put all the food away and was washing the china by hand. I scooted him out of the way with one hip and took over. Martin picked up a towel and began to dry.

"I checked on Clare. She was asleep on what I'm guessing is her mother's bed. I took off her shoes and covered her with a quilt. She didn't flutter an eyelash." Teo leaned against the silvery expanse of refrigerator door and ran his hand through his hair.

As I've mentioned, I'm not among those whose worlds are rocked by the sight of Mateo Sandoval. However, I will say that the hair through which he ran his hand is a kind of gold-inflected brown, which is somewhat unexpected, given the fact that the hand itself, along with the rest of his skin is a slightly lighter, not ungolden-y caramel color, and these factors combined with the clear green eyes (a steadfast rather than a changeable green), fine health, and a tendency to flush give Teo a kind of overall vividness that one doesn't encounter every day. I only bring this up to say that anyone who spends any kind of time with Teo quickly recognizes that this—let's call it radiance for lack of a better word—increases and diminishes with Teo's moods. The radiance serves as a kind of barometer for Teo's emotional state and is an especially useful tool because, unlike some people I know and am, Teo doesn't spend a great deal of time describing his emotional states, especially when the states aren't so happy.

As Teo leaned against the refrigerator door, he was almost not glowing at all. I wondered if maybe he was worried about more than just Clare. Maybe he was missing his wife. Maybe he'd been working too hard. I promised myself I'd ask him about it as soon as we were alone. But because the next time we were alone, I was caught in maelstrom of personal turmoil, I'm sorry to say this was a promise I didn't keep.

"I hope she sleeps for a long time," said Martin. "She needs it."

"She does. It wasn't just what happened, Lloyd showing up. She's been storing up exhaustion for weeks and weeks," I said and told Teo about the list in her room.

"Jesus," Teo said, and his voice was so concerned it was on the edge of being angry. "How the hell did she manage all that? You know, she told me about that list, or some version of it. She sat in a diner the day after her eleventh birthday, which both she and her mother completely forgot, and wrote down a plan for every day."

Martin put down the plate he'd been drying. "I wish she hadn't felt like she had to keep her mother's illness a secret. She could have told someone. It would've made life so much easier for her. She could've told me."

That's when it happened, when the whole house of cards I'd been keeping upright through sheer force of will, along with generous doses of avoidance and denial, came tumbling down with a *whoosh*. And there was no moment of portent, as there had been before Lloyd showed up, no lull before the storm, nothing to herald the coming of what was undeniably as bitter an end as anything ever came to.

After Martin spoke, Teo said two words: "She did."

I turned around, a wet plate still in my hand. Teo wasn't leaning against the refrigerator anymore. He was standing up straight, not in a challenging way. He had his hands in the pockets of his jeans, and he had a strange look on his face, as though his own words had taken him off guard.

Martin just stared at Teo, but I saw his face turning red, which was new. When he spoke, he stammered, which was new as well.

"Cornelia, I—I—uh . . ." he said, and then stopped.

"Teo," I said slowly, "what do you mean? Tell me what you mean."

When Teo spoke, it was to Martin, not to me, which, when I thought about it later, I understood was a gesture of respect to Martin. He wouldn't talk about Martin in the third person while they stood in the same room. "Clare called you. Weeks ago, maybe longer than that. She told you about her mother's erratic behavior, the buying sprees, the strange hours she'd started keeping. Clare told you how her mother took her out of school and said things to her that scared her. She told you she thought her mother was sick."

Martin turned to me. "What she told me, it didn't sound bad, it didn't sound like what it was."

My hands were shaking, and I thought, oh, God, I'm going to drop this plate, so I turned and dropped it into the sink. It hit the bottom of the marble sink and cracked in two. I could see the pieces through the soapy water.

Without looking away from the broken plate, I said, "Martin, did she tell you she was scared?"

"Yes. Sure, she said that, but I didn't understand how difficult things were. Not even close. She told me all these little details—towels, wine, cookbooks. Maybe I added them up wrong, but I really didn't believe there was anything terrible going on."

That's when every warm feeling I had for Martin, every happy memory and good thought, rose up out of my body and left me—whisked themselves away like ghosts. As crazy as it sounds, I felt them leave. They wouldn't stay gone, not all of them, but as I stood there at the sink, I felt the space where they used to be: a cold place in the center of my chest. I shuddered.

"Cornelia, please," Martin said.

"You knew she was scared," I said. "That's all you needed to know. Who cares if it didn't make sense to you? She was asking you for help. That alone should've told you she was desperate. It *did* tell you. She came to you for help and you turned her down."

I started crying then. "No wonder," I said. "No wonder she didn't tell anyone else. She probably thought no one would listen."

Martin came to me and took me gently by the arms. Over his shoulder, I watched Teo turn and leave us.

"Cornelia, you know me." Martin had tears in his eyes, but they didn't change anything. "You know who I am. I made a mistake. It was a terrible mistake. But don't let the mistake get the last word. Do you see what I mean?"

I did.

"I love you. Let that matter too. Don't leave me now. I can't lose you now. Do you understand that?"

I did. I understood, and I was already gone.

16

Clare

In the middle of a dream in which she was walking through fog, Clare heard a door slam, and the sound was like a tug, like a shiny hook taking her by the belt loop and lifting her sharply out of the fog, out of sleep altogether. No, was her first thought. Not again. For a few groggy seconds, it was nighttime, and she was back in her house, alone with her mother's roaming in the frangible, untrustworthy quiet night-time always brought.

She sat up in bed. Her mother's bed. She saw that she was fully dressed, and the present came back to her in a rush. It *was* nighttime; she *was* in her house; but her mother was gone. Clare was flooded first with relief and then with guilt at the relief. "I don't mean I don't want her here," she whispered to whatever or whomever might be in the business of listening to and granting desires. She couldn't risk any misunderstandings.

When she'd opened her front door to the man in the tiny glasses, her hope that her mother would come home for Christmas had, with a mocking sneer, deserted her. So when she heard the door slam, the idea that it could be her mother returning did not even enter her mind. When she was awake enough to worry, her first thought was that her father had driven separately; Teo and Cornelia might be getting into Teo's car and leaving her with her father. She threw off the quilt someone had put over her and ran into her own room in the front of the house. If someone was leaving, she prayed into the darkness, let it be her father.

It was. As Clare watched, he walked across the front lawn toward where his small car gleamed silver and spaceship-like against the snow. Halfway there, he turned back, took a step toward the house, then stopped, rubbed his forehead with his palm, turned again, and walked the rest of the way to his car. As soon as he started his engine, Clare padded down the stairs. When she got to the bottom, she heard another door open and shut—the back door this time—and she moved noiselessly through the house into the mud room, which had a window that looked out onto the backyard. Carefully, she moved a row of boots and gardening clogs and sat down on the old wooden bench by the window.

The backyard was startlingly bright, and Clare realized that her mother must have set the floodlights to come on at nightfall, as she always did when they went away. Briefly, she wondered at the mysterious nature of her mother's mind, how easily it slipped between confusion and clarity, how, in certain respects, it remained so capable. The woman who made plane reservations and set timers was also the woman who walked out into the cold in a summer dress.

Clare didn't consider all of this for long, though, because out the window, just feet away, she saw Teo sitting in one of the white Adirondack chairs and then saw Cornelia approaching him, holding a glass of wine in each gloved hand. When she was sure they weren't looking, she slid the window open a few inches. Cornelia handed a glass to Teo and sat down in the other chair. From her place in the dark, Clare could see both of them clearly, could see their little clouds of breath and tears starting in Cornelia's eyes. It was like watching a play. I'm spying, Clare thought. And she felt bad about it, but not very bad. Her life was being decided all around her. If she couldn't control what happened to her, she could at least try to keep up.

"He lied to me. Not that that's the worst of it. Not that it even matters, relative to everything else. But he lied to me, twice—three times if you count what just happened. A few hours ago, upstairs, he said he wished he'd known what was happening. He sounded so . . . I felt sorry for him. Idiot that I am." Cornelia's voice was vibrant with bitterness.

"Why are you an idiot? For trusting someone you love?" Teo said. He sounded tired, flattened out.

Cornelia shot him an astounded, baffled look. "Teo! Is that what you thought? No, not that. It's not as bad as that. Liked. Liked a lot. Never loved." She paused. "Did I seem to be in love with him?"

Teo swirled the wine around in his glass thoughtfully. Then he looked at Cornelia. "No. I mean, I don't know what you look like in love. But no, I guess not. I guess I just figured you were since he's—" Teo broke off. What? Clare wondered. He's what?

Cornelia shifted her gaze to the sky, even though Clare knew that with all that light out there, the sky wouldn't be much of anything but black. "I wanted to be," she said softly. "I got swept up in wanting to be. I overlooked so much."

Teo gazed at the sky too. "Anyone would have, I bet. I don't think love is blind, but wanting to be in love, that's probably blind. You couldn't help it."

"No, don't give me that kind of credit. If I'd been blind . . . But I wasn't. I saw, but I put aside or explained away. I refused to add things up." Cornelia sighed. "And the truth is, I wasn't stunned when you said what you said in the kitchen. If I found out someone else—you, for instance—decided to ignore a child's cries for help, I would be stunned."

"Oh," breathed Clare. She pressed her fingers to her mouth, but Cornelia and Teo hadn't heard her. So that was it. Her phone call to her father.

Cornelia stopped looking at the sky and looked at Teo, fiercely. "Not even stunned. I'd smite whoever said it down in his tracks. The lying bastard."

Teo tilted his face away, but Clare thought she saw him smile. When he turned back to Cornelia, though, he was somber.

"I'm sorry I didn't tell you earlier. Or maybe I should be sorry I told you at all. Or told you like I did, in front of Martin."

Cornelia poked him in the shoulder. "Stop. I won't allow it. You know and I know that you did try. Or started to try. Last night. Before I turned into a rattlesnake and bit you."

Clare didn't know what Cornelia was talking about, but she saw that whatever had happened last night, no one was mad about it now.

Cornelia clapped her hands to her forehead and gave a frustrated hiss. "What is the matter with me? *Why* did I want so badly to be in love with him?"

Teo laughed and said, "You mean what did you see in him? Come on, Cornelia!"

"Quiet, you." She stabbed her forefinger in his direction and glowered.

"If the resemblance were any stronger, he'd probably be in violation of copyright laws." Teo laughed again.

"You find yourself so amusing, don't you, little boy?" Cornelia was shaking her head, but smiling at the same time.

"The Grant estate could sue."

They both laughed. Clare didn't follow any of what they said, but she understood the laughing. She understood that a few minutes ago, Cornelia had had tears on her face and now she and Teo were laughing together.

Clare remembered that the two of them had grown up together, and she wondered if this was how brothers and sisters acted around each other all the time. Probably not. She considered the brothers and sisters she knew. Cornelia and Teo were sort of like brother and sister, but also were something else. A kind of energy danced between them. It dawned on her that this was what a friendship between a man and a woman looked like, and she felt dizzy and privileged, as though she'd gotten a glimpse into a new world.

"And it's not just that," said Teo, as their laughter subsided. "Charm, wit, sophistication, what even I can tell are great clothes. I bet his apartment looks like something out of a magazine. If I Googled 'Cornelia's dream man,' he's exactly what would show up on the screen."

"Am I hopelessly shallow?" asked Cornelia, wistfully, and Clare knew she wanted a serious answer, even if the question didn't sound entirely serious. As she spoke, Cornelia leaned her head against the back of her chair and looked into Teo's face. He looked back for a second.

"Nope," he said, and his tone was brisk. "Nothing hopeless about you."

They sat drinking their wine and staring straight ahead. If the light outside hadn't been so brilliant, they would have seen Clare for sure. Then Cornelia spoke. What she said nearly sent Clare running out into the yard.

"He went for a drive. When he comes back, I'm telling him it's over. Because it's over. I'm leaving."

Teo sat still, not looking at Cornelia or saying anything. Clare's breathing began to come hard.

"I can't be with him, Teo." Her voice was defiant.

Still, Teo kept silent. Cornelia stood up and began to pace. Clare felt desolate. It was over then, the safe feeling, the not being alone. Over, over, over. The word repeated itself in her head with the force of heavy footsteps, something bad coming closer and closer.

"I just can't do it. You know I can't, Teo. It's unthinkable." Cornelia's voice got higher as she paced.

"It is. It's unthinkable," said Teo evenly. "And it would only be for a little while. Just until they find her."

Cornelia stopped in front of Teo, her arms wrapped around her middle. Standing there, hugging herself, with her back to Clare, she was tiny, like a little girl.

"I'm supposed to what? Pretend to be in love with him?" Cornelia almost spat the words.

Teo stood up fast and put a hand on Cornelia's shoulder. "No," he said. "Of course not. Just talk to him, work on your relationship."

"*Pretend* to work on our relationship?"

Teo grimaced, his hand still on Cornelia's shoulder. He seemed to be ashamed of something, but Clare didn't know what. But he didn't look away from Cornelia's face.

"No one could expect me to do that," said Cornelia, angrily.

"No," said Teo, his gaze steady.

"I just want to get away from him," said Cornelia, pleading.

"I know you do," said Teo kindly. *So* kindly, Clare thought, Teo couldn't have any reason to be ashamed. Clare believed he was the nicest man in the world.

Cornelia reached up and held on with both hands to Teo's arm. She was crying.

"You're right," she said, hollowly. "I can't leave her. Of course, I can't. Especially not now, after everything I know."

Her, Clare thought. I'm the her she means.

"It's not fair," said Teo. "I'm sorry." He pulled Cornelia to him and hugged her.

Clare wished she could hug her too. Clare whispered, "Thank you, thank you, thank you," whispered it over and over, filling the small room she sat in with the words.

"Teo," said Cornelia, almost whispering, "what if I mess up?"

"Mess up what?"

"You saw Clare's face when she opened the door tonight. She's fragile. I don't know how to be responsible for a child that fragile."

"You won't mess up."

Cornelia pulled away from Teo. "OK. But you, you have to go, OK? Tomorrow."

"I know." Teo nodded. "I will."

"I can't stand to have you watch," said Cornelia. "And anyway, you have your life. We can't have you getting fired. By the hospital or by

Ollie." She laughed a brittle laugh and wiped her face roughly with her hand. Then she said, "Let's go in."

Teo picked up their wineglasses.

"But Teo," Cornelia said, suddenly sounding almost frightened, "if I call you, will you come back?" Then, in a more normal tone, "Because Clare might want you. I think she's in love."

I am, Clare thought and smiled to herself.

"Yeah," said Teo. "If you call me, I'll come back."

Clare ran up the stairs to her mother's room and slipped under the quilt. Her heart was pounding. For a long time, she lay awake, thinking of how finding out how her father had treated Clare had made Cornelia want to leave him, and of how, for the same reason, Cornelia was staying. For her, Cornelia had decided to stay. She must like me, Clare thought happily. Teo, too. They must both like me. Holding this thought close, she fell asleep.

When Clare came downstairs the next morning, Cornelia was sitting alone at the kitchen table with her forehead resting on her crossed arms. It was the precise position the younger kids at Clare's school used for their ten-minute rests after lunch, and Clare had always liked how it felt inside the small space her arms made: private, alone with the sound of her breath and, at the same time, linked to the other children in the darkened room who were each alone in the same way. But here, at the table, Cornelia was the only one with her head down; she really was alone.

Clare noticed the way Cornelia's cropped hair tapered down the back of her head; she noticed the slight depression in the center of her neck and one bump of vertebrae above her shirt collar. Cornelia lives in her body just like I live in mine, Clare understood suddenly. She's the main character in her story, just like I'm the main character in mine. Clare couldn't have explained these thoughts or accounted for her feeling of astonishment as she thought them. The thoughts seemed obvious, but were not. Somehow, they were revelations.

"Cornelia?" said Clare softly. Cornelia lifted her head, raising her shoulders as though the sound of her name had startled her. Clare wondered if she'd been sleeping. When Cornelia saw Clare, her shoulders relaxed, and she said, gently, "Hey, there. Hungry?"

"Starving," answered Clare. She poked around the kitchen and found two pies, untouched—apple and pumpkin. They didn't eat dessert without me, she thought, and this fact filled her with warmth.

"Cornelia," Clare said mischievously, "let's have pie."

Cornelia laughed and said, "You know, suddenly, I'm starving too. If you'd cut me a big old slab of apple, honey, I'd be much obliged."

As they ate, Clare asked, "Did Teo leave?" and Cornelia looked taken aback for a second. Then she said, "Teo is one of those lunatics who gets up at daybreak and goes running in the cold. I expect him back any minute begging us to put him in the oven to thaw. Will he fit, do you think?" They both looked at the giant oven.

"Maybe we can do half of him at a time," said Clare.

"Good idea." Cornelia smiled, then she said, seriously, "But he *is* leaving today. His patients need him."

"Oh," said Clare, taking care to sound disappointed. She was, actually, but she knew he'd come back if Cornelia called him. She knew she'd see him again. "I guess Ollie needs him too."

"Sure, she does. Ollie doesn't always know that she needs people, but she must need Teo."

"Who wouldn't need Teo?" said Clare. "He's needable."

Cornelia twinkled her eyes at Clare. "Now, now, Clare, you mustn't let men drive you to mangling the English language, no matter how sweet they are."

"Not men, just Teo." Clare laughed. "OK, what's a better word?"

"How about necessary?" Cornelia said. "Teo is necessary."

At that moment, the front door slammed. Teo trotted into the kitchen, panting, and immediately bent over with his hands on his knees. When he caught his breath, he stood up, then sat on the floor with his back against the wall. He wore a red sweatshirt with STAN-

FORD in white letters across the front. He was red-cheeked, and his eyes sparkled. Clare stared. He looks exactly like a rose, she thought, which instantly struck her as funny. She chuckled.

"What?" Teo said to the two staring people.

"Were your ears burning?" asked Cornelia. Teo cupped his hands over his ears.

"They're burning now. My whole head is burning. I think that's a good sign, because two minutes ago my whole head was numb."

"Which, I believe, would make you a numbskull," said Cornelia.

"Wouldn't be the first time," said Teo, shrugging. "Where's Martin?"

"Martin's showering, I think. Or probably shaving by now. Showering, shaving, two things you might consider, Sandoval. And your hair is crying out for a decent barber. Screaming out. Actually, at this point, an indecent barber would do." Cornelia's tone was light as a feather, but Clare noticed that when she talked about her father, she didn't meet anyone's eyes.

"Stop trying to make me over," said Teo, standing up. "It can't be done." He lifted what was left of Cornelia's pie in his fingers and shoved the whole thing in his mouth.

"Barbarian," said Cornelia primly, touching her napkin to the corners of her lips.

Clare heard her father coming down the stairs, his shoes heavy on the bare wood. It's the day after Christmas, she thought with disgust. Hasn't he ever heard of sneakers?

But when her father walked into the kitchen, she felt sorry for being so hard on him, even if it was only to herself. Inside his sweater and wool pants he seemed smaller, and his eyes looked shadowed and dark in his pale face, as though he hadn't slept at all. She wondered how long he'd driven around thinking about Cornelia, and even though Cornelia would break up with him before long, Clare guessed, she was glad he didn't know what Cornelia had said last night in the yard. Clare remembered that sad, desperate note in her voice when she'd told Teo, "I just want to get away from him." Just thinking about her father hearing that made Clare shiver.

"Martin," said Cornelia, and something about the way she said it made Clare wonder if she'd been thinking the same thing.

"Good morning, all. Ah, I was wondering where those pies had gotten to," he said. Even his voice was smaller.

Clare stood up. "We turned them into breakfast, Dad. Do you want pumpkin or apple?"

He smiled at her, into her eyes, and then said, "I'll have what you had, Sparrow."

Teo stood up. "Somewhere around here, there's a shower with my name on it."

"Make it a long one," called Cornelia, holding her nose as Teo sprinted out of the room.

"Teo does not smell!" said Clare to Cornelia with mock indignation.

"He was too frozen to smell much, at first, but as he began to thaw . . ." She took hold of her nose again.

"It appears that love isn't just blind, it dulls the olfactory nerves too," teased Clare's father.

Clare felt mildly shocked that her father had even noticed her crush on Teo. Of course, Cornelia may have pointed it out to him. But this morning, in his new smallness, with his sparkle dimmed, his edges drooping, her father seemed softer toward Clare. He seemed to notice her more than he usually did. She blushed a little at the thought that he knew she had a crush, which made her consider the fact that until that moment, she hadn't cared if Cornelia and Linny and even Teo knew. Not so long ago, being with people who knew such a fact would have embarrassed her mightily. But the atmosphere Teo and Cornelia carried around with them was playful, affectionate, and, what else? Accepting. When Clare entered this atmosphere, she felt free, as though what she thought and said were just fine.

"I don't think love is blind," said Cornelia in a hushed tone, and

Clare's father turned toward her abruptly. "True love is probably the most clear-eyed state of being there is."

Clare's father looked intently into his coffee cup, as though there were an answer to what Cornelia had said inside it.

"Maybe you're right. Maybe with true love, you see and you love anyway," he said finally. Then he shifted tones. "Who coined that phrase, by the way? 'Love is blind.' "

"Oh, Shakespeare, probably. At least, it's in Shakespeare, but it may have been something people said, a whatchamacallit. Not idiom. A commonplace?"

"I believe the technical term is 'something people said,' " said Clare's father, growing just a fraction brighter. At least, it seemed that way to Clare. A fraction? She tried to remember what you measured light in. A watt?

"Like 'Twinkle, Twinkle, Little Star,' " said Cornelia, which Clare didn't get at all. Right away, though, her father brightened a bit more.

"Exactly. Did Mozart compose it or did he just write variations of an existing folk song?"

"I believe the technical term is 'something people already sang,' " joked Cornelia, and her smile wasn't her usual smile, but Clare's father didn't appear to notice. Or maybe he was just glad to be talking like they were, batting a feathery subject back and forth. Like badminton, thought Clare, and wished she could say it out loud because it was a good simile. Oh, it popped into her head: a lumen. A lumen, right?

But even as she thought about how to measure light and her father and Cornelia talked about "Twinkle, Twinkle," Clare could feel the presence of seriousness and worry. It was as though another conversation, the real one, lurked underneath, like a riptide in the ocean. What Clare saw in Cornelia's face told her Cornelia felt this too. Cornelia at the kitchen table, her head in her arms flashed into Clare's mind; she'd help Cornelia, if she could.

"Maybe we should leave today," said Clare, "and go back to

Philadelphia." Out of this house, Cornelia wouldn't have to see Clare's father so much. They would live at their own apartments. She would stay with Cornelia, of course.

"Maybe we should." Cornelia's voice loosened with relief, which made Clare proud. She'd helped. "If you're ready. Oh, and after tomorrow morning, you and I will be on our own for a few days. Your father leaves for London tomorrow."

Clare felt buoyant at the news, but she tried not to let it show.

"I'll just be gone a few days," said her father. He paused, then said, "Unless you want me to stay, Clare. If you do, I can postpone the trip."

Cornelia darted him a startled glance; for a few seconds, she seemed confused, as though she couldn't decide what to think of this offer.

"That's OK, Dad. You can take the trip," said Clare. "I think I'll just go write a new note for Mom."

After she wrote the note, she started back toward the kitchen, then stopped. Upstairs, over the sound of water running, Teo hummed a song Clare didn't know. He was shaving, probably. Then Clare walked back to the kitchen as silently as she could and looked in. Spying again.

Her father had moved to a chair next to Cornelia's, and he leaned in toward her. "Keep the faith is what I want to say," said her father in a pained voice. "If you have any faith left in me."

"I'm trying, Martin," said Cornelia. Her mouth pulled down at its corners after she said it.

Clare's father picked up Cornelia's hand and stared at it; with his other hand, he touched each of her fingers, as though he were counting them. Then, hoarsely, he said, "May I?" Cornelia nodded, and Clare's father kissed the back of her hand, then turned it over and kissed the center of her palm, holding her palm against his mouth for a long time. Clare pressed her own hands to her heart. Afterward, she slipped out and sat in the living room, sorting out her ideas about what she'd seen.

What she came to was that even if someone wasn't perfect or even especially good, you couldn't dismiss the love they felt. Love was always love; it had a rightness all its own, even if the person feeling the love was full of wrongness. Cornelia had said that her father had ignored a child's cries for help. Even a man who would do this could be in love, with a love that mattered. Sitting upright in her living room, in a hundred-year-old chair, Clare trembled in the face of this truth she'd discovered all on her own, and she felt ancient and part of life.

Teo found her sitting like that. He entered the room quietly and said her name. When she looked up at him, she saw that his hair still shone wet from his shower and that his face was clean-shaven and golden-brown. Gosh, she almost said aloud, talk about lumens.

Before Teo left, he shook Clare's father's hand. Then he leaned over and kissed Cornelia on both cheeks. "Isn't that how they do it at your café?" he said with a grin. Cornelia nodded, but she took hold of Teo's coat sleeve, and Clare saw a flash of what might have been panic on her face. "I'll see you soon," said Teo firmly, and Cornelia let go.

"Want to walk me out, Clare?" asked Teo, and Clare did, of course. Teo offered his arm, and Clare took it and practically danced out the door. In her other hand, she held a brown paper bag, something for Teo to take with him.

As they stood by Teo's car, Clare took her gift to him out of the bag. It was the story she'd written; she'd done her best to smooth out the cover.

"I made it for my mom for Christmas," said Clare simply.

"You should save it for her," said Teo. He slipped a loose strand of hair behind Clare's ear.

"I can make her another one. This is for you and Cornelia. To share. So you'll have to bring it back when it's her turn." Clare paused. "And I think it should be her turn soon, OK?"

"OK. Thank you." Teo smiled, then he handed Clare a folded slip of paper, "Here's my number. You call me whenever you feel like it, all right?"

Clare nodded, holding the paper with both hands.

Teo stared up at Clare's house for a second, then said, "Clare, you think you could do something for me?"

Clare bounced on her toes a little. She would do anything. "Anything," she said.

"Call me if you need me. And call me if you think . . . If Cornelia seems to be in trouble, call me then, too. Would you do that?"

"I promise," said Clare solemnly. Then, quickly, before she could chicken out, she kissed Teo's smooth, brown cheek.

In her father's car, on the way back into the city, Clare wrote in her journal and her father and Cornelia talked. They stuck to broad, impersonal subjects. Their voices rippled smoothly over the surface of movies first, most of which Clare had never seen, and then poetry—the Metaphysicals, whatever they were, and Emily Dickinson, whose name brought to Clare's mind the image of a fly buzzing on a windowsill, and Edna St. Vincent Millay, and Auden and other names Clare didn't know. Only once did Cornelia's voice turn serious and reflective.

"It's true. I have a long history of prizing irony. Irony and cleverness. Overprizing, I think," she said.

"No worries," said Clare's father casually. "One can never prize irony and cleverness enough."

"You can, though. I'm starting to think you can. The older I get, the more I love Whitman."

Clare remembered a man talking to a blade of grass. Remembered, also, a rest stop on the New Jersey turnpike. "I celebrate myself and sing myself!" her mother always called out when they passed the sign. Oh, Mommy, Clare thought. Come home.

"Whitman can be very clever," said Clare's father.

"Of course," said Cornelia, impatiently. "But cleverness isn't the point. No one ever loved Whitman for his cleverness. His heart is the point, and his enormous generosity, and his exuberance." She sounded furious.

"Better reasons to love someone, you think? Better characteristics to be loved for," said Clare's father, sounding suddenly weary, weighed-down. What are they talking about, Clare wondered.

"Martin, don't think . . ." Cornelia sighed. "I didn't mean to get carried away. Or snippy. OK? I'm just talking about poetry. Poetry rattles me sometimes. It turns me into a beast. OK?" She lifted her hand to touch his knee, but hesitated. He took the hovering hand and held it.

"OK," said Clare's father. "Even when you're a beast, you're not really a beastly beast." He seemed happy again.

It doesn't take much to make him feel better, thought Clare. Then she wrote it in her journal. After it, she wrote, "He needs to believe that she loves him back."

17

Cornelia

There's a kind of tenderness that's only possible in the predawn hours, a blue-gray, lonely tenderness that comes from dim lights and sleepiness and immense quiet. A kind of tenderness and a kind of hope. I've always found it hard to feel angry in the half-hour before the sun comes up, and when Martin came to my door to say good-bye the morning after we returned to Philadelphia, I didn't feel anything close to anger. It's not that I'd forgotten the way he'd cut Clare loose, abandoned her to her sick mother and her fear. I hadn't forgotten a single thing. But when I saw him standing in my doorway, his face was so pale, so stripped bare of sophistication and sparkle, like the face of a child, he hardly looked like himself. Or maybe he looked so much like himself that I hardly recognized him. For the first time ever, I saw Martin and didn't see his handsomeness; I only saw that he was human.

Then Clare came out of the bedroom, and Martin said, "Hey, there, Sparrow," and his voice sounded just the way he looked, naked and sad, and he held out his hand to her.

When she walked over, he put his hands on her shoulders and kissed the top of her head, then her cheek. I could see the astonishment in her eyes.

"Sparrow, I was wrong not to listen to you when you called to say your mother was behaving strangely." He paused. I could hear Clare's breath quicken.

"I'm sorry for not listening. And for not helping."

Clare's body tensed, and I could tell how confused she was. This wasn't how her father talked to her; it just wasn't. She stood rigid and stock-still in her pajamas, and I was tempted to jump in, to explain or break the moment, but I didn't. After a long time, Clare managed a nod. Then she said, "I'll see you when you get back, Dad," and she turned and walked back into the bedroom.

Martin watched her go, and when he kept watching for a few seconds after she'd disappeared from view, I couldn't help it: I took his hand. He turned but didn't come closer to me, and we stood like two people shaking hands, sealing a pact across a stream of running water.

"While I'm gone, will you think about us? About whether you can see your way to giving us another chance?" His voice broke, which was almost enough to break my resolve, too, and send me rushing into his arms. Almost, but not quite.

"Martin" was all I said.

"I don't deserve you. But I want to become someone who does," he said.

"And Clare?" I flared. "Do you want to become someone who deserves Clare?"

"Yes. I want that." He looked at me with a gaze that was half-plea, half-challenge. "Will you help me?"

No seemed to be the wrong answer to this, but so did yes.

"Please think about it," he said, but he didn't sound very hopeful.

"Yes. OK, Martin. I'll think about it." I sighed and immediately wished I hadn't because the sigh made my words sound impatient and probably insincere, as well. His hand inside mine was warm and real; I could feel the bones in it. I thought about what I'd said to Teo about pretending to work on my relationship with Martin, and I understood that if I wasn't going to break it off with him, I couldn't just pretend, no matter how hopeless it seemed. "No, Martin, I mean it. I'll think about it."

Then he nodded, kissed me fiercely on the mouth, and left.

All that day, Martin's good-byes hovered over Clare and me. What we needed was hours alone with our thoughts, but because we were together, we spent our time as quietly as we could. Clare read and wrote in her notebook, and I read and dusted and cleaned my kitchen. In the afternoon I did laundry, and Clare helped me fold it, and I could tell she liked doing this for the same reasons I did: the clothes fresh as bread in their baskets, warm in our hands, the neat stacks and full closets afterward. Then, that evening, Clare and I went to Linny's to eat her specialty dish, spaghetti and meatballs, and to let her funny talk and big, kind spirit fill in our lonely spaces. Linny moves around the world with such firm, certain steps, being with her can make you forget your own confusion, at least for a little while. Then Clare and I walked home together through bustling, noisy streets and went to bed.

At five o'clock the next morning, I woke up. My apartment door stood open. Clare was gone.

Do I have to describe it to you? The white-hot, pounding panic; the breath rising to a wail; the desperate, out-loud prayers? Everyone knows this moment, and if you don't know it, you will. We've all seen it. The mother on the beach, the father in the department store, the baby-sitter in the park who only turned her back for three seconds, just three seconds, and what we all know is that no matter how briefly the moment lasts, it's always endless. And even if the child is just chasing a seagull or hiding in a clothes rack or petting a dog a few feet away, for that endless moment, the child is gone forever.

It took me twenty minutes to find her. Twenty minutes of running through the dark city like a madwoman, making deals with God and the devil, cursing myself, and calling out "Clare" over and over. The calling is the worst part: You throw the name into the air and hear how already it's becoming impersonal, just another sound in the world, and you only half-believe it will ever attach itself to anyone—your anyone—again.

She was wearing the fur coat and sitting at an empty, chained-up café table, feeding something to a pigeon. I sobbed out her name and tore across the street to kneel before her in a cold puddle of streetlamp light, patting her face and her arms, making sure she was real and unbroken.

When I could breathe enough to speak, I said, "What happened? What happened to you?"

"I went for a walk," Clare said, and the calm contained in her eyes and her voice should have done nothing but reassure me; I know that. Relief should have fallen from the sky like spring rain, and I should have hugged Clare and taken her home.

But that's not what I did. What you have to remember is that I'd organized my life in such a fashion that I'd never had to take much responsibility for other people, for their well-being or their whereabouts. I'd never had anyone to keep track of, so I'd never had anyone to lose, and if you've never had anyone to lose, you don't know the proper way to behave once you've found her. Which is just an excuse, of course, because although I didn't know, I could have imagined the proper way to behave.

But I didn't. My imagination failed. The predawn magic failed me too. I'd been so scared, so stretched thin with fear, and I snapped. I got mad. I got furious. I leaped to my feet and paced and yelled, and I only wish I could say that I've forgotten what I yelled, but I remember every awful word.

"What were you thinking? What the hell were you thinking? I woke up and you were gone and I've been running screaming through the freezing cold streets and, oh God, what if I hadn't found you? Anything could've happened to you out here. Anything! What is the matter with you? What is the *matter* with you?"

"I'm sorry," Clare began in a small voice. But I cut her off. And then I said the worst thing of all, the worst thing I could have said.

"I knew it. I knew I shouldn't have gotten myself into this. I must have been out of my mind to think I could do this."

And as angry as I was, I truly didn't mean that the way it sounded. I didn't mean I didn't want her.

Clare stood up, then. I could see her body shaking inside the coat, but her voice was so steady it was chilling.

"Don't do it, then," she said, viciously. "Just leave me alone."

She took off the fur coat and threw it on the ground in front of me. "Take this if you're so freezing cold. I don't want it. I hate all of you anyway."

And she took off running.

When I caught up with her, we were in Rittenhouse Square. Clare was sitting on a park bench, and I sat down next to her, keeping a couple of feet of space between us. She didn't look at me.

The colored globes of Christmas lights hung in the trees above us like little worlds, and I could see a few lit windows in the buildings around the square, shadows moving behind curtains. Away from the bench I sat on with Clare, people were making coffee, stepping into hot showers, letting themselves ease into the winter day that lay untouched before them.

Still not looking at me, Clare spoke and what she said scared me more than waking up to find her gone: "I wanted to disappear."

"Clare," I said bleakly.

"No, I mean, I wanted to know what it was like to just leave. I wondered . . ."

"What?" I asked.

"I wondered what would happen to me if I were all alone. Like, if no one knew where I was or who I was, would I still be me? Or would I be someone else?"

"And what happened?" I asked, with a full heart. "Were you still you?"

"Yes." She sighed. "I started worrying that you'd wake up before I got back," and suddenly the hard bitterness I'd heard under the street-lamp was back in Clare's voice. "That's how I knew I was still me. Because I worried about scaring you, and because I wanted to go back."

For a second, I thought her anger was for me, but when I saw her face—that battered, betrayed look in her eyes—I understood.

"You think your mother isn't worrying about you?"

Clare squeezed her eyes shut and shook her head. "She isn't. She left and forgot me. Like my father always does. If my mom were worried, she'd come back."

My own words from minutes before echoed in my head: *What is the matter with you?* How could I have yelled at this girl for walking out and leaving me? Who in the world had been more walked-out-on than Clare? I slid over next to her and wrapped the big coat around us both.

"Cornelia?" Clare said finally, "I want to tell you something, but I'm afraid to."

"Don't be afraid, honey," I told her, with my hand on her smooth hair.

"Sometimes, I'm so mad at her for leaving," whispered Clare. "It makes my stomach hurt. Sometimes, I hate her."

After she said it, I could feel her body relax, as though she'd been straining to hold on to a heavy weight and had finally put it down. Her breathing slowed, like a person falling asleep, but her eyes were open.

"Did you think that if you told that to anyone, your mother wouldn't come back?" I asked her, and she stared into the dark and nodded.

"Telling the truth about how you feel is good. Good and honest and brave."

She nodded again.

I said, "Clare, I'm sorry I yelled at you."

"That's OK," she said.

"I was scared I'd lost you," I told her. "And being with you is the best thing I've ever gotten to do."

She didn't say anything. Then she smiled. "You're wearing your pajamas."

I looked down at myself and nodded. "Yep, I am."

"So we'd better hurry up and go home."

That night, when Martin called, I decided to be good and honest and brave too. I decided to tell him the truth about how I felt.

"Martin," I said gently, "I've thought about it, and I don't think I can be in love with you."

"Oh," he said, and I heard the breath catch in his throat. "I really hoped you could be."

"I hoped so too," I said.

"There's no chance at all?" he asked, and his voice staggered over the words.

I started to cry. "I don't think there is," I said. "I'm sorry."

"No," he said kindly. "Don't be sorry, Cornelia. I appreciate your trying." He was such a gentleman.

"Martin, I have to say something else."

"Something else?"

I took a deep breath. "Clare. She needs me. She's so full of hurt. She needs me."

"Oh."

After a silence, Martin said, "You were afraid to tell me that you don't love me because you were afraid I wouldn't let you see Clare anymore."

I couldn't speak.

"Oh, Cornelia." Martin sighed.

"It isn't just that she needs me, Martin. She needs us both. Earlier today. Well, earlier today, I saw how big a job it is to keep her safe, to keep her fears at bay. One person can't do that for her alone. I know I can't, anyway."

"You want us to take care of Clare together?" he asked, and there was a note of hope in his voice when he said "together" that made me nervous, but I knew as well as anyone how hope hangs on. He'd hang on to hope a little while more, no matter what I said to him.

Maybe I took the easy way out. I don't know. Maybe I should have told Martin, then and there, not to hope, that we'd never be together the way he wanted. But later, I'd be glad I hadn't told him this. Later and forever after, when I remembered that conversation, I'd be glad I hadn't told him anything but "Yes."

18

Clare

The next evening, while Clare and Cornelia were doing the dishes, the telephone rang, and Cornelia answered it. She carried the phone into the kitchen, tucked it against her shoulder, and began drying a plate with a towel.

"Yes, of course I remember you. How are you?" There was a long pause. "What are you saying?" said Cornelia, and Clare saw her put the plate down very carefully and saw her whole body begin to shake. Clare's heart started to beat faster. *Mommy.* She mouthed the word, silently; inside her head, the word was a long, earsplitting shriek.

"He's what? He can't be," said Cornelia. "No."

He. Not Clare's mother. *Mommy.* She could breathe again. *Mommy, you're safe.* I'll stay alive, then, Clare thought.

"Oh, no. Oh, no, no, no, no," whispered Cornelia into the phone. She dropped her arms to her sides, the phone dangling from one hand. She stared at Clare without seeing her. Clare had never seen anyone's eyes look like that. It's something terrible, she thought. It's not my mother, but it's something terrible. Clare started to cry.

Cornelia brought the phone back to her ear. "I need—I need. Could you call me back in a little while? Yes. Thank you." She pressed a button on the phone.

"Oh, Clare," she said, brokenly, and as Clare waited for her to say more, the colors in the room got brighter, seemed to buzz with brightness. The only pale object in the room was Cornelia; even her lips were white.

"Teo," gasped Clare. "What happened to Teo? Tell me."

For an instant, Cornelia's face cleared, then it grew strange again. "Not Teo, Clare. Martin. There was a car accident in London. Martin's dead."

Entirely without meaning to be, Clare was rocked by an immense relief. Not Teo! She clutched her stomach and bent over, and her sharp exhalation was an "Oh!" of gratitude. Then, as she realized what else Cornelia had said, she straightened and stared at her, dazed.

As though remembering herself, Cornelia rushed to Clare and took her in her arms. "Oh, Clare," she cried. "Oh, Clare. I'm so sorry. Your father's dead."

19

Cornelia

Before I say anything else, I need to say this: Martin's death doesn't belong to me.

It's not that I wasn't sad about it; I was. But the tragedy of his death isn't my tragedy; it isn't even Clare's, although there's enough in that story to break anybody's heart. The fact that rises over every other fact: Martin's death belongs to Martin. I knew him for an intense three months; he was himself for every second of forty-four years, and then he was taken away from himself. Martin was a baby, fresh inside the glove of his newness, turning his head toward his own name, and then he was a child learning the world, and then he was a man. Do you see what I mean? Forget about cosmic unity, an overarching plan into which every event on Earth fits: Martin lost his chance at life too soon. There's the tragedy. Don't think I believe I'm saying anything new. I just needed to say it.

But I also need to move on to me (there it goes, that "I, I, I" thrumming like an engine or a heart), to my story because it's the only one that's mine to tell.

Who was I in the days that followed that phone call? I can hardly say. Certainly not what most other people seemed to regard me as: a lost girl, a tiny almost-widow. I stood there at the funeral I'd planned with Martin's secretary, Theresa Blum, and his lawyer, Woods Rawlings, holding Clare's hand, imagining what the people around me, and there were a lot of them, saw when they saw me—a child-sized, straight-backed, black-clad figure, heartbroken but stoic, my little head held high on my little neck—and I wanted to throw up. Apart from a child, no one seems to invite pity more than a woman of small stature, and pity poured out of everyone's eyes, pressed itself into my hand when it was shaken, and freighted down everyone's voices, as they expressed their deepest sympathies. If I sound angry at them, I'm not. What I felt was mortification and a desire to set the record straight.

There are people whose deaths make you ache with sadness. And then there are people whose deaths prevent the sun from rising, deaths that turn the walls black in every room you walk through, deaths that send storm clouds and a wail swirling through your head so that you can't hear music and you can't recognize your furniture or your own face in the mirror. As for this second kind of grief, I never touched it, never even got close enough to brush it with my fingertips.

I was not in love with Martin Grace. I was not. If it seems cold-hearted to have held fast to that fact, to have repeated it inside my head even as Chopin's funeral march filled the air around me, think of how much worse it would have been, at that moment especially, to pretend to anyone, especially to myself, that I was in love with him. To slip downward into that lie would have been obscene, unforgivable.

Martin loved me, though, and you mustn't think I didn't value that. Not to pontificate or anything, but this I know: There's a kind of holiness to love, requited or not, and those people who don't receive it with gratitude are arrogant beyond saving. At Martin's funeral, I held fast to that fact too, held fast and then, in the last seconds, let it go. I released my thanks into the air like birds, with the hope that, if they didn't find Martin, they'd at least add themselves to whatever accumulation of goodness might be out there.

I remember having these thoughts, feeling these emotions. I remember being cold and knotted, dry-eyed and dry-hearted. But so much of what happened smudged and muted in my head even as it was happening. It was, as they say, a blur. Although it was a blur punctuated by stark, staggeringly clear moments—Technicolor moments, so vivid they were almost cruel.

There was the opulent conference room of Woods Rawlings's opulent law firm, and his turning his round, robin's-egg-blue eyes on me like two headlights and asking, across the glossy lake of table, why Clare had been staying with her father.

"That's a bit unusual, isn't it? An extended visit. Is Ms. Hobbes away? Not ill, I hope," he said in his elegant voice with its Tidewater vowels cooing away.

"Not ill," I replied, all tranquility. "She needed some time for herself, to travel and think. Replenish. Martin could hardly refuse, since she's spent so many years raising Clare single-handedly. I'm not sure where she is just now, to tell you the truth, although she mentioned Spain as one of her destinations." I didn't look away. I didn't even blink.

There was Linny standing in my doorway in a red cowboy shirt.

"Cornelia," she said neutrally, waiting for a cue from me. How are we handling this? I could hear her ask. What's our angle? What do you need?

"So Hayes told you where to get one," I said, flicking one of the pearl snaps with my finger.

"He did, but"—she winked—"this one's his." And she gave me a sly, coquettish grin, a smile so utterly Linny that I ate it up like a fresh pear, like manna from heaven, and it nourished my soul.

There was Teo showing up as if by magic the morning of the funeral, wearing a navy jacket and khakis and smelling like rain.

There was the ravishing redhead in a Chanel suit throwing herself into my arms after the funeral. "Forgive me," she sobbed raggedly. "I shouldn't even tell you this, and it ended ages ago but, God, I loved him. I was mad for him."

There was me making waffles for Clare and hearing Martin's voice, warm and reverberant, behind me in the room. Heard it, as sometimes happened when he spoke to me, with my whole body, so that not only did the tiny bones in my ears vibrate, but also the bones of my spine, the nerve endings in my fingertips. His voice was so present and living that I whipped around to see him and dropped the carton of eggs on the floor. "Your stillnesses," he said. "Those listening stillnesses."

And there was Clare, Clare who—surrounded by me, Teo, and Max (scrawny and ferocious in head-to-toe purple)—had glided through the funeral and through the reception afterward as serenely as a cloud, giving her hand to people who plainly, until that day, had not known she existed. Most of all, there was Clare—oh, sweet child—in the middle of the night, wild-eyed, asking, in a raw voice I will carry in my head forever, "Cornelia, am I an orphan now, Cornelia? Am I an orphan?"

20

Clare

"*Did* you ever read *A Little Princess*?" asked Clare from under a pile of coats.

She and Teo were on assignment, shopping for a new winter coat for him. It was the day after her father's funeral, a freezing, azure day with the kind of sun that is all blinding brilliance and no warmth. "A shrill sun," Cornelia had said that morning as the three of them left her apartment building. "Like a soprano singing her head off in your ear." Clare had found that interesting, but Teo had said, "Someone *really* needs to chunk a snowball at you," even though there wasn't any snow.

"He's just mad because I'm making him shop," Cornelia had said, putting her arm around Clare conspiratorially. "I'm depending on you, Clare. If he starts heading anywhere near Army/Navy surplus, you're authorized to shoot him."

"I knew I shouldn't have shown up with a haircut," groaned Teo. "Give her an inch, and she takes a mile."

"Clare, could you please explain to Teo that with beauty comes a certain responsibility to that beauty? He's never accepted that fact, not fully," said Cornelia, shaking her head. Clare noticed faint, bruise-colored semicircles above the points of Cornelia's cheekbones. It occurred to her that this playful back-and-forth with Teo only appeared effortless.

"With beauty comes responsibility, Teo," said Clare sternly.

"And you might say a word or two about moth holes," said Cornelia.

Clare had pointed solemnly to the holes in Teo's peacoat. "Moth holes. You have some," she said.

"That was three words," grumbled Teo.

His choices had been a fancy men's clothing boutique and a department store, and when Teo had mumbled something about allergies and cleaning fluid that made no sense to Clare, Cornelia had squeezed his arm sympathetically and written down the address of the boutique.

"A boutique," Teo had intoned dully. But it wasn't so bad, Clare thought. In fact, she liked it, the vast old building with its fancy moldings—flowers and grapes—and a painted mural aglow on the remote ceiling.

The salesman, a short, sleek, elegant man who reminded Clare of a seal, listened to her description of what they were looking for and then sized Teo up with his large, shiny black eyes. When Teo took off his coat to find the size inside, the man said, "Not necessary, but I would be happy to . . ." and he held his hand out with his fingers together (like a karate chop, thought Clare) so that Teo could hang the coat on it as though the man were a coatrack.

He'd stood Teo in front of a huge three-way mirror and then had left Teo and Clare alone with at least a dozen coats. Teo would try one on, get Clare's opinion, and then toss the coat onto her lap.

Just as she was asking Teo about *A Little Princess,* the salesman glided up with an inscrutable smile.

"I've read it," he said smoothly. "And how are we doing with the coats?"

"You've read it?" asked Clare with surprise.

"The monkey. A monkey comes to the attic to visit the little girl. I liked that monkey." The salesman spoke dreamily, looking off into the distance. Then he glided away.

Teo and Clare stared at each other and burst out laughing, trying to stay quiet so as not to hurt the man's feelings. Clare buried her face in the coats and laughed until her sides ached.

When they'd recovered, Teo said, "I didn't read it. But I wish I had. I didn't know it had a monkey in it."

"This girl, Sara Crewe, her father dies," said Clare.

Teo stood in a coffee-bean-colored coat that was shaped a lot like his old peacoat, looking at Clare in the mirror, waiting for more.

"And it's terrible. The night after she hears, she lives through 'a wild, unchildlike woe.'" Clare watched Teo's face. "And there's another word: anguish. 'The anguish of her young mind.' Doesn't that word sound like what it is? Doesn't it sound like the worst thing you could feel?"

"It really does," said Teo after a pause. Clare loved this about Teo, the way he didn't push or get impatient, but listened and let her make her own way to what she wanted to say.

"When Cornelia got that phone call, I was there, and I knew someone was dead, and I was afraid it was you. And I felt—anguish." She had to get it out. "And when I found out it wasn't you, I was so glad."

She breathed and stared at him in the mirror, then she clenched her hands into two fists. Time to finish. "I felt sad when I found out who it really was. But I felt happy that you weren't dead before I felt sad that he was. I felt happy *more*. So what that must mean is that even if I didn't want him to die, I didn't want you to die more. And he's my father. That seems—evil." She unclenched her fists and spread her fingers, letting go. Teo might hate her now, but she'd said what she needed to say.

Teo sat down next to her on the floor, and said, "Sometimes, you meet a person and, right away, it seems like you've known that person for a long time. I feel that way about you. Like I know you even better than people I've known for years."

Clare nodded.

"So, I hope it's OK if I ask you to trust me about something, even though we haven't known each other very long."

Clare stared down at Teo's long hands, then up at his green eyes. Without stopping to think, she'd trusted him from the first minute she'd met him. And even though she liked to understand everything, to ask questions and follow an idea through to its conclusion, she didn't mind not understanding her faith in Teo.

"I trust you," she said simply.

"Here's what I think: You are a good person. You're made of good materials. That's just a fact. Ollie would say it's in your cells, that it's built into your DNA just like your brown eyes. Wherever it comes from, just being you is being good."

Clare concentrated on the words, trying hard to press them into her memory and wishing they were solid objects that she could keep and carry around with her.

"I don't mean you can't make mistakes like the rest of us. But you're luckier than the rest of us because if you just do what feels the most like you, you'll be fine. And forget about evil. There's just no way."

Clare sat under the coats, next to the three gleaming rectangles of mirror, with the store's mellow lights falling on her and the bright day outside, and she felt illuminated too. She thought relief and gratitude must be shining out of her skin.

"Thanks," she said finally, hoping he could see how much she meant it.

Teo smiled and started to stand up, but Clare reached for his coat sleeve and held its unexpected buttery softness in her hand. Teo sat down again.

"You know what?" she said, nearly whispering. She cleared her throat and spoke up. "He didn't love me."

It was a fact, not a complaint. It felt important just to have it out there. She expected Teo to contradict her, even though she knew she was right. But he just said, "Then he missed out."

Clare touched the sleeve of Teo's coat again and said, "I like this one."

Teo looked down at the coat and said, "Doesn't itch. Will hide dirt. Might get Cornelia off my back, the little monkey." He grinned at her. "We'll take it."

*   *   *

That evening, after dinner, Clare went into Cornelia's bedroom to write what Teo had said to her about being good in her journal. Getting the words right mattered, but so did describing his voice when he talked and capturing the feeling that filled her as he spoke and after he spoke. She thought about that word "capture," how it put a writer on par with a fur trapper or big-game hunter, and how it implied that stories were whole and roaming around loose in the world, and a writer's job was to catch them. Except of course that a writer didn't kill what she caught, didn't stuff it and hang it on a wall; the point was to keep the stories alive. She felt skeptical about this way of thinking about writing, she decided, but was glad to have considered it.

When she heard Teo and Cornelia move from the kitchen, where they'd been doing dishes, to the living room, putting down her notebook and stepping to the doorway of the bedroom to listen to them came automatically.

"I fired our friend Lloyd," announced Cornelia, flopping onto the couch.

"You did?" asked Teo. Clare couldn't see his face, but his voice sounded odd, cautious maybe.

"He didn't inspire confidence. Not in me, anyway. Did he in you?"

"Not especially. But Martin was pretty concerned with being discreet, not letting her friends and neighbors know what was up. Maybe if Lloyd had a longer leash?"

Cornelia sat up, suddenly full of fire.

"But don't you see? A longer leash is the last thing we want right now. Discretion matters more than ever." She spoke in a low, charged voice, like someone who would rather be yelling.

"Cornelia . . . ," Teo began, sounding wary.

"Viviana's traveling. Clare's staying with me until she gets back. That's our story. It works. If people get wind of the real situation. Well, think about it, Teo."

Clare tried to think about it, but she wasn't sure what she or Teo was supposed to be coming up with. She waited to see what Teo would say next.

"Cornelia, maybe it's time to get the police involved." A chill traveled over Clare.

"No," said Cornelia. "No, no, no. How could you suggest that?"

Clare didn't know how he could either. Teo didn't say anything.

"Teo, we sit here discussing Clare's life. Deciding her fate like those fat old ladies with their thread and scissors."

Clare had no idea what this might mean. Fat old ladies?

"Fat old ladies?" said Teo.

"I always picture them as fat. Probably, they're not fat. Forget it. What I'm saying is, let's include Clare. Let's call her in here right now."

Clare remembered what Teo had said about her being made of good material. Was it good to spy on people who cared about you? She took a deep breath and stepped out of the bedroom. Teo and Cornelia stared at her.

"I was spying. Not spying, but I was listening to your conversation, which I guess is—spying." She paused, feeling her heartbeat in her temples. "I'm sorry. I'm afraid of not knowing what's going on."

"Of course, you are," Cornelia said gently. "We should have had you in here all along. I think we were afraid we'd have to say things that might be hard for you to hear."

Clare walked over to the sofa and smoothed her hand over the embroidered shawl draped over its back. She hated to sit against something so beautiful without at least touching it first, letting it know she'd noticed it.

Cornelia stood and, with a swift motion, lifted the shawl off the sofa, set it floating in the air like a great butterfly, and then let it alight on Clare's shoulders.

"Will you forgive us?" asked Cornelia. Clare didn't know what to say; she couldn't quite figure out what Cornelia and Teo would need to be forgiven for. She just nodded, then sat down on the sofa and tucked her feet underneath her. Cornelia smiled and did the same.

"Teo thinks we should consider calling the police. Get them to help find your mother."

"I don't want police," said Clare. She didn't like how she sounded, like a baby who might stomp her feet and throw a tantrum. But she didn't want police. The thought of police made her feel sick.

"Teo?" said Cornelia. Teo flushed and shifted uncomfortably in his chair.

"As far as I can tell," he said in his steadiest manner, "the system is designed to help families. To keep families together. When they find your mother, they'll help her in the ways she needs to be helped so that she can take care of you the way she always did."

"I want her to be the way she used to be. I don't . . ." Clare hesitated. "I can't go back to, to living with her when she's sick. But . . ."

She looked from Cornelia to Teo. "But if we call the police, will I be able to stay with Cornelia while they look for my mom? Will I be able to stay here while they're making her well?"

Cornelia picked up Clare's hand and squeezed it. Clare saw that her eyes were wet.

"Maybe," said Teo. "I think they try to keep kids with people they know."

"Maybe, but maybe not," Clare said bleakly. "Right? Maybe not." She pictured Anne Shirley in the orphan asylum and the mean woman she'd lived with before ending up there. There'd been one sad tree in the yard of the asylum, and Anne's only friends had been imaginary girls. Clare felt stricken.

"I think I'll just wait here until my mom comes back," she said faintly. "And then, maybe you can help her find a doctor."

Teo rubbed his eyes with both hands, then looked at Cornelia.

"Clare's been through too much upheaval already," said Cornelia decisively. But Clare saw that the expression in her eyes was far less certain. "You have to see that."

"Of course, I see that," Teo said, frustration edging his voice, "but have you thought about . . ." He shut his eyes for a few seconds. Then he put his elbows on his knees and leaned toward Clare.

"I'm sorry, Clare, but I have to say this," he said.

"Don't," Cornelia said bitterly. "Just don't. This insistence on the truth, it's brutal, do you know that? Who are you, Atticus Finch? Bob Ewell fell on his knife. Just accept it!"

Clare knew who Atticus Finch was. Scout and Jem's father. A hero. And Bob Ewell. Clare remembered how he'd chased the kids, how Scout had bounced around, befuddled inside her turkey costume. Or was it a ham? And how did Atticus and Bob fit in to what she and Teo and Cornelia were discussing, anyway? To her own amazement, Clare laughed.

"Clare?" Cornelia turned toward her, big-eyed.

"I'm sorry, but—Atticus Finch? I'm just so confused." She laughed again. What could be wrong with her all of a sudden? The laughter took over her whole body; she gave in.

"It's you," Teo said coolly to Cornelia. "You're just so weird."

Cornelia lowered her brows, but the corner of her mouth tweaked upward. The wire of tension between Cornelia and Teo had snapped. Clare let her laugh run its course, like a fever; afterward she breathed raggedly, wrung out, but ready. The shawl had slipped off her shoulders; now, she pulled it up and held on to it with both hands.

"I know what you were going to say, Teo," Clare said quietly, at long last. That's how it seemed, at long last. At long last, these words, this moment.

Teo kept his eyes on her. His clear, kind, green gaze made her feel strong. He loved her; she knew that with a sudden certainty. Her heart leaped up.

"What if my mother never comes home," Clare said and wondered how she could say it. The worst—the poisonous, nightmarish worst. She'd finally said the worst out loud.

"Oh, sweetheart." Cornelia's voice shook with compassion, but with something else, as well. Cornelia sounded proud of her.

"Yes, we have to consider that possibility, as remote as it is." Teo gestured around the room after he said it, gestured to the three of them. "This isn't something we could keep up forever." Clare liked it that he said "we."

"You're right." Cornelia nodded. "But we can keep it up for a little while, can't we?"

"What if we wait until school starts?" Clare could be decisive now. She felt years older. "Once school starts, it will get too hard. It's too far to drive there from here every day, and my teacher Ms. Packer, she already suspected something was wrong. When she sees Cornelia instead of my mom . . ."

"When does school start?" asked Teo resignedly.

"People go all these fancy places for break, so it's long. We go back the tenth."

"That's ten days from now," Cornelia said. "If she hasn't come home in ten days, we'll take other measures to find her."

"Other measures?" said Teo skeptically. "Sounds like a euphemism for you scouring the country in a trench coat and an El Camino."

"Very funny," said Cornelia. "As if I'd be caught dead in an El Camino."

"What's an El Camino?" Clare asked Cornelia, who began taking sudden notice of her fingernails.

"She has no idea," said Teo. "If Viviana isn't home in ten days . . ."

"We'll call the police," Clare pronounced firmly. She had a sudden thought, "Hey, it's New Year's Eve."

"You're right! I hadn't noticed. No champagne for you, missy, not even a soupçon!" Cornelia pretended to scold. Then she got serious. "There's one wonderful year ahead of you, Clare. Wonderful, filled with wonders. Mark my words!" Cornelia sounded so fierce, as though she would will Clare's wonderful year into existence whatever it took. If anyone could do it, she could, Clare believed, this small woman next to her who wasn't really small at all.

It dawned on Clare with the colors and the glowing sky of a real dawn: Cornelia loves me too.

21

Cornelia

It happened. To me.

Soon after Martin's death, it happened, as it happens to most people at some point or another, if they're lucky enough or maybe unlucky enough depending on how you look at it and the circumstances surrounding it. But I don't really believe that, do I? And you don't, either. We don't really believe that such a turn of events (because it's a turn, if anything is, a dizzying, whip-lashing, astonishing turn) could ever be unlucky. When it happens—the great sea change, the alteration of one's life into something rich and strange—when it singles one out, one is always lucky, lucky automatically. I'm talking about transformation, and the transformation I'm talking about is always a gift. A blessing.

As I was saying, it happened to me, soon after Martin's death. Some might say too soon, but it's not as though I were in charge of the timing. I wasn't the director of this particular scene. I don't know who was, but I know it wasn't Cornelia Brown. She wasn't the writer, either. She played the role she was given to play.

A sea change. I adore that term. Shakespeare, again, of course. From *The Tempest*. Except that Ariel was singing about what happens to a drowned man's body at the bottom of the sea, and while there was a kind of drowning involved, I was in a car and as alive as I had ever been. I was the body electric. I shimmered with life. I crackled.

What the hell am I getting at? "With the rich and mighty, always a little patience," as the wise man wrote, and although I'm not rich or mighty, I am the one telling this story. Patience, friend. Trust me; I'll get there. I've gotten us this far, haven't I?

And I didn't fall in love with Teo Sandoval, if that's what you're thinking.

It started with a phone call. Actually, it started in the primordial ooze at the dawn of time or even before that, but since you could say that for anything, that all moments were mere prelude to the one you're describing, I'll skip to the phone call. It was the second of two phone conversations with my mother, the first of which took place the night I heard about Martin's death. As soon as I could punch buttons on a phone, I called her. What did you think? That I was different from the rest of humanity? When disaster strikes, I want my mother. I want her, I want her, I want her.

As she always does, she answered after the first ring. Rude to keep people waiting is what we grew up hearing, contemptibly rude, even if getting to the phone meant flying over furniture like something out of Cirque du Soleil. If every fourteen-year-old in America needs a cell phone strapped gleamingly to her or his body at all times, my mother is surely a candidate for one. However, she claims cell phones open up whole new avenues for rudeness (with which not a soul could argue), and besides, my parents don't get reception on their particular street, for reasons no one can determine. Turns out we'd been living in a mild, magnolia-scented version of the Bermuda Triangle for all those years, which doesn't surprise me a bit.

In any case, I'd called her out of wanting her in a large vague way and also in a large specific way. Specifically, I wanted her to tell me that I wasn't responsible for Martin's death. More specifically, I wanted her to tell me that I did not cause his death by refusing his (second; I hadn't told her about the first) invitation to London, and that I did not cause his death by telling him I wasn't in love with him, that my voice in his head saying I wasn't in love with him did not cause whatever distraction or carelessness may have been his on that London street. I wanted her to tell me that beyond being unwarranted, feeling guilty was presumptuous, even arrogant, and utterly unproductive. Because shortly after hearing Martin was dead, guilt fell on me like a piano.

And she did, in a few tidy sentences, my mother did all of the above. And she did it with such patience, concern, and goodwill that I realized for the first time her real reason for running to the phone: She was the mother of four children. It took thirty-one years to realize this. Shame on me.

But the second phone call, the one I meant to describe, came later, a couple of days after Martin's funeral. Teo had just gone back home to Brooklyn, and I could feel Clare's missing him, could see a faintly unmoored expression on her face, even when she smiled at me, which she did fairly often, brave girl.

I can't say I didn't feel a bit lost myself. After all, as the Schoolhouse Rock song tells us, "It takes three legs to make a tripod or to make a table stand; it takes three wheels to make a ve-HI-cle called a tri-CY-cle." Three *is* a magic number, especially when the third is Teo, whom Clare had called needable and spoken truth.

But after he left, after we watched him get into his car and drive away, I stood with Clare on the sidewalk and waited for panic to seize me in its icy fist, and here's the thing: It never did. I was nervous, yes. Walking with Clare alone across the shifty terrain of Martin's and Viviana's absences would be tricky business, and I wasn't at all sure I was up to the job. But when I looked at her with her hands in her pockets, tipping her head back for a moment, eyes closed against the winter sun, she seemed so firmly planted on the earth that I believed we would figure it out.

And we would have, too, if not for the second phone call, the one my mother made to me, the phone-call cum straw-that-broke-this-camel's-back.

To put it simply, Mrs. Goldberg died.

To put it less simply and more stupidly, as did one obituary, she "succumbed to Alzheimer's," as though she could have done anything else, as though she'd given in, the weakling. She died in a nursing home, which, no matter how expensive, could not have been a home, not to Mrs. Goldberg, who knew, above all the things she knew, what a real home was.

"She's in a better place now, love" was my mother's—inevitable—summing up.

"No platitudes, Mom, please. She wasn't a platitude person," I said bitterly.

Silence, into which I sobbed.

Then my mother said, "I only meant she's all right now. You just seem to be taking the news so—hard." She sounded slightly put out.

Nowadays, everyone and their grandmother labels behaviors and responses and so forth as "inappropriate," but my mother's been using the word for years. And while for many people it's just a means of feeling detached and intellectual while calling someone a jerk, as Eleanor Campbell Brown defines "inappropriate," the word specifically describes behavior or even emotions that are "beyond that for which the occasion calls," with slight connotations of jerkiness hovering around, so slight that she would probably say I'm imagining them altogether.

In any case, she finds my responses inappropriate with some regularity, and I'm sure she was biting her tongue not to say the word now. Because I was, I was taking the news so hard. I'd loved Mrs. Goldberg for most of my life. In addition, in recent days, I had been under no small amount of strain. If in crying for Mrs. Goldberg I was also crying for Martin (which I'd not yet done, not a single tear) and for Clare and for Viviana and for myself, perhaps I might be forgiven. Perhaps, if the crying was for all of us, its duration and intensity were precisely that for which the occasion called.

This crying, in all its unseemly, indecorous inappropriateness, may have gone on ad nauseam, if not ad infinitum, had I not caught sight of Clare standing in the doorway of my bedroom, white-faced, holding on to the doorjamb as though it were the mast of a storm-tossed ship, and staring at me with terror in her eyes.

"It's OK, honey," I gasped, beating the crying back like a brush fire. "Not Teo. No one you know. Everything's OK."

She just nodded, but I saw concern replace the fear, and she sat down on the floor, to watch over and abide with me, true friend that she was.

"Cornelia, there's something else," ventured my mother.

Oh, no more, not one thing more.

"What?" I asked.

"Ruth said her mother remembered you in her will." My mother sounded uncomfortable. Uh-oh, I thought. Mrs. Goldberg's behaved inappropriately, even from her grave.

"She left me the pearl necklaces," I guessed.

"In a way, yes. She left you her house and its entire contents."

I was speechless.

"And she's asked that you go through her belongings and give her children whatever you think they might want. The rest is yours."

I plunged further into speechlessness.

"Ruth sounded fine. Apparently, apart from the house, Mrs. Goldberg's estate was substantial. The value of the house is quite small in comparison. Still, it's rather awkward, isn't it?"

As stuffy as this sounded, I knew my mother's disapproval came from a heartfelt concern for Mrs. Goldberg's children. That a mother would risk hurting her children's feelings as Mrs. Goldberg had, or as my mother thought she had, was unthinkable.

"Ruth and Bern are probably fine. They know she loved them," I said, and this was true. When Mrs. Goldberg loved you, you knew it.

"The funeral is the day after tomorrow. I told Ruth you probably wouldn't be able to come, with Clare there and everything. But once Clare's mother's back from her trip, you'll need to come down and go through Mrs. Goldberg's things."

"OK, then," I said blandly. "Thanks for calling, Mom."

I hung up, and Clare was on her feet in an instant and sitting close to me on the bed, her face clouded with worry. When she put her arms around me, I heard Mrs. Goldberg's voice saying, "child of my heart" as she had the last day we'd spent together in her house, and I couldn't help it; I started crying again. Crying and telling Clare, as I'd once told her father in this same room, about Mrs. Goldberg—who she was and who she was to me, how I'd been expecting her to die and how I couldn't bear it that she had.

While I can be a bit overdramatic at times—when my mother finds my emotional responses to be out of measure, sometimes, *sometimes*, she has a point—I wasn't doing that now. I'd tipped over an edge and had fallen onto rocky, unfamiliar turf, into a place where I would turn for solace to a child of eleven who'd lost so much herself that just tallying it all would make anyone sick and weary. I didn't mean to turn to her, but as she rubbed circles between my shoulder blades with her hand, I needed to be comforted in precisely that way; I couldn't help needing it.

When the phone rang, Clare whispered, "I'll be right back," and she went into the kitchen to answer it. I heard her talking, and then she brought the phone in to me.

"It's Teo," she said.

"Teo," I said miserably into the phone. I could hear noises and voices, something that sounded like an intercom. He must have been calling from the hospital. I imagined him standing there in his scrubs on the phone to me, with that whir of life and death around him. Death and illness every day. How awful for him, I thought. A good sign, I see looking back, to be thinking of another person. A sign I might not collapse under a load of self-pity. I wasn't thinking that then, though.

"My mom just called," he said. "I'm sorry, Cornelia."

"I can't believe it." But that wasn't right. "No, I believe it. I just. I don't want her to be dead. I don't want her to have gotten sick and died."

"It feels all wrong to me, too," said Teo. "But for me she was a kind of good fairy. I think all the kids felt that way. For you, she was something different. I remember noticing one day how you looked at each other. She was like family, wasn't she?"

"Like a good fairy and family. Both."

No platitudes from Teo, of course. But also none of this "her suffering is at an end" business, which you might well expect from a person who spent more time than most with bodies in pain—bodies whose own cells turned traitor in terrible ways. He didn't get all scientific on me, either, pointing out the technical whys and wherefores of Alzheimer's path of destruction, its inexorable burning-and-pillaging march to the sea. There are facts and then there is knowledge that has nothing to do with fact. Teo is a guy who understands this, doctor or no.

"I'm going down for the funeral. Ollie can't get away, but I'm going. Unless . . . unless you want me to come be with Clare, while you go." His voice sounded a little hesitant.

"I'd do it," he continued. "I will do it. It just might seem . . . People might . . ."

I understood what he was getting at. A male nonrelative staying alone with a young girl who'd only known him a short time. What a crazy world. In a flash, I knew what I was going to do.

"Thanks, but no. Clare will be with me."

"OK," Teo sounded relieved. "Everyone will understand why you're not there."

"No," I corrected. "We're going, Clare and I together. Today. We'll catch a train down."

"Cornelia. You can't. OK? Listen, I don't know if you're breaking any laws by having Clare with you, not reporting Viviana's disappearance, all that stuff. But you might be. Do you know that?"

"I guess I might be," I said. The thought had occurred to me, but necessity had snuffed it out like a match.

"So, you have to see that whisking Clare off to another state is a bad idea."

The phrase "crossing state lines" popped into my head. But I was not a kidnapper. I was a woman taking responsibility. Lying and breaking rules had never appealed or come naturally to me, but if taking responsibility meant weaving a vast tapestry of lies and law-bending, so be it.

I thought about the house I'd grown up in, the trees and yard and my parents and thought about the solid, picture-perfect, kept-intact-at-all-costs cheerfulness that had driven me nuts when I'd lived there. That house was the best place for Clare right now, for both of us. I knew this in my bones.

"Teo, it's not just the funeral." I sighed, then I sang, softly, *"Taaayo, Taaaay-yo-oh."*

"Yeah, I know," he said. "I know you want to go home. I don't blame you. But I just don't . . ."

Teo's not the only one who knows when to keep mum. I waited.

"All right. Jesus, Cornelia. All right."

"All right," I said, relieved.

"And forget the train. I'll pick you two up in the morning."

Three, it's a magic number. Teo felt it too.

"I'm going anyway." He sounded brusque and offhand, but I wasn't fooled for a second.

At this juncture, I'd like to say a few words about cars. I don't own one, which some would label as downright un-American of me, on par with, say, holing up in a shack in Montana and refusing to pay taxes or with failing to take proper care of my lawn. Quite deliberately, I'd arranged my life in such a way that I almost never had to set foot in a motorized vehicle of any kind, buses included. These boots were made for walking, walking, walking—leaving size-five footprints all over town—and I'd rather spend the gas money on really beautiful ones: hand-crafted, high-heeled, and made in the mountains of Italy.

But don't picture me on a soapbox, preaching about greenhouse gases and the paving-over of America, although those up on that particular soapbox make quite a bit of sense, when you think about it. But the reasons the soapbox people give for living car-free lives are not my reasons, alas.

Cars just don't interest me, for one thing. Once when someone at the café asked what kind of car Martin drove, the best I could come up with was "silver-ish."

For another thing, I'm chickenshit, as I think I've told you, and cars are plain scary.

Having said all that, however, I must also say that some of my most treasured memories involve being in a car. Or maybe not individual, individuated memories so much as a general recollected sense of joy and well-being. Childhood happiness means car rides, sleepy ones, in the backseat with hazy, golden light pouring in or hazy silver light, depending on the hour, leaning against Ollie or Toby or Cam, music on the radio, the sound of our parents talking—and always our parents, there, up front, capable, keeping watch, protecting us with a boundless benevolence, carrying all of us down the right road.

Magic can happen in a car, a warm, intimate magic born of being in an enclosed, particular place and, simultaneously, being nowhere, passing through. No one leaves her troubles behind, not really, but you can believe you have. You can believe you're in an in-between space where trouble can't find you, and Clare and I believed this as we sat together in Teo's car, sunshine pouring in on us. Teo believed it too, maybe, although if he had troubles of his own, he wasn't telling me. Magic worked on all three of us, though, and all three of us, for a little while anyway, were unburdened, light of heart.

Clare was sleeping in the backseat, her face as peaceful as I'd ever seen it, and I'd just finished telling Teo a funny story whose funniness turned on the fact that I am ludicrously short (showing you what a very good mood I was in) when Teo got this ruminative expression on his face and said what no one has ever said to me before: "You know, I don't think of you as short."

"You don't?" I asked, incredulous. "What do you think of me as?"

Because when someone voices an opinion that outrageous, you must pursue it like a bloodhound.

Teo paused, as though searching for the proper word and then said, "Runty" with admirable deadpan.

"You'd make a great stand-up comedian," I said in a bored voice. "If you weren't so staggeringly unfunny."

"Seriously," said Teo seriously. "I guess you are short, but I've never thought of you that way."

"You think of me as . . ." I waited.

"Essential," he said.

I laughed because it was unexpected and also because, although I didn't know what it meant, I liked it.

"I mean, if you gave some guy the assignment of creating a woman using as little material as possible but without cutting any corners, he'd make you."

"Why, Teo, that's so—sweet?" But it was sweet. No one had ever told me my corners were uncut before.

"I don't know if it's sweet, but it's true. When you're around other women, they end up looking sprawling and overdone, like whoever made them got carried away."

"Went way overbudget," I said.

"Right." Teo glanced over at me. "Although, the person who made you may have gotten a little extravagant with your face, but probably because he had some left over to spend."

"Economical guy that he was." I laughed, and so did Teo, but when I turned to see *his* face, he looked a bit embarrassed, or not embarrassed exactly, but shy.

Now, don't go thinking I fell in love with a man because he told me he didn't think of me as short. First of all, I'm not nearly so frivolous or so insecure as that. And second of all, I didn't fall in love with Teo.

What happened was this.

Like most people, when I'm in a warm car, tucked up in the front passenger seat with a cold day outside and sunlight lying over me like a yellow blanket, I get sleepy. Sometimes I get sleepy enough to fall asleep, and this was one of those times. I drifted off—an easy, golden drifting.

I slept. I woke. When I woke, I saw Teo's hands on the steering wheel, his wrists emerging from the once-rolled cuffs of his soft denim shirt. The shirt, blue; the wrists and hands, brown, dusted over with a light, gold-dust dusting of glittery, butterscotch-colored hair. Shirt, wrists, hands. I saw them more clearly than I'd ever seen anything, and the sight of them moved me as I'd never been moved in my life.

This person, I said to myself, this one person, of course, of course, of course. The words became my breathing and my pulse, the whole world reverberated with them. "Of course." I didn't think the words "I love you," so obvious were they, so *given*, thinking them would have been sheer superfluity.

But I did love him. Teo. I was in love with him. I would always be in love with him. Of course, I was. Of course, I am. Of course.

So, you see that I didn't fall in love with Teo Sandoval. Falling is a process and what happened to me wasn't process. It wasn't sequential or gradual. It wasn't falling.

A sea change. Transubstantiation. One minute, I was a woman not in love with Teo, and the next minute, I was a woman in love with him. Bones, blood, skin, every cell changed over into something new.

"Teo?" I said, awestruck.

"Yeah. Teo." He smiled, thinking I was only half-awake. "Remember me?"

Remember him?

I had just buried my lover; I was on my way to another funeral; a child, possibly motherless, possibly kidnapped, rode in the backseat; and I was in love with my sister's husband. Trust me, no one plans for her life to become the plot of a Bette Davis movie. No one wants that, and all of it would come crashing down on me. Soon. But just then, in that car, for the duration of the ride, I was allowed to forget everything *but* Teo. Call it denial, if you want. I call it grace.

Teo. His eyes. His mouth. His shoulders inside his shirt. I'd never wanted to touch someone so much, and at the same time, I didn't need to touch him at all. In love, I grew large, boundless. I was not contained between my hat and boots. I rose up. I embraced Teo. I surrounded him.

Clare slept in the backseat. Out the window, mountains emerged, subtle and ocean-colored. I sat in one seat. Teo sat in the other. And I held him all the way home.

22

Clare

"I hope when I said it was quiet around here, you didn't think I meant literally," said Cornelia wryly, and Clare laughed because they weren't even in the house yet, had just gotten out of Teo's car, and were standing on the wide, circular drive, and already Clare could hear the noise: music and shouting and someone singing unbeautifully but with great enthusiasm, *"Let it snow, let it snow, let it snow."*

"I wonder if he knows it's not snowing," said Clare.

"What he doesn't know could fill the Grand Canyon," said Cornelia. She pointed at a dark blue, old, beat-up Jeep Cherokee with a University of Vermont sticker in the back window and said, "Cam."

"And Toby," she said, pointing to a dark green, slightly younger, slightly less beat-up Jeep Cherokee with a CU Boulder sticker in the back window and another one that said VT inside a green oval.

Clare's gaze took in the cars and then the yard with its big trees wrapped up in switched-off Christmas lights and then the house itself—redbrick with white trim, black shutters, and a black door with a brass knocker shaped like a pineapple. On either side of the door hung a wreath studded with pinecones and red berries. The house was not nearly as capacious or as castle-like as Clare's own house, which had an actual turret with a pointed roof, but Clare liked its broad shoulders and the way it rose solidly up out of the ground as though it had never not been there. And she liked that its yard spread out around it like a skirt but that it wasn't so wide that you couldn't see the houses on either side of it. A regular house on a regular street, she thought. A neighborhood.

"Onward?" asked Cornelia, tugging a piece of Clare's hair.

"Onward," said Clare, a little nervously, then turned to Teo, who was getting bags out of his trunk. "Can you come too?"

"Are you kidding?" said Cornelia, smiling at Teo, "If he left without saying Happy New Year, he'd be boiled in oil."

"Yuck." Clare grimaced.

"I would," agreed Teo. "Boiled twice. Once here and again at my parents' house. If my mom asks how the Browns are and I don't know . . ."

"Better come with us, then," said Clare, "Boiled twice is bad."

Cornelia smiled at Clare reassuringly, "Don't worry, honey. The natives are friendly. Loud but friendly. And only some of them are loud." With that, she took Clare's hand and, instead of going to the front door, led Clare, with Teo following, down a curving brick path to another door on the side of the house.

They stepped into a mudroom with a stone floor, sky blue walls and ceiling, pell-mell rows of boots and shoes of all different sizes, and milk crates filled with a tumbled stew of mittens, gloves, hats and bright tangles of scarves. Jackets and coats hung from brass hooks on the wall. Teo helped Clare off with her cardinal-red wool jacket, and Clare hung it up, feeling glad to see it add itself to the riot of color.

She felt a pang as she remembered her mother's mink, still on Cornelia's coatrack where she'd left it. But then she relaxed. That was OK too. The mink meant she'd be going back. Her mother would find the note they'd taped to Cornelia's door, and she would call, and Clare and Cornelia would go back, and her mother would come get her at Cornelia's apartment, and her mother would wear the coat home. There in the festive clutter of that little room, Clare had no trouble believing this, accepting it even as a sure thing, like a promise from a true friend who would never lie.

Almost as soon as they'd stepped from the mudroom into the kitchen, before the smell of baking and the sound of Christmas music had fully registered on Clare's senses, a tall, rangy boy in a red ski sweater bounded in, shouted, "Hey!" scooped Cornelia up and, cradling her baby-fashion, galloped around the kitchen.

"Mom, Dad, Tobe! They're here!" the boy—Cam, Clare guessed—bellowed.

Another boy, shorter, with curly hair, appeared. The first boy tossed Cornelia into the arms of the other boy, who spun around in time to the music.

"Erggh!" shouted Cornelia. "You are such *puppies!*"

Toby stopped spinning and bounced Cornelia in his arms as though testing her weight.

"Man, you're fat. No offense or anything, but you are one fat individual, Cornelia." He put her down and turned to Teo. "What do you think, Dr. Sandoval, am I right or am I right?"

"Too many cheesesteaks." Teo grinned. He put out his hand, and Toby shook it first, then Cam.

"Still ugly as ever, I see," said Cam to Teo. Then, to Clare's surprise, he stage-whispered in her ear, "*Uglier* than ever, but don't tell him I said that."

Before she could answer, Cam seemed to remember something. To Cornelia he said, "Sucks about Mrs. Goldberg. You doing OK?"

"Sucks, indeed," said Cornelia dryly, then she softened. "I'm doing pretty OK, Cammy."

"Fat, though," added Toby. "Fat as a blue-ribbon hog."

He looked at Cam, who gave him a high five.

"That's a relief," said Cornelia, "We'd been here two whole minutes without a single high five. I thought you two might be sick. Spinal meningitis, maybe."

She put her arm through Clare's. "These are my hooligan brothers for whom the frat-boy flame burns eternal. Hooligan brothers," she said, "this is Clare."

As they were shaking hands with her, two more people entered the room: a man with wire-rimmed glasses, cropped gray hair, and a sweater vest (like a professor in a movie, thought Clare) and a pretty woman with blue eyes—cat eyes, like Cornelia's.

The woman went straight to Cornelia and folded her into her arms. She hugged and Cornelia hugged back. Finally the woman let go. She held Cornelia at arm's length and stared hard at her face. "Let me look at you, baby," she said. As Clare watched, Cornelia stood, as docile as Clare had ever seen her, and let herself be looked at. Then Cornelia smiled a sweet, sweet smile. "Hi, Mom," she said softly.

The man, Cornelia's father, ruffled Cornelia's cropped, unruffleable hair, then looked over her sleek head at Teo. "Still ugly as ever, I see, Teo," he said cheerily.

Clare stood there in the middle of Cornelia's family, and something happened to her, something tremendous.

She felt like she was floating on a deep cushion of cinnamon-scented air. She felt as though she were the one who'd been scooped up, cradled, and tossed around. Inside her chest, she felt her heart beat: blossoming and shutting, blossoming and shutting, blossoming. Before either of Cornelia's parents had said a word to her, before Cornelia's mother had touched her cheek and said, "Clare, of course." Before she'd been sat down to a feast of turkey, stuffing, and cranberry sauce sandwiches and cinnamon buns rich with yeast and butter—the best food she'd ever had. Before she'd thrown a football with Cam and Toby, the air stinging in her lungs, before she'd lit candles for dinner. Before she'd taken an evening walk in the starlit, Christmas-light-lit night with Cornelia, who had pointed out the sledding hill and Teo's house, the spot where she'd first been kissed, her favorite climbing tree, and had stood before Mrs. Goldberg's house with tears on her face. Before Clare had beaten Cornelia's dad at checkers, before she'd slept in the attic bedroom under the fragrant weight of flannel sheets and hand-pieced quilts with stars beaming outside the window. Before she'd written the word "home" in her notebook.

Before any of this, as she stood in the kitchen and pressed one hand to her chest, before and even more so afterward, Clare knew: She was in love.

23

Cornelia

It was the look on Clare's face that decided it for me, that set the whole plan piecing itself together in my head like a jigsaw puzzle—a child's jigsaw puzzle, really, because the pieces were large and simple, although the final picture they made took my breath away.

Rapt. When Clare stood in my family's kitchen that first day, Clare was rapt, rapturous, enraptured. Clare was a flesh-and-blood girl, and her story was no fairy tale, but she got bewitched all the same—bewildered, too, probably—and in about two blinks of her brown eyes. But if those eyes were telling the truth, and they always did, she wasn't bothered a bit.

It has a certain allure, my family home, I can't deny that. (In recent months, for example, it had lured Cam and Toby right back into it "temporarily," although they had no discernible plans to leave.) A scrubbed, oak-y, apples-in-a-blue-porcelain-bowl variety of allure that is no less alluring than any other variety. More alluring, if you were Clare at that particular moment in her life. At that particular moment in her life, what reflected off the copper pans hanging from their rack and the clean, tile counters and the faces of my family was hearth light, home light, the very light of comfort and joy, and Clare fell before it, dazzled.

I'd expected her reaction. I wanted it. It's why we came. All the same, as I watched Clare enter the merry, laughing, genuinely good-hearted tumble of humanity that is my family fold, I wanted to tell her, "Love it, honey, but don't love it too much."

I know how that sounds, but I'm not referring to the individual people, who are certainly lovable and much beloved. Beloved by me, in fact, much. As I live, I love them. Believe that. It's the package, really, that I'm talking about. The allegorical Happy Family—robustly happy, as polished and fully realized as a pearl. Our family is as happy as Martin was debonair: unassailably, impenetrably, consummately. We are a pretty picture hung on the gleaming nail of my mother, who is the most consummate one of all, and carved into our pretty frame are the words: DON'T ROCK THE BOAT.

But sometimes, a boat needs to rock; a boat needs to head straight for the heart of a storm and come out on the other side, weather-beaten but with flags flying. Pictures. Boats. Do I mix my metaphors? Very well, then, I mix my metaphors. Sometimes, when you're in a tight spot, only a mixed metaphor will do.

To put it another way, in my family I have comrades—hearty and loyal—when what I need are intimates, and I've never figured out how to get us all to make the switch. I've never found a way in.

But sometimes souls need still waters, and just now, Clare had a soul like that. Clare, my Clare, she needed an unrockable boat. She deserved one.

But back to my plan. If it began its forming, as I said, after I took one glance at Clare's bewitched and shining face, then the last piece of it clicked into place the next day, at Mrs. Goldberg's funeral. (If you feel my story is heavy with funerals, downright cluttered with them, trust me when I say that this is the last one you'll get.)

I sat between my father and Toby in the black dress that was making its second appearance in the space of a week and which I planned to rip from my body and burn to cinders the first chance I got, and I listened to person after person tell stories about Mrs. Goldberg's life.

I even told one myself. For an old lady who wasn't the least bit sweet, not "sweet old lady" sweet, and who neither was the least bit adorably crusty, who wasn't an old lady in any of the easy ways people expect and like, Suzette Goldberg was universally loved. Loved for her magnificence and beneficence and brains and humanity, as all of us should live so long to be loved.

I spoke, I listened, and my heart broke, which is to say that it didn't break at all but became suddenly aware of its own wholeness in such a way that it hurt like hell. Mrs. Goldberg loved me; she'd singled me out. Quite suddenly, I understood that such a woman, in leaving me a house and a houseful of treasures, meant to leave me more. A chance. More than a chance. A challenge. She'd thrown down a gauntlet disguised as a pair of opera gloves. There, Cornelia! What will you do next?

Fight for Clare is what I'd do. Fight like a wolverine to keep her. Become a whirlwind of teeth and claws. Draw blood. Hire a lawyer, go to court, ten courts, if I had to. Fight and win.

Clare would help me. I remembered her that first day in Martin's apartment, how she'd looked at her father and darted him three true, piercing words, what I know now to be an accusation—no, more than accusation. A verdict, guilty: "She. Was. Sick." I remembered the cold burn in her eyes. The girl had steel. Besides, Clare was no waif blown by fortune's breezes, but a heroine, the queen of happy endings, the girl in the novel who ends up living with someone who adores her. Anyone could see that.

And I had the house, Mrs. Goldberg's gift. I'd hold it up for everyone to see. A home. The word, with all its golden freight of connotation, was there, unmistakable, in the pitch of the roof, the perfume of the lilacs, the wavy glass windows, and the gently sloping lawn. *Enter,* the house breathed from every brick. *Enter and be home.*

And I had the family—mine. Irreproachable and glad to help raise their daughter's adopted child. My Happy Family's happiness made me crazy, but don't think I wouldn't use it. I'd trot them out, one by one, Toby and Cam, red-cheeked and resplendent in lacrosse gear, my sweater-vested father, a healer by trade, and my mother. I'd stick her in a goddamn gingham apron, if a gingham apron were required.

Because that was part of the plan. Coming home. Or leaving home and coming here, to live, if not in the bosom of my family, then just down the road from it. Here, where Clare would run over tended lawns, eat homemade pie, feel safe and settled in her bones, peaceful in her heart, and where her face would shine all the livelong day.

Easy, from your vantage point, to see what the whole plan rested on: the permanent disappearance of a woman Clare loved, a woman whose permanent disappearance I'd never wish for, never ever. As easy a fact for you to see as it was, somehow, for me to put aside, God and everyone else forgive me. God and everyone else, and you. You forgive me too.

Just before the graveside service (the part of a funeral out of which I usually bow, but this was Mrs. Goldberg; I'd see the thing through to the end), as I stood in the remarkably mild December air, a hand rested on my shoulder, rested and then sent a streak of heat down the entire left side of my body. My eyes traveled from the hand—so sublime, the human hand, such an intricate construction—up the dark brown coat sleeve to the face, the face among faces, the only face. His chin, his teeth in his mouth, the incomparable curve of his cheekbone. My Teo.

Not mine. Not mine. Not mine. Ollie's. Ollie's husband, Teo. The single hour in the car with Teo, the hour in which I'd loved him with a joy that was endless had ended. He was Ollie's again. Ollie's husband, Teo. Never forget.

Now, Voyager, Splendor in the Grass, Dr. Zhivago, Roman Holiday, even *Casablanca*—of course, *Casablanca.* All those films in which the woman doesn't get her man, those films of yearning unsatisfied, hearts unappeased. You like them; I've liked them too. But I'll tell you what:

try belonging body and soul to a man who will never belong to you; see how well you like those films then. "Don't ask for the moon—we have the stars!" Sure, Bette, but as I stood there in that cemetery quivering under Teo's touch, my entire being was biting out the words, "Pardon my saying so, but fuck the fucking stars!"

If I sounded bitter, that's because I was. Bitter and walking around in pain like a woman on fire.

But consider the alternative: *In This Life*, also starring Bette. Bette as a woman named, for utterly unexplained and inscrutable reasons, Stanley, who steals her sister's husband and sends herself and nearly everyone she knows spiraling into desolation and despair, ruin and wrack, the deepest pit in hell. You don't have to be a film scholar to interpret that message: If you steal your sister's husband, expect a body count.

Not that I could steal him, if I tried. No one could. Even if Teo were unhappy with Ollie, he had too much integrity to run off with her sister or anyone else. And maybe he wasn't unhappy at all. I tried to hope he was happy, for his sake, deliriously, on-cloud-nine happy with Ollie, but I couldn't quite manage it, not yet.

"*Are* you OK?" Teo asked me, and the question could have set me howling with unhinged, ironic laughter. Could have, but didn't. After all, he was still Teo, and I didn't just love him in the new searing, soaring way, but in the old familiar way too. I squeezed his hand.

"OK-OK," I said, "Not great-OK. But I'll live."

And I would.

What do you do when you're in love with the last man in the world you can have?

You plan a life, a real life, without him.

24

Clare

Clare had spent the morning baking with Cornelia's mother and as she stood with Cornelia on the front porch of Mrs. Goldberg's house, she could still smell the scent of gingersnaps in her own hair, and for a moment it seemed as though the aroma came not from her but from the house itself, from the bricks and pillars and roof. A fairy-tale house, but with nothing wicked inside; Clare was sure of that. Still, as Cornelia turned the key and Clare heard the bolt slide back, Clare held her breath. And she kept her eyes fixed on Cornelia's back, on the place between Cornelia's shoulder blades, as the two of them crossed the threshold.

Then Clare looked around and gasped. There was magic inside, but not the kind she'd expected. No sheets over the furniture, turning chairs into lonely ghosts; no velvet, dusty, deep-purple hush like the petals of an African violet. Instead, the magic of a house not haunted, but alive, waiting. Light sluiced in through the windows and spread shine over the floors and tables. A living room, Clare thought, and then: A *living* room. Nothing dead here. Nothing forgotten. Even the sofa seemed to open its arms to her, and without thinking, she walked over to it and sat down.

"Oh," she heard Cornelia say, and then again. "Oh," and Cornelia took two steps into the room and sank slowly to her knees like a person in a church. Clare kept quiet, allowing Cornelia to be alone with the house. After a few seconds, Cornelia settled down cross-legged and took off her coat.

"Hello, house," she said happily.

"It's alive," said Clare.

"It is."

The two of them gazed around the room at the pale gold wallpaper and at the two silver candelabra on the mantel and at the marble fireplace, and Clare wondered if Cornelia was expecting, as she was expecting, flames to blossom on the wicks and a fire to appear, orange and snapping and singing, in the grate.

Then Clare noticed another scent, not gingersnaps, but something fragile and cool. She sat up and looked closely at the bowl of white flowers on the table in front of her. She leaned in and inhaled, then touched a finger, gingerly, to one creamy petal. She pulled her hand back and stared at Cornelia.

"Real," she whispered. "They're alive too."

Cornelia came over and touched the flowers, and for a few seconds, Clare knew they both believed in miracles.

Then Cornelia said in a soft, sad voice, "Gardenias. Of course, gardenias," and then, "Marielle."

"Marielle?"

Cornelia wiped her eyes and smiled at Clare. "She's cleaned Mrs. Goldberg's house for as long as I can remember. My mom said Ruth and Bern have had her coming in every few weeks to dust and air the place out. She must have rushed back here from the funeral today."

"She left the flowers for us to find," said Clare.

"Maybe. I don't know, though. I wouldn't be surprised if she left them every time she comes. I'd be surprised if she didn't. Mrs. Goldberg adored gardenias."

And somehow to Clare, this seemed no less magical than flowers that stayed alive for years, that one woman could so love another woman that she kept doing nice things for her even after she was gone. Like love was a habit you couldn't break.

"I'll show you everything. The whole place. The parlor with the seashells, the two-hundred-year-old kitchen table . . . soon," said Cornelia, turning to Clare with shining eyes. "But let's head straight for the attic. Right now. What do you think?"

"I think, yes," said Clare. "Right now."

And as she followed Cornelia up the attic stairs, she found herself not just walking, but placing her feet precisely and trailing her hand fluidly along the wooden rail, as though walking up the steps to the place Cornelia loved best were a dance, something to do in just the right way. And then with one clean motion, like they were blown in by wind, Clare and Cornelia were through the door and standing inside the sloped, honey-brown walls of Mrs. Goldberg's attic.

25

Cornelia

I showed Clare a picture of Mrs. Goldberg as a girl of eleven.

"My same age." Her voice was breathless, and I saw she felt what I felt in this room: enchantment. In the whole house, but in this room especially. Even when I began to tell the story and to tell it in the hushed, rhythmic storytelling voice Mrs. Goldberg always used, Clare didn't take her eyes off the photograph.

"Mrs. Goldberg's family was from New York, but she spent her eleventh summer at the home of her aunt and uncle, a farm not so far from here. Her cousin Sarah was also eleven, and the two of them were watching Sarah's brother Albert and some of his friends play baseball. One of the boys stood taller than the others and had serious blue eyes. Mrs. Goldberg wasn't yet in the habit of noticing boys, but she noticed him." I glanced at Clare.

"I notice boys, sometimes," Clare said, shyly. "Well, not boys my own *age*, but . . ." She broke off, smiling.

"Hmmmm," I said. "I wonder who you mean. Anyway, this boy wasn't her age either. He was seventeen."

"Oh!" exclaimed Clare, as though noticing a boy of seventeen were more surprising than, say, noticing a man of thirty-four.

"And while she was noticing him, he stood in the outfield, and her cousin Albert hit the ball right at him and, instead of catching it, the tall boy missed, and the ball whacked him on the side of the head."

"Oooooh." Clare flinched.

"And before she could stop herself, Mrs. Goldberg burst out laughing."

"That's awful."

"She thought so too. She was horrified, in fact. And she ran over to where he lay kind of rolling back and forth on the ground, and she knelt down, introduced herself, and apologized. The boy smiled a slow smile at her, put out his hand and said, 'I'm Gordon Goldberg. And I guess I did look funny going down like a shot duck.' 'More like a bowling pin,' said Mrs. Goldberg, and Gordon laughed and passed out."

"And they were in love."

"She was," I told Clare. "It took him about six more years, but then he was hook-line-and-sinkered. They were married for over three decades, until he died."

"She never married anyone else," said Clare with assurance. "There's only one true love for everyone, right?" A humdinger of a question. A doozy.

"I don't know. Maybe for some people, there can be more than one." I said this to Clare. What I didn't say: "Oh, let me, let me be right. If I'm not right, my goose is cooked."

Clare and I shared a comfortable silence for a while, looking at the pictures of someone else's family. Then I felt Clare's gaze and looked up.

"My mother married my father," she said, thoughtfully. "That's weird, isn't it? They must've been in love. And then my mother didn't marry anyone else. I mean, she hasn't, yet. But I don't think it's because my father was her true love, do you?"

"I don't know," I said honestly. I thought about the redhaired woman at his funeral. Just because I couldn't fall in love with Martin didn't mean no one else could.

Clare didn't say anything, but the silence we sat in now wasn't easy; it was the silence of something coming.

"I saw my mother." I couldn't read what was in her eyes. She seemed to be seeing something with them that wasn't in the room. "One night. After she was sick, I saw her. With a man. They were . . ." She stared at me, unable to finish. Fear. That's what was in her eyes. Fear and revulsion. I had to think fast, to undo what seeing what she'd seen had done to her. I couldn't have her growing up with those feelings about sex.

"I don't know your mother's reasons for having sex with that man. Sex. You know about that, right?"

"Yes," said Clare and I noted the note of exasperation in her voice, the what-a-dumb-question note, with relief.

"What they were doing, it wasn't wrong in and of itself. If it was part of your mother's being sick, then it might not have been the best thing, but it wasn't any more wrong than all those cookbooks she bought. Do you see what I mean?"

"I think so," said Clare, and after a pause, "I don't think she was in love with him. I mean, maybe she was, but I don't think so."

I took a breath. "People have different ideas about that, and you'll have to make up your own mind. You want to know what I think?"

"Yes."

"I think it's OK not to be in love. If you like the person and trust him and if you've decided all on your own that having sex with him is what you want to do, I think it's fine." For the record, I'd thought this for a very long time and did not speak out of my present condition of eternally unrequited love and possible future of never loving another man as long as I lived, although I'll say this: Loveless life or not, no way was I becoming a celibate. Come on.

"Have you ever been in love?" asked Clare, suddenly blindsiding me. I hoped she didn't notice my discomfort, but since I sat there frozen and blinking, with a hot flush creeping over my neck and face, she would have had to have been blind as a bat not to notice.

"Yeah, sure," I said, so casually I practically yawned the words. Then I shrugged one shoulder, completing my transformation into a caricature of a casual person.

"With who?"

"Oh, just—someone." *Oh, just someone?* Was it possible to be more lame? It was not. I sighed. "Someone who doesn't love me back."

"I bet you're wrong," said Clare instantly. "I bet he does."

"Thank you for that, Clare, but nope, nope, nope. For one thing, he's married to someone else." I scanned her face for an "aha!" look, but lots of people— maybe every lovable man on the planet, although I sincerely hoped not—were married to other people. She gazed back at me, innocent as a newly hatched bird. "And his feelings toward me are purely fraternal." I threw that in for veracity's sake, and I saw Clare's confused look, but no way was I explaining. I rushed on. "And, as if that weren't enough, I'm not his type."

"How could you not be someone's type?" asked Clare, with an honest disbelief I found adorable.

"No ambition." But this wasn't quite what I meant. "No divine purpose driving my life. I'm not passionate enough, maybe."

Clare laughed. Then she got serious. "Sorry. But that's funny, you not being passionate enough. You're passionate about *everything!* The Philadelphia Story and Teo's mom's pancakes and Mrs. Goldberg and all the stuff in this attic and pajamas and Walt Whitman." She laughed again.

I laughed too, even though I was so touched I could've cried.

"And me. Even me. You're passionate about me, too, right?" Oh, Clare. Even you?

"From the bottom of my heart, yes," I told her.

"What are you going to do with all this stuff?" asked Clare, gazing around.

"I've thought about that. I want Ruth and Bern, Mrs. Goldberg's kids, to have whatever they want. Everything, if that's what they want."

"I knew you'd say that," said Clare with satisfaction.

"But first, I'm going to go through and catalogue every object, even every photograph. Catalogue it and write down the story that goes with it, the one Mrs. Goldberg told me, because everything in here matters and has a story."

"So, when they're deciding what they want, they'll know how much each thing matters. It wouldn't be fair to just show them the object, right?"

"Right," I said, amazed at Clare's understanding. "And whatever they end up taking, the stories will go with them."

"Good idea," said Clare. She sat, thinking.

"Your apartment is just like this, isn't it, Cornelia? It really *belongs* to you. I thought that right away, as soon as I got there. How you chose everything, and all of it's important. You're exactly like Mrs. Goldberg." It was the nicest thing anyone had ever said to me.

From the big attic window, I could see the shiny leaves of the magnolia next to the house, bare now of the white rice bowls of blossom that would deck it in summer and, beyond that, I could see the magnificent, ancient white oak that dropped its fat acorns and mantle of shade in Mrs. Goldberg's yard. And beyond that, the other houses on the street with their chimneys and hedges and flowerbeds, dusk skirting their rooftops. Each house a receptacle of mystery and dailiness, each holding a family inside its walls. And in the distance, the rim of Blue Ridge, encircling us all.

"Cornelia?" said Clare.

"I was just thinking how Mrs. Goldberg gave all her stories to me," I said, tears blurring my eyes. "And how, if you want, I'll give all mine to you."

26

Clare

"*Are* your hands aching?" Ellie asked Clare. Cornelia's mother wanted Clare to call her Ellie, short for Eleanor.

Clare set down the sharp, scissor-shaped shears she'd been using, took off the gardening glove, and uncramped her fingers, spreading and closing them, finding satisfaction in the unfamiliar stiffness.

"Yes," she said. "But it's a good ache."

They were pruning the butterfly bushes in the backyard. It had taken a while for Clare to get comfortable with the pruning, to understand that she wasn't killing the plants. It seemed drastic—severe—cutting the stems back to just eight inches from the ground, and she winced at the forlorn sticks poking up out of their cold patch of dirt.

"I know it looks bad, but these shrubs only flower on new wood," explained Ellie. "We're doing the plants a favor. The butterflies, too. Wait until summer; you won't be able to tell where the blooms end and the butterflies start. And the hummingbirds. They'll be thanking us too."

Clare smiled into the bush she was working on; Cornelia's mother wanted her back in summer, didn't just want her, but expected her. Clare imagined the two of them sitting on the redwood bench in the yard, sipping iced tea and watching the whirring hummingbirds like tiny machines, the butterflies afloat around the bushes. Still, even after her brain knew she wasn't harming the shrubs, it took a while for her hands to believe. They'd hesitate, just seconds, before they cut each twig.

"You're doing a beautiful job," said Ellie. Clare smiled into the bush again.

"Have you ever read *The Secret Garden*?" ventured Clare.

"Oh, gosh, let me think. Sure I have, but it was ages ago. Did Ollie love that book or Cornelia?" Even when she was talking, Ellie didn't stop working. Clare admired the absolute certainty of her movements. Like Teo cutting the vegetables. She wondered if she'd ever be that good at something.

"I bet Cornelia did," said Clare. "There's this kid in the book, Dickon, who can tell right away if a plant is dead or not. I guess they all look dead, but he can find the new wood. When he finds a live one, he calls it 'wick.' He's sort of magic, I think."

"Some people are like that; they just have a sense. But I'll tell you what, Clare, I read a lot of books and magazine articles before I learned much of anything." She smiled at Clare, a rectangular smile like Cornelia's. "Killed a lot of plants, too."

"At home, we have a gardener, Mr. Field, which is a good name for a gardener, I think. He comes once a week, but I don't think I ever really paid attention to what he does." Clare wished she had. "I guess I just thought you put them in the ground, and they grow."

"That's true for some plants," said Ellie. She pointed to another type of bush. "That crepe myrtle pretty much takes care of itself. But if I don't prune my hydrangea just right"—she pointed to another bush, a big one—"it doesn't do a thing."

"We have hydrangea too," said Clare, excitedly. "They're my favorite, the way the flowers grow in whole bouquets. And I like the color. So deep blue, it's almost purple."

"Blues are my favorite," said Ellie. "Well, when you're back home, you'll have to get Mr. Field to let you help. My kids were never interested. Maybe it's part of the reason Ollie and Cornelia live in cities, so they don't have to take care of anything."

Ellie didn't sound disappointed or accusatory, just matter-of-fact, so it was really more to herself than to Ellie that Clare said, "That doesn't seem true about Cornelia."

She flushed. She didn't mean to contradict. "I'm sorry." Cornelia's mother smiled and waved her hand in a way that meant "You've got nothing to be sorry for."

"But even though Cornelia doesn't have a garden, she's always taking care of things, taking care of things *carefully*. Like everything in her apartment is old, and a lot of it is fragile—it looks fragile to me—and she's so gentle with it. She doesn't even use the dishwasher because she's afraid the cups and stuff will crack or the gold trim will get worn off the plates. And she dusts the surfaces of her little paintings with a feather-duster. And you can just tell by the way she holds things that she loves them." Clare knew she was talking her head off, but it felt nice to say good, true things about Cornelia out loud and to someone, instead of just writing them in her notebook.

For the first time since they'd started, Ellie stopped working. She rubbed her chin with the back of one gloved hand, thoughtfully, and looked at Clare. "You know what? You're right. I'd never thought about it quite like that. Cornelia and I don't usually love the same things, but what she loves, she takes care of."

"People, too," said Clare, effusively. "Like me. After my mother disappeared, my dad came and picked me up and brought me to her café. And I couldn't help it, I just burst out crying in the middle of the floor. Cornelia came over and just hugged me in this strong hug for so long."

"Your mother disappeared?" Ellie looked confused, but Clare didn't notice.

"And she didn't even know me," Clare went on. "She'd never seen me before. And I found out later that she didn't even know my dad had a daughter. But she started taking care of me, like it was just the normal thing to do. I bet not very many people would do that."

"You're probably right," said Ellie quietly. "Cornelia's always been a good girl. A good, generous girl. I'm glad you found your way to each other. Did you have a very bad time before that?"

Clare's breath stopped in her throat. Cornelia had told Ellie that Clare's mother was on a trip. Clare couldn't believe she'd forgotten that.

But when she turned to Ellie, her nervousness disappeared. And she began to explain, explain everything. Why Cornelia had lied and what the truth was. Once she started, it was simple. Breathe in, breathe out, trim the stems, open and shut the shears, and talk. When she'd finished, she glanced over at Ellie. The look on her face seemed somewhere between mad and worried; Clare hadn't expected such an expression.

"I'm sorry you had to experience all of that. Your mother leaving more every day and then really leaving you," she said in a hard voice.

"But she didn't mean to," Clare said urgently. "She was sick."

She watched the line of Ellie's mouth soften.

"Of course she was," she said kindly. "Of course she didn't mean to. She loves you." Clare felt the anxiety that had been rising in her chest subside.

"I knew someone who was sick like that," said Ellie briskly. "Not exactly like that. She was sick for a very long time—years—and never did anything to make herself well. Nothing. Except drink, which didn't work, naturally."

Clare didn't know what to say. Ellie took a glance at her, then dropped her shears and threw her gloves on the ground. She put a hand on each of Clare's shoulders.

"Oh, honey, what am I doing? I'm so sorry. Ancient, ancient history." She looked amazed. "I didn't think there was any anger left in there. I could just kick myself for spilling it all out in front of you."

"That's OK," said Clare, and it was. She smiled. "Cornelia calls me 'honey' too."

"You know what I think?" said Ellie cheerfully. "I think your mother is doing every *single* thing she can to get back to you. If I were you, I'd just stop worrying and enjoy yourself until she gets here."

Clare was enjoying herself, truly and without guilt, not so much because she felt as certain as Ellie that her mother was coming back, safe and sound. She had moments when she did feel certain, but more often, she put the whole question of whether and when her mother would come back aside. The truth was that she'd lived for a long time with fear like a demon hanging on to her doggedly and yelling in her ears, and living that way hadn't helped anything; it hadn't brought her mother home. She didn't want to feel sick and tired of life, and the worry had made her feel like that.

The night before the pruning, Clare had lain in bed floating just this side of sleep, and in a peaceful, hazy way, she had explored the idea of what would happen if her mother didn't come back. The answer came to her at once, drifted up like a blow-up raft in a blue swimming pool. I'll live with Cornelia and Teo, she thought. And even though she'd wake up the next morning, remember and understand that that didn't make any sense, it was the thought that had carried her, painlessly, past the demon, and into sleep.

Two days later, Clare sat at the computer table that stood at the far end of the attic bedroom, alone in the house, or as alone as anyone ever was in that house. In fact, Toby and Cam were in the yard playing a game the point of which was to keep a little sack filled with beans or sand or something from hitting the ground. From where she sat, Clare could see them out the window. But Dr. B (everyone called him Dr. B or just B, which amused Clare, as though Brown were too long to bother saying each time you spoke to him) was at his office, and Ellie was grocery shopping—"marketing," she called it.

Cornelia was back at Mrs. Goldberg's, where Clare had been too, until fifteen minutes ago. They'd been cataloguing, as they had been for the past couple of days, and Cornelia had been typing the objects' stories into her laptop. Clare loved the attic, so full and with stories floating in its sunny air like mist, and she loved the peace of being there with Cornelia, talking or just listening to Cornelia's quick fingers send out flurries of taps as she typed.

But today Clare had left early, saying she and Ellie were going together to Ellie's usual salon for haircuts.

"Uh-oh," said Cornelia. "Don't let that Ellie talk you into anything drastic. No Mohawks or purple streaks, you hear?"

But Clare knew Ellie wouldn't be home yet, that their appointments weren't for another hour. She sat bolt upright at the computer, staring tensely at the screen. The room was dim at that time of day, and she hadn't turned on any lights. In the semi-dark, the computer glowed with a light that seemed somehow dangerous to Clare, like radiation, even though she knew this was silly.

"Just do it," she hissed to herself. "Do it!"

And she did it. When she was finished, she took a black pen and, with practiced care, forged her mother's signature. Then she printed out an address on the envelope she'd taken from a box in the roll-top desk downstairs, placed a stamp on the envelope, folded the sheet she'd signed in thirds, and slid it in. As she held the envelope, ready to lick it shut, she stopped. She moved again to lick it shut, and stopped again. Then she made a huffing sound, got up, and stuck the envelope underneath the pillow of her made bed.

A few hours later she saw Cornelia walking across the lawn, her laptop swinging in its red case, and Clare ran to meet her, the envelope in her hand.

"Well, look at you!" said Cornelia with pleasure. "Turn around."

Clare's chestnut hair hung a couple inches above her shoulders. The back was cut a little higher than the front so that two pointed wings of hair swung forward.

"It's marvelous! Perfect!" sang out Cornelia.

"Watch this," said Clare happily, and she shook her head hard from side to side. When she stopped, the hair settled right back into its shining bob.

"I adore it," said Cornelia. "So Vidal Sassoon."

Clare almost asked what that meant, Vidal Sassoon, but she didn't want to get sidetracked. She had business to take care of, and if she didn't take care of it now, she was afraid she never would.

She handed Cornelia the envelope.

"I almost mailed it without showing you," she said somberly. "But then I couldn't. Like when you called me in to talk to you and Teo that time. We should make decisions together."

Cornelia raised her eyebrows, then took the letter out and read it.

"Oh, Clare," she said.

"We only have two days left," said Clare.

"And you're not ready to go." Cornelia sighed. She touched Clare's hair, making it swing.

"People come back late from vacation all the time. Really. And all they're doing is skiing or some dumb thing like that."

"Don't let Cam and Toby hear you say that," said Cornelia with a tired smile. "Skiing is their religion. They think if you're a good boy, when you die, you go to Courchevel."

"What's that?" asked Clare.

"Some dumb ski resort in Switzerland."

"Are we talking about skiing now?" asked Clare hopefully.

"No, I guess we aren't," said Cornelia. "To tell you the truth, I don't feel ready to leave, either. Which is what makes this so hard." When she said "this," she gave the letter a shake.

"What do you mean?"

"I mean I have to put what I want aside and figure out what's really right. For you."

"I can't," said Clare, her voice trembling. "I can't go back yet. I just can't. I can't even imagine it."

"Clare, this letter only buys you a week," said Cornelia. Her eyes were full of concern.

"I know," said Clare quickly. "I know, and I promise we'll go back then. I'll be ready."

Cornelia stared hard at the letter and then at the ground. Clare waited.

"If you need it that much, Clare, honey, all right. One more week."

Clare hugged her and kissed her on the cheek. Wow, she thought, someday soon, I'll be taller than Cornelia.

"There's something else," said Clare suddenly. She wanted to be completely honest with Cornelia. It was important.

"What's that?"

"The other day, when we were pruning, I slipped. I told your mom my mom was sick, about how she left. Everything."

"You're kidding me." Cornelia didn't sound mad, just shocked.

"You're not mad?"

"Oh, honey, no. It was your secret to tell. I just can't believe my mother's kept quiet about it for two days. I would've sworn she'd have called in the National Guard on the spot to find your mother. How interesting." She seemed completely mystified. Then she said, "Well, I won't bring it up, unless she does."

"We'll mail this, then?" said Clare, touching the letter with one finger.

"There's a box at the end of the street. Let's go together right this minute," said Cornelia.

They started walking, but then Cornelia stopped. As she paused, everything seemed to pause, lightly, like an evening on tiptoe, the trees still and listening.

"You're such a brave girl, Clare, do you know that? I love that about you." She dropped her eyes for a second, looking down at Clare's hand; she took the hand and squeezed it. When she looked back at Clare's face, her expression was happy and sad, both, an in-between, twilight expression for an in-between half-lit hour. "I love *you*," she said. "You should know that."

At that moment, Clare didn't feel at all like a girl rattling around inside a shaken-up life; under the slate-blue sky and its scattered early stars, what she felt was lucky and so glad to be herself. The words were right there, where they'd been waiting. "I love you, too," she said.

27

Cornelia

Sometimes a house can sit there for years, in desperate need of having its roof blown off, and then out of nowhere, there's a little *whoosh,* and the dang thing is gone, blown off and spinning away, first a black speck, then the blue sky closing over it as though it were never there. And the people inside, what do they do when it's gone? Probably, it varies from house to house, but when the house was the Browns' and the *whoosh* was a Christmas card no bigger than my hand, they did this:

"Jesus Christ," wailed my father, pacing the kitchen, nearly in tears, and this from a man for whom "Jesus Christ" is the limit; one man's "Jesus Christ" is another man's "Jesus Mother*fuck*ittohell Christ," and my father is that first man. "Jesus Christ! This'll kill Rudy. I'll tell you that. It'll kill him."

"It's totally her fault," fumed Toby, holding a soccer ball and punching it. "She thinks she can just *change* her mind. Like, 'OK, I changed my mind. *See* ya.' "

Cam shoved a cookie the size of a dessert plate into his mouth and sputtered, crumb-ily, "She's a woman! What'd you expect! Women are so fucking—whimsical." And this impressed me, I have to say, impressed me twice, once because of the both-parents-present expletive and again because of the word "whimsical," which I'd have sworn the boy didn't know. That's how far he's been pushed, I thought, driven to S.A.T. prep course vocabulary from some ten years back. Hats off to you, Mr. Kaplan.

Clare sat at the table, also snacking, but looking less like a nice girl chewing a cookie and more like the proverbial cat who's sinking her eye-teeth into the proverbial canary. All smug satisfaction. I think I even saw her lick her chops, afterward.

I'd been working in Mrs. Goldberg's attic for hours and, all unsuspectingly, had walked in on a world gone mad. I turned to the one person in the room who appeared, more or less, to be functioning normally. The cords in her neck were stretched a bit tightly, but other than that, she looked as calm and collected as ever.

"Mom, what in God's name is going on?" I asked, and she had the presence of mind to give me a reproving stare, as though "God's name" didn't pale to near-invisibility next to "fucking" and "Jesus Christ." Still, I took it as a good sign.

She handed me a card in an envelope.

"There's a way to do a thing, if it needs to be done," she said tersely. "And this was not the way."

I looked the envelope over, then took out the card, a Christmas card, belated by nearly three weeks. A card from my sister, Ollie. The lateness was no surprise. The surprise was that she'd sent a card at all. And, in all fairness, this particular little card had an excuse for being late. It came from the Galapagos Islands.

"The Westermarck effect," said Teo drearily.

As soon as I'd been able to breathe normally, I'd called him.

The Westermarck effect was how Ollie had explained her leaving, explained in person to Teo, which was decent of her because leaving a note was much more her style, as evidenced by the Christmas card. She'd given him only twenty-four hours' notice, though, before hopping on a plane, which seemed somewhat less decent to me. But who am I to judge?

I thought for a moment.

"Oh, right, that thing where a butterfly flaps its wings in one country and sets off a tornado halfway around the world," I said.

"That would be the butterfly effect," Teo said, and the smile I heard in his voice came as a vast relief, although it was somewhat disappointing to shelve my image of a heedless lepidopteran in Beijing—a blue swallowtail is what I'd been picturing, for no particular reason—giving a flutter and creating in Brooklyn a mighty breeze that blew Ollie clean out the door of her apartment and into the well-muscled arms of Edmund Battle. I thought about the uproar and discombobulation I'd just left downstairs. Chaos theory, indeed.

"The Westermarck effect is some built-in mechanism we all have to keep us from marrying our own siblings."

"Oh. But you and Ollie aren't siblings . . . Are you?" Suddenly, anything seemed possible.

"No, Cornelia, we're not." Teo's voice was dry as dust. "But according to the theory, because most males and females who grow up together are siblings, all males and females who spend their childhoods together are programmed not to be sexually attracted to each other. It's instinct."

No, it most certainly is not, I was on the verge of yelling. Dr. Westermarck and the scientific method be damned! I imagined marching into a lab somewhere, Teo in tow, and offering myself up as living disproof of this cockamamie theory. "Look!" I'd shout, victoriously, "I can't keep my hands off him!" And just thinking about my hands on him turned my face hot and my breath shallow because, I'm not sure if I mentioned it before, but in addition to being in love with Teo, I was also practically radioactive with desire for him, in danger of spontaneously combusting, of sending up my own miniature mushroom cloud at the mere sound of his voice.

"Do you believe that?" I asked, seriously. There was a long pause on the other end. I almost jumped headfirst into the pause with an inchoate tumble of verbiage maligning Westermarck, the know-nothing bastard, the dastardly fraud, and his bullshit effect, but I restrained myself.

"What I believe is that I was a goddamn idiot to marry a woman I wasn't in love with." Teo's voice was so flat, so deflated, that I couldn't even feel a flicker of joy at the news he'd just given me. Besides, if he had any sense, and he had plenty, barking up the Brown family tree again was about the last thing Teo Sandoval would ever do. Westermarck effect or not, why would anyone chance it?

As we sat there in our own separate unhappinesses not saying anything, I began to consider what I hadn't so far considered: that if Ollie had left weeks and weeks ago, then Teo, the very soul of honesty, had, for weeks and weeks, been living a lie, living some of it right alongside me, alongside me and Clare both. Cooking in my apartment and out sitting in the Adirondack chairs in Clare's yard and driving in his car, the lie had been with us the whole time, like an extra person, a stranger we couldn't see. The thought made me cringe, but I decided to save the "Why didn't you tell me?" This conversation would be about Teo's hurt, not mine.

"Cornelia, I meant to tell you," said Teo finally. "I *came* there to tell you, that day in the café."

"It's fine," I said. "Don't worry about explaining."

"But when I got to you, so much was happening. Clare and Martin. And then the accident. How could I bother you with my trivial, asinine . . . shit?" If Teo, who, under normal circumstances, was the last person to undermine the importance of anything remotely important, was calling the dissolution of his marriage "shit," he was in pretty bad shape.

"Oh, Teo." I sighed.

"But that's just an excuse, I think. You would have made room for my stupid mess. I know that about you. You would've listened."

"I would've. I'd listen now, too." Now and for the rest of my life, to whatever you have to say. Just try me.

"I know. Forget what I said about not wanting to bother you. That sounds—I don't know—noble. And I wasn't noble." He almost spat the word "noble." Teo sounded so disgusted with himself, I could hardly bear to hear it. "I was glad to plunge myself into other people's heartache, to tell you the truth. Remember when you said it was easy for me to come in and be a hero to Clare?"

"Teo," I said, alarmed. "You know I didn't mean that."

"You didn't, but you were right. It was easy to come in and feel like I could help, like I could fix something. I was so sick of myself and of Ollie. All of it. Nothing there I could fix"—he made a bitter sound—"and nothing worth fixing."

"What happens now?" It would have been kinder, I know, to allow him to direct the course of the conversation, but I couldn't help myself.

"Divorce," said Teo bleakly. "Which is no picnic in New York. No such thing as nobody's fault in New York. Either I have to say terrible things about Ollie or she has to say terrible things about me, and then it could be over fast. That's what Ollie wants. Or . . ." Teo seemed to just give out, too tired to go on, but I would not be deterred.

"Or?"

"Or we separate, live apart a year and, at the end of the year, our separation quietly becomes a divorce."

"You want to do that, don't you?" Of course he did. Goddamn, goddamn integrity. Jeez, Teo.

"I hate the idea of our blaming each other. On record. It was a mistake we made together."

"How did it happen? Can I ask that? How did you and Ollie end up together?" Because if you're going to act like a hard-nosed investigative reporter, the kind people call intrepid when what they really mean is detestable, you may as well go all the way.

"Right after Edmund left, Ollie and I ran into each other in Midtown. We've known each other forever, you know? We like each other. We never pretended to be in love. Ollie was through with true love; she thought she was, anyway."

"And what about you? Were you through with true love?" God, I was relentless. But I needed to know.

"No, not exactly. But I felt pretty sure that the right woman—the real thing, I guess—wasn't going to . . . happen. And I was disgusted with the person 'casual relationships' were turning me into." His quotation marks around that phrase just sizzled with bitterness; I could hear them. I'd felt it too, that dating, having some fun, playing the field were euphemisms for as Machiavellian a game as was ever invented. In such a game, no one's soul was safe. Then he added, vehemently, "And I was *sick* of sick people."

He paused, like a child who'd just said something awful and was waiting for someone to start yelling. I didn't yell. When he spoke next, his voice was calmer.

"Ollie said that people marry for love all the time, and it goes up in smoke. We thought, why not take a chance; maybe the love would come later. Ollie cited all these cases of countries with arranged marriages that worked out fine."

I had to smile at the word "cited." Ollie was always and forever Ollie.

"You went into it with the spirit of adventure," I said encouragingly. And I could imagine how it happened, how they got caught up in that sense of adventure. Let's go for it! Birds do it, bees do it, even educated fleas do it. I could see wanting to be part of life in all its coupling and ongoingness; lately, in fact, I'd become something of an expert on that kind of wanting.

"I'll sure as hell never do that again," he bit out. "We said that, that it was an adventure. But really, we were just reckless. Thorough, though. We managed to hurt every single person who cares about us. I don't think we left anyone out." He paused, then he said with icy resolution in his voice, "My days of taking chances are over."

My tattered heart sank into my shoes then, for if ever, oh, ever a risk there was, Cornelia Brown was one because. Because, because, because, because, because.

Ollie's sister. Teo's childhood pal. If he was through taking chances, there was no chance for me.

As soon as we hung up, I remembered something. Seconds later, I called him again.

"Cornelia," he said as soon as he picked up, even though I knew there was no little screen on his phone telling him who was calling. We both hated those screens. He thought they violated people's privacy. What if a person started to call, then had a change of heart? I just disdained the screens as yet another means of sucking the mystery from life.

"Teo," I began and was instantly incredibly self-conscious. "I just . . . well, I wondered . . . I—" I groaned, inwardly, and started over. "You said you came to Philadelphia to tell me about you and Ollie. Why? Why me and no one else?" You can probably see why I had to ask this, why I had no choice but to ask it. What would you have done?

"Because you're my . . ." Oh, God, what? My heart lodged itself in the very back of my throat and squatted there, pounding. "My pair of clear eyes."

Oh.

I considered. "Pair of clear eyes" is not the same as "heart's desire," but it is something.

"You're like an MRI, you know? I was sort of—bogged down in it all. I wanted you to help me understand it, to tell me how bad or not bad the damage was."

"Oh," I said. "OK."

He laughed. "I'll be honest, I wanted you to take one look and tell me it wasn't that bad."

I took a breath. Lost cause or not, I'd make my pitch.

"You want to know what I see, now?"

"We're on the phone, Cornelia."

"I know. I'm that good. I can see you when you're not here." Around every corner and every time I close my eyes, Teo.

"And what do you see now?"

"Bruising. Pretty deep, but I've seen worse. And you want to know what else?"

"What else?"

"I see a man who has a little chance-taking left in him. A man who should keep the faith."

There was a pause.

"Good night, Cornelia," said Teo in his voice.

Just that. Nothing more.

"Good night."

Good night, sweet Teo, good night, good night. Good-bye.

It never rains, but it pours. A solid, serviceable idiom if ever there was one, and it was about to pour like gangbusters directly into the Browns' newly roofless house, leaving all of us drenched.

That evening, my mother took Clare over to the Sandovals' house. A diplomatic mission, likely, although I didn't think it would be necessary. Civilized people don't blame parents for their daughter's behavior, no matter how feckless or adulterous, and the Sandovals were nothing if not civilized. And Teo had no doubt called them posthaste to deliver the news that, New York law notwithstanding, his and Ollie's split was a clear case of no-fault, which, when you think about it, actually means both of their faults, thus getting Ollie at least partway off the hook. Plus, and more important than all the rest, Ingrid and Rudy loved Ellie and B, and Ellie and B loved them right back.

My mother came home after about an hour, but Clare stayed for dinner.

"Clare started talking about Swedish pancakes in the kind of voice people use to talk about Mount Everest or the moon, and before she'd finished, Ingrid was measuring out the flour," said my mother. Then she came over to where I was sitting and first touched the cuff of my sweater, then circled my wrist with her fingers. She smiled at me. "She's a nice girl, baby. And she worships the ground you walk on."

"It's mutual," I said.

"Yes, I can tell," said my mother. She let go of my wrist, smiled again, and then left to go perform some task or other, to work out her fury and worry about Ollie and Teo by beating rugs or changing sheets or scrubbing nonexistent mildew from the bathroom tile. If it weren't so well on its way to being dark outside, I knew she'd be in her garden, torturing some plant into good behavior, into a future of breathtaking blooms.

I'm not much of a sitter and thinker either. I don't hack away at poor, innocent shrubbery but, especially in times of stress, I think things out by talking, as you may have observed, and I would have done just that, had there been the proper listener anywhere nearby. Linny was who I wanted. I could have picked up the phone, but Linny's a person who conveys half of what she means through little twitches of her mouth, finger flutters, shrugs, and almost imperceptible widenings and narrowings of her keen, keen eyes. I wanted her in person or not at all and, besides, even I can do with short bouts of tranquil contemplation now and then. Although, in this instance, the tranquility was a bit forced, which I guess means it wasn't tranquility at all.

After my mother left, I sat and thought. Thought about Teo, how he felt as lost to me as ever or nearly as lost. *"They're writing songs of love, but not for me."* That kind of thing. But mostly, I thought about Clare, about the nuts and bolts of how she and I would be OK. My mother was on the board of the private school we'd all gone to and, middle of the year or not, she'd pull strings and get Clare in. There was money enough from Martin, who had left everything to Clare, a fact that had surprised me, although it shouldn't have. Martin's blind spots had been large and appalling, but when he could see the right thing to do, he'd almost always done it. I was sure Martin's attorney, Woods Rawlings, would get Clare money if she needed it. But I hoped she wouldn't need it. I'd get a job, something real, and maybe take graduate courses as well.

I was no nearer to knowing what I wanted to spend my life doing than I'd ever been, apart from knowing I wanted to parent Clare—which was no small thing to know—and apart from knowing I wanted to grow old with Teo, which wasn't in the cards. But I thought about what Ollie had said about marriage, how you could jump in and learn later how to love. This had been a complete washout of course, but it was a philosophy I thought might be more ably applied to an occupation. I could read and write and speak well enough. Why not get a job in a library or a hospital or a museum or a law firm and then try sincerely and mightily to love it or at least like it a lot?

I had just conjured up a Goya-esque picture of myself working in a law firm and was in the process of crossing law firm off my list with the thick black marker I carry around in my head for just such a purpose when I heard a car in the driveway. Cam and Toby probably, coming back from whatever twentysomething boy movie in which they'd tried, no doubt successfully, to drown their troubles. To be fair, their hurt for Teo was real, and because, despite their requisite display of male loyalty back in the kitchen, they loved Ollie, too, they didn't quite know what to do with themselves. They'd be fine, though, eventually, as both of them could only sustain anger or concern for so long before becoming distracted by a soccer ball or a pretty girl or a movie with aliens and car chases. I'm not being mean. My little brothers are resilient, weatherproof. The world needs its Tobys and Cams, and I need mine.

The front doorbell rang. Not Toby and Cam after all. I opened the door to see a woman standing there, a very thin woman wearing a lovely camel coat that was much too big for her. Under the porch light, the color of the coat almost precisely matched her hair.

"Yes?" I said.

And then she inhaled deeply, as though she were about to dive into water, and her jaw tightened and something flinty entered her eyes. I knew I was watching a woman gather herself, and before she said anything, I knew who she was. Beneath the taut face with its sharply articulated bones, its red lipsticked mouth like a swagger, I saw another face, delicately beautiful and luminous with love: the mother in the photograph watching a girl watching a butterfly.

My mother came up behind me. Suddenly, I felt dizzy and hot. Without thinking, I clasped my mother's hand between both of mine and hung on.

"Cornelia. Honey." Puzzled, my mother looked over my shoulder, "Who is it, Cornelia?" she asked.

"Viviana," I said, hoarsely. "Clare's mother."

To my amazement, my mother's whole body stiffened, and when she spoke next, her voice—the voice of a woman whose cardinal rule was "everyone who comes to the door is a guest," who routinely asked the UPS delivery man if he'd had his lunch, how he took his coffee— her voice was ice, needle-sharp splinters of ice. "I hope you don't think you can just pack her up and take her home. You must know it won't be that simple."

I stood there aghast, sputtering. Without thinking, I lifted my hand as though to touch Viviana. My hand hung in the air for a few seconds before I dropped it, but I don't think she even saw. Her eyes, two gray wells of grief, all the flintiness gone, stared into my mother's face.

"Nothing." Her voice was as broken and lonely a sound as I have ever heard. "Nothing is simple."

28

Clare

Back home, where Clare had lived with her mother, the houses were like secrets, set far apart from one another, each with its long drive, its buffer of trees. Clare had liked that, the big spread of lawn and then the trees beyond, all around. Like living in a basket, she'd thought. Walking from one house to the next meant shortcutting through stands of evergreens or hardwoods because the main road that connected them all was narrow, winding, and without sidewalks. People did walk on the road, sometimes, or ride their bikes, but Clare's mother rarely allowed this and, although she begged to do it from time to time, Clare's awareness of the danger was sharp and took the fun out of it. Certainly, she'd never walked on the road after dark.

But as Clare made her way from the Sandovals' house to the Browns', she wasn't scared at all. There were streetlamps—a few— and every house was bathed in mild light, porch lights and driveway lights and little garden lights among the bushes. She didn't even need the flashlight that Ingrid had given her to carry, although she wouldn't have switched it off for the world.

"It's what we always did when Cornelia or one of the others headed home after dark," Ingrid had told her, in her remarkable voice. "The Browns did the same for our kids, flashlights going back and forth between us for years. Goodness, it seems like yesterday." So having that flashlight filled Clare with the sense that she was part of the present and the past too, that she, Teo, Cornelia, Cam, Toby, and even Ollie and Teo's sister, Star, who lived in England, were all kids together, playmates. As she swept her beam of light across the houses and lawns, across the trunks of the sycamores she walked under or through their branches, she felt snug and proprietary, as though the neighborhood belonged to her, and she were one of its children.

She saw the car first. The car and then the people on the porch. Cornelia, Ellie, and someone else. She saw them before they saw her. Before Clare knew she'd recognized her mother, she recognized her, her body did. It must have, because suddenly she was running across the grass and the air she ran through was singing in her ears, louder and louder. About thirty feet from the porch, she stopped short and stood as though frozen. There seemed to be no breath in her body.

"Mommy," she whispered.

She lifted her gloved hands to the sides of her mouth, like someone calling across a great distance. "Mommy," again a whisper.

Just as she was about to try again, her mother turned and saw her.

"Mommy!" Clare shouted. She wanted to run toward her, but she couldn't move.

Clare's mother clapped a hand over her mouth, then flew across the grass to Clare. When she was surrounded by her mother's arms, an emotion like nothing she'd felt before filled Clare, a complicated emotion— elation, dread dropping off of her like a heavy, smothering coat, and a high, thin, burning feeling almost like sadness—but when her mother pressed Clare's head against her body, when her mother leaned down so that Clare felt her mother's breath on her cheek, on top of the strange, new emotion or weaving itself around it was something else: a familiar peace, the stuff of the universe settling into its proper place. So familiar was the feeling that this was the first time she'd understood it *as* a feeling; for her whole life, it had simply been part of the condition of living, like her heart beating or her eyes dilating in sunlight.

"Clarey." Her mother whispered it into her hair. "Clarey. Oh, my girl, my girl, my girl."

After a while, her mother pulled away, just slightly, and looked at Clare's face for a long time.

"Your hair," her mother said at last. Then she smiled. "Oh, the sight of you. The sight of you, beautiful girl."

"The sight of you, too," said Clare simply, and her mother started to cry silently, the tears just sliding down her face.

It hurt to watch her mother cry like that, so Clare looked past her to Cornelia, standing on the front porch. Ellie stood behind her and, as Clare watched, Ellie put her arm across Cornelia's chest, a protective hug that Cornelia leaned back into.

"Mom?" said Clare softly. "Please don't cry. I want you to meet my friend Cornelia."

Her mother nodded, wiping tears away with both hands.

As they walked to the porch, another car pulled into the driveway— a long, low, red, peculiar car, the back half of which was a kind of shallow truck bed. It stopped and a woman and a man got out. The woman ran straight to Cornelia and cradled Cornelia's face between her hands. From the back, Clare recognized the woman's long, purplish coat. Linny.

Linny turned and shook a playful finger at Clare's mother. "You're fast, lady," she said.

Sitting in the Browns' family room, warming her palms with the mug of hot chocolate Ellie had handed her almost as soon as she'd sat down, Clare felt very glad to have Linny there, glad for her chatty, effervescent presence. Although her mother sat next to Clare with one arm around her shoulders, in the indoor, evening light of the room, lamplight and firelight, Clare felt more separate from her mother than she had outside. And even though she knew everyone there, except for the man she recognized as Hayes, who sat in the corner of the room looking vaguely uncomfortable and, except for his boots, not much like a cowboy at all, Clare felt shy. I feel shy with all of them, she thought.

Even Cornelia. And that struck her, the "even Cornelia" instead of "even my mom." A tiny shiver ran through her.

But Linny was telling a story. Clare turned her attention like a flashlight, placing Linny in the center of her circle of light and leaving the rest in dimness.

"I came to water your plants, Cornelia, which come to think of it, I never did do, so they might all be dead in their pots when you get back," said Linny.

"That's OK," said Cornelia. "I never liked those plants anyway." Clare realized by the way Cornelia looked at Linny that she felt glad Linny was there too.

"And she was standing there, just kind of staring at the door like a person who's tried knocking and is all knocked out and at loose ends."

"An apt description," said Clare's mother quietly.

Oh, where have you been, Mommy, thought Clare. This question was right there in the room with them—other questions too, but Clare didn't want to ask them. She didn't want the answers, not just yet.

"Thank you. And I recognized you. I recognized Viviana. By her eyebrows. You know how I am about eyebrows, Cornelia," said Linny.

"I do know, Linny. You collect eyebrows."

"Oh," said Clare. "Like Teo's are accents. *Accent grave, accent aigue.*" She demonstrated on her own face with her fingers.

"Teo's eyebrows," declared Linny, with the air of one stating a gravely important fact, "are works of art. Poems. Sonnets!"

Clare glanced over at Hayes, who seemed to be Linny's boyfriend, to see if this bothered him. He gave Clare a private smile and rolled his eyes as if to say, "Crazy old Linny." Clare smiled back. Hayes was pretty handsome too, sparkly-eyed, his nose crooked in a way that made him more handsome rather than less, so maybe he didn't mind what Linny said about Teo.

My mother is sitting here, and I'm thinking about the shape of Hayes's nose, thought Clare.

"Viviana's eyebrows are nice too, shapely, and they go farther past the outer corners of her eyes than your ordinary brow. Just like . . ." Linny turned to Clare.

"Mine," said Clare.

"But our note," said Cornelia, confused, to Viviana, "Clare and I taped a note to my door telling you my parents' phone number and address. Oh, God, you didn't get the note?"

"There was no note," said Clare's mother. She sounded tired, "I got the one at our house, so I called your apartment. When no one answered I went over there. Twice. Linny saw me the second time."

"And I tried on the spot to call you on your cell, Cornelia, but couldn't get you," said Linny.

"The Bermuda Triangle," groaned Cornelia. "When it comes to cell phones, my parents live in the Bermuda Triangle."

"Your parents *live* on Pleasant Street," corrected Linny. "Since that's unforgettable, I didn't forget it. I knew the town, too. But I didn't have their number. And it's not listed."

Cornelia's mother entered the room with a tray of coffee cups and plates of cookies. Clare noticed that she seemed tense. Back when they'd all stood on the porch, after Linny and Hayes had gotten there, Clare had seen Cornelia and Ellie exchange looks—brown eyes and blue eyes, the brown asking something and the blue answering—before Cornelia had turned and invited everyone in.

"Doctors," said Ellie, her voice still not quite her voice. "They never list their numbers."

"What could have happened to the note?" said Cornelia, a catch in her voice, "Viviana, I wouldn't have just left. But I didn't . . ." Cornelia stole a look at her mother, who was now pouring coffee from a silver pot. "I didn't want to leave word with anyone. We've been trying to keep all that's happened—private."

"Thank you for that," said Clare's mother.

"The lady who cleans your building. I bet she took it. You know how she hates you," said Linny.

"I know," said Cornelia distractedly. She was looking at Clare's mother.

"You're small. And skittery. Probably, she thinks you're a mouse."

"I'm not the least bit skittery," said Cornelia, turning her attention back to Linny. "And you know it." Her voice faltered again. "But maybe. Maybe it was the cleaning lady."

"The cleaning lady or the hand of fate," Hayes piped up cheerfully.

"As soon as I could get Hayes to pick me up in his car, I came down. We were fast."

"Eighty, eighty-five," said Hayes, proudly. "Got here without a ticket by the grace of God."

"But Viviana was faster. I remembered that circular drive and the mailbox shaped like a little house, but how . . ."

"Their name is on the box," said Clare's mother. She pulled Clare closer to her. Clare could see her mother's pulse beat under the thin skin of her temple. Clare saw Ellie looking at her mother too.

"Viviana looks tired," said Ellie to Cornelia. "I could call one of the hotels nearby for her or maybe the Calloway Inn?"

Cornelia's face turned red. "Mom," she began.

"Actually, I was hoping to have a word with you alone, Cornelia," said Clare's mother. "Could Clare stay here while we take a walk?" She turned to Ellie. "Thanks for your offer, but I saw a hotel on the way in."

Linny stood up. "We're staying at the inn, and we should head over there. I'm starving." Hayes stood up too.

"You'll go straight into my kitchen and let me warm something up for you, Linny-girl," said Ellie. "You too, Hayes."

"You don't have to ask us twice," chirped Linny. She gave Cornelia a long look. Cornelia pressed two fingers to her mouth and blew Linny a kiss.

When Clare, her mother, and Cornelia were alone, Cornelia said, "It's too cold to talk outside, but I have a place we can go. I think, though . . ." She touched Clare's hair for a second. "I think Clare should come along."

Clare's mother said, "I don't know if that's a good idea." There was an edge in her voice.

Clare looked from one woman to the other. She saw Cornelia knit her brows for a moment, then saw her sigh and close her eyes, briefly. When she opened them, she looked tired too.

"It's just that it's Clare's life. We decided that it's better if she knows what's happening."

"You decided." Clare's mother said, flatly.

"Mom," said Clare, a note of pleading in her voice, "I do. I need to know. So things just don't happen *to* me."

Clare's mother seemed to consider this. Her eyes softened. "Yes, OK, then. You'll know."

In Mrs. Goldberg's parlor, with its rows of seashells glowing on their magical shelves, illuminated with hidden lights, Clare and Cornelia sat and listened as Clare's mother told the story of where she'd been—told it in a calm, nearly uninflected voice, as though she wanted to say the words without really remembering what she was telling.

"I just drove. I thought about the airport and going to Barcelona, but when I found I was going in the wrong direction, I didn't turn around. I had a handbag full of cash, and when I got low on gas, I stopped and got it and then kept going. For a long time, I didn't stop or sleep. I just drove. I think"—she glanced at Clare, then continued—"I think I wanted to erase myself with driving."

Clare saw that Cornelia was sitting still, watching her mother's face, and listening. She admired Cornelia's steadfast listening, how she didn't fidget or look away. The quality of her attention, of her steady gaze wasn't challenging, just—something else. Respectful was the word that came to mind, but that wasn't exactly right. Friendlier than respectful. Clare tried to listen that way too.

The story wasn't so terrible. That is, what made the story not so terrible, the only thing that made it not so terrible, was that it could have been so much worse.

Her mother had driven, stopping once at a dingy motel to sleep for a few hours, and she'd ended up in northern Michigan at a hotel which was really quite grand, although it had been much grander in the past.

"Leave it to me," her mother said, her voice charged with irony, "to have a breakdown at two hundred dollars a night."

She'd stayed there for days; how many exactly she didn't know, and this was the point in her story where Clare understood that the bare facts were the least of what happened. When her mother described her stay at the hotel, her eyes changed, grew large and frightened and haunted.

"Bipolar," said Clare's mother. "The term doesn't convey the half of it. I didn't swing from one extreme to the next; I lived all kinds of extremes at the same time. Blackness and mania and a mind that wouldn't stop."

She reached over and tilted Clare's chin up with a finger. "You're sure? You want to hear it all?"

Clare turned the question over in her mind. She looked at Cornelia, who looked back with love on her face, but no answers. Cornelia would let her make up her own mind. She remembered Cornelia's voice, telling her she was a brave girl. Be brave, Clare told herself. She nodded.

"I was delusional," her mother said matter-of-factly, "The color of the hotel drapes meant one thing, the expression on the face of a chambermaid meant another. There was a man"—she broke off, looked at Clare, then started again—"a stranger I thought was someone else, a man I'd known years ago." She drew her arms tightly around herself. "Thank God he turned out to be decent. He didn't— hurt me, although I might have scared him half to death.

"Once, I thought about killing myself," she went on. Clare felt suddenly cold. "More than once. But once, I got as far as slinging a belt around a light fixture."

Her voice cracked. "Oh, Clarey, all I did was sit staring at it. I don't think I was close at all, not really." Hearing this should have made Clare feel better but, instead, she felt herself grow colder, pull away. She managed to nod. Her mother went on. "And the maid just took it down without a word or a glance, coiled it up like a snake and set it on the dresser." Her mother seemed amazed, as though this were the truly shocking event.

"It ended with my knocking on room doors in the middle of the night, asking crazy questions. People slammed their doors, called security. But one woman, her name was May, she took one look at me and pulled me inside. Can you imagine that? The compassion of it?" Her eyes grew misty.

The woman had used her computer to find a psychiatric facility nearby. "Not a madhouse," said Clare's mother. "A good place, thank God."

And some doctors had given her medicine and others had coaxed her into talking, and it had taken a while for her to come back to herself.

"And the minute I could, I called. Home, first. Then, Martin's. Then, around. Friends. Damn holidays, though, so many people were away. The Merry Christmas messages on their answering machines felt cruel, like slaps. I was still so dull from the drugs; we hadn't hit the right balance yet. Finally, I called Martin at work, and they told me he was dead and that you, Clare, were with Cornelia."

She shook her head, as though shaking something off. "Anyway, I found you."

Then, as Clare watched, her mother began to cry, first silently, and then with panting, jagged sobs. "I am so sorry, Clare." She repeated it several times.

Clare pressed herself against the back of the sofa; the image of her mother in the car, crying and saying she was sorry for everything, flashed into her mind.

"Stop crying. Please, stop." Her voice was a rough whisper. She saw Cornelia straighten and put a hand on each arm of her chair as though preparing to stand.

"I don't like that crying, Mom. Please, stop." Clare's voice was growing shrill.

Her mother stopped. Clare could see her wiping her face, swallowing her sobs. Then her mother turned to Cornelia. "I want to thank you. For everything. I know Martin—" She broke off. "I know Clare needed you. Thank you."

Cornelia's eyes filled with tears, and she shook her head but didn't speak.

"I'm better now, Clare," said Clare's mother, "and I want to take you home."

Of course, thought Clare. Of course this is what would happen. It's what was supposed to happen. Her mother would come and take her home. But a wave of nausea rolled over her and, with it, the old raging, spinning storm of fear. "Cornelia," Clare said faintly, and Cornelia was there kneeling in front of her, her arms tight around her. Clare felt as though Cornelia's arms were the only thing keeping her from blowing away.

"I can't," Clare gasped out. "I can't go yet. I'm scared to go. I can't." Cornelia rocked her and said, "Shh, it'll be OK, honey. It'll be OK."

Clare heard her mother stand, and she looked up. Her mother's face was desolate, but Clare couldn't go to her.

"I'll get a hotel. I'll come back in the morning. We'll talk then, OK?" Her voice was so sad. Terror shot through Clare.

"No," she almost yelled. "You can't go away again."

Cornelia said, firmly, "No. Let me go talk to my mother. You'll stay with us."

When she was gone, Clare's mother pulled Clare onto her lap, and Clare curled up there, and they sat that way for a long time. Clare didn't want to talk. She only wanted to be held in these arms that were the first arms ever to hold her, against the familiar shape of this body. If they didn't speak, just touched, her mother could be the woman Clare was safe with, the one she'd always known.

29

Cornelia

It was my mother's mother, a woman dead since my mother was twenty years old, who'd done it. Who'd put the hard bewildering fury I'd heard on the porch that night into my mother's voice. Into her heart, too.

When I was a kid, eleven or so, about the time I began to wear "Cornelia" like a rash, I'd asked my mother what she could have been thinking. Why had she named me after a great-aunt whose chief claims to fame were having perfect attendance from kindergarten through graduation and inventing an apple bundt cake the secret ingredient of which was chicken fat? Why hadn't I been named after my maternal grandmother, for instance? Susan. Susan I could have used.

And I'd seen it then, just a flash of glinting, diamond-hard anger. Heard it, as well, when my mother snapped, "I didn't spend two seconds considering Susan as a name." When my mother smiled and said in her ordinary voice, "And perfect attendance is no mean feat," I had let it drop, believing the early deaths of mothers to be reason enough for anything and a mystery best left unfathomed by the likes of me.

And that was part of it, the early death, but not the most of it. The most of it was what came before the death.

"She was a drunk," said my mother bluntly after I'd left Clare and her mother at Mrs. Goldberg's and run home to find her stoking up the fire in the fireplace like a person killing something. "Today, they call it self-medicating."

My father walked into the room to hear this, and he said, angrily, "Cornelia, don't."

"I didn't," I said. And I hadn't. But I did want to know, to have the moment cracked open like that smoldering log, so that I could see whatever fire was inside.

My mother straightened, and my father went over and took the fireplace poker out of her hand. "B," she said tenderly, "it's all right."

My grandmother had been a drunk, a wild one, but even when she wasn't drunk the wildness could take her over like a demon. She'd yanked the shelves out of the refrigerator once, letting what they held crash to the floor. When my mother told me this, she didn't even blink. This and more. This and worse.

"I swore nothing like that would ever touch this family," and her whole body tilted forward when she said it, so great was her ferocity. It was the scene in *Gone With the Wind*, Scarlett raising her fist into the air, Georgia in ashes around her, the morning sun turning the world red.

When she said that, I understood. I saw the truth all at once, like an image on a movie screen, how this single statement, my mother's resolve, ran like a strong, rigid seam through the foundation of this house, through the supporting walls and wooden beams, and through the upbeat normalcy of every single day.

My mother walked out, then, and my father sat down beside me, staring into the fire.

"It's what she's been protecting us from all this time," I said with wonder in my voice.

My usually mild father shot me a look and said, almost viciously, gesturing around the room, "Did you think all this was for free? Happiness isn't what happens when you whistle along, pretending bad things don't exist. No, don't say anything, Cornelia. I know that's what you think goes on in this house. But you're wrong. Happiness is *earned*, like everything else. It's achieved. The problem is that your mother's made it look too easy. Which is exactly what she wanted." It had to be the longest speech he'd ever made to me. When it was over, he pulled my head toward him and kissed me. He stood to leave, then turned back.

"And invite Clare's mother to stay. Toby'll double up with Cam."

"It's OK with Mom?"

"I don't know if it's OK. But she's already vacuumed, dusted, cleared out a couple of drawers, and changed the sheets."

When I went to bed that night, there was too much in my head to let me sleep: Viviana, Teo, Clare, my mother, and my grandmother jostling for space, struggling to get heard, sending their voices echoing. So when, without a word, Clare came in and lay down next to me, I was still awake and, without a word, I rubbed her back until she fell asleep.

"I said, 'Hayesy, get thee to a winery!'"

Linny and I were in a café downtown eating lunch. I'd seen a flicker of panic cross Clare's face when I'd said I was going out for a while, but she and Viviana needed time alone. And, at that moment, I craved Linny like other people crave cocaine. You know those movies in which a vagrant breeze blows their lines of white dust to the floor? All that frantic scrambling around on hands and knees? Like that.

"Did he obey?" I asked.

"He did not, the recalcitrant brat. Took off for what's-his-name's house instead. You know, that president. The name escapes me."

"Thomas Jefferson."

"Bingo. Turns out Hayes worships Thomas Jefferson, says he's a genius. He quoted this long thing some guy said about him to a bunch of Nobel Laureates eating dinner at the White House. Something like, 'There are more brains in this room than have ever been assembled here, except for when Jefferson dined alone.' Dined alone. I remember that part."

"I believe the guy who said it was a guy called John F. Kennedy. Heard of him?"

I sat happily watching Linny devour a catfish sandwich for so long that she finally said, "Cornelia?"

"I'm just basking in your presence." I beamed at her.

"I thought you might be," said Linny, licking her finger. "I said, 'Hayesy, get thee to a winery! Cornelia wants to bask in my presence.'" Linny got serious. "Listen here, lovey. You won't lose her, you know. You'll stay friends, keep in touch. She doesn't live that far away."

My friend Linny, she wouldn't hurt me for all the stars in the galaxy. But every word she said—lose her, friends, keep in touch—stung me like a wasp. When it came to the subject of Clare, I was a person with no top layer of skin. Even the air burned.

Linny must've seen this, because the next thing she said was, "But could we put the issue of Clare aside for a moment?"

I nodded my gratitude. "You want to talk about Hayes?"

"We have been talking about Hayes," said Linny coyly. "Remember? Get thee? Thomas Jefferson? Dining alone?"

"Linny."

Linny pursed her lips and gazed off into the distance. "Like. We're in like. Lots of like, even. And I can envision it going in a good direction." She moved her hand like a plane taking off. Then she snapped to and touched the end of my nose with a touch that was almost a bop. "But what I see there, on that face? We're not in that."

I leaned back in my chair, flabbergasted. How did she do that? "How do you *do* that?" I asked her.

"Omniscience." She shrugged, all modesty. Then she said with sudden seriousness, "Not Martin. You haven't looked back and realized . . ."

"No."

"Thank God for that," said Linny fervently, because despite her general tongue-in-cheekiness, Linny can be as fervent as anyone when the situation calls for it.

She eyed me. If I'm an MRI, Linny is a superdeluxe-souped-up-superfabulous MRI, one that sends its magnets resonating smack-dab into the unexplored hinterlands of a person's soul. I composed my features into a mask of inscrutability, feeling like a suspect trying to beat a lie-detector test.

"Oh," she said, finally and decisively. "Well, *that's* not without complications," and coolly took a sip of ice water. Damn that Linny anyway. She grinned. "But welcome to the land of the living!" Then, she tilted back her head and warbled, *"I could cry salty tears. Where have I been all these years?"* Etcetera. Etcetera. When sung properly, it's not a short song, especially if you hum all the in-between instrumental parts, which, naturally, Linny went ahead and hummed.

A smartly dressed man at the table next to us leaned over and asked politely, "And how long can we expect *that* to go on?"

I gave him a helpless look. "If she weren't unstoppable, I'd stop her."

"Ah," he said. "Then we'll leave it up to the Lord." Which was either deliriously funny, or I was just delirious.

When my fit of girlish giggling was over, I kicked Linny under the table. "The waiter's coming. Hatred just dripping off his face. Do you want to get bounced before the pecan pie?"

"Ooh." Linny recoiled. "A dripping waiter. Cornelia, you should be appreciative of how appreciative I am of the music you make me listen to."

"I'm appreciative of your appreciation; it's your use of it as ammunition I don't appreciate. Shot with my own gun. Anyway, that's not how it was."

"Humph!" Linny humphed skeptically, which I suppose is the only way to humph. "How was it?"

"I didn't come to my senses one day and see the light, not a light that was already on. There was no light *to* see, and then suddenly, on the car ride down here, there was light."

"Like Genesis. *Creatio ex nihilo*," said Linny dryly, fiddling with her fork.

"Yes!" And I began a passionate launch into my transubstantiation metaphor, of which I was enormously fond and which, had I not been in an excited state, I would never have exposed to Linny's scathing glance. But I was in an excited state, and so not only launched but failed to taper off forlornly anywhere close to quickly enough.

"OK, could we put aside the religious imagery now?" asked Linny. "Because, frankly, it's freaking me out. Here's the deal: You've been in love with Teo since you were old enough to be in love with anyone, or probably before that, and you just now figured it out."

"No," I said feebly. "Transubstantiation, *creatio ex*—forget it."

"Forgotten. So what are you going to do about it?"

I told her about Ollie and Edmund and the Westermarck effect and how, if she'd forgive the mixed metaphor, with all the fish in the sea, no way Teo would dip into the Brown family well again—come on—and why risk losing his friendship, and about the purely sororal light in which he viewed me, and how anyway, sororal light or not, I just wasn't his type. All of that stuff.

"He's not your type either. Which apart from meaning you're blind and insane, also means maybe there's a world where types are rendered meaningless, and you are now living in that world."

"You think I should tell him. I knew you'd think I should tell him. It's not that simple."

"Just say this," said Linny and, to my horror, she began humming the opening bars of "Night and Day," which I took as a sign that I should throw money on the table, hustle her hastily out of the café, and think about what she'd said, later.

It's one thing for your best friend to uncover, with an annoying lack of effort, the deepest secret your heart holds; it's quite another for a near-stranger and, if you're being honest, semiadversary to do the same thing.

I guess it was inevitable, a heart-to-heart between Viviana and me. The obligatory female-bonding scene, the cozy, shoes-kicked-off chumming-it-up over a bottle of Chardonnay with Aretha Franklin belting out "Respect" in the background. But despite the inevitability and obligation, or maybe because of them, this was precisely the scene I'd been avoiding.

Look, I was glad the woman was alive. Of course I was. I was so glad she'd come back to her daughter. But I wasn't the first person to hold on to a dream long after it had turned to dust in my hands, and my dream of raising Clare had been the dream of a lifetime. I would let it go, drop my handfuls of dust and get on my way, but if it was hard for me, if the process filled me with a private, searing grief, who amongst you would blame me?

I loved Clare. Loved? I love Clare. Don't forget that.

"I love Clare." I told Viviana, too.

It was late. I'd been curled up in an armchair with my old copy of *Anne of Green Gables* and a glass of wine (a shiraz, just for the record) when Viviana had walked into the room. She looked better than she had a couple of days ago, less frail, more life in her eyes, and her pale face had taken on a smooth translucence, like sea glass, as if she'd undergone a sea change of her own. Ariel's song again, but in reverse. This was a woman who'd been drowned and come back from drowning. These are eyes that were her pearls.

"Would you like a glass of wine?" I asked Viviana. She shook her head.

"Can't," she said. "My medicine." Then she corrected herself. "My medication." There was the faintest note of bitterness in her voice.

"Is it—awful stuff?" I asked, tentatively.

"It brought me back," she said briskly, and I understood that the edge in her voice was meant for herself, not for me. "Back to Clare."

We talked about Clare for a while and, as she had in Mrs. Goldberg's parlor, she thanked me and, as they had in Mrs. Goldberg's parlor, her thanks cut me to the quick.

"Please," I said, my voice shaky, "don't thank me. I can't stand to be thanked. As though I were just anyone. A kind stranger. I love Clare."

"Yes, I see that. I see that you're not just anyone," she said softly. Then, she said, "Can I ask you a question you absolutely don't have to answer?"

I smiled. "Well, when you put it that way, why not?"

"Were you in love with Martin?"

This took me off guard, but I said, "No. Almost." I shook my head. "Not even almost. But I really, really wanted to be, for a while there anyway."

"I'm glad. I'm glad you didn't lose the man you were in love with." I could hear the relief in her voice. Then she said, "I can't believe he's dead."

And I realized when she said it that I hadn't thought about how Martin's death was also something she'd come home to. Of all there was for her to absorb, there was his death, as well.

"Does it hurt?" I asked.

"I think it does, some. But mostly what I mean is he seemed like a person who couldn't die."

I knew what she meant.

"He was so replete, so handsome and charming, always saying the right thing. He seemed untouchable, like a famous person or a character in a book. Maybe he began to seem that way because of all the distance we put between each other over the years." Then she gave a wry laugh. "No, he seemed that way when we were married, too. That was the problem."

"Our problem, too. I could never know him well enough." How odd, I thought, to be talking to Martin's ex-wife about him—odd, but at the same time entirely natural. "And he didn't love Clare enough. I couldn't live with that."

"I couldn't either. I hated him for it for a long time." Nothing shocking about that. The marvel was that she didn't hate him, still.

"You know, it's funny," I said. "I tried so hard to fall in love with Martin. And then, *boom*, without trying at all, I fell in love with Clare." I'd been about to say, "And Teo, too," but I caught myself in time.

"Clare and who else?" said Viviana, to my amazement. There was challenge in her voice. I stared at her. Medicated or not, this woman was sharp, a fact I suddenly knew she wanted me to know.

"I'm sorry," she said, not sounding sorry. "I shouldn't have asked that. But you are in love with someone besides Clare." It wasn't remotely a question.

"It doesn't matter," I said finally.

She smiled at me. "Love always matters," she said.

I was in no position to argue.

30

Clare

Teo found Clare and her mother in the garden. Clare had been showing her mother the bushes she'd pruned, those sad clusters of sticks.

"It seems funny to call them bushes, though," Clare had said. "There's just nothing bushy about them."

Her mother had laughed, and Clare felt the old pride she'd always felt when she could make her mother laugh, but even as that old pride filled her, the experience of feeling it was nothing like what it used to be. Clare decided that it was like going to a house where you'd always lived and finding strange furniture in it and being afraid to sit down.

Clare remembered how her mother had described her illness, not like she was swinging between two poles, but like, all at the same time, she was feeling ways that, together, made no sense. That's sort of how Clare felt with her mother now, ever since she'd come back. Clare could be so happy and, all the while, under the happiness drifted a wariness and an unease and a desire to get away. Clare couldn't stand it that she felt like getting away from her mother, but she couldn't deny it. There were times when she wanted to open the door, start running, and not stop.

So when Teo came around the corner in the coat they'd picked out together, Clare was overcome with gladness at the sight of him. When he hugged her, her eyes filled, and she hung on for a few seconds longer than she ordinarily would have to let the tears disappear into the softness of his coat.

"Teo," she said, letting go of him, "this is my mom, Viviana. Mom, this is Teo."

"I've heard so much about you," said Clare's mother warmly, reaching out to shake his hand.

"Welcome back." Teo smiled.

Clare watched them together, standing in the winter sun, under the same blue sky: her mother and Teo with his smile curling up at the corners and his green eyes in his brown face. That's how she used to look, thought Clare. Not exactly, of course, but as though sunlight didn't just fall on her but also came out of her.

Teo could marry my mother, she thought suddenly. Then Teo would be my father. But before she got any further, another idea appeared, even more suddenly, like a wind whisking fog away from something that had been there all along: Cornelia loves Teo.

Clare didn't know how she knew this—or maybe there were so many tiny reasons for her knowing that she couldn't even name them—but as soon as the thought came to her, she saw it was absolute truth. And here was another truth: If Cornelia loved Teo, and she did, then they should be together. They had to be together. She wondered what they were waiting for.

"I thought Clare might want to go for a walk. But we can do it later," said Teo.

"I think you should do it now," said Clare's mother. "I think that's a good idea. If you want to, Clare."

Clare bounced up and down on her toes. "Yes, I do. I want to."

Her mother laughed. "I figured that you did."

When they were alone, walking down the Browns' driveway, Teo said, "My mom likes you a lot. She liked the way you ate her pancakes."

"I know," said Clare. "She said I reminded her of Cornelia. I thought it was really great that she said that. Does Cornelia know you're here?"

"No," said Teo. "Ellie said she was over at Mrs. Goldberg's house. Cornelia's house now, I guess. I talked to Ellie and B for a while. I had some explaining to do." He looked uncomfortable.

"I know about Ollie," Clare said tentatively, aware that she was stepping out into grown-up territory, onto ground strewn with grown-up mistakes: loveless marriages, other men, runaway wives, divorce like a storm on the way. As she walked, she imagined that the ground under her feet even felt different. Different but steady. She decided to go further. "You'll probably feel better soon," she ventured. "I mean, you seem kind of fine."

"What a mess," said Teo, kicking a rock off the sidewalk. "I'll probably feel like an idiot for a hundred years. But you're right, I am kind of fine."

He smiled at her and added, "Thanks," and Clare felt a quick pulse of exhilaration. From the first minute she'd met Teo, she'd needed him, and that was a usual sort of needing: a child going to an adult for comfort. But if she was comforting him now, that meant something different, didn't it? Clare knew it did. She looked happily down the path of sidewalk before them, long and bright white beside its row of trees. If she could comfort him, they were friends.

Clare pointed to a maple in someone's yard—the Wangs' yard, she remembered—although she couldn't remember if the Wangs still lived there. "That's where Cornelia got her first kiss."

Teo looked at her, startled, then grinned. "She told you about that?" Something about the way he said it made Clare give him a sharp glance. Oh, she thought. Cornelia had told her about the kiss, but not who'd given it to her.

"Yep," Clare said. "She said it was the best kiss she's ever had." The lie came out of nowhere, and Clare wondered if she'd feel bad about it later.

"Really," said Teo, startled again. Then he added, "That's difficult to believe."

"No, she really said it," said Clare quickly.

"OK," said Teo, narrowing his eyes at her for a second. "But I didn't mean that. I just meant it's hard to believe that some kiss you got from another kid when you were fourteen would be the best one of your life."

"Sometimes, hard-to-believe things are true," Clare said. "Lots of times."

Then she said, "Cornelia's working really hard on Mrs. Goldberg's attic. She's on the computer all the time, looking stuff up about the silver and crystal and everything. Did you know Mrs. Goldberg has a silver nutcracker with a squirrel on it that probably used to belong to Robert E. Lee?"

Teo laughed. "No, I don't think I did know that."

"She looks up other stuff too. Like, oh—you know—that Westermarck thing?"

"Yeah," said Teo slowly, not looking at her.

"She found out Ollie was wrong. If you meet a person after the age of three, even if you grow up with them, the effect doesn't happen. It only happens if you meet them *before* you're three."

Teo stopped walking. "You're kidding." His brow was furrowed. Then it unfurrowed, and he started walking again. "That's exactly the kind of information Ollie never gets wrong. I think she probably just told me that so I wouldn't feel bad."

Clare didn't think she liked the sound of that. She didn't want him to like Ollie *more* because she'd lied.

"I don't know why Cornelia was so interested to find that out. I mean, she seemed very excited. Very. Isn't that weird?" This was somewhere in the vicinity of the truth, although Cornelia hadn't actually said a word to Clare about looking up the Westermarck effect on the computer. Clare had found a printed-out page with a star drawn in ink next to the part about before three years old. Surely a star meant Cornelia was excited.

Teo didn't say anything, and when Clare looked at him, she saw that there were streaks of pink burning in his cheeks. Clare breathed in and touched her hands to her own face. Then Teo looked Clare right in the eye. "You know what? I never believed in the Westermarck effect anyway. I knew it wasn't true."

They walked for a few minutes, not talking.

"Teo," said Clare, "did you love growing up here? Because I think I would've loved growing up here."

Teo leaned back against the pretty, mottled cream-and-brown trunk of a sycamore tree and looked up into its branches. "It was great, actually." His voice was thoughtful. "Everyone sort of took care of each other, which doesn't always happen in a neighborhood. We were lucky."

"I like thinking about you and Cornelia being kids here. Sometimes, I walk down the street and just imagine it." She gazed around. "In a place like this, what happened with me and my mom? It wouldn't have happened."

Teo said gently, "People get sick everywhere, Clare."

"But there would've been someone for me to tell, if we'd lived here. Someone might have been able to help us before she ended up leaving."

"Maybe so," said Teo simply.

Clare took a few steps closer to him. "Teo, my mom showed me these pills she has to take. They make her stay well. That's why she showed me because she wanted me to understand that she could stay well now. And she said that as soon as we got back home, she'd find a good doctor she could talk to. She showed me the pills to make me feel better." Clare clasped her hands together. "But they were so small, those pills. It scared me how small they were. Do you know what I mean?"

Teo said, "Yeah, Clare, I think I do."

Clare's eyes filled with tears. "I don't want to be alone with her. I don't want to go home and have us be alone again, like we were. But if I tell her that, it'll make her so sad. I know it will."

Teo put an arm around Clare's shoulders. "Sometimes, you just have to say exactly what you feel."

"You do?" said Clare. She pressed her cheek against his coat.

"In certain situations, you can't worry about how people will react. You just have to be as honest as you can and let what happens afterward happen."

For dinner that night, there was beef stew and a thick braid of homemade bread, glossy with brushed-on egg yolk. Clare had brushed on the egg yolk herself; in fact, she had helped make every dish. When Ellie had praised her chopping, she'd glowed.

Teo had ended up spending the whole afternoon at the Browns' house, first talking to Clare's mother on the front porch, both of them watching Toby and Cam teach Clare how to play hacky sack, and then, after Cornelia got home, sitting with her at the kitchen table, talking while Clare and Ellie cooked.

Even as she'd chopped onions and peeled potatoes and chatted with Ellie, Clare had watched Cornelia and Teo together as carefully as she could. To her own surprise, she found herself thinking of Ollie on the island Cornelia had told her about—Ollie watching the birds, their hops and wing-flutters and the curves of their beaks. I'm watching love, she thought, her heart beating fast. What does being in love look like? What does it make you do?

Clare wished she had her notebook. Notice everything, she told herself, like a scientist. Blinks and breaths and head turns. The pitch of Cornelia's voice, the motion of her hands, the pauses in her speech. Love was mixed up in all of it, like gold in a pan of sand. Sift. Sort. Pay attention.

Mostly, Cornelia and Teo seemed like their usual selves. But Clare had noticed Cornelia when she'd first walked up to find Teo sitting on the porch, how instantly not just her mouth, but her entire body seemed to smile. Was this how she always smiled at Teo? Clare tried to remember. Clare thought she'd seen her mother notice it too, and when Cornelia kissed Teo's cheek and messed up his hair with her hand like he was a little boy, Clare had seen her mother lock eyes with Cornelia for a second with an expression on her face that Clare recognized. "I know what you're up to," the expression said.

At the kitchen table, Cornelia and Teo kept space between each other and didn't touch. Clare looked at the space. She wondered if the air between Teo and Cornelia felt different from usual air, if it felt different to Cornelia, maybe warmer, or if maybe Cornelia were filling up the air with something no one could see.

And then, as she held a peeled potato as smooth as an egg in her hand, Clare saw it: the fleeting, unguarded look on Cornelia's face when Teo turned to say something to Ellie. Cornelia gazed with intensity at Teo's profile or maybe the side of his neck. There, Clare thought. Love. And she felt her own cheeks flush at the sight.

Clare waited until dessert to say what she had to say. When everyone had a mouthful of lemon pound cake, Clare spoke up. "Today, I decided about a few things. Actually, I've been thinking about them for a while, but today, I decided to tell all of you"—she took a breath—"what I've been thinking."

Clare's eyes met Teo's, and he didn't nod or say anything, but he crinkled the corner of his eyes at her which, for some reason, made her decide to stand up. She stood there, beside her chair, with all the faces before her and felt like she did when she had to give a report at school. Nervous in an excited, electric kind of way.

"I'm so glad my mom's back." Clare turned to her mother, who smiled at her, even though her eyes looked worried. "Mom, I missed you so much, and I knew you'd come back. Or, most of the time, I knew. And I want to be with you every day, just like always."

Clare felt her voice get choked-up, so she waited for a few seconds. No one seemed to mind. "But, I'm afraid to be alone with you, back at home. When you were sick, I would lie awake, listening, scared of what you might be doing. And even though you're well right now, I know I would do that again. Just lie there, listening with that bad feeling."

"And, I'm sorry, Mom, I don't want to hurt your feelings"—Clare looked at Cornelia, who had tears in her big, tilted eyes—"but I would miss Cornelia too much." The tears spilled over onto Cornelia's cheeks, and Clare saw Toby, who sat next to Cornelia, put his arm along the back of her chair.

"And I love this place. It's the best place I've ever been. So, I decided that I want to live here forever. In Mrs. Goldberg's house. With my mom and Cornelia." Clare fixed her gaze on the cake at the center of the table, so that she wouldn't have to even try to read the faces of the people around it. "That's what would make me happy. So just think about it, please."

She sat back down and smoothed her napkin back into her lap. No one spoke for at least a full minute. And when someone finally did, it wasn't Cornelia or Clare's mother, but Ellie. In her clear voice, she said, "Well, and I was just thinking today while we were cooking that I could make a call or two and get Clare into St. Anne's just like that." She snapped her fingers. As Cornelia and Clare's mother and the whole table stared at her, Ellie broke off a forkful of cake and lifted it.

"Just in case," she said brightly, "Clare ends up staying." With a smile and with everyone still staring, she popped the forkful of cake into her mouth.

31

Cornelia

My life—my real life—started when a man walked into it, a handsome stranger in a perfectly cut suit and, yes, I know how that sounds. Or I know how it might sound, to the kind of person I used to be, one who spent her days skirting around the edges of adulthood, commitment, responsibility, accomplishment—whatever word you use to describe diving into the deepest part of being human. Take your pick; they're all woefully inadequate, but they're also all we have.

If you're the kind of person I used to be, you might think that real life means going after what you want and getting it. I thought that, as I skirted those edges (and don't get me wrong, I liked that skirting; there was joy in it—most of the time, that skirting was the lightest kind of dancing), gazing into other people's real lives—Ollie's, B's and Ellie's, Teo's, Mrs. Goldberg's, to name a few—like lit-up houses, places in which real people did the work of real life. I believed they'd all achieved their hearts' desires or were in the process of achieving them. There. That's what I mean: I believed the process of achieving them was life.

But in the months that followed Martin's gracing of Café Dora's doorway, I'd figured out that a real life didn't mean attaining my heart's desire, but *knowing* it, meant not the satisfaction, but the longing. Knowing what you love and why, I found out, is as real as it gets.

I love Mrs. Goldberg because she got sick and died, but is as alive as anyone I know. I love the trees in her yard and the treasures in her attic because they were her trees, her treasures. I love my family's house because it is my family's. I love Linny and Toby and Cam and Ollie because it is impossible not to. I love my gentle father for his fierceness and my happy mother for her sadness. I love Teo because he is the best man I know and because my arm bones ache when they're not holding him and because I am myself. I love Martin for bringing Clare into my life, and I love Clare because she is brave and loving and smart and full of hope. Oh, how I love Clare.

I wanted to be Clare's mother, and then Clare's mother came home, and the home she came home to was my own.

I decided to do it. It took thirty seconds' contemplation and one nod from Viviana to decide. I decided to move back to the street I'd grown up on and live in Mrs. Goldberg's house with Clare and Viviana. It wasn't what I'd hoped for, and I didn't see how in the world it could work, but I decided to jump in and figure out later how to do it. How to do it and how to love it. I got on the phone that night and broke the news to Linny and began my campaign of persuading her to go to law school down the road from where I'd live, and I quit my job at the café, hired the cheapest moving company I could find, and talked my landlord out of six months' rent and into taking down my chandelier.

And then, that night, I went into my room to find a story about a girl and a bear and a bleak, enchanted winter lying on my bed. I remembered the battered cover. The story had been in Clare's backpack the first night she'd slept in my apartment, and I assumed Clare had left it on the bed, until I opened it to find a sheet of paper. The words written on the paper said *Clare's Christmas gift to us. A book she made for Viviana, but Clare decided you and I should share it instead. Your turn. Be brave. Love, Teo.* I pressed a finger to his name and kissed the page like the lovesick girl I was, and then I read the story. I read it and I finished reading and I thought about it until the sun came up.

The story was gorgeous and devastating, and it left me with a choice of two possible interpretations, like two paths. Both paths were rutted, difficult; either one would jar my bones and rattle my soul, but one was easier than the other. The easy interpretation was that Viviana's illness had terrified Clare so completely that she had longed for an endless sleep, the particulars of which I couldn't bring my imagination to imagine. The easiness lay in the conclusion that a child who had been this frightened should not be made to live alone again with the woman who had frightened her. The child needed me.

But there was something different one could take from the story, something both difficult and difficult to explain. When winter fell, it wasn't only Annika's world that the brute frost drained of life, but her very own flesh and hair and eyes, and, despite all his strength and goodness, even John the Bear couldn't help Annika. Only spring's return, getting her old world back, would save her. If you looked at the story this way, you'd see that there's a power at the heart of mothers and their children—a mysterious connection no one else can touch. I could live with Clare and Viviana for a hundred years without ever coming close.

Two roads diverged in a yellow wood. *Be brave,* Teo had written. I stood at that fork in the road and waited to be brave enough.

So when Viviana appeared in Mrs. Goldberg's attic the next evening and asked, "What will you do?" the question stopped me dead. I closed my laptop carefully, putting it to sleep. How simple, I thought; if only I could do that to Viviana. Turn her and her questions off long enough to make a run for it.

"What will I do?" I echoed, buying time. I knew exactly what she was asking.

Except I didn't. Because the next thing she said was, "Here. What will you do here? Get a job? Go back to school?" Not on the spot after all, I felt giddy with relief.

"Oh. Gosh. I wish I could say I had a plan."

Viviana sat down on the floor next to me and picked up the Art Deco cigarette lighter I'd been writing about. I watched her hold that elegant object in her hands, which were precisely shaped and almost creaseless, as though they were Art Deco as well.

"I know how you feel," she said.

"Are you sure about this?" I wasn't sure I wanted an answer to that, but I asked anyway. "Pulling up roots, living here, away from what you know."

"I know Clare," said Viviana, pausing to let the words resonate with me. And they did resonate. "I know the difference between her wanting something and her needing something. And this?" Viviana gazed around the attic and then out the window. "She needs this."

Then Viviana looked at me and the tightness went out of her features. She sighed. "It's not the leaving that will be hard. It's the staying. The being watched over and the sharing. Sharing Clare. I don't mean that unkindly."

I could tell she didn't, and I was amazed at how we could do this, Viviana and I, shift from wariness to intimacy, the way we could become two women talking.

"Maybe it's not sharing, really. Maybe her world's just getting bigger."

Viviana nodded. "It needed to get bigger. I see that. A world of two is too small." She cleared her throat. "So, back to you. What will you do here?"

I looked around the attic. "I need to finish going through all of this. That comes first. So, I'll get some kind of job until I'm done. After that, I'm not sure. More school, maybe."

"What would you study?" asked Viviana with real interest.

"I don't know, exactly. I love doing what I'm doing, though. I started out just writing down the stories Mrs. Goldberg told me about her belongings."

"A labor of love," said Viviana. "Clare told me how much Mrs. Goldberg meant to you."

"Yes." I felt flustered at this, for some reason, and moved quickly past it. "But it turns out there are other stories attached to so many of these objects, ones I don't think even Mrs. Goldberg knew. Stories I found online and in the university libraries." I picked up a funny silvery turban and put it on. "Like this."

Viviana smiled at the sight of me in the hat.

"I know," I said, "can you imagine? It's by Lilly Dache, a French-woman who became the most famous New York milliner of her time. I mean, who knew there were famous milliners?" I couldn't explain just why this sort of thing excited me, but it did. "And the silver. There are pieces dating back to the eighteenth century. And that old wrought-iron gate over there I *think* was made in Philadelphia by a former slave. Everything comes from someplace. Everything's been held in so many hands."

I took the hat off, embarrassed at my own gushing. The fact that I was going to live with this woman and her child loomed between us, and I sat there and talked about hats and gates.

"So, art history maybe?" said Viviana, nodding. "Conservation? Or material culture." She stopped talking, set down the cigarette lighter, and looked at me. "There's a wonderful program in Delaware, of all places, with a museum nearby housing the most astonishing collection, entire interiors re-created. Parquet floors, plaster moldings, furniture, paintings—everything. I've done some parties for a woman on the board. I'm sure she'd write a letter for you." She stopped.

Delaware.

"Viviana," I said in as neutral a voice as I could muster, "what are you asking?"

"It's really not far," she said crisply. "You could come back here, come—home, every weekend. Home to your house."

"What are you asking?"

Her bravado disappeared. "She goes into your room every night. I hear her."

She wouldn't cry, I could tell, and I felt grateful for that. She sat there in her calm, upright blondness, her eyes proud like a marble statue's, but I could feel the tension under her cool surfaces. Ruthless, I thought. This woman would be ruthless if she needed to be. I admired her for it.

"I need to be the one she needs," said Viviana steadily. "She's my life."

I wanted to speak, but I couldn't figure out what to say.

Viviana stood up and started for the door. Then she turned back to me.

"Please," she began. And I cut her off. This proud woman pleading for her child would be more than I could bear.

"Don't," I told her. "Don't say please."

And Clare's mother left me alone with myself.

32

Clare

"*I* can't decide if she's beautiful," said Clare halfway through the movie, "or if she just looks better than anyone I've ever seen."

Cornelia sat on the floor, leaning against the big armchair Clare sat in. When Clare said this, Cornelia tilted her head back to look at Clare and laugh. "Exactly! She's just—marvelous!"

She was marvelous, Tracy Lord, in her white dress with her frowny mouth and sculpted little face and those long eyes whose expression could switch from scornfulness to hurt without a blink.

When Clare had first seen Dexter, she'd gasped out, "Wow."

"The wowest." Cornelia sighed.

"But not only that," began Clare, "he looks like . . ."

"You." Cornelia smiled, then added, "And your father."

I look like my father, Clare thought. People had always said this, and it used to bother Clare. But, somehow, it didn't bother her anymore. Martin Grace was her father. Gone or not, he was part of who she was, and it looked more and more as though who she was was who she wanted to be.

I have my father's eyes, she said to herself. And a tiny bright window of insight opened: Just because my father didn't love me doesn't mean I can't love him, someday. The window shut, but Clare felt a newness inside her, a beginning. I have my father's eyes, she thought again.

When the movie was over, Clare said with satisfaction, "That's how movies should always end. With all the good people getting what they want."

Cornelia switched off the television and turned around to face Clare. Seeing Cornelia sitting there, cross-legged in her jeans made Clare remember how small she was, like a child.

"Clare, I need to tell you something." She paused. "You are part of my family, not just a friend. You'll always be part of my family."

This was wonderful, just what Clare wanted to hear. She should have felt happy, but she felt scared, instead. Cornelia's voice and the expression in her eyes made her look more like a child than ever, like a child trying to sound stronger and braver than she feels.

Clare nodded, then said, "Why don't we watch the movie again, from the beginning?"

"You and your mother will live in Mrs. Goldberg's house." Clare saw that she was trembling. "And I will come visit you all the time."

"No," said Clare. "You can't do that, Cornelia. You already said you would stay."

The anger in her own voice startled Clare. She sounded furious, when what she was was sad and scared. But she couldn't stop the angry sound and, pretty soon, she felt angry too.

"We'll spend holidays together and weekends. And you can come visit me whenever you want. In Philadelphia or wherever I end up." Then she added quickly, "But wherever I end up, it won't be very far away. I promise you that."

"You *promised* you would stay." The words hurt Cornelia, Clare could see that and, as angry as she was, she couldn't feel any satisfaction in Cornelia's pain. But her own disappointment was so sharp and awful.

"I promised because I wanted to be with you so much. I still want it. But you need to be alone with your mom." Cornelia's hands were so tightly clasped together, they were turning red.

"What if she gets sick again?" flashed Clare. "Did you even think about that?"

"You'll come right over here and tell Ellie and B. And you'll call me and I'll come, no matter what. And we'll all help." Cornelia said it as though it were a solemn vow.

"Oh, honey—" Cornelia's voice broke and she reached a hand toward Clare. But Clare got up and left her there, small and sitting on the floor, looking like her heart was broken.

33

Cornelia

It makes sense that Mrs. Goldberg's attic, that place I loved, would come to hold some of my story, along with all the other ones it held. It made sense that Teo would find me there—a sapphire blue dress of Mrs. Goldberg's slung across my lap, shimmering—calm but with a sharp sadness that felt like a permanent addition to my heart.

"What light through yonder doorway breaks?" was what sprang to mind when he came walking through it. And I had to smile at that, because I couldn't have been less in the market for a story about star-crossed love. I wanted my stars clean and steady and spelling out a happy ending straight across the sky. But if you're like I am, you don't treasure that play for its tragic ending but for its flawless rendering of love achieved. When your man has to leave you in the morning, the bird singing outside is always the nightingale, never the lark, and when your man appears in an attic doorway, the moon is always humbled by his radiance. Or the sun, if it happens to be daytime when he arrives.

Teo arrived and sat down across from me in a burnt-orange leather armchair, a chair whose only story seemed to be that Gordon Goldberg had purchased it himself and, for fifteen years, had steadfastly refused to relinquish it, even in the face of his wife's offended sensibilities. Teo took off his coat, which made me inordinately happy. Take off your coat, I thought, and stay forever.

"I've lost her," I told Teo. I showed him my empty hands. Somehow, I knew he knew about Clare.

"She won't stay mad," he said.

"I know she won't."

"She'll grow up here, where we grew up. You'll always belong to each other."

"But not in the way I wanted us to belong to each other." It was the simple truth.

"You wanted to see her every day."

"I wanted to see her every day. I wanted her to climb in bed with me at night when she couldn't sleep. I wanted her to come home to me with stories about school." I slid my hand over the blue satin, smoothing it, even though it couldn't get any smoother than it was. "And I came so close to having that. But it wouldn't have been right." I looked up at him. "Teo, I just wanted to do the right thing."

I wanted him to tell me that I had done the right thing, but instead of saying something ordinary, Teo said something miraculous: "Of course you did. That's how you are. Why do you think I love you so much?"

Before you get too excited, remind yourself that there was never any question of Teo's loving me; he's loved me since I was four years old. This I know; this I've always known. But even this piece of irrefutable, twenty-seven-year-old knowledge did not prevent my heart from beating faster than a bird's.

And imagine this: a lifetime spent wanting "I love you" to be poetry served up on a platter, a line from a movie script, and there I was, about to fly heavenward to hear it stated like accepted truth, like it didn't need stating at all. As though Teo's loving me were the trees and sky, the world we'd always lived in. Which I guess it was. But I needed something from him.

When I could speak, I said, "I need something from you."

And he smiled his wide, warm smile and said, "You know you can have it." And even this didn't necessarily mean what it would've been so easy to let myself believe it meant, since Teo Sandoval was as naturally magnanimous a human being as had ever lived. Everyone who knew him knew that. Be brave, I told myself.

"Clarification," I said, my voice shaking. "That question you asked me a second ago? Clarify it, would you? Because for you to mean that the way I want you to mean it—" I broke off. Be brave. "I would do anything." Tears burned my eyes. "Just—anything."

And he looked at me with kind concern and said, "You've been hit hard, haven't you?"

"Oh, Teo. I've been *slammed*."

Teo didn't answer, but instead sat looking at me with that compassion on his face. Dizziness struck; I faltered. "But you haven't, I guess."

"Oh, yeah, I have." He kept his eyes on my eyes. "But so long ago, I've had some time to get used to it."

"How long ago?"

"That's my secret." He smiled. "I don't plan to keep any others from you, but that one's mine."

If you're thinking swells of music, heavens raining down celestial light, and a shining path into the future opening up before me, you've got it wrong. Instead: Mrs. Goldberg's attic, ordinary afternoon sun, Cornelia sitting on the floor, Teo sitting in an ugly orange armchair. All anyone could ask for.

"Enough clarification?" asked Teo.

I am as skilled as anyone at being coy. And I know that there's a time for being coy and then there's a time for tossing what you're holding to the floor, striding across the room, and dropping into your true love's lap, relying on all your strength and on all your eighty-five pounds of weight and on the help you know gravity will give you, because nature and all its forces are on the side of love, to pin him to the spot.

"I love you," I told him. "And a little more clarification would be good." I put my arms around his neck, my face inches away from his, so as to leave him no choice but to do what he did, which was kiss me. I kissed Teo. Teo kissed me. We gave each other the kiss of a lifetime, of a hundred lifetimes. A thousand.

Yes, it's true, what I said earlier: A real life doesn't mean getting what you want; the achievement, the privilege, too, is knowing what you love.

But getting what you love? Having what you love love you back? Oh, my friend, it's miracle: your one tiny life's head-on collision with divinity.

When you are in love, you want to spread the word, to tell the fish in the ocean and the lamppost on the corner and to send the news spinning itself out across continents and seas, so that all of creation might rejoice with you.

When you are in love with your sister's husband, or with your wife's sister, you have to tell your family first.

After you and your beloved have touched each other into immortality, you have to descend the attic stairs on ordinary human feet and cut across lawns to your respective family homes with your heart in your throat and your fingers crossed hard and spend the next forty-eight hours facing what there is to face.

Conversation One: My father, that same afternoon.

> Cornelia: Daddy, Teo and I are in love.
> Daddy [*with startled eyes behind his glasses*]: You're serious?
> Cornelia [*buying time, splitting hairs*]: Do you mean do I mean what I just said or do you mean am I serious about Teo?
> [*A pause.*]
> Daddy: If it's you and Teo, it could only be serious, so I guess I mean do you mean what you just said.
> Cornelia [*from the bottom of her heart*]: I do.

Daddy [*grinning*]: Teo doesn't look much like Cary Grant.
Cornelia [*grinning back*]: I can't imagine what you're talking about.
Daddy: Don't tell Ollie but, Cornelia, it's what I've always wanted.
[*Daddy's eyes shining. Cornelia standing humbly in their light.*]

Conversation Two: Toby and Cam, early evening, as they throw a
football and shout friendly insults at each other.

Cornelia [*shouting over friendly insults*]: Hey, you guys, you'll never
    guess what Teo and I are in. Love.
[*Toby's arm arrested mid-throw. Football thudding to the ground.*
Cam cantering over like the golden retriever he is.
Finally . . .]
Cam [*whining*]: But I got him after Ollie. I *called* it!
Toby: Shut up, dude. He's mine!
[*Wrestling.*]
Cornelia: I adore you guys, you know that?
[*Toby and Cam looking pleased and sheepish.*
Pleased, sheepish, and adoring moment broken by the inevitable pick-
    ing up of Cornelia and the inevitable bodily tossing of her like a
    medicine ball from one brother to the other, as the evening star
    looks on.]

And you don't need to point out that the above conversations went
worlds better than any bombshell-dropping daughter and sister has the
right to expect. I got off easy, I knew it, and I was properly grateful, believe me. Grateful, grateful. I went to bed that night radiant with familial love.

You also don't need to point out that in telling my father and my
brothers first, I hadn't exactly rushed boldly in and seized the bull
by the horns, bearded the roaring lion in its den. But think about it:
If you're dropping a bombshell, why not choose the easier targets
first, then tackle the really tough ones later, with a good night's

sleep under your belt and the glow of the early victories on your brow?

So there, you see? It wasn't cowardice; it was strategy.

Conversation Three: Clare, at the breakfast table the next morning, alone with Cornelia.

Cornelia: Clare, I have to tell you something.
Clare [*not looking up from her cereal bowl*]: . . .
Cornelia: It turns out that I'm in love with Teo. And you know what?
Clare [*not looking up from her cereal bowl*]: . . .
Cornelia: He's in love with me.
[*Clare meeting Cornelia's eyes with hers. Her eyes full of Cornelia can't tell what.*]
Cornelia [*taking a deep breath*]: I'm going to New York with him to-morrow. I mean, not permanently, but for a few days, until I can stand to be away from him. Then I'll go back and pack up my apartment and move there. Eventually. And you know, it's New York. It's not far at all. And I'm going to learn how to drive, so I can come see you all the time. Teo, too, he'll visit a lot, whenever he can, with me or without me. Because we love you so much, and we can't stand to be away from you for very long either. Clare, honey, please say something.
[*Nothing. Then . . .*]
Clare: Whatever.

Oh, Clare.

After we ate a silent breakfast together, I went up to my room and called Linny. I told her what I'd told everyone else.

She said, "Cornelia. I'm so delirious with joy, I can't even make a joke."

"You can't?" I asked her. "Because, Linny, I could really use one."

Linny considered this and then said, "I can't make a joke, but I can ask you about sex. Will that do the trick?"

"I think it might," I said.

"Are you having it?"

"Linny. It hasn't even been twenty-four hours!"

"Give or take twenty-four years."

I thought about arguing, re-submitting my transubstantiation theory, but quickly recognized this thought for the self-abnegating lunacy it was.

"We're not having it," I said.

"Oh, God, Cornelia." There was sudden horror in Linny's voice. "You're not putting it off until he's divorced, are you?"

A good question, pertinent. So good and pertinent, in fact, that Teo had asked me his unhorrified but equally urgent version of the self-same question during a stolen half-hour on the oriental rug in Mrs. Goldberg's attic the night before, asked it after I'd pulled back, panting, at the feel of his hand sliding under my sweater and making its electric way along my rib cage.

"We're playing by the rules, then?" he'd asked, raspy-voiced. The hand retreated, which is what I wanted, definitely wanted, because why would I have pulled away if I didn't want it, except as soon as it was gone, I'd have given my eyeteeth to have it back.

"Teo. She's my sister." I sighed, knowing the same thought was in both our heads: how, husband or no husband, no way in hell was Ollie forbearing from a single thing, how no doubt even at that very moment, even as Teo and I lay side-by-side, frustration faintly tingeing our elation, Ollie and Edmund were on their pebbly beach, disporting themselves before God and tortoises.

But in my mind's eye, alongside this all-too-lurid picture, was another one, more lurid still, of a lifetime of my looking in mirrors to find the goggle eyes of Bette Davis staring back. Who could face that kind of future? Could you?

I told Linny the same thing I'd told Teo: "We'll abide by the letter of the law while entirely ignoring its spirit each and every chance we get."

To which Teo had replied, with affectionate laughter, "Only you would say that."

To which Linny replied, with affectionate disgust, "You are so fucking weird."

Then, lamely, I added to Linny what I'd added, lamely, to Teo: "That's the plan for now, anyway."

To which Teo had said chivalrously, "Nope, better not leave that door open. I might be tempted to try to change your mind."

To which Linny said derisively, "For now? Ha! You won't make it a week, sister."

Then she asked, "By the way, since they weren't in love and so forth, did he and Ollie . . . ?" Linny is not one to leave a stone unturned, not even that one.

"Linny, they were married for two years," I said calmly. "One assumes they had sex."

"One assumes? Come on, I know you asked him. I know you did," she said knowingly.

"I don't know why you'd say that," I said.

"Cornelia."

Damn that Linny.

OK, I had, I'd asked him. By way of testing a pet theory that my love for Teo existed on a plane above jealousy, I'd asked, and his answer hadn't stung a bit. My jealousy-proof heart beat on, triumphant.

"They did. He said it was fine." His exact words.

"Fine? Around here, we call that damning with faint praise," said my friend Linny and, jealousy-proof or not, I'll admit it, the evil grin I heard in her voice was music to my ears.

That night as I was packing, my mother came into my room with a pair of my oldest jeans, an ironed, knife's-edge pleat down the center of each leg.

"Don't forget these," she said.

I sat down on the bed.

"Mom."

She sat down next to me.

"You've sure shaken things up around here," she told me, and my heart dropped, because I knew as well as I knew anything that shaken-up things were the last things my mother wanted.

"I love him with my soul," I said, because I knew this, too.

She looked at me. "Well, why wouldn't you? He's a wonderful boy."

"He's the best man in the world."

"Your father is the best man in the world." The force of her love for her husband rolled over me like a wave. Wow, I thought. Has that been in there all this time?

"Look at us," I said. "Two lovesick peas in a pod." And she smiled at me.

"When will their divorce be final?" she asked. So I gave her the explanation Teo had given me, along with his plan to wait a year.

"A year?" said my mother sharply. "That's crazy." And I felt like I was the one who was crazy. Or else she was. I'd been sure she'd want Teo to do the noble thing and wait.

"He won't say terrible things about Ollie." I sighed. "He just won't."

My mother's eyes gleamed. "But Ollie might be persuaded to say bad things about him, don't you think? With a well-placed nudge from her mother?"

"Mom!" I was out-and-out shocked.

She lay a hand on my cheek. "Baby," she said, "why the surprise? I've always been on the side of love. Didn't you know that?"

When I thought about it, I realized I did know it. Of course. I'd known it all along.

The next morning, Clare didn't come down for breakfast.

"I'm sorry, Cornelia," said Viviana. "More sorry for her than for you, because she'll hate it that she didn't say good-bye. Later, she'll hate it."

Then she paused, and I braced myself for another thank-you.

But Viviana just smiled and said, "When you come visit, you'll have three places to stay, now. This house, Teo's parents' house, and Mrs. Goldberg's house."

An invitation. I smiled back at her.

"Your house, now," I said.

After a long conversation that had involved my insisting on giving it to them, and Viviana's insisting on buying it, I'd agreed to sell.

"And Clare's house," I added happily, even jubilantly, because that's what love does: You give up a house that's been your heart's home most of your life and come away feeling like you've been handed the sun and moon.

"Plan on extended visits," Viviana told me.

She waited a long time. She scared me with her waiting. But, as I was putting my bag into the trunk of Teo's car, suddenly there she was. Not there, then there, then in my arms.

"Call me honey," Clare said, her cheek against my cheek.

"Oh, honey, honey, honey," I told her, "Clare. Child of my heart. Honey, I hate to leave you."

I hated to leave her. I was sick with leaving her.

"But you'll come back," she said, "and see me soon."

"You know I will."

Then she looked at my face with her matchless brown eyes and smiled.

"I want you and Teo to get married," she whispered, "and be together forever." She was crying. "I want all of us to be together forever. I wish someone could promise me that."

I kissed her. "Is that the hardest promise you've got? Because that's an easy one."

I remembered Teo saying, "Why do you think I love you so much?"

"Our loving each other is just the world we live in, like the grass under our feet," I told Clare. "No matter where we are, it's the world we live in. Do you know what I mean?"

And into my shoulder, Clare was nodding yes, yes, yes.

I waited to cry until Teo and I were driving away, and then I couldn't stop.

"How can I leave her?" I said. "I can't leave her."

He reached over and held my hand.

"Do you think she knows how I love her?" I asked him.

"I know she knows," he said.

Suddenly it seemed vitally important that everyone I loved know exactly how and how much. I felt feverish with wanting them to know. I turned to Teo.

"Do you know how I love you?" I demanded.

"Yes."

"No, I mean, I'm not fooling around here," I said vehemently. "This isn't—dating."

"I know."

He drove and I stared at him, at his glowing beauty that was beautiful because it was beauty, but mostly because it was his. Teo looked like no one who had ever lived. I was seized with a frantic thought.

"Teo," I said, "I don't love you for your beauty."

He laughed. "Uh-oh," he said. "What else is there?"

Like no one who had ever lived, I thought. Except maybe Lawrence Olivier, the tiniest bit, but only around the cheekbones.

We rode for a long time after that without saying anything.

"And I should probably just tell you that I want to have a baby. Not right away, but soon. Really soon." I just said it. I rushed right out on that limb and stood there for all I was worth, with wind in my face and birdsong in my ears, not looking down or anywhere but at Teo.

"OK," said Teo, so serenely that I thought he must have misunderstood.

"With you," I said. "I want to have a baby with you. Soon."

He didn't laugh. He pulled the car to the side of the road and kissed my wet face.

"The sooner the better," he said.

And we keep driving, the mountains blue and beneficent in the distance, then gone. Gone but not gone. The mountains, Clare, Mrs. Goldberg, my mother and father, Ollie, Cam, Toby, Linny, Martin, Viviana, all right here. You, too. My heart is large; it can contain everything at once, and the road I'm on with Teo, can you see it? It runs forward and backward and no matter which way we travel on it, the direction is the same. You know the direction I mean: Homeward.

Acknowledgments

I offer heartfelt thanks to the following people:

Everyone at Dunow, Carlson, and Lerner, especially my agent, Jennifer Carlson, for her immense sanity and patience and for believing in this book before it *was* a book;

All the folks at Dutton, especially my editor Laurie Chittenden for her clear eyes and ever-judicious guidance, along with her kind assistant Erika Kahn;

The amazing Shari Smiley at CAA;

My treasured brain trust—Ralph Ashbrooke, Julianna Baggott, Susan Davis, Dan Fertel, Rebecca Flowers Schamess, Annie Pilson, Kristina de los Santos, and David G. W. Scott—early readers who provided advice and resounding cheers along the way;

Mark Caughey and Kym Pinder for keeping my edges sharp and for turning over the little house in Vermont to me and Cornelia and Clare;

Diane Sheehan, my lucky children's third parent;

Arturo and Mary de los Santos, my parents, for steady, steadying love;

My children Charles and Annabel who wear me out, make me laugh, and grace my life every day;

And, most of all, thank you to my husband David Teague: leading man, first reader, resident genius, and joyful collaborator. There aren't enough words in the world.

About the Author

An award-winning poet with a Ph.D. in literature and creative writing, **Marisa de los Santos** lives in Wilmington, Delaware, with her husband and their two small children. *Love Walked In* is her first novel.